MAIL ORDER BRIDE SERIES
NO. 9
1877
USA
AL & JOANNA LACY

SO LITTLE TIME

So Little Time

MAIL ORDER BRIDE 9

AL & JOANNA LACY

Multnomah®Publishers *Sisters, Oregon*

SO LITTLE TIME
published by Multnomah Publishers, Inc.
© 2002 by ALJO Productions, Inc.

International Standard Book Number: 1-57673-898-1

Cover design by Kirk DouPonce/UDG Design Works
Cover illustration by Vittorio Dangelico

Scripture quotations are from:
The Holy Bible, King James Version

Multnomah is a trademark of Multnomah Publishers, Inc.,
and is registered in the U.S. Patent and Trademark Office.
The colophon is a trademark of Multnomah Publishers, Inc.

Printed in the United States of America

For information:
MULTNOMAH PUBLISHERS, INC.
POST OFFICE BOX 1720
SISTERS, OREGON 97759

Library of Congress Cataloging-in-Publication Data
Lacy, Al.
  So little time / By Al and JoAnna Lacy.
    p. cm. -- (Mail order bride; bk. 9)
  ISBN 1-57673-898-1
  1. Overland journeys to the Pacific--Fiction. 2. Women pioneers--Fiction. I. Lacy, JoAnna. II. Title.
  PS3562.A256 S6 2002
  813'.54--dc21   2001007866

02 03 04 05 06 07 08—10 9 8 7 6 5 4 3 2 1 0

This book is affectionately dedicated to
Janice Dawson,
our dear and precious friend and loyal fan,
who herself has known the meaning implied in the title of this book.
We love you, Janice. The Lord bless you!

2 PETER 1:2

So teach us to number our days,
that we may apply our hearts unto wisdom.

PSALM 90:12

Redeeming the time, because the days are evil.

EPHESIANS 5:16

Time was—is past: thou canst not it recall:
Time is—thou hast: employ the portion small.
Time future—is not and may never be:
Time present—is the only time for thee.

Prologue

The Encyclopedia Britannica reports that the mail order business, also called direct mail marketing, "is a method of merchandising in which the seller's offer is made through mass mailing of a circular or catalog or advertisement placed in a newspaper or magazine, in which the buyer places his order by mail."

Britannica goes on to say that "mail order operations have been known in the United States in one form or another since colonial days, but not until the latter half of the nineteenth century did they assume a significant role in domestic trade."

Thus the mail order market was known when the big gold rush took place in this country in the 1840s and 1850s. At that time prospectors, merchants, and adventurers raced from the East to the newly discovered goldfields in the West. One of the most famous was the California gold rush in 1848–49, when discovery of gold at Sutter's Mill, near Sacramento, brought more than 40,000 men to California. Though few struck it rich, their presence stimulated economic growth, the lure of which brought even more men to the West.

The married men who had come to seek their fortunes sent for their wives and children, wanting to stay and make their home there. Most of the gold rush men were single and also desired to stay in the West, but there were about two hundred men for every single woman. Being familiar with the mail order concept, they began advertising in eastern newspapers for women to come West and marry them. Thus was born the "mail order bride."

Women by the hundreds began answering the ads. Often when men and their prospective brides corresponded, they agreed to send no photographs; they would accept each other by the spirit of the letters rather than on a physical basis. Others, of course, did exchange photographs.

The mail order bride movement accelerated after the Civil War ended in April 1865, when men went West by the thousands to make their fortunes on the frontier. Many of the marriages turned out well, while others were disappointing and ended in desertion by one or the other of the mates, or by divorce.

In the Mail Order Bride fiction series, we tell stories intended to grip the heart of the reader, bring some smiles, and maybe wring out a few tears. As always, we weave in the gospel of Jesus Christ and run threads of Bible truth that apply to our lives today.

Introduction

AMERICA'S CIVIL WAR BEGAN ON APRIL 12, 1861, and lasted three days short of four years.

On April 6, 1865, General Robert E. Lee and his Army of Northern Virginia drew up to the Farmville and High Bridge crossings of the Appomattox River in Virginia, and while they were crossing the river, General Ulysses S. Grant's Army of the Potomac surrounded them. The Confederates were forced to lay down their arms without a shot being fired.

Lee quickly saw that this was the Confederacy's last stand, and after negotiations with Grant, agreed to surrender. Three days later, on April 9, at the former county seat known as Appomattox Courthouse, Lee surrendered to Grant, thus effectively ending the Civil War.

Five days later, on April 14, tragedy struck.

MAIL ORDER BRIDE SERIES
NO. 9
1877
USA
AL & JOANNA LACY

FIVE MEN HUDDLED IN A DARK ALLEY in a residential section near the intersection of Pennsylvania and Louisiana Avenues, their hard faces alabaster masks in the moonlight. Their horses were tied next to a small barn nearby. It was just after ten o'clock in Washington, D.C., on the starlit night of April 14, 1865. A brilliant full moon was rising into the sky behind some low, long-fingered clouds on the eastern horizon. Lewis Paine, Samuel Arnold, Michael O'Laughlin, Edman Spangler, and George Atzerodt were looking toward the street expectantly.

"What do you suppose is holding them?" asked a nervous Edman Spangler. "Shouldn't they be here by now?"

"Who knows?" said Lewis Paine. "Why don't you go take another look?"

"I'll do it," said Spangler, heading toward the street.

The others watched as Spangler hurried to the end of the alley, and keeping in the shadows, looked northwest on Pennsylvania Avenue. He stared that direction for a long moment, as buggies and carriages with burning lanterns for headlights passed by; then he turned and hurried back to his cohorts. "Naw. Ain't no sign of them, yet."

Michael O'Laughlin took a deep breath. His back was rigid and his voice unsteady. "Something's gone wrong, I just know it."

Waving him off, Lewis Paine said, "Now, don't go giving up, Mike. They might have to veer around some mounted policemen, who'd wonder why they're riding so fast. Those two guys know what they're doing. Have a little faith."

A feeling of panic nudged the back of Samuel Arnold's consciousness. "Lewis, what if Mike's right? What if something did go wrong? What if they were caught right there on the spot?"

Paine gave him a scowl. "Like I said, Sam. Have a little faith."

"I'm gonna go check." Arnold hurried toward the street.

George Atzerodt sighed, watching Arnold move away. "It shouldn't be taking this long, Lewis.

Arnold called back in a hoarse whisper, "Here they come!"

Rapid hoofbeats were heard as Samuel Arnold was scurrying back to his friends, and seconds later, two riders turned into the alley. The five horses that were tied at the small barn whinnied at the presence of the other horses, and the two carrying the riders whinnied in return.

By the bright moonlight, the riders caught sight of their cohorts huddling close to the barn.

The five men saw quickly that one of the riders was bent over in the saddle, his hand gripping his left leg. The other one was riding close, holding onto his arm. They rushed to the pair as they drew rein, and Lewis Paine asked, "Is it done?"

A gloating smile stole across David Herold's face. "It is done." He leaned from the saddle in an effort to keep his friend from falling from his horse.

"Great!" said Paine, while the other four were silently rejoicing at the good news. He then looked at the injured rider, frowning. "What happened?"

"I think I broke my leg in the escape," said the injured man through clenched teeth. His forehead was clammy with cold sweat. "No time to explain right now. We've gotta get outta here!"

"Yeah, in a hurry!" said David Herold. "People along the way—both afoot and in vehicles—have taken notice of us galloping down the street. They'll tell the police. We're going over the Navy Yard Bridge as planned. All of you move out there on the street. When the police come, tell them you saw two riders, in a hurry, turn east on Louisiana Avenue."

"We'll do it," said Edman Spangler.

A worried George Atzerodt stepped up to the injured rider. "Can you stay in the saddle?"

"I'll have to." The reply was through gritted teeth as the man kept a tight grip on his left leg. "Believe me, I'm not gonna fall off. I did what I went there to do tonight, and they're not catching me. I'm getting away. Hurrah for the Confederacy!"

"We're sorry you're hurt," said Michael O'Laughlin, "but at least it's done! The South has its revenge!"

"Even if this leg is broken," said the man bent over in the saddle, "it's worth it."

Still gripping his friend's arm, David Herold said, "Let's go!"

While the two men were riding away, the five Confederate sympathizers were hugging each other.

George Atzerodt laughed. "The Confederacy just scored a monumental victory, even though we lost the War!"

The others laughed in agreement, then Lewis Paine said, "All right, boys, let's get out there on the street."

The quintet dashed out onto Pennsylvania Avenue, and with Paine in the lead, they ran the opposite direction from the way their friends had gone. They drew up under a street lamp at the next intersection.

People in horse-drawn vehicles and those riding horseback glanced at them as they passed by.

"I sure hope they get over the bridge all right," said O'Laughlin.

"They will," Spangler said in a confident tone.

Suddenly they heard the rapid pounding of hoofbeats, and looked up the avenue to see four uniformed riders galloping toward them. The officers spotted the five men grouped under the street lamp and pulled rein.

"You men see two riders go by here like they were in a horse race?" asked one of the officers.

"Yes, sir," said Lewis Paine. "They were riding like the devil himself was after them. They turned left down there on Louisiana Avenue."

"Thanks," said the officer, and they put their horses back to a gallop as they headed down Pennsylvania Avenue. The Confederates watched them slow down at the next corner, turn east on Louisiana Avenue, and whip their mounts to full speed.

Lewis Paine laughed heartily. "Well, those hotshots won't catch them, I'll guarantee you that!"

The five men laughed together, rejoicing once again in the tremendous victory gained for the Confederacy that night.

2

THE NAVY YARD BRIDGE SPANNED the eastern branch of the Potomac River from Washington, D.C., into Maryland at the foot of Eleventh Street in the southeast section of Washington.

At ten-thirty on the night of April 14, 1865, in the guardhouse at the Washington end of the bridge, Union Sergeant Silas Cobb had just welcomed an old friend from his hometown of Springfield, Illinois—Ward Hill Lamon, who had ridden a borrowed horse to the bridge to see him.

The sergeant introduced his fellow guards, Corporals Eddie Cavin and Mike Hankins, to Lamon. He said that Mr. Lamon was his father's attorney, and that they were close friends.

Smiling warmly, Cobb laid a hand on Lamon's shoulder. "I really appreciate your coming by to see me, Ward. Dad wrote and told me you were coming to Washington on business and were going to have dinner at the White House with President and Mrs. Lincoln...what was it? April 11?"

"Yes. Just last Tuesday. It was my privilege to spend the entire evening with them."

"So you know Mr. and Mrs. Lincoln personally, do you, Mr. Lamon?" said Corporal Hankins.

"Yes," said Lamon. "I got to know them quite well when they lived in Springfield. Mr. Lincoln and I both worked in the same law firm from 1836 until he was elected to Congress in 1847."

"You must have gotten to know him quite well," commented Corporal Cavin.

"Yes. Quite well, indeed, and there's not a man on earth I admire as much as I do him."

"President Lincoln has carried a tremendous load during the Civil War," said Sergeant Cobb. "How were his spirits when you spent the evening with him just two days after the war was over?"

Lamon reflected on the question. "Well, in one way, he was superbly happy and jovial, but in another way, he seemed quite melancholy."

Cobb's brow furrowed. "What do you mean?"

"When the surrender of General Lee to General Grant at Appomattox Courthouse was the subject, there was pure elation. He did, however, speak of his utmost respect for General Lee as a soldier and a gentleman. He admires General Lee very much."

The three soldiers nodded.

Lamon went on. "It was after dinner when we were relaxing in the Red Room at the White House that he seemed to become melancholy. Mrs. Lincoln noticed it and asked if something was bothering him. He was reluctant to share the reason for his depression, but she pressed him about it, and he told her it was because of a nightmare he had a few nights before. He said it had haunted him ever since, but he would rather not talk about it.

"As I said, I know the Lincolns quite well, and back when we were in the same law firm, Mrs. Lincoln and my wife became quite close. One time, Mrs. Lincoln shared with us that since her childhood, she had been afflicted by dreadful nightmares. So I wasn't surprised when Mr. Lincoln brought up the nightmare that Mrs. Lincoln would not let the subject drop. 'You frighten me, Abe,' she said. 'I want to know about it.'

"Well, by now, the president evidently regretted having aroused the morbid fears that sprang from his wife's nature, for he said he wished she hadn't asked him about what was troubling him. But despite her husband's reluctance, Mrs. Lincoln insisted that then and there he describe the nightmare. At last, he agreed.

"He began by referring to the Bible, and how in both the Old and New Testaments, God and His angels came to men in dreams. He went on to say that since the Bible was completed and man now has the full written revelation from God, that he believed people on earth learn God's truth by reading the Bible, not from dreams. He wanted to make sure that both of us understood that he wasn't taking the nightmare as a message from God.

"Mr. Lincoln said that one recent night, he had gone wearily to bed after waiting up late for important dispatches. Almost immediately he had fallen into a deep slumber and soon had begun to dream. 'There seemed to be a deathlike stillness about me,' he said. 'Then I heard subdued sobs, as if a number of people were weeping. In my dream, I left my bed and wandered downstairs. Finding no one, I roamed from room to room, seeking the source of the sorrowing sounds. I kept on until I arrived in the East Room. There I met with a sickening surprise. Before me was a catafalque, on which rested a coffin. In the coffin was a corpse in funeral vestments. Around it were stationed soldiers who were acting as guards; there was a throng of people, some gazing mournfully upon the corpse, whose face was covered, with others weeping pitifully.'

"Mr. Lincoln asked a soldier who in the White House had died, and the soldier said solemnly that it was the president. He had been killed by an assassin."

"Oh, how awful, Ward," said Sergeant Silas Cobb. "That must have upset Mrs. Lincoln."

"It very much upset her," said Lamon. "In fact, she said she wished she hadn't pressed him to tell it. But Mr. Lincoln took hold of her hand and said, 'It was only a dream, Mary. Let's say no more about it.'"

Corporal Eddie Cavin rubbed his upper arms. "Brr! Just the thought of it gives me chills. Imagine—President Lincoln being assassinated."

"Gives me chills, too," said Corporal Mike Hankins.

Ward Lamon smiled. "Well, gentlemen, for Mr. Lincoln's nightmare to become a reality would require an act of violence running against the tide of American history. Of the fifteen men who have preceded Mr. Lincoln as president, all have died of natural causes."

"Right," said Cobb, "and just recently it was in the newspapers that Secretary of State William Seward said in a speech to Congress that assassination is not an American practice. And he doesn't believe it ever will be."

"I sure hope not," said Mike Hankins.

Ward Lamon said, "Well, Silas, I really need to get on back to my hotel. I have to catch the early train to Chicago in the morning."

Sergeant Cobb shook the attorney's hand, saying how much he appreciated him taking the time to come and see him. Cobb walked him through the seven-foot sentry gate where his borrowed horse was waiting. He stepped back inside the gate and locked it, and the three guards watched Lamon mount up and ride away. When the night had swallowed him and they were returning to the guardhouse, Eddie Cavin said, "I sure was glad to hear Mr. Lamon say what he did about how President Lincoln admires General Robert E. Lee. In spite of the hard feelings between the North and the South, I very much admire Robert E. Lee, myself. He is a kind and humble man. I really—"

Cavin's words were cut off by the sound of rapid hoofbeats drumming down Eleventh Street toward the bridge.

"The moon's bright," said Cobb, "but you boys better get your lanterns so we'll clearly see whoever this is."

Both corporals dashed inside the guardhouse, picked up lanterns that were already lit, and hurried back to the sergeant, who was moving toward the sentry gate. Seconds later, they were able to make out two riders slowing from a gallop to a trot as they neared the bridge. The horses were breathing hard as they drew up.

Cobb peered between the bars of the gate at their shadowed faces. "I'm Sergeant Silas Cobb. What can we do for you, gentlemen?"

One rider was holding onto the other, who was bent over in the saddle and clutching his left leg. While steadying his injured friend, the rider said, "We need to cross the bridge, Sergeant."

"Sir," said Cobb, "since the Civil War began four years ago, the Navy Yard Bridge has been shut off to traffic after nine o'clock at night as a security measure. It is now nearly eleven. Even though the war is over, the enforcement of the regulation is still intact, except in extreme situations."

"My name is Harold Smith," said one rider. "My friend is

injured. He needs to get home to Beantown, Maryland, as soon as possible."

"Beantown?" said Cobb. "That's a pretty good stretch. Maybe you'd better get him to a doctor here in D.C."

David Herold felt his temper heat up. "This is an extreme situation, Sergeant. My friend needs to get to his own doctor in Beantown."

"He's hurt pretty bad, huh?" said Mike Hankins, lifting his lantern higher in order to see the injured man, whose head was bent low. "What happened?"

Herold's nerves were tight as he said, "Well, he—"

"Hey, Sergeant!" blurted Hankins. "I know this man! It's John Wilkes Booth, my favorite actor."

Booth's head came up.

Eddie Cavin gasped, raising his own lantern. "Mr. Booth, I've seen every play you've done here in Washington!"

"I have, too!" said Cobb. "You're great!"

Masking his anxiety, the dark-haired, mustached Booth said, "Thank you for your kind compliments, gentlemen. My friend Harold Smith and I have been on an errand here in Washington. We had been delayed some, and by the time we were ready to leave, the moon hadn't come up yet. So we waited a little longer in order to have the moonlight to ride by. We both live in Beantown. And for reasons I don't have time to discuss—in addition to the fact that I really need to see my own doctor—we are asking you to let us cross the bridge and be on our way."

Cobb asked, "What is the nature of your injury, Mr. Booth?"

Booth gritted his teeth. "Just as we were mounting back there in town to head for home, this big dog came out of the shadows and started barking. My horse shied, and I fell from the saddle, landing on the leg. If I can get to Beantown tonight, I'll haul my family doctor out of bed so he can do whatever is necessary right away."

Brow furrowed, Sergeant Silas Cobb said, "I'll let you through on one condition."

"What's that?"

A smile creased Cobb's features. "I want your autograph."

Relieved, Booth said, "Sure."

"I want one, too," said Hankins.

"So do I," piped up Cavin.

Looking at Cavin, Cobb said, "Corporal, go into the guard-house and get a pencil and some paper."

Setting his lantern down, Eddie dashed into the guardhouse, and returned quickly with three separate slips of paper and a pencil.

When John Wilkes Booth had signed all three pieces of paper, the sentries thanked him. They opened the gate and waved as the two riders trotted across the bridge and vanished into the Maryland night.

As John Wilkes Booth and David Herold galloped southeast, the full moon was clear-edged and bright against the deep blackness of the night.

Booth's leg was hurting fiercely. The wind created by the speed of the horses ruffled his hair, blowing wisps across his pale fore-head. Booth looked at his partner and called out above the thunder of the pounding hooves, "Dave, I—I'm dizzy! I'm afraid I'm gonna pass out and fall from the saddle."

"Let's stop!" shouted Herold, pulling rein.

Booth yanked back on the reins, calling for his horse to stop, while gripping his leg and trying to stay in the saddle. Just as the panting horses came to a halt, Booth gasped and peeled out of the saddle, hitting the ground with a loud whump.

Herold quickly dismounted and knelt beside him. John Wilkes Booth was out cold.

Herold's ears picked up the gurgling sound of a brook some-where nearby. Rising to his feet, he looked around until he found the sound some thirty or forty feet from the road. Dropping to his knees again, he took Booth's slender body into his arms, rose to his feet, and carried him into the deep shadows of the trees where the water flowed freely with the speckled moonlight dancing on its sur-face.

Laying Booth down and stretching him out on the bank of the brook in the dappled moonlight, Herold dropped to his knees and splashed cool water in his face. "John...John...c'mon. Wake up."

Booth rolled his head back and forth, ejecting a low moan. After a moment, he opened his blurry eyes. He made out the vague form of David Herold looming over him and ran his tongue over his lips. "Dave, I'm sorry. I couldn't help it."

"It's all right," said Herold, patting his shoulder. "Just lie there for a while till your head clears. You want some more water on your face?"

"Might help."

Scooping the cool liquid from the brook in his cupped hands, Herold splashed his friend generously until he asked him to stop.

Booth lay there a little longer, blinking against the haze that seemed to hang over his vision. "This leg's gotta be broken," he said. "It wouldn't do this to me if it wasn't."

"You're probably right. I don't know if Beantown has a doctor, John, but there is a good one in Bryantown, which is just four miles past Beantown. I hear he's real good. Name's Dr. Samuel Mudd."

"All right. Let's go to him. How far's Beantown, now?"

"I'd say about ten or twelve miles from right here."

Booth gritted his teeth. "Four more miles after that?"

"Yeah. Only four. You can make it. Just lie there till your head gets completely cleared up. Then we'll go. I don't want you falling out of the saddle again."

Booth nodded. "Could you give me some of that water to drink?"

"Sure," said Herold. Cupping his hands, he dipped what water he could hold and dribbled it into Booth's open mouth.

When Booth had taken his fill of water, he lay there and looked up at his friend. "Just a little longer, and I'll be ready to go."

"Sure," said Herold, shifting to a sitting position. "John, let me ask you something. Wasn't there any other way you could have gotten out of Ford's Theatre than jumping from the president's box to the stage?"

"No. I only had one way out. The hall behind Lincoln's box is very narrow. If people had come into the hall at the sound of the shot, I would've been caught for sure."

"Couldn't you have used your gun to make them get out of the way?"

"It's a single-shot Derringer, and anyone who knows guns would see that. There was no way but to jump from the elevated box to the stage."

"That's only about ten feet, isn't it?"

"Yeah."

"That's not so far. What did you do, land wrong?"

"Exactly. My foot caught in the U.S. Treasury Guards' flag that was suspended from the center column of the box. You've seen it."

"Yeah."

"I was in a big hurry to get outta there, and somehow my foot caught in that thing. I landed on my left foot, but it must've been slightly twisted when I hit the stage."

Herold shook his head. "Well, no doubt you were recognized by the people on the stage and many of them in the audience. The Federals will know who they're looking for long before they're told about it by those guards at the bridge."

Booth was grimacing in pain and did not reply.

"If you're up to it, we'd better get back in our saddles. Once the Federals find out we went into Maryland, they'll have the troops on our trail."

Booth nodded and raised a hand. "Help me up."

Herold helped Booth to his feet. Booth stood wavering for a few seconds, then seemed to find his balance. Although he had to resist the urge to drop back to the ground, he let Herold assist him toward the horses. His limbs felt sluggish, as if their blood flow had become viscous.

Soon they were riding again, and Booth seemed fixed in his saddle.

Just over an hour later, they passed Beantown, but Booth's pain was getting worse. His head stayed clear, for which he was thankful. Knowing he was only four miles from the doctor gave him the strength to hang on.

As they headed toward Bryantown, Booth said, "Dave, I need to slow down. This leg is killing me."

"Sure," said his friend. "Let's just go at a walk."

While they rode, Booth said, "Dave, Dr. Mudd is going to want to know my name. You've seen this tattoo I put on the back of my left hand when I was fourteen."

"Oh. You mean your initials."

"Yeah. I'll tell him my name is James W. Boyd."

"Good idea. We sure don't need the troops on our trail any sooner than they already will be."

When they rode into Bryantown, Herold led his friend down the main street to the business section, then turned at a cross street. Half a block from the main street, they came upon Dr. Samuel Mudd's office.

Reading the sign by moonlight, they learned that the doctor's house was behind the office. They guided their horses to the rear and drew up at the porch of the darkened house.

"Dave, I'll need you to help me down."

Herold dismounted, stepped up to the left side of Booth's horse, and lifted his friend down.

When they reached the porch floor after climbing four steps, Booth leaned against a post, trying valiantly to stay on his feet. Putting all of his weight on his good leg, he wiped a palm over his eyes and took several deep breaths, willing himself not to pass out again.

Herold stood close, observing him, then said in a low tone, "You all right?"

"Leg...hurts bad...and I'm...dizzy," Booth replied, straining his words through clenched teeth.

"Just hang on." Herold turned and banged his fist on the door.

Booth closed his eyes and leaned his head against the post that was supporting his body.

All was still inside the house.

Herold banged on the door again; this time louder and longer. "Come on, come on, Doctor."

He was about to pound on the door again when he saw the light of a lantern through the curtains on the window. The lantern glow came nearer and the door opened, revealing a tiny silver-haired woman in a voluminous gown and robe, who was wiping her eyes. A long, fat braid hung over one shoulder.

Face flushed with sleep, she peered at the two men as she held the lamp up to get a good look at them. Their appearance at that time of night was a little frightening to her, but noting the man leaning against the post who was grimacing in pain, she said, "Gentlemen, I'm sure you are wanting to see my husband, but he has been out on a farm most of the night, delivering a baby. He got home a half hour ago and just got to sleep. He is very tired. Could you come back in the morning?"

Suddenly she heard a wrenching moan come from the man leaning against the post and watched as he slid down the post and collapsed on the porch floor.

Turning and kneeling beside Booth, Herold looked up at her. "Please, ma'am. My friend needs the doctor's help right now."

Muriel Mudd widened the door and said, "Bring him in and put him on the couch. I'll awaken my husband. He'll want to take him to the office, but it'll take a few minutes for him to get dressed."

Muriel turned and hurried into the parlor. While Herold picked Booth up and carried him into the room, she lit a lantern that sat on a small table, then rushed toward the rear of the house, carrying the other lantern.

Booth was conscious, but a bit woozy as Herold eased him down onto the couch and did what he could to make him comfortable. "Hang on, John," he said in a low voice. "The doctor will be here in a few minutes."

Nearly ten minutes had passed when Dr. Samuel Mudd appeared, running fingers through his thinning gray hair. Managing a sleepy smile, he said, "Mrs. Mudd says we have a man here in severe pain."

"Yes, Doctor," said Herold. "My name is Harold Smith, and my friend is James W. Boyd."

Nodding, Mudd knelt down beside the couch, noting that Booth was clutching his left leg, eyes closed. "It's the left leg?"

"Yes, Doctor. We're from Lexington Park, down near Point Lookout."

"Oh, sure. I know where it is. Just off Chesapeake Bay."

"Yes, sir. James and I were in D.C. on a business matter, and when we were mounting up to start back a few hours ago, a big dog came out of the shadows and started barking at us. James's horse shied and he fell out of the saddle and landed on his leg. I think it's broken."

Mudd picked up the lantern from the small table. "Let's get him over to the office so I can examine it and take care of him."

"I'll carry him, Doctor," said Herold.

"Fine, Mr. Smith," said Mudd, heading for the door. "Follow me."

Moments later, Dr. Mudd led Herold into the office as he carried Booth in his arms. There was a strong odor of medicines and disinfectants as the doctor led them into the examining room.

MAIL ORDER BRIDE SERIES
NO. 9
1877
USA
AL & JOANNA LACY

3

LYING ON THE EXAMINING TABLE, John Wilkes Booth steeled himself as Dr. Samuel Mudd rolled up the left leg of his trousers. David Herold stood close by, looking on.

After rolling the pant leg above the knee, Mudd looked the area over between the knee and the ankle without touching it. "Mr. Boyd, something's definitely not right, here. I think you have a fracture of the fibula, but I won't know for sure without examining it with my hands. That will be painful for you unless I give you a strong dose of laudanum. Are you willing to take that?"

Booth nodded. "Yes. If the leg is fractured, it needs to be set, and I want it taken care of."

"Good," said the doctor, turning to his medicine cabinet. "I'll mix you a strong dose and after fifteen or twenty minutes, I can begin my examination. If the bone needs to be set, the laudanum will take the edge off the pain. We'll just leave your shoe on."

While Mudd was mixing the powder with water, Herold asked, "Doctor, am I right that the fibula is the outer and smaller bone in the leg between the knee and the ankle?"

"Yes. If it was the inner bone, the pain would be greater when I correct the fracture, and it would be much more difficult for him to walk when I put it in a splint."

The doctor returned to his patient and gave him the mixture to drink. Booth made a face as he swallowed it.

Mudd grinned. "I know it doesn't taste good, Mr. Boyd. Laudanum is tincture of opium, and nobody likes the taste of opium. However, if I have to set a broken fibula you will be plenty glad you have it in you."

The doctor returned the cup to the counter of the medicine cabinet. "All right, we'll give it time to take effect." He moved back to the side of the table, and glanced at Herold. "Mr. Smith, I'm curious."

Moving closer to him, Herold asked, "About what, Doctor?"

"Why are you two gentlemen riding at night? Wouldn't it be much better to ride in the daylight?"

Booth looked at his friend and noticed him stiffen slightly.

"Well, it's like this, Doctor," said Herold, "we're in a hurry."

Booth's eyes widened.

"You see," Herold went on, "James's mother also lives in Lexington Park, and she is very ill. Her doctors say she will not live much longer. He was hesitant to leave her for this trip, but it was very important, so he came with me. He's wanting to get back to see her before she dies."

"Oh," said Mudd, lowering his head to look at Booth. "I'm sorry, Mr. Boyd. We'll get this taken care of as soon as possible."

The physician kept checking the clock on the wall, and when twenty minutes had passed, he carefully examined the leg. Booth winced a few times while Mudd was doing his examination.

Finally, the doctor sighed and said, "Just as I thought. The fibula is definitely fractured. I will set the broken bone, then wrap it tightly and put it in a splint. You will experience some pain when I set the bone."

Booth and Herold exchanged glances and Herold commented, "Like the doctor said, James, be glad for the laudanum."

Booth could feel his body tensing up. "Yeah. I am."

Mudd said, "Mr. Smith, it would help if you would stand there at the head of the table and put your hands on your friend's shoulders. He may want to move some. Hold him down, and hold him still. All right?"

"Yes, sir," said Herold, moving to the head of the table. He looked down at Booth and laid his hands on his shoulders. "It'll be all right, James. You're tough."

Booth did not comment, but as Dr. Samuel Mudd took hold of his leg, the tension in his muscles was now an uncomfortable strain.

There was a sudden, sharp pain in the leg as Mudd hastily set the bone, accompanied with the snapping sound of the bone going partially back in place. Booth clenched his teeth, grunted, and bowed his back. Herold pushed his shoulders down, holding him tight against the table. There was another sharp pain as the doctor completed the setting, and Booth's head began to swim. Even through the laudanum fog, he was gripped in a vice of pain. He seemed to be floating off the table, and the sounds of Dr. Mudd's work were fading. His head felt like a boulder atop a pillar of stone, rocking…rocking.

When John Wilkes Booth regained consciousness, the pain in his leg was barely noticeable. The two men were standing over him.

Dr. Mudd said, "The splint is on, Mr. Boyd. How do you feel?"

"A little weak," said Booth, "but I'm not hurting much."

"Good. Now, your friend is in a real hurry to get going, so let's sit you up and see what you think about riding a horse."

Herold helped his friend to a sitting position, and though Booth felt a bit light-headed, he said, "Not bad. I think I can ride." His thoughts ran to the sentries at the Navy Yard Bridge, who by now had probably learned of Lincoln's assassination and had advised the authorities that the assassin and his accomplice had ridden into Maryland. "I'm sure I can ride."

"Actually," said Dr. Mudd, "you shouldn't ride a horse for a few days. You're suffering from shock. You should stay here and rest."

Booth shook his head. "Can't do it, Doctor. We've really got to get home. Just give me some of that painkiller stuff to take along the way, and we'll be going."

Mudd sighed. "Then while I'm preparing some laudanum to send with you, why don't you sit down over here on this chair? Rest just a bit longer before you try sitting in the saddle."

Booth's brow puckered. "Can I stand on my left foot, Doctor?"

"Yes. Just be careful as you put your weight on it. The splint will keep it from hurting too much. It would really be best if you would use a crutch under your left arm for a while when you walk. Then you could keep from putting too much weight on the foot."

As he spoke, Mudd went to the medicine cabinet and began to pour some laudanum powder into a small cone-shaped paper container.

"Do you have a crutch, Doctor?" asked Herold.

"Yes," he replied without looking up. "I sell them for two dollars."

"We'll take one. Now, we also need to pay you for your work. What do we owe you?"

The doctor finished filling the paper container, twisted the top to close it, and handed it to Herold. "Well, let's see, Mr. Smith. I suppose ten dollars would cover it. Nine dollars for the work and a dollar for the laudanum he's taking with him. With the crutch, it'll be twelve dollars. By the way, it's two teaspoons to eight ounces of water when you mix the laudanum dosage."

Herold nodded and slipped the paper cone into his jacket pocket. "James, come over here and sit on the chair as the doctor said, while I pay him."

"I can pay him," Booth said stubbornly.

"You just sit down on the chair," said Herold, grinning. "You can pay me back later."

Booth eased off the table slowly and gingerly stood on his feet. "Little pain, but it's not bad." With that, he limped to the chair and sat down.

When the doctor had been paid and had placed the crutch in Booth's hand, Herold said, "Okay, James. Let's go. Your mama's waiting. I'll go bring the horses around here to the front of the office."

Minutes later, Muriel Mudd came in from the house and watched with her husband as the two men moved outside and Booth used the crutch as he approached his horse. The men talked for a couple of minutes, and decided that Boyd should ride on Smith's horse with him, at least for a while.

When they were settled, with Smith riding behind Boyd, they rode away with Boyd's horse being led by the reins.

Standing in the open door of the modest frame office, watching the two men ride away in the moonlight, the aging physician placed an arm around his wife. "Honey, something about those two fellows just doesn't ring true."

"Really?"

"Mm-hmm. Something says they didn't tell me the truth about why they're riding at night."

Muriel sighed, a shiver going through her body from the cool night air. "Well, I guess it doesn't make any difference to us. Your job is finished."

"Yep. Sure is," he said, shrugging his bent shoulders as they turned and entered the office, and he closed the door behind them.

As they were riding down the road, Booth said, "So where do you suggest we go, Dave?"

"We need to keep heading south, that's for sure. "Let's just go on down to Lexington Park, even though your mother isn't really there."

"But what if the Federals decide to check with that doctor, since they probably know my leg is injured, and he tells them we were going to Lexington Park?"

"We won't stay there long, but at least it's a large city. If we move around, nobody will notice us."

Booth shrugged. "Okay. For now, Lexington Park it is."

By the time the sun was lifting its rim over the eastern horizon, Booth's pain was starting to make itself known. "Dave, I'm gonna need to take some more of that stuff."

"We're coming up on Golden Beach," said Herold. "Since it's a good-sized town, I'll put you over there in the forest to hide, and go in and get us some breakfast. It's been a while since I've been in Golden Beach, but I remember a couple of cafés. It's best that we not be seen in town together. Who knows what news might have gotten here by now? Anyway, you can take the laudanum with your breakfast."

"Sounds good to me."

Some thirty minutes later, Herold chose a spot in a dense part of the forest, looked around, and said, "Nobody should see you here."

Herold dismounted, then helped Booth down. While Booth stood leaning on the crutch, Herold tied the horses to a couple of small trees, then dragged a fallen log from between a couple of bushes. "Here. Sit down."

Booth carefully eased down onto the log, using the crutch to balance himself. His face showed the pain he was now experiencing. Herold said, "You take it easy. I'll be back in a little while."

Booth watched his friend threading his way through the trees. It took only seconds for him to vanish from view.

The twenty-seven-year-old man who had shot Abraham Lincoln thought about his mother, who lived in a rural area outside of Baltimore. He knew she would be proud of him for exacting vengeance on Lincoln. Though the Booth family lived in Maryland, they were Southerners at heart, and the day after the Civil War was officially over they had a family gathering, and all agreed that Abraham Lincoln was a blight on the country.

Booth's mother had even made the statement that the "New America," as it was now being called, would never reach its potential with Lincoln in the White House. His actor brother Edwin had reacted to their mother's words by saying, "If I had the intestinal fortitude, I'd catch ol' Abe out in the open and shoot him dead."

Adjusting himself on the log, John Wilkes Booth smiled. "Well, Edwin, you needn't be concerned about ol' Abe, now. I took care of him." He thought on it a moment. "Hah! But you probably already know that by now."

Booth wanted to go to his family so he could gloat in what he did, but he knew the Federals would be keeping an eye on his family in case he showed up there.

In Golden Beach, David Herold moved down Main Street and soon came upon the Chesapeake Café, which was already busy with a good number of customers in booths and at tables. The clock on the wall indicated that it was ten minutes after seven.

Approaching the counter, Herold told the friendly man who greeted him that he needed two breakfasts to go, and told him what he wanted.

After writing the order down, the man said, "I suppose you've heard about the president being shot."

Feigning ignorance, Herold put a shocked look on his face. "Shot! No. What happened?"

"That Shakespearean actor John Wilkes Booth crept up behind Mr. Lincoln at Ford's Theatre last night and shot him in the head."

"Oh no! They caught Booth, I take it."

"No. He got away. In fact, he and an accomplice are somewhere in Maryland right now. Union cavalry patrols are swarming all over the state, looking for them high and low."

"Mmm. I see. Well, too bad the president is dead."

"Oh, he isn't dead."

Herold's jaw slacked. "I thought you said Booth shot him in the head."

"I did. But a wire that came to our police chief at six o'clock this morning said Mr. Lincoln is still alive. Mrs. Lincoln is at his side."

"Hmm. I see."

"Well, excuse me. I'll get this order to the cooks."

Herold moved to an unoccupied table and sat down. Four men at the adjacent table were talking about the assassination attempt. Herold heard one man marveling how the president could still be alive. The others agreed.

Another man then told how late last night, the sentries at the Navy Yard Bridge told army officials that John Wilkes Booth and a man who gave his name as Harold Smith had given them a story about having to get to Beantown in a hurry and were allowed to cross the bridge. This had taken place less than two hours after the president had been shot.

Soon the food was ready, and packed in a cardboard container. Herold talked the man into selling him a cup, paid him, and hurried down Main Street, dreading to tell John that he had not killed Lincoln, after all.

Because of the increasing intensity of the pain in his leg, John Wilkes Booth slipped off the log, lay flat on his back on the ground, and rested his head on the small end of the log.

He closed his eyes and whispered, "Come on, Dave. This thing is getting unbearable."

Even as the words were coming out of his mouth, Booth heard footsteps. He opened his eyes and saw his friend hastening through the forest toward him.

Drawing up, Herold frowned and said, "You all right?"

"Yeah. I had to lie down to ease the pain. It's getting pretty bad."

"Well, I've got a cup. First thing will be to get the laudanum in you. Then you can put breakfast on top of it."

Booth watched as Herold poured water from his canteen into the cup, then put what he estimated would be the two teaspoonfuls of laudanum and stirred it with his finger. Kneeling beside Booth, he said, "Can you sit up?"

Without replying, Booth did so. Herold handed him the cup, and Booth gulped it down, making sure he got the last drop.

Herold sat down on the log and took the food out of the cardboard container. Laying it before Booth, he took his own food and said, "Better get it down, John. Otherwise that laudanum might make you sick to your stomach. We still have a way to go, and I don't need you passing out on me."

Booth chuckled and put a mock sneer on his face. "Don't worry, pal. Lincoln's dead. Nobody can stop me now." As he spoke, he reached for a biscuit with ham and cheese layered inside it.

The dread inside David Herold was building. While they ate, he told Booth how he had learned from the friendly man at the counter in the café that the Union Cavalry was swarming all over Maryland looking for "that Shakespearean actor John Wilkes Booth" who had shot President Lincoln and his accomplice.

Booth swallowed a mouthful of food. "Didn't take them long, did it?"

"No. I heard some men at a table in the café talking about it, and one man told them how the federal officials had talked to the sentries at the Navy Yard Bridge late last night. They identified you, of course, and told the officials that your partner had told them his name was Harold Smith."

Booth had taken another bite.

"I think we'd better get out of Maryland as soon as possible, John," said Herold. "We've got to get into Virginia."

Booth swallowed the food. "You're right. As soon as possible."

Herold cleared his throat nervously. "Uh...John...there's something else I need to tell you."

Booth didn't like the tone in his friend's voice. He was about to take another bite, but stopped short, frowned, and looked at him warily. "What's that?"

Herold cleared his throat again. "Well...that man at the counter in the café also told me that Lincoln is still alive."

Booth sucked in his breath. "He's lying! I put that bullet in Lincoln's head! It had to have killed him instantly."

"The man would have no reason to lie. Those men in the café I told you about; they were talking about what a wonder it is that the president is still alive. By some miracle, John, the man who set the slaves free is still alive."

Booth glowered, his body stiffening. His eyes flashed with fire. "He can't live! He just can't! I laid my life on the line to rid the world of him, and—" Booth jerked in a spasm of pain.

Herold laid a hand on his shoulder. "Settle down, John. You're gonna make your leg worse."

Booth relaxed and nodded. "Yeah. You're right. How can he still be breathing, Dave? A bullet in the brain means instant death."

"Maybe you missed his brain. But with a slug in his head, how's he gonna live? Maybe he'll still die."

"I hope so," Booth said with a tremor in his voice. "Dave, we need to work fast on getting outta Maryland."

"Yeah. We sure do. I just thought of somebody who can help us."

"Who?"

"I know of a Maryland man who was a Confederate agent during the War. His name is Thomas Jones. During the War, Jones helped many Confederate couriers cross the Potomac River back and forth between Maryland and Virginia. He lives in the Tall Timbers area on the Potomac, near Maryland's Zekiah Swamp, southeast of Lexington Park about seven or eight miles. Jones knows the shoreline well. He can help us find the best place to cross and take us in his boat."

"You say he lives in the Tall Timbers area, but you don't know exactly where?"

"No, but with a little ingenuity, we'll find him."

"Sure. We need to get to Thomas Jones real quick, Dave."

"You feel like riding your horse, or do you want to ride with me some more?"

"The laudanum is taking effect. Let me try riding my own horse."

The fugitives rode steadily southward toward the Tall Timbers area of Maryland, but only at a leisurely trot.

When night fell under heavy clouds, they camped in the woods near Leonardtown. Herold went into town and returned with food. Booth was given another dose of the laudanum mixture, then as they ate, he said, "Dave, did you hear anything in Leonardtown about Lincoln still being alive?"

"No. But I heard more about Union army troops combing Maryland with a vengeance, desperately wanting to catch you. The federal authorities in Washington are calling you the coward who shot President Lincoln, and are saying when you're caught, they're going to hang you publicly on Pennsylvania Avenue right in front of the White House."

For an instant, a blood-freezing image rose at the back of Booth's mind: his lifeless body hanging at the end of a rope with a crowd of people looking on with pleasure. He shook himself mentally. "Coward, huh? What do they mean, coward? I had the guts to walk right into Ford's Theatre, climb the stairs to the private boxes and shoot the big-shot president, didn't I? Lots of other people wanted him dead, but I was the only one who did anything about it. Where do they get the gall to—"

A flash of lightning high in the clouds cut off Booth's words, and was followed instantly by a deep rumble of thunder.

Herold looked up. "There's an old shack about a hundred and fifty yards from here. I noticed it when I was going into town. It's abandoned, I'm sure. We'd better get to it."

"Let's do it," said Booth.

More lightning provided light for them as they led their horses toward the shack, with Booth limping along, using his crutch.

Suddenly the rain came in a downpour, accompanied by a powerful wind. Branches whipped at their faces and caches of water tipped from overhanging tree limbs, soaking their clothes and hair. The horses whinnied as the galelike wind seemed to push them back. Booth and Herold leaned into the wind, heads down, struggling for every hard-won step.

After a while, lightning showed them the shack. They picked up pace as much as possible and drew up to the door. They tied the horses to the shack on the opposite side from where the wind was coming and scurried inside.

More lightning showed them a dirt floor and some old, broken chairs. Other than those, the shack was empty. They sat on the dirt floor and did what they could to wipe the water from their faces and to squeeze it out of their hair.

Speaking above the rumble of thunder, Herold said, "John, the best thing we can do is try to sleep."

"I know," said Booth, "but it's going to be pretty hard with all this noise around us."

"Well, let's try."

Both men lay on the floor for some time as the storm continued to assail the shack, then it began to abate. By the time the storm was gone, and all was quiet, both men were asleep.

The angry crowd that had gathered on Pennsylvania Avenue kept roaring the word "Coward!" as John Wilkes Booth was ushered from the police wagon toward the gallows that had been hastily constructed next to the iron fence that surrounded the White House. His hands were shackled behind his back.

Between the tall, vertical iron rods of the fence, Booth caught a glimpse of the impressive white presidential structure as strong hands pushed him closer to the steps of the gallows platform. A single noose dangled from the heavy beam that ran the length of the gallows, tossed by the slight breeze.

His knees went watery as they pushed him up the steps, and the terror that gripped him moved into his midsection, eating at his stomach. When Booth reached the floor of the platform, his eyes fell on the outline of the trapdoor. Revulsion swelled the muscles of his throat, sealing off the air to his lungs.

The crowd continued to scream at him, making the word *Coward!* burn into his consciousness.

When the strong hands halted him beneath the swinging noose and on the trapdoor, Booth's chest was in spasms. He felt his heartbeat throbbing behind his eyes, in his ears, and in his throat.

And then…they dropped the noose over his head and cinched it up tight around his neck. Above the pounding of his heart and the roaring of the crowd, he heard one of the police officers ask, "Where's the hood? Aren't we going to put the hood on him?"

"No!" came the answer. "The crowd wants to watch every contortion of this cowardly assassin's face when he hits the end of the rope!"

Down below, Booth saw the hangman place his hand on the lever that would release the trapdoor and drop him to the end of the rope.

Booth's mouth stretched into a hideous angle as the trapdoor gave way, caught forever at the moment of a chopped scream as he plunged downward.

Suddenly John Wilkes Booth found himself sitting up in the shack with moonlight streaming through one of the dirty windows. He gasped. "No-o-o! No-o-o!"

A sleepy-eyed David Herold sat up and peered at him. "John, what's wrong?"

"I…I was having a nightmare!" he said, partially choking on the words.

"About what?"

"I…I was being hanged in front of the White House with a huge crowd looking on! They were calling me a coward."

"Well, settle down," said Herold. "It was only a dream. You're fine. Go back to sleep."

"I…I can't. I might dream the same thing again."

Herold's brow furrowed. "You're never going to sleep again? Come on, pal. You need your rest. We can't get to Thomas Jones and across the Potomac into Virginia if you're worn out."

Booth palmed cold sweat from his face. "All right. I'll go back to sleep."

THE ANGRY, WILD-EYED CROWD that had gathered on Pennsylvania Avenue kept shouting out the word *Coward!* as John Wilkes Booth was ushered from the police wagon toward the gallows next to the iron fence that surrounded the White House grounds. His hands were shackled behind his back.

Booth's knees were turning watery as they pushed him toward the steps, and he suddenly dug his heels in the ground, screaming, "No-o-o! No-o-o! Not again! You can't hang me again! No-o-o!"

"John!" came the voice of David Herold into his nightmare. "John! Wake up!"

Suddenly Booth came awake, opened his eyes, and saw the form of his friend bending over him in the pale moonlight. The trees of the forest swayed in the breeze above him. Their gnarled and twisted limbs seemed to stretch their arms toward him in a sinister embrace.

Booth gasped and swallowed with difficulty. "It was the same nightmare again, Dave. They were calling me a coward and were going to hang me."

Herold sighed. "That's two nights in a row, John. Was it exactly the same as last night in the shack?"

"Exactly," said Booth, sitting up and rubbing his eyes. "It's horrible, Dave."

"Well, maybe that'll be the last one."

"I hope so." Booth sleeved cold sweat from his brow. "I can't take much more of this."

They were near the edge of the woods. Herold looked across

the fields to his left and set his eyes on the farmhouse and out-buildings some three hundred yards away. "Well, since we found Thomas Jones's place just after midnight, thanks to those nice people in Tall Timbers, I'm sure he'll have us across the river by tomorrow night. Maybe once you're in Virginia, you won't dream like that anymore."

"I sure hope you're right. So when are we going to knock on Mr. Jones's door?"

"Well, I suppose we'd better wait till he's had breakfast. Since he's got milk cows, he'll no doubt do the milking before breakfast. We'll just have to keep an eye on the place." He paused. "Do you think you can get back to sleep now? It can't be more than two o'clock."

"I'll try."

"Good. Come sunup, we'll eat this food we picked up in Tall Timbers for breakfast and get some more laudanum in you. How's the leg?"

"Hurting a little, but not too bad. I can wait till morning."

The morning sun was shining down from a partly cloudy sky, and the birds were singing in the trees as the fugitives stepped onto the porch of the Jones house. John Wilkes Booth was leaning on his crutch as David Herold knocked on the door.

Seconds later, they heard light footsteps inside, and when the door came open, they were looking at a woman in her early fifties with her dark hair pulled back in a bun. There were silver strands at her temples and crinkles at the corners of her eyes. She smiled. "Hello. May I help you, gentlemen?"

"Are you Mrs. Jones?" asked Herold.

"Yes."

"We need to talk to your husband if possible. It is very impor-tant."

"Does my husband know you?" she asked politely.

"No, ma'am. But I know about him. My name is David Herold. I'm a Marylander, but I'm a true son of the South, as is my friend here."

Mrs. Jones let her eyes stray to Booth, who was leaning on his crutch a couple of steps behind Herold. "Oh, my. You're hurt."

"He is, ma'am," said Herold, "and his injury is related to the reason we need to see Mr. Jones."

"Who is it, Beth?" came a masculine voice from inside the house.

"A couple of men who are asking to see you, dear," replied Beth, turning her head toward him to speak.

There were rapid footsteps and a tall, slender man in his mid-fifties with a handlebar mustache appeared. He noted the man with the crutch, then set his pale gray eyes on Herold.

Looking at Herold, Beth said, "This is Mr. David Herold, dear. Both of these men are Confederate sympathizers, and live here in Maryland. I didn't get the other gentleman's name."

"David Herold," repeated Jones. "Your name has a familiar ring, but I don't believe I know you."

Herold smiled. "Let me see if you know the name of my friend. Does John Wilkes Booth ring a bell?"

Jones's mouth sagged and his eyes widened. "Oh, my!"

"Thomas!" Beth gasped. "This is the man who—"

"Yes! Who shot Abraham Lincoln! And now I know why Mr. Herold's name is familiar! Beth, I'm going to take them out to the barn. I must hide them quickly."

Beth nodded. "I'll stay right here. If I should see a cavalry unit coming, I'll ring the dinner bell as a warning."

Booth hobbled swiftly on his crutch in order to keep up with the other two men as they led the horses across the yard. When they were inside the barn, Jones faced them. "Mr. Booth, you did the country a great favor! But the federal cavalry is known to be combing this area with slavering mouths. Like beasts of prey, they want to catch you in the worst way. With my reputation as a Confederate agent, I dare not keep you in my home. My place is bound to be searched any day."

"What we were hoping, Mr. Jones," said Herold, "was that you could get us across the Potomac into Virginia."

"I'll be glad to do that, but it's too dangerous to try it right now. The federals are combing the river bank. I will take you to a place in the swamp where you can hide. You'll have to stay there till the army has given up on finding you in these parts and has turned their search elsewhere. You'll have to remain in the swamp until it is safe to cross the Potomac. My boat won't hold your horses, so you'll have to leave them behind."

"We'll find some after we get into Virginia," said Herold. "Main thing now is to get out of Maryland."

Booth looked Jones in the eye. "Have you heard about Lincoln? Is he still alive? The last we heard, he was."

Jones smiled. "Lincoln is dead. I found out late yesterday afternoon from a neighbor who had just been in Washington that the archenemy of the South died at 7:22 the morning after you shot him. Abraham Lincoln's tombstone will say he died on April 15, 1865."

Elation washed through Booth like warm water. Popping his palms together, he said, "Great! All the pain I've suffered is worth it!"

"Word is that you hurt your leg when you jumped onto the stage from the president's box to make your escape," said Jones.

"Right. I broke it. Found a doctor Dave knew about, got the bone set and the splint put on. It's been rough traveling with it like this, but like I said, it's worth it."

"You're a brave man, Mr. Booth," said Jones.

Booth looked at Herold and smiled. "That's better than what they tell me I'm being called in Washington, huh?"

"Sure is," said his friend. "In Washington, they're calling him a coward."

Jones chuckled dryly. "I guess it depends on which side you're serving. Well, let's get you two out into the swamp. Mrs. Jones and I will see that you have plenty to eat and drink."

It was almost nine o'clock the next morning when Thomas Jones appeared in the swamp carrying food for his guests.

Herold mixed the laudanum first, which Booth drank down quickly. While they were wolfing down their food, Jones said, "I just got word from a neighbor who was in town early this morning that the newspapers are reporting the whole story of the assassination, including that you two are being hunted all over Maryland. He told me the paper he read said that Lewis Paine, Samuel Arnold, Michael O'Laughlin, Edman Spangler, and George Atzerodt have been arrested by federal authorities as conspirators with you two in the assassination of the president. Were they really in on it with you?"

"Sure were," said Herold.

Booth frowned. "Did your neighbor say how they were detected and caught?"

"He didn't give me much in the way of details, but it had to do with a boardinghouse in Washington, D.C., where Lewis Paine was staying. Anna Surratt, the woman who owns the boarding-house is a Confederate sympathizer, and the day after Lincoln was shot Paine was bragging to her about the part he and his four cohorts had in helping you two get away. A young man who was a guest in the boardinghouse overheard it all and reported it to the federal authorities. Within a couple of days, all five had been arrested and jailed."

Booth pulled at an ear nervously. "They'll probably hang them."

"I'd say so," said Jones.

For the next two days, Booth and Herold continued to hide in the swamp. They were brought food and newspapers by Thomas Jones. The newspapers were full of the accounts of the assassination, the president's death, the arrest of the five accomplices, and of the dogged search for the assassin and his accomplice throughout Maryland by the federal troops.

Just before dawn on Thursday, April 20, Jones made his way through the heavy brush, carrying a partially loaded gunnysack, and found the two men asleep. Standing over them, he said in a hoarse whisper, "Mr. Booth! Mr. Herold!"

Herold was first to stir and open his eyes. "Yeah?"

"Just wanted you to know that the cavalry is moving through the immediate area, and should be gone sometime this afternoon. They will search my place, I'm sure."

Booth began to stir.

Lifting the gunnysack, Jones said, "There's food and water in here for your breakfast, lunch, and supper. I dare not come out here until the troops are gone, and I have no idea when they'll show up. Once they're gone, and are positively out of the area, I'll come out and let you know."

Booth opened his eyes and focused on Jones in the dim light. "Something wrong?"

"Not really," said Jones. "I explained it to Mr. Herold. He can explain it to you."

With that, Jones laid the gunnysack down and said, "I need to get back to the house. I'll take you across the Potomac to Sandy Point, Virginia, under cover of darkness tonight."

Thomas Jones guided his boat up to the bank of the Potomac River near Sandy Point, jumped out, and pulled the bow up on dry ground. The moon was behind a bank of clouds, but there was enough light for David Herold to safely help his injured friend from the boat.

"Well, gentlemen," said Jones, "you're on your own, now. I hope you find a good place to hide from here on out."

"We'll be fine, Mr. Jones, now that we're in Confederate territory," said Booth. "And thank you so much for all you've done for us."

"My pleasure," said Jones. "I'd do it all over again, if needed."

As he spoke, Jones shoved the boat off the bank and hopped in. Taking the oars in hand, he began rowing back across the river.

"Thanks, again!" called Herold.

Jones waved a hand.

"Well," said Herold, "we'd better get going. First thing is to steal us some horses, so you won't have to hop very far on that crutch."

It was almost dawn on that Friday morning when the fugitives came upon a small farm where they spotted several saddle horses in the corral. Leaving Booth at the corral gate, Herold worked fast. He found saddles and bridles inside the barn, and soon they were riding away.

Less than an hour later, they caught sight of a cavalry unit riding out of a farmer's yard. Rushing their horses down into a gully, they pulled rein, fear showing on their faces.

"Wouldn't you know it?" said Herold. "They're searching for us in Virginia, too."

"So what do we do now?" asked Booth.

Herold pondered it a moment. "Keep riding, and keep our eyes peeled for more cavalry units. Let's head south. I think the farther we go in that direction, the safer we'll be. The farther we get from D.C., the more true, loyal Southerners there are. We'll find somebody who will hide us till the Federals give up. If not, we'll go on down into the Carolinas. Somebody, somewhere down there will help us."

Herold dismounted and cautiously climbed to the lip of the gully. After studying the land around him for a few minutes, he returned to his friend and said, "They seem to be gone. Let's ride."

After riding for almost an hour, keeping their eyes peeled, Booth and Herold caught sight of another cavalry unit. This one was riding away from a small settlement where they had been talking to a group of people and were turning their direction.

"Come on!" said Booth, veering his horse off the road into the dense forest they had been skirting.

Herold followed, and they hastily threaded their way deeper into the forest a good hundred yards before stopping amid a thick stand of trees.

When they felt they had given the cavalry unit plenty of time to pass the forest and be a good distance away, they returned to the road and kept moving south.

Saturday proved to be difficult, too, with federal troops combing the area. When the fugitives were hiding in another thick stand of trees at midmorning, watching the soldiers talking to a farmer and his family in their yard, Herold's voice was lined with discouragement as he said, "John, we don't have a chance. There are too many army units. They're going to stay on our trail till they catch us."

Booth frowned at his friend. "Dave, this doesn't sound like you.

Come on. We are gonna make it. We have to. If they caught us, I'd be the one to hang, but because they consider you my accomplice, they'd lock you up in prison and throw the key away. We can't let that happen. We've got to keep our chins up. Sooner or later we'll find somebody who will help us—like you said. After so much time goes by, the federals will find other things to do rather than hunt for us."

Herold sighed and nodded. "Sure. You're right. We have to keep going and not give up."

Late that afternoon, they rode their horses across a broad place in the Rappahannock River where the water was shallow, and found a secluded spot in the nearby woods to rest for the night.

That evening, Herold left Booth and went to the nearby town of Loretto to get food.

The next morning—Sunday, April 23—they ate a late breakfast, and with a fresh dose of laudanum in Booth's system, they rode down the road that led to Loretto and soon found themselves approaching a church on the outskirts of the town, where many buggies, wagons, and saddle horses were collected in the parking lot. As they drew near, they could hear the congregation singing.

Suddenly, they caught sight of a cavalry unit as it topped a hill on the same road no more than a mile away.

"Over here!" blurted Booth, and plunged his horse into a thick stand of trees a few yards from the road.

When Herold caught up to him, they dismounted, tied their horses to low-hanging branches, and each took a position behind a tree trunk, eyes riveted up the road.

They watched the troops draw up to the church, turn into the yard, and dismount. They counted eight men in uniform as they entered into the building two by two.

Booth started to say something to his friend, but Herold looked over Booth's shoulder, raised a vertical forefinger to his lips and said, "Sh-h-h!"

At the same instant, Booth heard male voices and turned to see what Herold was looking at. Two middle-aged farmers were coming from a field behind the stand of trees, toward the road, talking. As they passed by without noticing Booth, Herold, and their horses, they were discussing the federal troops who had just gone inside the church.

"Yeah, Lester, I heard that the Federals will be entering churches all over this part of Virginia today. They want to ask more people at one time if they have seen Booth and Herold, and if nobody in the congregation has seen 'em, then to encourage 'em to keep their eyes peeled for those two."

"Personally, I hope they get away," said the other. "They are true sons of the South."

Booth and Herold looked at each other and smiled.

While the troops were inside the Loretto church, some twenty miles west another federal cavalry unit rode into a churchyard on the outskirts of Bowling Green, Virginia, and began dismounting. Through the open windows, they heard the congregation just finishing the last line of "A Mighty Fortress Is Our God."

Inside the church, the song leader stepped away from the pulpit while the people were easing onto the pews. Pastor Olan Granger left his chair, moved up to the pulpit, opened his Bible, and said, "John, chapter four in your Bibles, please. John, the fourth chapter. We will begin reading in verse one, and read down through verse—"

Suddenly the pastor's words were cut off by the sound of heavy footsteps in the foyer, then the doors opened, and every eye in the congregation turned to see seven uniformed men enter. Six remained just inside the double doors, while the seventh made his way up the aisle. "Pastor Granger, I apologize for interrupting your service, but I need to speak to your people. It is very important."

Noting the man's rank by the insignia on his uniform, Granger nodded. "Please come up here, Lieutenant."

"Thank you, sir," the lieutenant said politely.

When he stepped up on the platform, the pastor asked, "Does this have to do with your search for John Wilkes Booth?"

"It does, sir."

"All right. You may address the congregation."

The officer moved up beside the pulpit and ran his gaze over the faces of the people. "Ladies and gentlemen, my name is

Lieutenant Edward Doherty. As most of you already know, the federal government is on an all-out search for John Wilkes Booth, who assassinated President Lincoln, and his accomplice, David Herold. They were last known to be in Maryland, but military leaders in Washington, D.C., believe they may now be in Virginia."

While Doherty was giving a vivid description of the fugitives, the children in the congregation were looking on, wide-eyed.

On the second pew from the front, a family named Garrett was sitting together. Ten-year-old Rya Garrett, who was positioned between her parents, gripped her father's hand and looked up at him. Her eyes were round and luminous in the ashen pallor of her skin. "Papa," she whispered, "I'm scared."

Richard Garrett bent his head down with his wife and other children looking on, and whispered, "Sweetheart, there is nothing to be afraid of. We aren't in any danger."

Taking comfort in her father's words, she nodded, and the fear left her big blue eyes.

Having given the detailed description of the fugitives—including the fact that Booth had been treated for a broken left leg and was wearing a splint on his leg and using a crutch—the lieutenant said, "I must ask you now, have any of you seen either or both of these two men?"

There was dead silence.

Doherty took a deep breath. "All right. I am asking that if you should spot them, that you notify your local law enforcement authorities. They will, in turn, notify the army. Booth and Herold are dangerous men. Under no circumstances are you to try to capture them yourselves."

Doherty thanked the pastor for allowing him to speak to the congregation, then led his men from the building.

Pastor Olan Granger ran his gaze over the faces before him. "As you know, we have already been praying that Booth and Herold will be captured. Lieutenant Doherty told you that they are dangerous men. My concern is for the innocent people in their path. The fugitives are desperate to escape capture. They no doubt will harm anyone who would seem to be a threat, and of course, must hide themselves as they travel to avoid capture. They will have to use people to do this, which will put those individuals in danger."

The people in the pews were nodding their agreement.

Pastor Granger led the congregation in prayer, asking God to hasten the capture of the two fugitives, then preached his sermon.

After the service, as people were leaving the building and heading for their wagons, buggies, and horses in the parking lot, the Garrett family was standing beside their buggy, talking to other members of the church about the two fugitives and the danger they were presenting to the people of Maryland and Virginia.

Twelve-year-old Saul Garrett was in conversation with his best friend, McClain Reardon, who would soon turn thirteen.

"McClain," said Saul, "I stayed all night with you the last time, so it's your turn to stay all night with me this time. Can you come home with me on Tuesday after school and stay all night?"

McClain, who had a thick shock of black, wavy hair, grinned and said, "I think Mom will let me come." His eyes ran to his parents who had just shaken hands with the preacher and were headed toward them. "Here they come. I'll ask her."

Hal and Ruth Reardon drew up and were greeted by Richard and Laura Garrett.

McClain said, "Mom, excuse me, but could I ask you something?"

"Sure, son," said his mother.

"Saul wants to know if I can go home from school with him this coming Tuesday and stay all night."

Laura Garrett said, "Ruth, Saul already had permission from us to make the invitation. We'd love to have him again."

Ten-year-old Rya had picked up the conversation and was looking at McClain with adoring eyes. Observing the scene with great interest, she smiled to herself when Ruth Reardon turned to her husband and asked if there were any special chores he had planned for McClain to do on Tuesday after school. Hal Reardon said it was all right; he had no special chores planned for McClain any day this week.

Rya's smile broadened. "McClain, I'm glad you will be coming to spend the night at our house again."

Grinning at her, McClain said, "Thank you, Rya. I always enjoy staying at the Garrett farm."

Everyone in the group was looking on as Rya giggled and said, "Even when Saul makes you help him with the chores?"

"I don't mind," said McClain. "When he stays at our place, he always helps me with my chores."

Seventeen-year-old Jack Reardon chuckled. "McClain, I hope Saul does a better job helping you with your chores than he does on his own chores at home. I have to go around and finish his work half the time."

Saul playfully punched his big brother's upper arm. "Hah! It's usually me having to finish your sloppy work for you so Papa doesn't tan your hide."

Everybody laughed, and Hal and Ruth Reardon told Richard and Laura Garrett they would see them in the evening service. They headed for their wagon with McClain between them.

Rya kept her shining eyes on McClain while the Reardons were climbing into their wagon. She had admired McClain Reardon since she first met him as a very young child. Her beaming face showed how happy she was that McClain would be spending the night once again with her older brother. She kept her eyes on McClain until the wagon rounded a bend and he disappeared from her sight.

Her big sister, Ella, who was fifteen, noted it and smiled to herself.

"Well, we'd better head for the farm," said Richard. "Your mama's got a roast in the oven." He turned to Jack. "You want to drive home?"

"Sure!" said Jack, his eyes dancing.

"Okay," said Richard. "Let's go."

As the Garrett family was climbing into the wagon, Saul elbowed Rya in the ribs. "Boy, little sis, are you ever stuck on my best friend!"

Rya blushed, but did not deny it.

While Jack was climbing into the driver's seat, Richard helped Laura up beside him from the other side of the buggy, then sat down next to her.

As Rya sat down on the second seat between Saul and her big sister, Ella giggled as she patted her arm and said, "Honey, you might as well forget about a romance with McClain. He's too old for you."

Rya looked longingly toward the last spot she had seen McClain, but did not reply.

5

As THE GARRETT BUGGY ROLLED DOWN THE ROAD toward their farm with Jack Garrett at the reins, Ella spoke up from the second seat. "Papa, have John Wilkes Booth and his partner left Maryland and come into Virginia?"

Looking over his shoulder at Ella, Richard said, "I would think they'd come to Virginia because it is a Southern state, honey. Maryland does have a small percentage of people who are Southerners at heart, but it's a Northern state. Virginia may have a few people who remained loyal to the North during the war, but the vast majority are true Southerners. Since Booth and Herold are going to need help evading the federal troops, it seems to me they would come to Virginia. And that's why the Federals think they are in Virginia right now."

"If I was them, I'd sure want to get out of Maryland," put in Saul.

"But actually they are Marylanders, aren't they, Papa?"

"Yes, they're in that small percentage of Marylanders who are Southerners at heart."

"Then why wouldn't they stay in Maryland, Papa?" queried Rya. "Wouldn't their family and friends help them hide?"

"They would if called upon, sweet stuff. But the federal authorities are watching their families and friends real close, you can be sure of that. Booth and Herold know that, so they won't go anywhere near them."

"Oh," said Rya.

"Booth must have had a deep hatred for President Lincoln," said Laura as the sound of the horses' hooves clopping on the road and the squeak of the buggy wheels filled the air. "He had to know he was taking a real chance to shoot him in a place filled with people like he did."

"Hatred does strange things to people, honey," said Richard, meeting her gaze. "Like the crowd that day in Jerusalem who called for the Lord Jesus to be crucified when Pontius Pilate asked what he should do with Him. Their hatred for Him turned them into a frenzied mob."

"Bad people," said Rya. "Jesus was so good to them."

"That He was, honey," said Laura. "To show them that He was the Son of God, He healed sick people and even gave them food. He showed them nothing but love and kindness."

"Bad people," repeated Rya. "Papa?"

"Yes, sweet stuff?"

"Since President Lincoln was an enemy of the South, and John Wilkes Booth was a Southerner at heart, was it right for John Wilkes Booth to shoot him?"

"Mr. Lincoln wasn't really an enemy of the South, Rya. He was an enemy of slavery. He didn't believe that one human being should own another human being. And besides that, so many of the slave owners were brutal to their slaves. Mr. Lincoln knew that and condemned their brutality. But to answer your question, it was definitely not right for John Wilkes Booth to shoot and kill him. What he did was murder, and murder is never right."

"Never," put in Laura.

"What about when a policeman shoots and kills a criminal during the act of a crime, Papa?" asked Jack. "Is that murder?"

"No, it's not."

"But the sixth of the Ten Commandments says, 'Thou shalt not kill.'"

"Son—and I want all of you to listen to this—when law officers have to kill lawbreakers who are a threat to the lives of innocent people, it is not murder. No more than when soldiers fight on battlefields to defend their country and their families from aggressors, and kill the enemy soldiers."

"But Papa," spoke up Ella, "the Bible still says, 'Thou shalt not kill.'"

"You've got your Bible in your hand, honey," said Richard. "Open it to Matthew chapter nineteen."

Saul and Rya looked on as their sister opened her Bible. "Okay, Papa. I've got it."

"All right, look at verse seventeen."

"Uh-huh."

"Notice Jesus is talking to a man about keeping the commandments?"

"Yes."

"Now, read us verse eighteen."

Ella cleared her throat. "'He saith unto him, Which? Jesus said, Thou shalt do no murder, Thou shalt not commit adultery, Thou shalt not steal, Thou shalt not bear false witness....'"

"Jesus goes on, listing more of the Ten Commandments," said Richard, "such as honoring your father and mother and loving your neighbor as yourself. But look again at the one that corresponds with 'Thou shalt not kill.' What did He say?"

"'Thou shalt do no murder.'"

"Do you see it, children? Jesus is interpreting for us what 'Thou shalt not kill' means. It means 'thou shalt do no murder.' He is the only one we can always trust to interpret Scripture without error because He is the one who gave it to us. So when law officers have to kill criminals in the line of duty, and when soldiers have to kill the enemy to protect their homeland and loved ones, it is not murder.

"When David killed Goliath with his own sword, it was not murder. He and Goliath came face-to-face, and Goliath told David he was going to kill him and feed his body to the birds of the air and the beasts of the field. For David, it was self-defense. It was kill or be killed. When it is self-defense, it is not murder.

"We find in the Bible that God sometimes told the armies of Israel to go out and slay their enemies. Whether it was the Philistines, the Syrians, the Ammonites, or some other enemies, they were always armed, and the Israelites met them on a field of battle. Killing their enemies in battle was not murder."

"That makes sense, Papa," said Jack.

"Now, back to Rya's question: it was not right for John Wilkes Booth to murder President Lincoln because he considered him an enemy of the South. Booth did not shoot Mr. Lincoln on a battle-field. Mr. Lincoln was unarmed and was posing no threat to Booth's life. What Booth did was murder and it was terribly wrong. Do you all understand?"

All four of the Garrett children said yes.

"Good," said Laura.

"May I remind you," said Richard, "that we should still be loyal Southerners. Booth and his accomplice do not represent true Southerners. True Southerners will sharply disagree with what Booth did. And something else—although as Christians, we must be against slavery, we are still Southerners and will remain loyal to the South, even though the war is over."

On Monday afternoon, John Wilkes Booth and David Herold were nearing the town of Bowling Green when they saw a lone rider coming toward them.

As they and the rider drew nearer each other, Herold straightened in the saddle. "John, this fellow coming our way is a friend of mine. We'll get some help now."

Booth focused on the rider. "Who is he?"

"Willie Jett. His reputation as a Confederate soldier in the war is well-known. He was a tough sergeant and a hero in battle. He's a true son of the South. We've known each other for years."

"Good," said Booth. "It's about time things were turning our way."

Herold lifted a hand and waved as the gap between them was closing.

Recognizing Herold, the tall, slender Willie Jett smiled and waved back.

As they pulled rein and met up, Jett said, "Dave, there are a bunch of troops all over this area looking for you. And this has to be John Wilkes Booth."

"John, shake hands with my old pal, Willie Jett," said Herold.

Leaning from their saddles, Booth and Jett shook hands.

Jett said, "John, I'm proud of you for ridding the country of Abraham Lincoln. In my eyes, you're a real hero."

Booth smiled thinly and nodded.

"But like I said," Jett went on, "there are lots of troops in these parts, looking for you two."

"We know," said Herold. "We're doing our best to elude them."

"Well, if you need a place to hide, I'll find it for you."

The fugitives grinned at each other, then Herold said, "We sure do need a place to hole up."

"Well, with my reputation as an ex-Confederate soldier, it wouldn't be safe for you at my place. The troops have already been there twice. They don't trust me one little bit. They'll be back again."

"I've been traveling under the name of Harold Smith," said Herold, "and John's telling people his name is James W. Boyd. Show him your tattoo, John."

Exposing the tattoo on his hand, Booth said, "Did that when I was a kid. So I had to come up with a name that matched these initials."

Jett studied the tattoo and nodded. "I know where I'm going to take you, Mr. Boyd and Mr. Smith. I'm acquainted with a farmer some three miles south of Bowling Green who is unswervingly loyal to the Confederacy. His name is Richard Garrett, and his family is as loyal to the South as is Richard. I know the Garretts will hide you if we make some changes."

"Changes?" said Booth.

"Mm-hmm. We'll have to tell the Garretts that you, Sergeant James W. Boyd, are a Confederate soldier who was wounded in the battle at Petersburg, Virginia, on April 2. And your friend Harold Smith is trying to get you home to Fairfax. However, your battered, broken leg is hurting you severely, and you need a place to rest for a few days. I'll tell Richard and Laura that if the Federals who are looking for Lincoln's assassin and his accomplice should come upon Sergeant James W. Boyd, they would arrest him for not reporting to the Union authorities since the war is over. They'll gladly hide you, I have no doubt."

"But how will I convince them I was in the Petersburg battle, dressed like this?" asked Booth, pointing to his clothes.

"I was coming to that," said Jett. "I'll give you one of my old Confederate uniforms. We'll rip it up, put some chicken blood on it, and soil it good, so it looks like you've been in battle. How's that sound?"

"Plenty good," said Booth.

Jett looked at Herold. "And I'll give you a change of civilian clothes, Dave. The federal troops have been giving your descriptions to people all over these parts, including what you were wearing when you crossed the Navy Yard Bridge and when you visited that Dr. Mudd."

"Anything like that will help," said Herold.

"There must be more changes, too," said Jett. "The troops have described your physical features in detail. Since you both wear mustaches and your hair rather long, you need to shave off the mustaches and we need to do something about your hair. I'll cut your hair real short, John. And, Dave, since your hair is blond, I suggest you let me shave your head completely. Your being a bald man will really disguise you. With that light-colored hair, when your head is shaved, it'll look like you've simply lost your hair. Okay?"

The fugitives exchanged glances then both agreed.

"Good," said Jett. "I'll take you to my house long enough to get these things done, then we'll go to the Garrett farm. The Garretts won't suspect who you really are."

Booth smiled. "Let's go!"

Some two hours later the three men were riding toward the Garrett farm south of Bowling Green. Their horses were moving at a leisurely pace.

Hanging onto his crutch with one hand and the reins with the other, Booth looked at Jett. "I realize we needed these changes, Willie, but if this Garrett family is so loyal to the Confederacy, why can't we tell them I'm the man who shot Lincoln? Wouldn't they look at me as a hero, like you do?"

"Well, let me explain something. I was about to tell you this anyhow. The Garretts are true Southerners, with unwavering loyalty to the Confederacy. But they're a bit fanatical in their religion. They believe that born-again, washed-in-the-blood stuff. I can tell you that they wouldn't go along with your killing Lincoln, John. They wouldn't welcome you, nor give you a place to stay if they knew your true identity. But they will welcome you and hide you if they think you are Sergeant James W. Boyd, a wounded Confederate soldier who is trying to get home to his family in Fairfax without Union interference."

Booth grinned at Herold, then looked at Jett. "Well, I think we can put up with the Garretts' religious fanaticism if it means we're safe from the federal troops."

"We sure can," agreed Herold.

When the Garrett farm came into view, Willie Jett pointed ahead and said, "That's the place, right up there. The one with the big red barn."

Moments later, Jett moved his horse out ahead and led the fugitives through the Garrett gate, down the tree-lined lane, and up to the front porch of the big white two-story house. As they were dismounting, they noticed a wagon turn off the road and head down the lane.

Jett focused on the wagon's occupants. "Those are the Garrett children," he told Booth and Herold. "No doubt coming home from school."

In the wagon, as Jack held the reins, he said to his siblings, "I wonder what Willie Jett is doing here and who his two friends are."

"I guess we're about to find out," said Ella.

At the house, Laura came out the front door, having noticed the three men through the parlor window. "Hello, Willie," she said with a smile as she crossed the porch. "Nice to see you."

"You too, Laura," he said warmly. "Is Richard on the place?"

"Last I knew, he was out at the barn," she said, glancing at the approaching wagon. "I'll have Jack tell him he has company when he takes the wagon and team back there."

Even as Laura was speaking, Richard came around the corner of the house, carrying a hoe. He smiled and hurried his pace when he saw his old friend. "Hey! Willie! Good to see you."

At the same moment, Jack pulled the wagon to a halt, and the Garrett children listened while climbing down from the wagon as Willie was introducing James W. Boyd and Harold Smith to their parents.

Willie then introduced Jack, Ella, Saul, and Rya to Boyd and Smith, then began telling the Garrett family the story he had devised. While the family heard the story, they observed Boyd in the torn, bloody, and dirty Confederate uniform with the sergeant stripes on the arms. The sympathy they felt showed on their faces.

When Jett was finished with the concocted tale, Richard said, "We will be most happy to give you a place to rest up, Sergeant Boyd. And Mr. Smith, we appreciate what you're doing to help the sergeant get back home to Fairfax."

"We sure do," said Laura. "We have a large guestroom with two beds upstairs. It's at the rear of the house, where you can have your privacy, and it's very quiet. You'll be able to rest all you want."

"We know the federal troops are leaving no stones unturned in their search for John Wilkes Booth and David Herold," said Jett. "If, in their search for them, they should come upon Sergeant Boyd here in your house, they will arrest him for not reporting to the Union authorities, since the war is over. He'll need a hiding place as much as he'll need a resting place."

"That's for sure," said Richard. "I was about to bring up that very thing. I want the sergeant to be comfortable, but even more, I want him to be safe. We'll keep our eyes peeled for any approaching cavalry unit, and if we see them coming, we'll quickly put Sergeant Boyd in the attic. There's a small closet up there that can't even be detected unless you already know it's there."

"And, of course, if the troops should come on the place," said Laura, "it won't make any difference if they find Mr. Smith. We'll just tell them he's our guest, which he is."

Richard looked at Booth. "Sergeant Boyd, I'm wondering if it will be difficult for you to climb the stairs to the attic with your leg in the splint. If we see the Federals coming, you'll have to move fast."

"It may be a bit tricky," said Booth, "but I think I can do it."

"How about we let you try it?" asked Richard. "Just so we'll know."

"Fine with me."

"Well, I'd better be going," said Jett. "Laura, Richard, I really appreciate your helping these two men."

"Our pleasure, Willie," said Richard. "Any friends of yours are friends of mine." He chuckled. "Especially if they are Southerners."

Willie laughed. "You know very well the only friends I have are Southerners!"

Jett mounted up, told Boyd and Smith good-bye, and trotted his horse up the lane. When he reached the road, he hipped around in the saddle and waved. Everybody waved in return, then he rode away.

Jack stepped up close to the two men. "I want to welcome you to our home. And Sergeant Boyd, I want to say that I'm proud of you because you didn't report to the federal authorities. You're a brave man."

Booth released a sheepish grin. "Thank you, Jack."

Ella moved up, with Saul and Rya following on her heels. "Sergeant Boyd," she said in a tender tone, "I'm sorry you were wounded at Petersburg, and I hope you get home to your family real soon. Are you married?"

"Uh...no," said Booth. "But I have my parents, brothers and sisters, aunts, uncles, and cousins in Fairfax. I'm anxious to get home to them."

"Anything I can do to help you, Sergeant?" said Saul.

"Not that I can think of right now," said Booth.

"I'll be glad to help you, too, if I can," said Rya.

Booth forced a smile. "I appreciate that. Thank you."

Laura set soft eyes on her husband. "Darling, since you have those weeds to hoe in the flower garden, and the boys need to put the wagon and team away, as well as put our guests' horses in the corral, the girls and I will take our guests up to their room and get them settled."

"All right," said Richard. "It's a deal." An impish grin curved his mouth. "That is, if you'll still have time to cook supper."

Laura laughed and swung a fist playfully, clipping his chin. "The old stomach first, eh?"

"Well, I'm just a growing boy!" said Richard.

Booth and Herold laughed, then Laura said, "All right, gentlemen, let's get you up to your room."

Richard began his hoeing job. Saul took the reins of the two saddle horses and led them toward the barn. Jack jumped in the wagon and drove it around the house in the same direction.

As they were climbing the stairs, Laura and the girls noticed that Booth was experiencing some pain as he took the stairs slowly, implementing the crutch. Laura asked if he would rather be on the ground floor. He told her he would be fine.

When the guests had been shown their room and the adjoining washroom, they thanked Laura for being so kind to them.

Booth eased down on his chosen bed and sighed.

Rya, who was the curious one of the Garrett children, stepped up close to him. "Sergeant Boyd, what happened to your leg in the battle at Petersburg?"

"Rya," said Laura, "you shouldn't ask such questions."

Booth smiled at her. "That's all right, Mrs. Garrett. I don't mind telling her about it. Well, little lady, I was in charge of six cannons during the battle. When the firing was hot and the smoke was thick, two of my men were both hit with rifle bullets while they were moving their heavy cannon up a slope to a different place to fire on the enemy.

"I saw that the cannon was going to roll down the slope, and we might lose it. I rushed up to stop it, and a bullet hissed by my face just as I touched the cannon. The near miss threw me off balance and I fell. The cannon went rolling down the slope, and one of the wheels ran over my left leg, cutting the skin and breaking the bone."

Rya's big blue eyes showed compassion. "I'm so sorry, Sergeant. I sure hope your leg will be all right."

"I'm sure in time it will be, honey," said Booth.

"You want to tell us more about your family in Fairfax?" asked Rya.

"Rya, we need to go and let these men rest," Laura said. "We also need to get supper started."

"All right, Mama. You'll both like Mama's cooking. Ella and I help, but the cooking is really Mama's."

"I'm sure we'll like it," said Herold. "Thank you, ladies, for your kindness."

Both men lay down on their beds as Laura and the girls left the room.

On their way down the stairs, they were met by Jack and Saul. "Mama," said Jack, "I thought we'd go up and let Sergeant Boyd try those attic stairs, so he'll know if he can get up there all right if the troops come."

"He may want to wait till he gets some rest, Jack," said Laura, "but you can ask him. The door's open."

Laura and the girls were busy in the kitchen when the boys entered some twenty minutes later.

"So how did it go?" asked Laura.

"It was quite a struggle for him, but he finally made it," said Jack.

"He almost fell twice," put in Saul.

"Oh, dear," said Laura. "Maybe we'll have to come up with some other solution."

"That's what I suggested," said Jack, "but he insisted it would be all right."

Laura shrugged. "Well, he's the one who knows."

An hour later, when everyone sat down to supper in the dining room, Booth looked at the dishes of hot food and his mouth watered. He hadn't had a real meal since the day before he had shot Abraham Lincoln.

Herold was also eager to begin eating. "Sure smells good, Mrs. Garrett," he said. "I think I'll start with the fried chicken." As he spoke, he reached for the plate of chicken.

Richard cleared his throat. "Ah...Mr. Smith, we always give thanks to the Lord for our food before a meal."

Herold's face flushed. He retracted his hand. "Oh. I'm sorry."

After Richard had led in prayer and everyone was eating, the Garrett family noticed that their guests were a bit on edge over the prayer being offered. Figuring to take advantage of the opportunity, Richard shared the gospel with them in a tactful and loving way.

Herold said, "I…I appreciate your telling us about your beliefs, Mr. Garrett. It's just that…well, my beliefs are different."

"I mean no disrespect," spoke up Booth, "but my beliefs are different, too."

"Well, gentlemen," said Richard, "if your beliefs are not founded on the Word of God, you will face the God of the Word in eternity and suffer the consequences for not believing and obeying the gospel. Only by repenting of your sin, believing the gospel, and receiving the Christ of the gospel into your heart as personal Saviour can you be saved. To die without Him will be to spend eternity in a burning hell."

Booth swallowed hard. "Uh…Mr. Garrett, thank you for explaining the gospel to us. I…uh…need some time to think it over. I've never heard it like this before."

"Me, either," said Herold. "Thank you for telling it to us."

"Of course. I understand. But please do think about it seriously, and I can tell you more about it later. Let's talk about something else for now. Since you've been traveling from Petersburg, have you seen any of the federal troops searching for John Wilkes Booth and David Herold?"

"Sure haven't," said Herold. "But we've been expecting to. I guess there must be hundreds of them covering Virginia and Maryland."

"Probably close to a thousand, with that much ground to cover," Richard said, setting down his coffee cup.

Laura's brow furrowed. "I sure hope they catch them soon. That Booth, especially, has shown that he's a violent man. Both of them are desperate men, for sure. And desperate men do desperate things. I fear if they aren't caught soon, someone else will get killed."

The guests dared not look at each other. Both men put food in their mouths and chewed it in silence.

Jack ran his gaze from one of them to the other. "How about it, Mr. Boyd, Mr. Smith, do you approve of what John Wilkes Booth did?"

The man posing as James W. Boyd said, "Jack, as a loyal son of the South, I feel that Lincoln needed to pay for freeing the slaves and putting many plantation owners into bankruptcy."

"I'm also a loyal son of the South," spoke up Richard, "but as a Christian, I cannot condone slavery. One human being should not own another as chattel. Every man should be free. I'm sorry about the plantation owners and their financial problems, but I had to agree with Mr. Lincoln's position on slavery."

"But since Lincoln was such an enemy of the South, Mr. Garrett," said the man posing as Harold Smith, "you should be glad that John Wilkes Booth assassinated him."

Richard shook his head. "No. I am not. President Lincoln was an enemy of slavery, not of the South. What Booth and his co-conspirators did was wrong. Murder is always wrong. God says so. Don't you agree?"

Booth and Herold exchanged quick glances. Fearing that they might lose their place of hiding if they disagreed, both lied, saying that they agreed wholeheartedly.

As soon as supper was over, Booth said, "Thank you for the excellent meal, Mrs. Garrett. It's been enjoyable. I'm really tired, and my leg is hurting some. If you will excuse me, I'll go on up to our room."

"I'll go with you, James," said Herold. "I'm pretty worn out, myself."

"We understand," said Richard. "I hope you get a good night's rest."

"We all understand," Laura said. "Saul, there's a pot of hot water simmering on the back of the kitchen stove. Would you pour some into a pail, mix it with a little cold water, and carry it up to their room so they can wash up and get some of the trail dust off?"

"Sure, Mama," said the boy, shoving his chair back. "I'll have it up there in a jiffy, gentlemen."

Herold stood up and said, "I'll go into the kitchen with you, Saul. When you get the water in the pail, I'll carry it upstairs and save you the trouble."

Shrugging his narrow shoulders, Saul said, "Sure, Mr. Smith. Let's go."

LATER THAT MONDAY NIGHT, when the Garrett children were all asleep in their rooms, Richard and Laura were in their own bedroom, preparing for bed.

Richard was at the closet in the corner, taking out shirt and trousers for the next day.

Laura was standing in front of the dresser, brushing her hair. She laid down the brush and began plaiting her hair into one long braid. In the mirror, she saw Richard pass behind her, hang the shirt on the back of a chair, and lay the trousers over the chair arm.

As he sat down on the edge of the bed and yawned, Laura held the braid in one hand and turned to look at him with a perplexed expression. "Darling, I want to ask you something."

Richard looked up. "Sure, honey."

"Has it struck you that there is something strange about our unexpected boarders?"

"Well, they were very nervous when I brought up the gospel."

"Oh, yes. I saw it, too, but it's something more than that. Somehow, I'm very uncomfortable with them in the house."

"Really?"

"Yes. Call it woman's intuition if you want to, but I get this strong feeling that all is not right with them."

Richard yawned again, covering his mouth. "Are you afraid?"

"Not really afraid. Just uneasy."

"I trust Willie, my love," said Richard, "and since he brought them here, I felt they were all right. But I also believe in your intuition. I'll keep a close eye on them. Now finish braiding your hair and get to bed. Morning will be here all too soon."

As Richard was sliding under the covers, Laura completed the braid, feeling relief that her husband would be watching their visitors. She crossed the room, doused the lantern, and snuggled in close to him.

Soon both were asleep.

The next day was spent with John Wilkes Booth in bed, and David Herold helping Richard do some work in the barn and the small shed near the barn where the horses were kept at night. All the while, Herold kept an eye on the road and the lane, fearing the federal troops might come along at any time.

That afternoon, when the wagon Jack drove from school pulled into the yard, Saul's friend McClain Reardon was aboard with the Garrett children. McClain was introduced to Harold Smith at the barn as the wagon and team were being put away. Jack told him that he and Saul had explained about his friend Sergeant James W. Boyd being wounded at Petersburg on April 2, and that Smith was helping him to get home to Fairfax. Richard was putting the horses in the shed as Herold walked to the house with the boys.

Moments later, after Saul and McClain came back downstairs from Saul's room, McClain was introduced to James W. Boyd, who was now in the parlor. McClain told him he hoped he would get home to his family in Fairfax soon.

When supper was on the dining room table and everyone was seated, Richard looked at Saul's friend and said, "McClain, we're so glad you could stay with us tonight. Would you lead us in prayer as we thank the Lord for the food?"

"It would be my pleasure, Mr. Garrett," said the boy.

When the amen was said, Booth and Herold were nervous again.

A few minutes after they had all begun eating, Saul said, "McClain, tell Mama and Papa about Tommy Stone."

The impostors' nerves tightened even more when McClain told Richard and Laura about the joy he had that very day in being able to lead his schoolmate Tommy Stone to the Lord at school during lunchtime.

"Isn't that great?" said Rya. "I like Tommy very much. It's wonderful to know that he's a Christian now."

"It sure is," said Richard. "This is very good news. McClain, you've led several of your friends at school to the Lord, haven't you?"

"Yes, sir," said the boy. "So many of our schoolmates don't have the privilege of being raised in a Christian home. I'm so thankful that I have that privilege, and I want to share the gospel with as many of them as I can. Tommy is coming to church Sunday and is going to be baptized."

"Wonderful!" said Laura.

Jack took a drink of milk and wiped the white film from his upper lip. "Talking about Tommy made me think of Derk Waters, McClain."

The Garretts all knew that McClain had led his schoolmate Derk Waters to the Lord just about a year ago. And only a month after Derk was saved, he was killed when he was thrown from a horse on the Waters farm.

Tears welled up in McClain's eyes. "Oh, yes. Derk. Can you imagine how happy he is in heaven with Jesus?"

Richard smiled. "I can guarantee you this, McClain. Derk wouldn't want to come back to earth again. This old world would be too dark a place now that he has basked in the light of the Lord's presence for a whole year."

McClain wiped away his tears. "That's for sure, Mr. Garrett. That's for sure."

Rya's adoring gaze was fixed on McClain. This did not escape the notice of her big sister.

When supper was over and Laura and her daughters were doing dishes in the kitchen, Ella smiled at Rya and said, "You really admire McClain, don't you, little sis?"

"Yes," replied Rya, returning the smile. "He's such a good Christian, and loves the Lord so much."

"He's going to make some young lady a wonderful husband," commented Laura.

I wish it would be me, thought Rya. *But he will be married long before I'm old enough to be a wife.* Then tugging at one of her auburn pigtails, she said, "He sure will, Mama."

—⁓—   —⁓—   —⁓—

When the Garrett sisters and their mother entered the parlor, Rya saw that Saul and McClain were sitting together on the parlor's smallest sofa. Boyd and Smith were on straight-backed wooden chairs next to them.

Rya moved up to the sofa. "McClain, would you like to see some of the pictures of horses that I drew?"

McClain smiled. "You've drawn some new ones since I was here last?"

"Uh-huh. Wanna see 'em?"

"Of course! You really have a talent with a pencil, Rya."

She giggled. "I just happen to have 'em right here in the drawer of this table by the sofa."

"Yeah, just happened to have them right there," Saul said in a playful tone.

While pulling several drawings from the drawer, Rya gave her brother a disdainful look. She returned to the front of the sofa, and with a little effort, squeezed herself between her brother and his friend. Saul frowned while she was wiggling to get settled and moved closer to the arm of the sofa, giving her a bit more room.

She gave him a big smile. "Thanks, Saul. You're such a wonderful big brother."

While Rya was showing McClain her drawings and explaining why she had made each one, Richard and Laura were talking to their boarders while Ella and Jack sat nearby, listening.

Looking at Booth and Herold, who were sitting together, Laura said, "Have you gentlemen heard about General Robert E. Lee?"

"Must not have," said Booth. "What about him?"

"It was in the newspapers a couple of days ago. Maybe you didn't see it because the front pages have all been John Wilkes Booth, the assassination, and his flight with David Herold to evade capture. Anyway, General Lee has just become president of Washington College in Washington, D.C."

"Oh, really?" said Herold. "That's good. He deserves a position like that and the honor that goes with it."

"He sure does," agreed Booth.

"Great man," said Richard.

"As far as I'm concerned," said Laura, "he was the greatest general in the Civil War, on either side. He showed more brilliance and more—" Laura's words were cut off by the loud sound of pounding hoofbeats and the blowing of several horses at the front of the house.

Jack jumped from his chair as his father started to get up, and headed for the parlor door. "I'll see who it is, Papa."

Booth and Herold exchanged a furtive glance, their eyes showing the fear they felt. Only McClain noticed it.

Jack was almost to the front of the house when a loud knock shook the door. When he opened it, the bright moon showed him a cavalry officer before him, with several uniformed men on horseback.

Everyone in the parlor heard a husky voice ask, "Is Mr. Garrett home, son? I'm Lieutenant Edward Doherty, United States Army. I need to talk to him."

"Yes," they heard Jack reply. Then, even as Richard was getting out of his overstuffed chair, Jack called, "Papa, federal troops are here! Lieutenant Edward Doherty wants to talk to you!"

While Richard was hurrying out of the parlor, Laura said, "I didn't know they rode at night."

"They want that John Wilkes Booth and his pal pretty bad, Mrs. Garrett," said McClain.

Booth pictured himself rushing out of the parlor and hopping down the hall on his crutch. Even though the hallway could not be seen from the front door, there was no way he was going to get up those steep stairs to the attic in time. He looked at Herold, ran his eyes to McClain, and both of them sprang off their chairs.

Booth left his crutch leaning against his chair and grabbed Rya, who was closest to him. In less than a heartbeat, Herold seized McClain. Both children looked shocked.

Laura stood up and started to cry out, but stifled it when Booth hissed in a whisper, "If you holler, I'll break your daughter's neck! And if any of you follow us, both Rya and McClain will have broken necks! We'll kill them, understand?"

With a hand over her mouth and fear in her eyes, Laura nodded.

Ella sat frozen on her chair, her face pale. Saul was the same on the small couch.

Herold pointed a stiff finger between McClain's widened eyes. Keeping his voice low, he said, "One peep outta you, kid, and you're dead. Do you understand?"

The boy nodded.

Rya gave her mother a fearful look as Booth dragged her through the door into the hall with Herold and McClain following. They could hear the voices of the lieutenant and Richard Garrett at the front door as they hurried toward the rear of the house.

In the parlor, a strangled moan escaped Laura's lips as if someone was choking her from the inside. Saul and Ella rushed to their mother, clinging to her.

Booth was limping as he held Rya by the arm, forcing her down the hall. She was numb with terror, and when her mouth came open as if she was going to scream, Booth locked her neck in the crook of his arm, lifted her off her feet, and clamped a hand over her mouth. She thrashed against him, kicking his legs, and when her booted feet struck flesh between the slats of the splint, he ejected a moan, then said angrily, "Be still and do as you're told, or I'll come back here when the troops are gone and kill your parents!"

Behind them, McClain was also struggling to free himself from Herold's strong grip. "Settle down, kid, or your parents will die, too!"

"Do as they say, Rya," said McClain quietly. "It'll be okay if we don't try to fight them."

With tears spilling from her eyes, Rya gave a little nod and stopped the effort to free herself.

They were almost to the kitchen. Booth remembered that Richard kept a rifle by the back door. He hoped it was still there.

When they entered the kitchen, he saw the rifle leaning against the wall by the door. He removed his hand from Rya's mouth and picked it up. They quickly passed through the back door into the night.

At the front door of the house, Lieutenant Edward Doherty was explaining that he and his men were searching for assassin John Wilkes Booth and his accomplice, David Herold.

"We're quite sure those two have come into Virginia, Mr. Garrett," said Doherty. "Let me describe them to you."

"That won't be necessary, Lieutenant," said Richard. "I heard you give their descriptions in church on Sunday morning. I haven't seen two men with shaggy hair and mustaches, and one of them with a splinted leg, traveling through these parts together."

The instant Laura Garrett heard the back door close, she rushed out of the parlor with Ella and Saul on her heels. She headed toward the front door where her husband was talking to the lieutenant. "Richard! Oh-h-h, Richard...!"

Richard turned from Doherty and opened his arms as he saw the intense fear and panic in Laura's eyes. "Honey, what's the matter?"

Throwing herself into his arms, Laura said with a shudder, "Boyd and Smith took Rya and McClain out the back door! Boyd said they will kill the children if anybody follows them!"

As Richard's body stiffened, Lieutenant Edward Doherty asked, "Who are Boyd and Smith?"

Richard cast a glance toward the rear of the house and said, "Boyd is a Confederate soldier who was injured in the Petersburg battle on April second. His friend Harold Smith is trying to get him home to Fairfax without Federal interference. We're allowing them to stay with us while Boyd rests up. But something's wrong."

"What kind of injury does Boyd have?" asked Doherty.

"It's his left leg. It was broken severely when a cannon wheel ran over it. The leg is in a splint."

"Mr. Garrett," said the lieutenant, "I'll tell you what's wrong. You've got John Wilkes Booth and David Herold! They must have shaved off their mustaches and gotten their hair cut."

"But Smith is completely bald," said Richard.

"He's blond. He had it shaved, and it just looks bald. I'm telling you, it's Booth and Herold who have taken the children."

By the pale moonlight, the fugitives headed toward the small shed that housed their horses.

"The shed is locked," said Rya. "Papa puts a big padlock on it at night because there have been some horse thieves around."

Herold started to say they would kick the door in, but remembered how solidly the shed was built.

"Dave," said Booth, "if I shoot the padlock off, or even if we try to break it off, they'll hear it and be here before we can saddle the horses and be gone. We'll have to hole up in the barn. Let's go."

As they headed toward the barn, Booth said, "When the troops come back here, we'll demand two of their horses and threaten to kill these two if our demands aren't met. We'll ride away with Rya on a horse with me and McClain on a horse with you. We'll warn those low-down Federals if they follow us, these kids will die. We'll make it. They aren't gonna take any chances on getting these kids killed."

The night sky was clear and the moon was bright as the fugitives took their captives inside the barn and closed the door.

McClain looked at the man who favored his left leg and held on to Rya. "You're John Wilkes Booth, aren't you?"

Booth fixed him with a hard glare. "Yes, I am! I killed that no-good Abraham Lincoln, and I'll kill the two of you if those soldiers don't do as Dave and I tell them."

Suddenly Rya broke down and started to weep.

"Stop that crying, girl!" snapped Booth. "Shut up, right now!"

Rya was so terrified, she could not control her weeping.

"Stop it, I said!" Booth demanded, shaking her.

McClain asked, "May I talk to her?"

Booth glared at him. "All right, go ahead," he said, shoving the girl at him. "You'd better make her quit bawling real quick, or I'll do it myself!"

Herold was peering out one of the windows that faced the house as McClain took Rya in his arms and began talking to her in a soothing tone, trying to quiet her.

Richard let go of Laura and darted toward the rear of the house.

"Hey!" called Doherty, moving inside and running after him. "Wait!"

Richard halted halfway down the hall and pivoted at the lieutenant's word.

"Where do you think you're going, Mr. Garrett?" asked Doherty, drawing up to him.

Laura, Jack, Saul, and Ella were now in the hall, accompanied by two soldiers.

There was a strong look of determination in Richard's eyes as he fixed them on Doherty. "That's my daughter and another farmer's boy they've got, Lieutenant. I'm going after them!"

With that, Richard turned and ran to the kitchen. When he saw that the rifle that usually leaned against the wall by the door was gone, he opened the pantry and picked up a second rifle, checking the loads.

"Wait a minute," said Doherty. "I understand you're wanting to free the children from those men, but you might just cause more problems, and even get them killed. My men and I are well-trained for situations like this. You wait here. We'll bring the children back safely."

Laura, the other three Garrett children, and the two soldiers drew up as Lieutenant Doherty laid a hand on Richard's shoulder. "Trust us, Mr. Garrett. We'll bring those children back safely."

Laura took hold of her husband's arm. "Please, Richard. Let them handle it."

"Listen to her, sir," said Doherty.

Richard looked at the lieutenant with tenacity etched on his countenance.

"Sir," said Doherty, "you are far too overwrought to take on those two men and make the proper decisions that will come with facing them. Don't endanger your daughter and that boy further. Let us do our job."

Laura squeezed his arm. "Please, darling."

Richard met her pleading gaze, then looked directly into the lieutenant's unswerving eyes. His shoulders slumped and he lowered the rifle so the butt rested on the floor. "Okay, Lieutenant, you win. But if you fail in your job, you will answer to me."

"We won't fail, Mr. Garrett," Doherty said levelly.

Jack, Saul, and Ella looked on, their faces void of color.

Richard took a deep breath. "Lieutenant, Booth and Herold have one of my rifles. They can't get into the shed where the horses are kept without making a lot of noise by breaking off a padlock or shooting it off. There haven't been any such sounds, so they're out there on foot."

Doherty turned to the two soldiers. "Go tell the others that we're going after Booth and Herold right now. I'll be there in a minute."

As the two uniformed men hurried away, Jack stepped up, his features twisted in agony. "Lieutenant Doherty, if those evil men see you and your troops coming after them, they'll kill Rya and McClain! Maybe if you let them go, they'll leave Rya and McClain behind when they know they're safe from capture."

Doherty shook his head. "No, son. Those two children are hostages now, but when Booth and Herold no longer need them, they'll kill them. Booth is a cold-blooded killer. I'm telling you, that's what will happen. We have to hunt them down quickly and get the drop on them in order to save Rya and McClain's lives. Being afoot, they can't get very far away. With the moon so bright, they'll be easy to find. When we catch sight of them, I'll deploy my men so as to surround them without them knowing it, then surprise them suddenly. When they find themselves facing seven gun muzzles, they'll surrender."

"Lieutenant," said Richard, "they just might be hiding out there in the barn."

"That's where I was going to start."

With that, Doherty turned and dashed up the hall. When he reached his men at the front porch, they got out of their saddles, guns ready.

Doherty explained the situation and his plan of action. Then marshaling his troops, he led them into the deep shadows of the trees in a wide perimeter, and the soldiers scattered to surround the barn.

Still looking a bit frustrated at being left behind, Richard put his rifle back in the pantry, then looked into the faces of his family.

Leading Laura by the arm, he sat her down at the kitchen table.

To Jack, Saul, and Ella, he said, "Let's all sit down. We must go to God, our great Protector, in prayer."

Inside the barn, McClain Reardon stood with an arm around a quietly sniffling Rya Garrett, holding her close to him, and speaking to her in soft tones.

"That's better, girl," Booth said curtly. "Now, just keep it quiet like that. Any more outbursts, and you're gonna make me mad. Believe me, girl, you don't want to make me mad. Abe Lincoln made me mad, and you know what happened to him."

With all of her little girl might, Rya was trying to keep her emotions in control, but she slipped from McClain's arm and crumpled to the straw-covered floor. Lying on her side, she pulled her shaking legs up close to her heaving chest and wrapped her arms tightly around them.

Still only sniffling, tears streamed down her ashen face, and her entire body jerked with fright.

McClain knelt beside her under the glaring eyes of Booth, and laid a tender hand on her shoulder. Although nearly as frightened as she was, he said, "It's going to be all right, Rya. The Lord will take care of us."

A sneer formed on Booth's face at the mention of the Lord. He glanced over his shoulder at Herold, who was still at the window, looking toward the house. "Shut up about that religious stuff!" said Booth. "I don't want to hear it."

"John!" came Herold's tight voice. "It's the troops! Here they come!"

MCCLAIN HELPED RYA TO HER FEET, and held her tight in his arms. Trembling, she laid her head on his chest and clung to him.

John Wilkes Booth limped to the next window from where Herold stood and peered out into the moonlit yard. Four uniformed men, guns in hand, were just drawing up behind a hay wagon that stood some twenty yards from the barn.

Booth cursed and cocked the rifle.

"I only see four, John," said Herold.

"Yeah, but there have to be others we don't see."

"What're we gonna do?"

"Stick with our plan, that's what we're gonna do."

Outside at the hay wagon, Lieutenant Edward Doherty and the three men with him looked intently at the barn, studying the moon-sprayed windows.

Suddenly, Sergeant Boston Corbett whispered, "Look, Lieutenant! There's someone at that window next to the barn door."

"Just as I thought," said Doherty. "They're in there, all right."

"Lieutenant!" whispered a corporal. "There's someone at that next window, too."

Doherty holstered his revolver and cupped his hands around his mouth. "John Booth! David Herold! We know you're in there! This is Lieutenant Edward Doherty, United States Army! We have the barn surrounded! Come out right now with your hands in the air!"

Booth's voice came back in a defiant scream. "We're not coming out! You know we have these two kids with us! If you don't do as I tell you, we'll kill them!"

Doherty did not reply.

"You hear me!" said Booth. "We want you to bring two of your horses up here to the double doors and leave them! Then take your men and ride outta here immediately! If anyone follows us, we'll kill Rya and McClain! If we make a clean getaway, we'll leave the kids on a farm somewhere, unharmed."

Doherty called back, "You mean like you left President Lincoln at Ford's Theatre unharmed?"

There was dead silence for a moment, then Booth shouted, "I mean it! If you don't leave us those two horses and ride outta here right now, we'll kill both of these brats!"

Inside the barn, Rya let out a tremulous whimper.

Booth looked back. "Shut up that noise, girl! Right now!"

McClain whispered, "Rya, stay as quiet as you can. Let's move back a little." Even as he spoke, he guided her into a shadowed corner next to a horse stall. Rya could hear the thumping of her own heart.

Lieutenant Edward Doherty's voice came back, edged with indignation. "Booth! If either or both of those children are harmed in any way, you and Herold will never live to see the sunrise! This is no idle threat!"

David Herold turned toward his friend. His body shook slightly and his voice was unsteady. "John, maybe we should give it up while we're still alive."

Booth turned from the window and gave Herold a puzzled look. "What're you talking about, giving it up?" Rifle in hand, he began pacing the moonlit barn floor, limping on his bad leg. "I just need time to think, here. There has to be a way out."

Herold began pacing with him, his body shaking the more. "Well, I can't think of a way, John. You'd better come up with something quick, or they're gonna storm this place."

"No, they're not!" snapped Booth as they passed each other, pacing. "They won't do that as long as those kids are in here. But that doesn't get us out. There has to be a way to make them do what I told them!"

"They aren't gonna bring us horses, John. We've gotta come up with something else."

"I'm not so sure," said Booth. "Just let me think."

Herold continued to argue with Booth, insisting they come up with something entirely different. Booth argued back, his temper rising.

While the fugitives were totally engrossed in their predicament and the solution, McClain pulled Rya back a little deeper into the shadows. Still holding her tight, he whispered, "I've got to get you out of the barn before those beasts harm you."

"But how?" she asked in a whisper. "McClain, they'll kill us both if they catch us!"

"I've been forming a plan. Please trust me on this, Rya. Having played around this barn with Saul all of these years, I know it like the back of my hand. There's a window at the rear of the barn, behind the wall where the grain bins are, right?"

"Y-yes."

"It is locked from the inside like those windows over there, right?"

"Yes."

Booth and Herold were arguing heatedly, and at the same time, Lieutenant Doherty's demanding voice was filtering into the barn.

"Well, now's the time," said McClain. "They're completely occupied with their problem. Let's go."

Rya swiped a sleeve across her face, ridding it of tears. She tentatively nodded her head.

At the house, Laura, Jack, Ella, and Saul were huddled on the back porch with Richard, who had them out of the line of fire in case shooting should take place. Nerves were taut, faces were stiff, and bodies were rigid.

They could hear Doherty shouting at Booth, and the muffled sounds of Booth's indignant replies.

Richard was at the edge of the wall, peering around the corner and watching the scene at the barn by the bright moonlight. "Lieutenant Doherty and three men are over there at the hay wagon. I saw the three other soldiers go behind the barn."

Laura, Jack, Ella, and Saul were clustered in a tight knot. Tears were coursing down the mother's cheeks as she felt her children trembling. *Please, dear God,* she said in her heart, *spare Rya and McClain. They both belong to You. Don't let anything happen to them!*

Laura's thoughts raced back to the day Rya was born. *She was my easiest delivery,* she thought. *She entered the world squalling, at the top of her lungs, her pinched little face as red as her hair. She has always been so full of questions and so eager to learn. That's why she was saved at such a young age. God has blessed her with such a tender heart and a sweet spirit. Oh, she has tried my patience at times, with her persistent ways, but she is a little bundle of love and such a joy to this family.*

Laura bit her lower lip as the scalding tears flooded down her face.

Please, dear Lord...please! Keep my baby girl safe. Let her live! Use her life to glorify You. Oh, God, I know Your grace is always sufficient. Help me to draw on that now, and to trust You explicitly as I should. And please take care of McClain. Such a sweet boy. He's so devoted to You. Just do what You have to do, dear Lord...but get them out of this awful thing safely! Let those two men be captured, and—

"Mama," came Ella's quivering voice, "Jesus won't let Rya and McClain be killed, will He? We prayed before we came outside that He wouldn't."

While Laura was attempting to speak past the lump that was in her throat, Richard cupped Ella's chin in his hand. "The Lord is going to protect Rya and McClain, sweetheart."

Swallowing the lump, Laura said, "That's right, honey. Our wonderful God will protect them."

Saul sniffed and wiped tears from his cheeks. "If anything happens to McClain, his parents will hate me."

Richard laid a hand on Saul's shoulder and squeezed it.

Trembling, Jack thought of how much he loved his little sister. Tears trickled down his face as he said, "I wish those vile men had taken me instead of Rya."

Laura patted his cheek.

Lieutenant Doherty could be heard shouting warnings at the fugitives, with Booth's stubborn replies coming from inside the barn.

Frustrated beyond endurance, Richard moved back to the corner of the house and looked toward the scene. "Maybe the Lord wants me to get in on this. I shouldn't have let Doherty talk me into staying here at the house. I'm going to get my rifle and go out there!"

"Please don't, honey," said Laura, moving to him. "There could be a lot of gunfire going on out there any minute. The children and I don't want to lose you. We've asked God to take care of Rya and McClain. You just told Ella He would. Let the soldiers do their job, as Lieutenant Doherty said."

Richard looked back at the moonlit scene at the barn again. "Something's got to be done, Laura. This can't go on much longer. If bullets fly, those children could be in real trouble."

"There are seven against two," Laura said evenly. "God can use the seven to get the two. Please don't go and make yourself a target."

Richard looked deep into the eyes he loved so dearly and sighed. "All right. But Laura, if something doesn't happen soon, I'm going to make it happen!"

Richard felt a small hand squeeze his arm, and looked down into Ella's tear-dimmed eyes. He felt a lump rise in his throat and gathered her into his arms.

The three soldiers at the rear of the barn were bellied down behind a water trough, guns ready. Suddenly they heard a squeaking sound, and all three tensed up.

"It's the window!" whispered Corporal Len Courtney. "Somebody's opening it!"

All three rifles were instantly trained on the window.

McClain saw moonlight flash on a gun barrel. "I'm McClain Reardon, and I have Rya Garrett with me!"

As the three soldiers dashed up to the window, Lieutenant Doherty could be heard at the front of the barn making commands for the fugitives to send the children out, then come out themselves.

McClain lifted Rya up and eased her through the window. Corporal Len Courtney leaned his rifle against the barn and took Rya into his arms. McClain climbed out himself.

Noting the quiver of her tense young body and seeing the wide stare in her eyes, Courtney said, "It's all right now, sweetie. No one is going to hurt you."

Rya saw McClain draw up between the other two soldiers as the voices of the fugitives still filtered from the front side of the barn, arguing between themselves.

The little redhead gave the corporal a lopsided grin. "Thank you for coming to our rescue."

"You are very welcome," said Courtney, easing her down on her feet.

Rya's knees were a bit weak, and they buckled a little. Courtney kept his hand on her shoulder until he felt her stance become steady.

"You all right?" he asked.

"Yes, sir. I'm a little weak, but I'm fine."

"Good," said Courtney. "Take her to the house, son. Quickly. Make a circle over there by those trees, and stay in the shadows. I don't think they can see that part of the yard from those windows, but if you're in the shadows till you get near the house, I know they can't."

"Yes, sir. I want to thank all three of you for your help."

"Our pleasure," said one of the other soldiers. "Now, go!"

As the children were running toward the house, Corporal Len Courtney said, "You two stay here and keep an eye on that window. I'll go let the lieutenant know that the kids are out of the barn and safe with their parents."

On the back porch, Richard was holding Laura, Ella, and Saul in his arms as they wept and prayed together. Jack was at the corner, keeping an eye on the scene at the barn.

Jack was looking at the four soldiers who stood behind the hay wagon, when movement in the shadows beneath the trees off to his right caught his eye. He focused on the two shadowed figures and could tell that they were running. When they appeared plainly at the edge of the shadows in the mottled moonlight, he recognized them.

"Mama! Papa!" he said in a hoarse whisper. "It's Rya and McClain!"

Richard and Laura, accompanied by Ella and Saul, dashed to the edge of the porch. At the same instant, the pair came out of the shadows and made a beeline for the porch.

Tears of apprehension suddenly turned into tears of joy as Rya and McClain bounded up onto the back porch and the family gathered them into their arms.

After at least a full minute of hugging and subdued voices praising the Lord, Richard wiped tears and said to the pair, "How did you get out?"

Everybody listened intently as McClain explained how they made their escape.

"McClain saved my life!" exclaimed Rya, keeping her voice low. She turned and hugged him.

McClain held her close and patted her back.

Laura wrapped her arms around McClain. "You precious boy! There is no way I can ever thank you for risking your own life to save my daughter's!"

McClain drew back a little in her embrace so he could look into her eyes. "Mrs. Garrett, Rya is a very special little girl. I had to take the risk to get her out of there."

Rya beamed up at him, her heart aglow. "McClain, you're my hero."

The boy blushed and hugged her again.

Inside the barn, Booth and Herold were still pacing fitfully, each in his own thoughts. Lieutenant Doherty's voice filled the night, warning them of the consequences if they didn't give it up and come out.

Booth stopped pacing and rubbed his left thigh. "Dave, I've got it."

Herold halted, facing his friend. "I'm listening."

"Our only hope is to take those kids out with me holding this rifle to Rya's head. We'll demand two revolvers and make them all throw the rest of their guns down and ride away. Then we'll force

Garrett to hitch his team to the wagon so you and I can drive away, holding the revolvers on the kids."

"It's the best idea yet," said Herold. "With guns on those kids, we'll be in control of the situation. Let's do it."

Booth looked toward the dark corner where he had last seen Rya and McClain. "Okay, you two. Come out here."

When there was no response or sound of movement, Booth's anger flared. His flushed face was like a marble mask. "You two get out here right now!"

Dead silence.

Mumbling a curse in a low voice, Booth limped toward the corner with Herold following. When they drew up, Booth ran his eyes back and forth in the shadows. "They're not here!"

"Well, they've gotta be somewhere in the barn," said Herold. "You wait here. I'll find them."

Just as Herold turned to begin his search, Doherty's voice boomed from outside, "Booth! Herold! Come out! Your hostages are safe now! They're at the house with their family!"

Herold gasped, looking toward the double doors. "He's lying!" Even as he spoke, he dashed past the stalls and headed toward the rear of the barn.

Seconds later, he returned to Booth, his face gray. "He wasn't lying, John. Those kids escaped through a window in the back of the barn. I saw more soldiers out there."

John Wilkes Booth swung the rifle carelessly, eyes bulging with hatred for the soldiers, and mumbled heated words Herold couldn't understand. When he stopped to take a breath, Herold said, "John, we don't have a chance. We might as well give up."

"Booth! Herold!" roared the lieutenant. "I want you out here right now! We don't want to kill you! Give it up so we don't have to!"

Ignoring Doherty's words, Booth looked at Herold. "Give up? No way! I still have this rifle. We aren't done for yet!"

"We can't fight that many men with one gun! Give it up!"

"What's the matter with you? Don't you know what they'll do to me if I give up? You'll only go to prison for the rest of your life, but they'll hang me! They'd like nothing better than to hang me in public right in front of the White House with thousands of people laughing and jeering! No way, Dave! No way! I tell you, we can make it. I just need more time to think."

Herold looked down at his hands, clasped in a tight ball of fear. "It's over, John. I'm giving myself up."

Before Booth could utter a word, Herold hurried to the double doors and opened them a crack.

"Dave!" hissed Booth. "You fool! Come back here!"

Herold turned and looked at his friend who stood in the moonlight that streamed through the windows. The moon struck Booth's eyes, reflecting a gleam that was full of lunacy.

Without comment, Herold widened the opening and shouted, "Lieutenant! It's David Herold! I give up! I'm coming out! I'm unarmed! Don't shoot!"

Four guns were trained on Herold from behind the hay wagon as he stepped out, his empty hands held high over his head.

"Come over here," commanded Doherty.

While Herold was making his way toward the wagon, Booth's voice boomed. "Dave Herold, you dirty coward! You dirty coward!"

As Herold drew up to the wagon and moved around where the soldiers stood with their guns pointed at him, Doherty asked, "What kind of weapons does Booth have?"

"Just Garrett's rifle," Herold replied in a broken voice. "And it is definitely loaded."

The lieutenant nodded. "Okay, men. Tie him up like I told you."

Two of the soldiers seized Herold, took him to a nearby tree, and tied him to it.

On the back porch of the house, Richard was once again at the corner, observing the scene at the barn. He spoke to his family over his shoulder: "Smith—I mean Herold—just came out of the barn with his hands in the air."

Laura moved up close.

"Apparently Booth is not going to give up," said Richard.

"They'll probably have to go in after him."

"I just hope none of the soldiers get shot," said Ella.

At the hay wagon, Lieutenant Doherty cupped his hands around his mouth and shouted, "You're all alone now, Booth! You don't have a chance! Come on out!"

Inside the barn, Booth was pacing once again. "If I surrender, you'll hang me!" he blared. "You're not hanging me! Do you hear? You're not hanging me!" His temples throbbed as he struggled for breath.

"Booth!" cried Doherty. "Don't make us come in and get you! I've told my men we want to take you alive!"

"Yeah, so you can put a noose around my neck!" said Booth. "I'm telling you, Lieutenant, you're not gonna hang me!"

"You've got exactly sixty seconds to come out that door, Booth!" said Doherty. "If you don't, we're coming in!"

Even as he spoke, Doherty led his men around in front of the hay wagon, holding his cocked revolver. The other three had their rifles cocked and ready as they fanned out on both sides of him.

"We've got to take him alive if possible," said the lieutenant.

Inside the barn, Booth stopped directly in front of the double doors, sucking hard for air. His mind went back to his recurring nightmare, and he saw himself being pushed up the gallows steps with the huge crowd jeering and calling him a coward.

Suddenly he opened one of the doors a few inches and cried out, "Draw up your men before the door, Lieutenant! I'll come out and fight the whole bunch of you!"

"We're not moving any closer, Booth!" said Doherty. "Do as I tell you! Put down that rifle and come out with your hands over your head!"

"I'm coming out to kill as many of you as I can! Prepare a stretcher for me!"

Doherty and his three men tensed up as the barn door suddenly swung open and Booth appeared, doing a limping, halting jump with the rifle aimed directly at Lieutenant Edward Doherty.

Off to Booth's right, Sergeant Boston Corbett took aim and

fired his rifle. Booth was struck in the neck and his rifle fired harmlessly into the ground as he fell.

The three soldiers who had been on the back side of the barn came running around the corner as the other four dashed to the spot where the assassin had fallen.

Doherty dropped to his knees beside Booth and noted the blood on both sides of his neck. "Let's get him over to the house."

As three of the soldiers were picking Booth up, Richard Garrett sprinted up. "Good work, Lieutenant."

Doherty nodded, smiled grimly, and said, "He's in pretty bad shape. Is it all right if we take him over on the back porch?"

"Sure."

The Garrett family, McClain Reardon, and the rest of the soldiers gathered around as John Wilkes Booth was carried up the steps and laid on the porch floor. David Herold was left tied to the tree near the barn.

Quickly, two lanterns were lit and placed so Lieutenant Edward Doherty could get a good look at Booth. Laura knelt down beside Doherty and bent over so she could see the wounds.

"Bullet went right through," said Doherty.

"I see," said Laura. "Ella, will you bring me some towels, please?"

As Ella ran inside the house, Booth looked up at Doherty, then at Laura, and with a gurgling sound, said, "I...I can't feel anything below my neck."

"Apparently the bullet severed your spine," said Laura. "I'm going to try to stop the bleeding as much as possible."

Booth closed his eyes, swallowed blood, and opened them again, fixing them on Laura. "It won't make any difference. I'm going to die." He paused, swallowed blood again, and looked up at Doherty. "I told you, didn't I?"

"What?"

"You wouldn't get to hang me."

At that moment, Ella returned and handed her mother the towels. Laura lifted Booth's head and wrapped them tightly around his neck. Richard stood a few feet away with his sons and daughters, and McClain stood beside him. The soldiers were positioned on the other side of the spot where John Wilkes Booth lay. Every eye was on the dying man.

Suddenly Booth's breathing became erratic. He looked up again at Doherty. "Tell Mother that I died for my country."

The soldiers looked at each other, shaking their heads.

Booth gritted his teeth. "Lieutenant, would you lift my arms so I can see my hands?"

Laura met Doherty's puzzled gaze and frowned.

Doherty shrugged, took hold of Booth's elbows, and lifted his hands up so he could see them.

Looking at his hands through hazy eyes, Booth murmured, "Useless. Useless."

With that, his eyes closed, and he breathed out his final breath.

Studying Booth's chest and seeing no more rise and fall, Doherty looked up and ran his gaze over the group. "The man who killed President Lincoln is dead."

Moments later, the Garrett family stood on the porch and watched the soldiers place a shackled David Herold on the horse he had stolen, as the lifeless body of the assassin was draped over the other horse.

Lieutenant Edward Doherty swung into his saddle, thanked the Garretts for their help, and led the troops into the night.

The Garrett family then gathered around McClain Reardon, thanking him one at a time for risking his own life to save little Rya.

Rya waited until the others had spoken their thanks to the handsome boy, then with tears running down her cheeks, she hugged McClain. "You will always be my hero."

As the weeks passed, the Garrett family slowly began to get their lives back to normal.

However, in the first week of June, they found themselves standing with other mourners in the Bowling Green cemetery as Pastor Olan Granger conducted the funeral service for Hal Reardon, who had died of a stroke.

Three days later, the Reardon wagon hauled up in front of the house on the Garrett farm at suppertime. McClain was at the reins with his mother beside him, and his sisters Lena and Ruby sitting on a blanket in the wagon's bed.

After Richard had led the group at the dining room table in a prayer of thanks for the food, Ruth Reardon looked around at the Garrett family. "I don't know how to thank you for being so good to McClain, Lena, Ruby, and me these past few days. You are the dearest friends we have."

"And you are the dearest friends we have," Laura said, her eyes filmed with tears.

Rya had managed to position herself next to McClain at the table. Even as her mother was speaking, she looked up and smiled at the boy who had saved her from John Wilkes Booth and David Herold.

McClain smiled back.

As they began eating, Ruth explained that with Hal gone, there was no way she and her children could manage the farm. She already had a generous offer on the place so she and her children would be moving to Blue Springs, Missouri, to be near her own family. They would be leaving within two to three weeks.

The Garretts were saddened at the news that the Reardons would be moving away, but also understood that it was better for Ruth and her children.

On Saturday, June 24, when Ruth Reardon and her children were ready to board the train at the Richmond depot for Kansas City, Missouri, the Garrett family was there to see them off.

When the conductor called for all passengers to board, the good-byes had been said, and the hugs passed around. Rya had done her best to cover the sorrow she was feeling.

As his mother and sisters were about to move toward the chosen coach, McClain set his gaze on Rya, who was looking at him with mournful eyes and furrowed brow. Her sad face was pitiful to behold. Tears were threatening, and she blinked rapidly to keep them from spilling down her cheeks.

"Mom, you go ahead and board," said McClain. "I need another moment with my friend."

Richard, Laura, and their other children walked slowly toward the coach with Ruth and her daughters.

Rya's long, dark eyelashes were spiky from the unshed tears. She tried to smile, but it wouldn't come.

McClain tugged at one of Rya's long auburn braids and grinned. "Hey, cheer up, little friend. We'll see each other sometime. It's not such a big world, after all."

Rya wrapped her slender arms around him as the tears finally spilled down her cheeks. "I'll miss you so much. You're my very best friend."

McClain kissed the top of her head. "And you're my very best friend, too."

Richard was watching close and moved up behind his little daughter.

As Rya dipped her head and let go of McClain, she felt her father's strong hands on her shoulders.

The conductor was giving his final call for passengers to board.

Rya raised her head and watched McClain until he hopped up on the coach's rear platform and moved inside. Then she tilted her head up and looked into her father's eyes, giving him a crooked smile.

"Let's go home, sweetheart," Richard said softly.

Twelve Years Later

ON MONDAY, MAY 7, 1877, the midmorning sun shone down from the azure Virginia sky, giving the land a golden hue. White puffy clouds rode the high westerly wind, patching the vast fields around Bowling Green with drifting shadows.

A lone army wagon rolled through the town and headed out into the country on a dusty road. Two uniformed men occupied the wagon, both enjoying the beautiful spring day. Corporal Bill Cameron held the reins, guiding the team along the road, and letting his eyes roam over the farms that surrounded them. Cattle, horses, and sheep dotted the green fields amid farmhouses, barns, and outbuildings which were surrounded by tall shade trees.

Cameron smiled at the man beside him. "I've always wanted to live in the country, Colonel. I was born and raised in the heart of Philadelphia with crowds of people and traffic and noise. It's so quiet and peaceful out here."

"That it is, Corporal," said the Colonel. He pointed to a lane they were approaching. "That's the place right there."

Cameron turned the wagon onto the winding lane and glimpsed the white farmhouse in the distance through breeze-stirred branches. "Nice place."

"Sure is. Looks the same as I remember it. These folks really take care of their property."

As they neared the house, they saw a man wielding a hoe in a flower garden that was close to the wraparound porch. The farmer looked up as the sound of the approaching wagon met his ears. He focused on the wagon, then the two men on the seat. His brow puckered as he pushed his hat back and laid the hoe down.

"He doesn't recognize me yet," said the colonel.

The corporal drew rein, and as the wagon stopped, the farmer stepped up close, squinted at the man who wore the insignias that designated him as a colonel and said, "You look familiar, sir, but I— Wait a minute! Lieutenant Edward Doherty!"

Doherty climbed down, smiled, and extended his hand. "Mr. Garrett, how are you?"

Grasping the hand and pumping it, Richard Garrett said, "I'm fine, Lieuten—I'm sorry. I mean Colonel. It's been…what? Twelve years? And how are you?"

"Just fine. Let me introduce you to my driver. I've told him all about you. Richard Garrett, shake hands with Corporal Bill Cameron."

As the farmer and the corporal shook hands, Cameron said, "So it was here on your place where the infamous John Wilkes Booth was shot and killed by Colonel Doherty and his cavalry unit."

"Sure was, and—"

Richard's words were cut off when he saw Laura coming out the front door, smiling at Colonel Doherty.

Doherty and Laura spoke of the twelve years that had passed, and each told the other they had hardly changed. Laura was then introduced to Corporal Cameron, who greeted her warmly, saying the colonel had told him all about her and the rest of the Garrett family.

"So what brings you here, Colonel?" asked Richard.

"Well, it's like this," said Doherty. "I am commandant at Fort McNair in Washington, D.C."

"Oh, really? That's on the south side of the city, right on the Potomac River, isn't it?"

"Correct. Corporal Cameron is my main adjutant, so he drives me wherever I need to go. I had some official business at the Fort Lee Military Reserve near Petersburg these past few days, so we were on our way back and I told Corporal Cameron I wanted to swing a bit out of our way so I could drop by and see you."

Richard's smile was from ear to ear. "Well, sir, we're honored that you would want to see us."

"Can you stay for lunch, Colonel?" Laura asked. "I realize it's only a little after ten o'clock, but if you and Corporal Cameron can stay till noon, I'll fix you a nice lunch."

"We can't stay that long, Mrs. Garrett. I wish we could, but they're expecting me back at the fort by four o'clock, so we'll need to pull away from here in about half an hour."

"Well, how about some nice hot coffee? There's some from breakfast still on the stove. I can have it piping hot in a few minutes."

The soldiers grinned at each other, then Doherty said, "Now, that we have time for."

Ten minutes later, as the men and Laura were seated at the kitchen table drinking coffee, Richard said, "Pardon me, Colonel, but I think congratulations are in order."

Doherty's eyebrows arched. "What do you mean?"

"I'll answer that when you tell me one thing."

"All right."

"How long have you been a colonel?"

"Four years."

"And how long have you been commandant at Fort McNair?"

"Four years."

"Isn't it pretty phenomenal for a man to go from Lieutenant to Colonel in just eight years?"

Doherty chuckled. "Well, in most cases, yes. But what propelled me forward in the ranks was the fact that it was my unit that brought President Lincoln's assassin down. I was promoted to major three weeks afterward, bypassing the rank of captain. Making it from major to colonel, then, was about in normal time."

"Well, congratulations," said Richard. "You deserve your rank."

"Thank you," said Doherty.

"He's a great commandant, Mr. Garrett," said Cameron. "All the men at Fort McNair respect him highly."

Doherty cleared his throat, adjusted his position on the chair, and said, "Enough about me. Now, Mr. and Mrs. Garrett, I want to know about you and your children. Let's start with you. How's the farm doing?"

"The farm is doing fine, sir," said Richard. "It's making us a decent living. The Lord has been good to us. Laura and I are enjoying good health."

"Good. Now, let's see, the names of your children. I remember your oldest boy's name is Jack. And I remember your youngest daughter, that cute little doll with the big blue eyes and the red hair. Her name is Rya. The other boy and girl, I can't recall."

"Ella and Saul," said Laura.

"Oh, yes. Of course. Ella and Saul. So I suppose all of them are married."

"All but Rya," said Richard. "Jack, Ella, and Saul and their families live in different parts of Virginia. We have three grandchildren, with one on the way."

"Wonderful. And Rya. Where is she?"

"She's in Richmond," spoke up Laura. "She's attending Richmond Teacher's College. Rya's twenty-two. When she first graduated from Bowling Green High School she was offered a job at the school in the business office. She was satisfied with the job for three years. Then one day, they asked her to be a substitute teacher because one of the regular teachers had suddenly become ill. She got a taste of what it was like to teach, and the first thing we know, she quit her job in Bowling Green and entered Richmond Teacher's College. It's a three-year course. She's just about to finish her first year."

"Well, bless her heart," said Doherty. "Is she still a doll?"

"More beautiful than ever," said Richard. "I realize I'm her father, but take my word for it: she's a very lovely young lady."

"I assume she lives in the dormitory on campus."

"Yes," said Laura.

"How often do you get to see her?"

"Every weekend. She catches a ride in a carriage owned by one of the male students who lives in Bowling Green."

"Well, it's good that you get to see her on weekends."

"We're thankful for that," said Richard. "Of course, once she graduates, only the Lord knows where she'll get her teaching job."

The colonel grinned. "And…ah…is there a young man in her life?"

Richard shook his head, smiling. "Not yet, at least. Oh, there's one who would like to be in her life, but she wants nothing to do with him. The right one will come along one of these days, but I hope it's after she graduates with her teaching degree. I'd like to see her finish school before she gets married."

"Can't blame you for that," said Doherty, finishing his second cup of coffee. "Well, Corporal Cameron, it's time we hit the road."

On Friday, May 11, a carriage slowed on the dusty country road and turned into the lane that led to the Garrett house. The sun's red glow was fading in the west and twilight was settling gray on the fields as Rya Garrett chatted with her three friends, saying she would see them on Sunday afternoon.

Melvin Foster hopped down and helped Rya from the carriage. She thanked him, then bounded up the steps of the front porch, waving to the two young ladies over her shoulder.

Wearing a big smile, Rya rushed through the front door. The aroma of fried chicken teased her taste buds, and she headed down the hall toward the kitchen. Bursting through the kitchen door with her wide, sparkling smile intact, she saw her mother at the stove and her father at the cupboard, repairing one of the doors. Rya had a youthful glow and flush to her skin. Her blue eyes were like crystal, highlighting the soft curves and lines of her beauty, and her long auburn hair was a striking, waving mass.

Both of them smiled and greeted her.

"Yum, yum, Mama!" she said. "You fixed my favorite dinner, and I'm starving! The food in the college dining room leaves a lot to be desired. Hello, Papa."

Both parents headed toward her, and she opened her arms to them. After she had hugged them both, Laura said, "Honey, you look especially happy this evening. What is it?"

"Yes," said Richard. "You always come home with a smile, but this one is brighter than usual. Tell us what's got you so happy."

Rising up and down on the balls of her feet, Rya said, "Oh, Papa...Mama! I've been offered a student teaching job, teaching summer school at Elm Park Elementary School in Richmond!"

—⁓— —⁓— —⁓—

That evening after supper, while mother and daughter were doing dishes and cleaning up the kitchen, Richard was finishing his repair job on the cabinet door.

There was a knock at the front door of the house. "I'll get it," said Richard.

Richard was humming a nameless tune as he turned the knob and opened the door. The tune died quickly when he saw the face before him.

"Good evening, Mr. Garrett," said Jason Lynch. "I would like to see Rya."

Richard's stomach turned sour. He had met twenty-three-year-old Jason on two occasions when he and Laura visited Rya at Richmond Teacher's College. Jason lived in Richmond and worked at the college as a maintenance man.

Richard also knew that Jason had been pursuing Rya, trying to date her, but that Rya had shied away from him. One reason was that Jason was not a Christian and wanted nothing to do with the Lord, the Bible, or church. Another reason was that he could be obnoxious at times. Rya had shared with her parents that she had found Jason very pushy and sometimes even repulsive. Richard recalled that Rya had once told him and Laura that because of Jason's aggressiveness, she had never told him the location of her parents' farm.

But there he stood.

Jason Lynch was slender and of medium height. His clothes hung loosely on him, and his face was lean and rawboned. Deep within protective wells, his pale gray eyes were the kind that seemed to look through a person, rather than at him.

Richard's first instinct was to brush Jason off and send him away without seeing Rya. However, wanting to keep a good testimony before him, he would be kind and let him see her briefly.

"Come in, Jason," he said, swinging the door wider. "You need to know, though, that Rya is spending the rest of the evening with Laura and me, and the entire weekend, too. You can see her for a few minutes."

Jason gave him a bland look. "I'll appreciate those few minutes."

Closing the door, Richard said, "She's in the kitchen with her mother. Follow me."

When the two men entered the kitchen and Rya saw Jason, a coldness washed over her.

Not even bothering to speak to her mother, Jason said, "Rya, your father says I can only spend a few minutes with you. Could I talk to you in private?"

"You can talk to him on the front porch, Rya," Laura said. "And...ah...hello, Jason."

"Hello, Mrs. Garrett."

Rya quickly led him out of the kitchen. When they were alone on the front porch in the pale moonlight, she gestured toward the porch swing. "We can sit here."

When they were seated, putting the swing slightly in motion, Jason said, "I know you always ride home from college and back again on Sunday afternoons with Melvin Foster. Could I come on Sunday afternoon and drive you back to Richmond? We could stop along the way and have a picnic. Just the two of us."

Rya frowned. "Jason, I've told you before that I only do things like that with Christian young men. I don't date anyone who is not a Christian."

A look of disgust captured Jason's features. "Rya, I ain't gonna try to turn you away from your religion. I just—"

"Jason, I will not bend on this issue. As I've told you before, I would love to see you get saved. Not only would it give you the assurance that you would go to heaven instead of hell, but it would make a big change in your life."

Jason sighed and took hold of her hand. "Rya, how many times do I have to tell you that I'm in love with you? Just because I don't look at religion the way you do is no reason to turn me away."

Rya set her jaw firmly and pulled her hand from his. "And how many times do I have to tell you that what I have is not religion? I have salvation in Jesus Christ. There's a big difference between religion and salvation. And you need salvation, Jason. Unless you become a Christian, there is no possibility that anything can ever develop between you and me."

Jason leaped to his feet, and his eyes flashed against the night.

"It's wrong for you to spurn my love, Rya!"

With that, he stomped off the porch, heading for his horse. Rya left the swing, and keeping her eyes on Jason, moved toward the door.

Settling in the saddle, Jason said, "I'll talk to you when you're in a better mood."

Rya watched him gallop away into the night, then turned and entered the house. Her parents were just coming down the hall from the kitchen.

"Honey, you're upset," said Laura. She came toward Rya and embraced her.

"What happened?" asked Richard.

Rya told her parents word for word what went on between her and Jason on the porch.

"I'm sorry, honey. You're just going to have to tell Jason you want no more to do with him."

Richard's eyes were flashing. "I'm going into Richmond tomorrow and have a talk with that young man. I'm telling him to stay away from you, Rya! Didn't you tell me he lives at that boarding-house on Broad Street, just around the corner from the campus?"

"Yes, Papa. That's where he lives."

The next morning, Jason Lynch was just getting out of bed when there was a loud knock at his door. Hurriedly, he put on his bathrobe and padded to the door. When he opened it, he was surprised to see Richard Garrett standing there.

Richard's features were stonelike. "Jason, I need to talk to you."

Reluctantly, Jason stepped back. "Come in."

"Jason, I don't want to be unkind to you, but I am going to put it straight so you'll understand. You need to find another girl to set your heart on. It is quite evident that there will never be anything between you and my daughter."

Jason stiffened. "I can't believe that. My heart is set on Rya. I could never love anyone else. I believe in time she will feel the same way about me."

"Wrong," Richard said. "For starters, nothing can ever develop between the two of you until and unless you become a child of God."

Jason's face flushed. "I am a child of God! All human beings are God's children."

"Wrong again," Richard said. "God says in John 1:12 that we have to become His children by receiving Christ as Saviour. All human beings are God's creation, yes. He is their Creator. But He is not their Father until they repent of their sin, believe the gospel, and receive His only begotten Son into their heart. Jason, you have to be born into God's family spiritually like you were born into your parent's family physically. Only being born again, as Jesus said in John 3:3, can make you a heaven-bound child of God."

"I don't believe that," Jason said, "and I know Rya does. But in spite of our disagreement on this, I feel quite confident that given a chance, I could make her love me and want to marry me."

"Wrong once more, Jason," countered Richard, looking steadily into Jason's pale gray eyes. "Your disagreement with Rya in spiritual matters would affect everything in your lives. There can be no compatibility between the two of you unless you become a genuine child of God. The Bible warns against a Christian marrying a non-believer, saying it would create an unequal yoke. There would be constant disagreement, and it would only make for a miserable marriage."

Jason set his jaw. "I want no part of this Jesus Christ stuff, but that shouldn't have anything to do with my relationship with Rya. I'll keep trying until I win her over."

Richard pointed a stiff finger between Jason's eyes and said in a knife-keen tone, "there is no relationship between you and Rya. You are to stay away from her. She wants nothing to do with you. Therefore, you are to leave her alone."

Jason's back arched. "Now, look, I—"

"You are to leave my daughter alone!" Richard's eyes burned with anger. "Am I getting through to you? Do you understand what I'm saying?"

Jason gave him a dull look. "I understand."

"Tell me what you understand."

In a low voice, and barely moving his lips, Jason said, "I understand I am to stay away from your daughter."

"Good." Richard turned and took hold of the doorknob. "And you had better not forget it."

When Richard Garrett walked into the house after putting the wagon in the barn and the team in the corral, he found his wife and daughter sitting at the kitchen table. They were sewing a new dress for Rya.

"Did you get to talk to him?" queried Laura.

"Yes."

"And how did it go, Papa?" asked Rya.

Pulling his regular chair from the table, Richard sat down. "We had a good man-to-man talk. Once he made it explicitly clear that he wants nothing to do with our Saviour, I told him that he is to stay away from my daughter. I told him, Rya, that you want nothing to do with him, and therefore, he is to leave you alone."

"Thank you, Papa. I...I'm really relieved. I've actually begun to be afraid of Jason. He frightens me."

"I can see why. But it's over now." Richard reached across the table and laid his calloused fingers on Rya's soft hand. "Honey, you are to let me know if Jason ever bothers you again."

"I will, Papa."

"Promise?"

"I promise."

On the following Monday, Rya Garrett was coming out of the college administration building, walking across the lawn amid the trees beside a fellow student named Walt Keaton.

"That was some enlightening lesson, Rya," said Walt. "I never realized until today that Napoleon Bonaparte's older brother had been king of Spain for five years."

"I remembered that Joseph Bonaparte had been king of Spain," said Rya, "but I sure didn't know that he had lived in the United States after abdicating the Spanish throne."

Suddenly, a slender form jumped out in front of them from behind a tree.

"Jason!" gasped Rya.

Ignoring Walt Keaton, Jason said, "I want to talk to you, Rya."

Walt did not like the angry look in Jason's eyes, and when Rya asked him if he would excuse her while she talked to Jason, he said, "I'm going to stay right here while you talk to him."

"Oh, so you have designs on her, do you, Walt?" Jason said.

"I'm her friend, and I don't like the tone of your voice."

Jason clenched his fists. "And I don't like your face. Maybe it needs to be rearranged."

"Jason, please," said Rya. "Don't start trouble."

"There won't be trouble if he leaves! On your way, Keaton. I want to talk to my girl alone."

"Walt, I appreciate your looking out for me," Rya said, "but Jason and I need to talk in private."

"All right," said Walt. "Since it's you saying so."

Walt walked just far enough to be out of earshot and leaned against a large oak tree, eyes fixed on Rya and the maintenance man.

Before Jason could get a word out, Rya said, "Let's get something straight right off, Jason. I am not your girl."

"I did not appreciate your father coming to my room Saturday and telling me to stay away from you. I am in love with you, Rya, and I want to marry you."

Rya wanted to scream at him. "I repeat, Jason. I am not your girl. I am not in love with you, either. And what's more, I am not interested in marrying you. Papa knows this, and chose to talk to you man to man so you would understand it and stay away from me. But here you are, going against his edict."

Jason let a quick gust of irritation come out of him. "I know you're in love with me, Rya, and you might as well accept the fact that we are meant for each other. I'm gonna have you as my wife, and you might as well face it!"

Hearing Jason shout at Rya, and seeing her cringe before him was too much for Walt Keaton. "That's it, Lynch! Get away from her! You're upsetting her! Go on. Get outta here."

Jason bristled, meeting Walt's hot stare.

Suddenly Jason swung a fist toward Walt's nose, but the stocky man dodged the blow and sent one of his own, smashing Jason on the jaw, knocking him flat.

Other students were gathering around as Jason lay on the ground, shaking his head. Walt grabbed Jason by the front of his shirt and lifted him to his feet. Jason's head wobbled as if he had a rubber neck.

Slapping his face with a palm to help revive him, Walt said, "You awake, Lynch?"

Jason batted his eyes and shook his head again to clear it. "Yeah."

"You get outta here right now, and stay away from Rya, or you'll get more of the same."

Jason sent a hazy glance at Rya. "I don't care what anybody says. I'll see you again." And he staggered away.

MAIL ORDER BRIDE SERIES

NO. 9
1877
USA

AL & JOANNA LACY

9

IT WAS MID-AUGUST, 1877. In south central Wyoming Territory, the hot day had closed and the cool, lonely night on the prairie settled in with its dead silence.

Travelers Mike Torvall and Jim Chaffee sat propped against huge rocks, their eyes on the crackling campfire. The Rocky Mountains loomed against the starlit sky a few miles to the west, and a small creek ran quietly southward nearby. Supper was over, and their tin cups, plates, and eating utensils had been washed and put aside. Their horses were tied to small trees on the bank of the creek. A soft wind fanned the embers and blew sparks and thin smoke away into the enshrouding circle of darkness.

The night silence split to the cry of a coyote. It arose strange, wild, and mournful, then faded away.

Staring into the fire, Torvall said, "Well, Jim, I guess we'd better turn in. My bedroll's lookin' better every minute."

"Yeah. Mine, too," said Chaffee. He turned his face southward, looking into the darkness. "We're only about fifteen miles or so from Rawlins. We can freshen up our food supply by noon tomorrow and move on down toward Colorado. It'll be good to see my brother again."

"How long did you say it's been since you saw your brother?"

"Almost eleven years. Rex and I were very close in our growin' up years, and I'm really lookin' forward to—"

Chaffee's words were cut off by the sound of their horses whinnying, and another horse somewhere near in the darkness answering them. Both men leaped to their feet, drawing their sidearms and earing back the hammers.

Torvall pointed north with his revolver. "Came from that way."

Abruptly they saw the lone horse coming slowly toward them as it drew within the circle of the campfire's light. The horse was bridled, but the man was bent over, riding bareback, and clinging to the horse's mane. He looked to be in his late thirties.

"He's hurt," said Chaffee. Both men rushed to him, easing their hammers down and holstering their weapons.

The horse stopped as the drifters stepped up to the rider. They saw that the front of his shirt was soaked with blood. His eyes were dull as he looked at them and said hoarsely, "I...need...help."

"Here, let's get you down," said Torvall, reaching up and wrapping his arms around him.

Chaffee helped carry him. They laid him on his back close to the fire, and both men knelt beside him.

Torvall picked up his canteen, pulled the cork, and said, "Let me give you some water."

The man took a sip, coughed, then took a good swallow. "Th-thank you."

Putting the cork back in place, Torvall said, "What happened?"

"Indians. Cheyenne. I...I'm a farmer. 'Bout five miles north of here. Name's Da—Dale S-Slater. They...they seemed to come out of nowhere. Attacked us while we were in the yard behind the house. Shot us all. Killed my wife and three children. Thought they had killed me. Burned the house. I...was unconscious for quite a while. Finally was able to get on my horse. Trying...to get to Fort Steele. Tell army what happened. Cheyenne on warpath...again."

Chaffee looked at Torvall. "Fort Steele is twenty miles east of Rawlins. Things have been pretty quiet with the hostiles in these parts, the last three months or so. Army needs to know about this. You stay here and take care of Mr. Slater. I'll ride for the fort right now."

Torvall frowned. "Shouldn't we get this man to a doctor in Rawlins, first?"

"I don't think he's in any shape to ride anymore tonight. After I alert the commandant at Fort Steele about this, I'll ride into

Rawlins, wake the doctor up, and tell him what we've got out here. Be best if we could get Mr. Slater in a buggy. The doc's got one, I'm sure."

As Chaffee was speaking, Torvall pulled his lips into a thin line, leaned down close, and put an ear to the wounded man's mouth. "He's not breathing, Jim." He then laid gentle fingers on Slater's neck, feeling for a pulse. He shook his head solemnly. "He's dead."

The sun cleared the eastern hills and vast prairie, and the cool air brought in by the night was fleeing as if before a charging foe. The gray shadows of Fort Steele's guard tower and stockade fence began to lighten.

Within the stockade, Colonel Ward Lamont—the fort's commandant—stood before his troops, who were in formation shoulder to shoulder and line by line. At the colonel's side were Mike Torvall and Jim Chaffee. The body of Dale Slater was draped over his horse in front of the commandant's office a few feet away.

"Men," said the forty-nine-year-old colonel, "you've all heard the testimony of Mr. Chaffee and Mr. Torvall. The Cheyenne are definitely on the warpath again. This is the fourth such incident in south central Wyoming in the last eight days. According to what Mr. Slater told these two men last night, the Cheyenne attacked his farm yesterday, shot the family down, and burned the house. Things have been quiet with the hostiles for too long, even as I told you last week. As you go out on your patrols, you must keep a sharp eye."

The wives and children of the fort's officers were standing close by, huddled together with deep concern showing on their faces.

Lamont cleared his throat and ran his eyes over the faces of his stalwart men. "As you know, I've been trying to get more Gatling guns for this fort. Washington has promised them, but so far, they have not been delivered by rail as I've been expecting. It is Captain Moore's turn to take our one and only Gatling on the next patrol. I'm hoping that soon every patrol unit will have one."

Captain Lance Moore raised his hand.

"Yes, Captain?" said Lamont.

"Sir, are we to concentrate our patrols on the areas where the farmers have been hit, rather than sticking to the routes we've been following?"

"Let's stay with the routes I laid out," said the colonel. "If we spread the patrols out to cover each of the areas where the Cheyenne have attacked in the past eight days, they'll be too far apart from each other. I want all patrols to be close enough together that if one gets attacked, there'll be another patrol close by who can join them."

The seven other captains exchanged glances, nodding their agreement with the colonel.

"All right, men," said Lamont. "Get a good breakfast down and we'll assemble on the parade in one hour."

As the troops broke rank and hurried in the direction of the mess hall, the colonel turned to Torvall and Chaffee. "You gentlemen are invited to eat breakfast with us."

Both men smiled.

"We'll just take you up on that, Colonel," said Chaffee.

"And you will see to Mr. Slater's burial, sir?" said Torvall.

"Yes, and that of his family. We'll bury them together on his farm. If there is livestock that needs caring for out there along with his horse, I will see to it that they are taken to a neighboring farmer."

Precisely an hour later, Colonel Ward Lamont stood before his mounted troops as the morning sun's heat brooded over the fort. Lamont gave them final instructions and saluted them as the patrols began filing out the gate one by one, each taking its assigned route.

Captain Jess Adams and Lieutenant Bart Springer sat on their horses in front of the unit of steely-eyed men. There were twelve men in the unit, including officers Adams and Springer.

Adams mopped his brow with a bandanna and watched the first three units moving out ahead of him. Number three was led by Captain Lance Moore. Adams focused on the wagon at the rear of Moore's column that carried the Gatling gun, and longed for one—considering the circumstances. When Moore's patrol was out of the gate, Adams turned around in his saddle and set his eyes on his sweaty troopers. The dark blue shirts of their government issue uniforms were plastered to their chests and backs.

Raising his hand, Captain Adams gave the signal to move out. "Forward, ho!" He led his troops through the gate and onto the hot prairie, riding two by two. They took a slightly different course northward from that of Moore's unit.

Immediately, every trooper's squinted eyes were moving back and forth across the sun-bleached land, alert for any sign of hostiles. A hot wind was beginning to blow, adding to the discomfort. After about twenty minutes, Captain Lance Moore's unit passed out of sight over a hill off to the right.

The morning wore on.

The creak of saddle leather, the clink of bit chains, the occasional whicker of a horse, and the shrill barking of prairie dogs peering from their holes were the only sounds to break the stillness. From time to time, a flock of blackbirds, disturbed by their passage, whirred out of bushes to wheel through the sky in dark, erratic flight. Wind-whipped buffalo grass and sagebrush dotted the prairie, and the ground was crisscrossed in many places by grass-bottomed gulches, ravines, and an occasional stream of water that wound through the land.

It was coming up on eleven o'clock when they topped a gentle rise. Adams spotted a creek in a low spot off to their right. Since leaving the fort, there had been little conversation among the troopers. Adams said to Lieutenant Springer, "Let's go down there to the creek and let the horses get a good drink."

Springer grinned. "The way we've all been hitting our canteens, I'm sure they need filling, anyhow."

Moments later, the troopers dismounted at the creek side and led their horses to the water, each man keeping an eye on the surrounding area. When that was done, the horses were led away from the bank, and the men knelt down and began filling their canteens.

Among the troopers were Privates Matt Koehn and Ernie Widner, who had arrived three days ago with several other men who had been transferred to Fort Steele from Fort Calhoun,

Nebraska. While dipping their canteens into the water, both men noted the sergeant who knelt beside them.

Koehn elbowed Widner. "Let's talk to him about it."

The sergeant heard his words, looked at them, and said, "Talk to me about what?"

"Well, Sergeant Reardon," replied Matt Koehn, "ever since we arrived at Fort Steele, we've had at least a dozen men tell us about you."

"What about me?" asked Sergeant McClain Reardon.

"They've told us about your prowess in fighting Indians," said Ernie Widner. "They say you've distinguished yourself time and time again during battle. Corporal Max Noland told us how you saved his life back in March when you were fighting Chief Black Hawk's warriors over by Medicine Bow Peak. You had to take on three warriors at one time to do it."

"Yeah," said Koehn, "and Sergeant Jake Ridgeway told us how you risked your life to save Captain Adams's life in a battle with a Blackfoot war party up by South Pass City last October. We'd just like to know more about you."

A familiar voice from behind said, "I can tell you firsthand about that battle by South Pass City."

All three turned to see Captain Jess Adams pulling the cork from his canteen. Kneeling, he dipped the canteen under the surface of the water, smiled at Reardon, then looked at the other two. "I'd be a dead man if it weren't for Sergeant Reardon's raw courage. We were fighting the Blackfoot hand to hand in a rocky gulch. Four warriors were closing in on me, no doubt because they saw my rank. There was dust and gun smoke everywhere. I had one bullet left in my revolver. Just as I took a step back and fired at the Indian who was closest to me, I stumbled over a rock and fell. The slug missed the Indian.

"Sergeant Reardon had already seen my predicament and was coming on the run. He fired and dropped one of them, then two of them turned on him while the other one raised his tomahawk to finish me off. Reardon fired between the two who were coming after him and dropped the one that was after me and then another, but also found that he had fired his last shot. He had to take on the fourth warrior barehanded. The warrior tried his best to kill Reardon with his tomahawk, but soon found out he was up against a real man. I won't go into the details, but the sergeant was cut twice with the tomahawk: once on the upper left arm and the second time on his ribs. But as you can see, he's still here. The Indian isn't. I wouldn't be here either, if it hadn't been for this brave man."

McClain's face tinted. "Aw, Captain, you'd have taken that last one out if I hadn't."

Adams lifted his canteen, took a long swallow, then dipped it back into the stream. "I'd like to believe that, Sergeant, but I don't. He was a fierce one and very muscular. He'd have killed me. I owe my life to you."

"Like I said, Sergeant," spoke up Matt Koehn, "we'd like to know more about you."

"I'll tell you this much," interjected Captain Adams, "because of this man's courage under fire and his excellent ability in fighting Indians, he went from private to corporal in his first six months at Fort Steele, and was made sergeant about a year later. If enlisted men could become officers today like they did in the Civil War, he'd be a general by now—even though he's only twenty-five."

Embarrassed, McClain shook his head.

"Another thing," said Adams, "he also assists the fort chaplain with church services on Sundays."

"What do you do, Sergeant?" asked Matt Koehn.

"Oh, what ever Chaplain Fremont needs or wants. Often, I teach Sunday school and he preaches."

"And when the chaplain gets sick or has to be away, he even preaches," said Adams.

"I'm impressed," said Koehn.

"Me, too," said Ernie Widner. "How long have you been at Fort Steele, Sergeant?"

"Be three years next month."

"Got a girl somewhere?"

"Not really. Had a few I dated at home, but around here, there aren't any."

"Where's home?"

"Blue Springs, Missouri."

"Family live there?"

"Mm-hmm. My mother and two sisters. Actually, I was born on a farm near Bowling Green, Virginia. When I was thirteen, my father died. Right after that, we moved to Blue Springs to be near my mother's relatives, who had lived there most of their lives."

"So where did you join the army?" asked Widner.

"At Fort Larned, Kansas. After graduating from high school, I decided I wanted some adventure in my life, so I joined the army. I was transferred to Fort Steele some four years later. I like it here. I really like serving under Colonel Lamont. I'm glad to be in Captain Adams's patrol unit, and as a Christian, I am especially happy to be assisting Chaplain Fremont."

Koehn chuckled. "You sound like a satisfied man. Are you planning on making the army your lifetime career?"

McClain shrugged. "Whatever the Lord wants for me. There might be something else down the line, but for now I know I'm where I'm supposed to be and doing what I'm supposed to be doing."

"You mentioned how you like serving under Colonel Lamont, Sergeant," said Widner. "We were told upon arriving at Fort Steele that he is planning on retiring soon. What do you think of that?"

"Well, the colonel is a Christian, too, and if the Lord is leading him to do something else, that's what he ought to do."

"Isn't forty-nine pretty young for a fort commandant to retire?" asked Matt Koehn.

"It is. Most of them, as you know, usually stay at it until they are about sixty. But, as I said, if the Lord is leading him to retire, that's what he ought to do."

"Well, men," said Captain Adams, "we'd better mount up and keep moving."

By midafternoon, the sun was a burning brand in the brassy blue sky as a band of mounted Cheyenne Indians pulled out of a draw and paused on the edge, looking across a sweeping valley. In the distance to the south, they could see the town the white men called Rawlins.

Chief Black Hawk sat on his pinto proudly with the hot wind plucking at the feathers of his large headdress. His dark eyes were like bits of stone as he pointed to a small farmhouse about a half mile eastward. "That is next one."

The warriors studied the scene. Behind the house were three outbuildings and a corral that surrounded a barn. Atop the barn were two men, just finishing the roof.

Black Hawk's twenty-year-old son moved his pinto up beside him. "That farmer and his family settled there many moons ago, my father. They have worked hard to put up their buildings, and it looks like they are almost done with the barn."

Black Hawk turned his head and looked at his son, scowling. "Do I hear a weak tone in voice of Sky Eagle? Is he thinking that we should not kill the paleface farmer and his family?"

Sky Eagle swallowed hard under the frown of his father. "Ah...I am only thinking that there must come a time when we cease our war with the white men, my father. They come from the East like snowflakes come in the winter. They will soon be greater in number than the Cheyenne and our brother tribes. Should we not seek to live with them in peace?"

While the other warriors looked on silently, Black Hawk slowly ran his gaze over the sun-washed land around him. He loved the prairie, the mountains, and the forests which had been home to his ancestors from time immemorial. "Sky Eagle speaks of hard work the white men have done to put up their buildings. Yes. They have worked hard cutting down trees in our mountains to make wood for house and buildings. Like all white men, they come here, settle on Indian land, cut down our trees, kill our deer and buffalo, expect us to welcome them."

Sky Eagle noted the cold, dark shine of his father's eyes, the thin, vicious trap of his mouth, and the forbidding hawk-like features of his face as he hissed, "We do not welcome them, Sky Eagle! The paleface invaders come to steal what not belong to them! Because in mind of white men Indian is ignorant, and he does not put the land to same use as whites, so they say we not deserve to live on this land. They have right to take it away from us."

The chief's features grew even darker than normal. His breath was heated and coming in short puffs. "They want our land, we bury them in it! There are two more farms beyond hills behind this one. We also kill those invaders today!"

As Black Hawk led his warriors toward the farm before them, their horses' hooves stirred clouds of dust that were instantly whipped away by the hot wind.

As Captain Jess Adams led his men over the rolling hills and flat spaces of south central Wyoming Territory, the hot afternoon dragged on. The windswept plains were ominously still.

Plagued by a growing feeling of uneasiness, Sergeant McClain Reardon left the corporal who was riding beside him and moved his horse up beside the unit leader.

"Yes, Sergeant?" said Adams.

"Sir, I've been in this Indian fighting business long enough to have instincts honed pretty sharp."

"You have. What's the matter?"

"Well, sir, with the Cheyenne on the warpath for sure, I just— well, I just have a feeling that things are too quiet. Something is in the air."

The captain was about to comment when suddenly they heard a sudden volley of guns roaring rapidly like a string of giant fire-crackers amid the familiar whoops and screeches of wild Indians.

Every man in the patrol tensed up as their leader pointed due north. "The fighting is going on just over that next rise, Sergeant. You were right. Things were too quiet."

Adams gave the command for his men to follow and led them toward the sounds of battle.

WHEN CAPTAIN JESS ADAMS AND HIS MEN topped the rise in a cloud of dust, they saw a battle going on between an army unit and a Cheyenne war party in a farmer's yard.

Adams signaled for his men to stop, and as they sat their horses to take stock of the situation, they saw amid the clouds of gun smoke that the Cheyenne warriors were in breechclout leggings, wearing shirts whose tails dangled against their thighs. All of them were wielding repeater rifles, their legs curved against the bare flanks of their pintos.

Lieutenant Bart Springer said, "Sir, that's Captain Lance Moore's outfit down there. A couple of his men are jumping onto the wagon to use the Gatling."

"Yes," said Adams. "I see two dead men sprawled on the roof of the barn, and a woman and two children lying on the ground by the front porch of the house. No doubt they're all dead. Captain Moore must have caught them in the act of killing the farmers. The battle is just getting started. Let's go!"

As they galloped down the slope toward the farmyard, the Gatling gun cut loose. Immediately warriors began falling from their horses, surprised by the rapid-firing, deep-throated Gatling.

The Cheyenne leader noticed the second cavalry unit charging down the hill. He wheeled his pinto about and signaled for his remaining warriors to follow him. They quickly galloped away and disappeared over a grassy hill. Riderless pintos followed them, manes flying in the wind.

When Adams and his men came to a halt in the front yard,

Captain Lance Moore hurried up. "Thanks for joining the fight!"

"We didn't get to help, but we would have been in the thick of it in a few more seconds," said Adams. He ran his gaze over the area and saw five Indians on the ground, along with two uniformed men who were each being attended to by two troopers. Other troopers were moving among the fallen Indians.

While Adams and his men were dismounting, Moore sent three troopers to see about the men who lay on the barn roof.

When Captain Adams moved up to the bodies of the woman and children who lay near the front porch, he groaned. Turning to Moore, he said, "You must've come along just as the Indians were shooting these people down."

"Exactly," said Moore, using a bandanna to mop perspiration from his brow. "Wish we could have arrived sooner. One bunch of them was cutting down the woman and children, while another bunch was shooting the two men on the roof."

Adams nodded. "I knew you couldn't have been here long when I saw your men use the Gatling. Do you know which Cheyenne village the war party was from?"

"I sure do. Their leader was Chief Black Hawk."

Adams gritted his teeth. "Black Hawk. Mmm. He's probably the fiercest of all the hostile chiefs of any tribe in Wyoming Territory."

"I agree," said Moore. "He's the worst."

The smell of dust and gunpowder still clung to the hot air.

Sergeant McClain Reardon was standing close by, listening to the captains talking, when his line of sight went to Moore's troopers who were moving among the fallen Indians. Lieutenant Carl Pierson was standing over a bleeding Cheyenne. The Indian was still alive, clutching the wound in his right shoulder.

McClain stiffened when he saw Pierson grinning viciously at the Indian while he pulled his revolver from its holster.

"No!" shouted McClain while running toward Pierson. "Don't do that! Don't shoot him!" As McClain drew up, Pierson snapped the hammer back and aimed it at the young warrior's face.

"I said don't do that!" said McClain, noting the blood flowing between the Indian's fingers as he clutched the wound. He also noted that the warrior's feathered rifle lay on the ground, out of his reach.

Pierson had a quick spark of anger flaring up in his eyes. "Why not?"

"What do you mean, why not? The man is still alive! He's wounded and unarmed! To kill a wounded, defenseless man is murder!"

Pierson fixed him with hot eyes. "You're talking to an officer, Sergeant!"

"Officer or no officer, if you pull that trigger, you'll face murder charges! I'll see to it!"

The wounded Cheyenne was staring up at McClain, unable to believe what he was seeing and hearing. His somber eyes went to Pierson.

Unaware that the two captains and other soldiers were headed toward him, Pierson pointed the muzzle of his gun at the Indian's forehead, fire flashing in his eyes. A thick vein on his temple throbbed as he snapped, "This dirty savage helped massacre this poor farm family! He deserves to die!"

McClain Reardon moved lightning fast and seized the revolver, trying to wrest it from Pierson's hand. They both stumbled a few steps as Pierson sought to resist him, and the gun fired, sending the slug harmlessly into the air. McClain then twisted it from Pierson's grasp.

Anger boiled up in Pierson's eyes. "I'll see you court martialed for this, Reardon! Give me that gun!"

The young warrior lay on the ground, wide-eyed, as Captain Lance Moore moved in and placed himself between the lieutenant and the sergeant. "There's not going to be any court martial, Pierson," said Moore. "Sergeant Reardon is right. To shoot this wounded, unarmed Indian would be murder."

"I don't see it that way, Captain!" rasped Pierson. "This savage and his companions murdered the white people who lived on this farm! If I killed him, it would be an execution, not murder. Every one of those beasts should be hunted down and executed. We oughtta wipe out every tribe. They deserve it!"

"Hold on, Pierson!" snapped McClain, moving aside a step so

he could look the lieutenant in the eye. "The Indians are only trying to defend what belongs to them. Their ancestors have freely roamed these plains, hills, and mountains for centuries. And now the white man comes, killing their game, and trying to take their land away from them. They are a primitive people, and killing the invaders is the only way they know to fight back."

While the lieutenant was struggling to come up with a reasonable reply, Captain Jess Adams was studying the face of the wounded warrior. "Hey!" he said. "This is Chief Black Hawk's son, Sky Eagle!"

Moore frowned, looked down at the young warrior, then back at Adams.

"You sure?"

"Yes. I've seen him with his father on several occasions. See the arm bands?"

"Yeah."

"They have the markings worn only by a chief's son."

"Hmm. I wasn't aware of that."

"It's an old Cheyenne custom," said Adams.

Pierson chuckled. "Well, isn't this something? Black Hawk's son, eh? Give me my gun back, Reardon! It'll teach Black Hawk a valuable lesson for his son to die after what he and his warriors did to these farmers!"

"No way, Lieutenant!" said McClain. "Black Hawk no doubt already thinks Sky Eagle is dead, or he wouldn't have gone off and left him."

"I say we finish him off!" hissed Pierson.

"Enough of that, Lieutenant," growled Moore, rubbing his chin and looking at Adams. "The other four Indians are dead. But what are we going to do with this one? We can't take him to the fort."

"Why not, sir?" asked McClain.

"Because there are other men at the fort who have the same attitude toward the Cheyenne that Lieutenant Pierson does. Doc Wallis wouldn't be too keen on trying to save the life of Sky Eagle, especially since he's Black Hawk's son. Remember, it was some of Black Hawk's warriors who attacked the wagon train that Mrs.

Wallis was on. And we had to bury her. We can't take him to the fort."

McClain bent over the young warrior, noted the blood running through his fingers, and more blood in the sod beneath his right shoulder. Then turning to his commander, he said, "Captain Adams, Black Hawk's village isn't more than a dozen miles from here. I'll bandage Sky Eagle up as well as I can, then I'll take him home where the Cheyenne medicine men can work on him."

"Reardon, you fool!" said Pierson. "You go into that village, and they'll kill you!"

"No!" said Sky Eagle, grimacing from the pain caused by his outburst. Looking up, he set his dull eyes on Pierson. "My people will not kill the white man—" He swallowed with difficulty and took a sharp breath. "My people will not kill the white man who brings their chief's wounded son home. They will thank him."

McClain looked into Adams's eyes. "Captain, may I have permission to take Sky Eagle to his village after I bandage him up?"

Adams shook his head in wonderment. "Permission granted, Sergeant. I believe I'm beginning to understand more about your Christianity. I'm seeing real Christianity right before my eyes. However, I think I should send four or five men with you."

"It is best that you do not, Captain," said Sky Eagle. "If my people see a band of soldiers coming toward the village, they will not understand. They will think they are coming to fight them. Please. I promise. Your Sergeant—" He looked up at McClain. "What is your name, Sergeant?"

"McClain Reardon, Sky Eagle."

The son of Black Hawk looked again at Captain Jess Adams. "Your Sergeant McClain Reardon will not be harmed."

"I'm sure he's telling the truth, Captain," said McClain. "Let me take him alone."

Adams sighed. "All right, since you insist. Use what bandage material you need and get going. I'll send some men to hide close to the village, so they can escort you back safely. We'll wait right here for you."

"Really, sir," said McClain, "you should get our wounded men to Doc Wallis. I'll be fine."

When Sky Eagle saw that the captain was about to refuse, he said, "Captain, when my father learns what Sergeant McClain Reardon has done for his son, he will send warriors to escort him all the way to Fort Steele. He will be safe."

"That's good enough for me, Captain," said McClain.

Adams sighed again. "All right. Get him bandaged quickly."

Carl Pierson extended an open hand to McClain. "I want my gun."

McClain smiled thinly, laid it in his palm, then turned toward Sky Eagle.

Smoke drifted in lazy streamers from between the lodgepoles atop the tepees in the Cheyenne village as the war party drew near. More than two hundred tepees were gathered in a great circle beneath tall pine and birch trees on the bank of a wide creek. Like the hub of a giant wheel, the chief's tepee was in the center.

Old men, young warriors, women, and children looked at the band of incoming riders with the five riderless pintos trailing behind, pointing and talking rapidly.

As the war party reached the edge of the village, a droop-shouldered Black Hawk slid off his pinto while the inquisitive people gathered close. The other warriors also dismounted, their faces grim.

Some of the Indians were running from tepee to tepee, announcing the return of the war party, which resulted in many more hurrying toward their chief and his band of warriors.

Many voices were calling for the chief to tell them what had happened. He raised a hand for silence. "Black Hawk will wait until everyone here." Even as he spoke, he saw his squaw, Meadowlark, coming from the central tepee, flanked by two women.

When the rest of the people had gathered, and Meadowlark was standing with her companions on the inside of the circle, Black Hawk ran his dismal eyes over the faces of the crowd. "We attack farm of new white invaders. Army come with big gun that shoot many bullets quickly. Gray Cloud, Falling Stone, Spotted Bull, and Young Crow all dead."

Women began to weep and wail.

Meadowlark's eyes were flitting from warrior to warrior in the war party that had followed their chief that day. Black Hawk saw it, choked up for a moment, then lowered his eyes groundward. "There is one other warrior who was killed. Son of Black Hawk and Meadowlark—Sky Eagle."

Meadowlark released a shrill cry, and Black Hawk hurried to her, folding her in his arms. While she sobbed and wailed, the chief looked at his medicine man. His voice shook as he said, "Tall Tree, will you conduct a mourning ceremony for those braves who have been killed today? We will return to the farm tomorrow morning and pick up the bodies."

Tall Tree nodded sadly. "We will begin the ceremony immediately, my honorable chief."

Tall Tree led everyone back to the center of the village, where a large fire was built. With everyone gathered in a circle around the fire, Tall Tree led in a mournful chorus of chanting voices while drums beat out rhythms that filled the late afternoon air.

When the mourning ceremony was over, the chief and his squaw went to the privacy of their tepee, where they clung to each other and wept over the death of their only son.

While the other families who had lost warriors that day were also mourning in their tepees, the rest of the people returned to their necessary work. The men were skinning deer and buffalo, brought in that day by the hunters. For the women, there were wild turnips to be gathered and buffalo hides to be staked out and scraped with crude fleshing tools. Dry hides were to be cut into shields and there was pemmican to be made.

When the sun was dropping behind the jagged Rocky Mountains, the shadows of the low places on the prairie stretched from the west and between them streamed a red-gold light.

Inside their tepee, Chief Black Hawk and Meadowlark sat side by side, clinging to each other and talking about precious memories that Sky Eagle had left them.

"Yes, my husband," said the squaw, "Sky Eagle was always a

good, obedient son. He made me proud."

Black Hawk nodded. "And he was a mighty warrior. He would have made our people a fine chief one day." Suddenly the shadowing in the wells of his deep-set eyes grew darker. His lips were thinned from the pressure of his thoughts. "If the greedy white men had not come to steal our land, this would never have happened. Our son is dead because the whites invade our land and we fight back. We must kill all white men! We must—"

Hands clapped outside the tepee. "Chief Black Hawk!"

Black Hawk rose quickly and pulled back the flap. "Yes, Red Fox?"

Glee danced in Red Fox's black eyes. "Come! Bring Meadowlark. There is something to see."

When the chief and his squaw stepped out of the tepee, Red Fox pointed to the south side of the village, where the people were gathering. "Look!"

Black Hawk and Meadowlark were stunned to see a white soldier riding into the village in the fading light of the setting sun, holding a wounded but living Sky Eagle in the saddle.

"Oh, Black Hawk!" exclaimed Meadowlark. "Our son is alive!"

The feathers of Black Hawk's headdress fluttered furiously as he ran to the spot where Sergeant McClain Reardon drew rein. Meadowlark was on her husband's heels.

Leaning against McClain, a dull-eyed Sky Eagle looked down at his parents. "Father and Mother, this white man must be treated kindly. I will tell you of his kindness to your son."

"Chief Black Hawk," said McClain, "I have bandaged the wound. The bullet is not lodged in his shoulder. It went completely through and came out the back side. Your medicine men must treat the wounds immediately."

Black Hawk quickly commanded two braves to take Sky Eagle down and carry him to Tall Tree's tepee. Tall Tree hurried the braves along as they carried the wounded young warrior amid the tepees. Three other medicine men followed.

McClain dismounted and accompanied the happy parents as they threaded their way through the crowd. Sky Eagle was laid on a blanket in front of the designated tepee. Tall Tree ordered the other medicine men to remove the bandages, then dashed into his tepee. Returning quickly with a buffalo hide bag in hand, he knelt beside Sky Eagle and examined the wounds.

After a few minutes, Tall Tree looked up at Black Hawk and Meadowlark, smiling. "White soldier did good work with bandage. Tall Tree will treat wounds. Sky Eagle will heal and be fine."

The crowd began rejoicing at the good news. Meadowlark wept for joy, and Black Hawk smiled broadly.

While Tall Tree was using his own medication and cloths to bandage the wounds with the help of the other medicine men, Black Hawk turned to the white soldier. "Black Hawk is grateful for white soldier's kindness to his son. I see you are a sergeant. Your name?"

"McClain Reardon, Chief."

"We must know how our son was spared, Sergeant McClain Reardon," spoke up Meadowlark.

McClain smiled at her. "Sky Eagle wants to be the one to tell you, ma'am. He asked me to allow him to do it."

The parents looked down at their son, who had his eyes fixed on them. The medicine men were still working on him. "Father and Mother, Sky Eagle will tell you the story when these men are finished."

Moments later, bandages in place, Sky Eagle began his story while the entire village stood, circling the scene. He told his parents that the other braves who were shot in the farmyard had been killed instantly. He went on to tell them about the white soldier who was about to shoot him and how Sergeant McClain Reardon had intervened and saved his life.

Black Hawk offered McClain his Cheyenne-style handshake and said with deep feeling, "Sergeant McClain Reardon, Black Hawk has not seen a white man with this kind of compassion for Indian before. Why is this?"

"Chief, have you heard the name Jesus Christ?"

Black Hawk nodded. "Umm…is Son of white man's God. We had man who was half white–half Cheyenne come to village many grasses ago. He is dead, now. He teach us English. He also tell us of white man's God, though he had not left gods of Cheyenne."

"Chief, I wish all white men had faith in my God and His Son, but they do not. It was Jesus Christ who came from heaven to die for the sins of all mankind—including Indians."

Black Hawk shook his head. "Our own gods appeal with Great Spirit for Indian wrongdoing."

"I know this teaching is your heritage, Chief, but let me say that the compassion you see in me for Indians is because Jesus Christ is my Saviour. He has given me love and compassion for all men—even my enemies."

Listening intently to the conversation, Sky Eagle said, "My father, Sergeant McClain Reardon does understand how Indians feel about white men coming into our land. Sky Eagle heard him explain this to other soldiers."

Black Hawk nodded. "It is good that you understand, Sergeant McClain Reardon. Few white men do."

McClain smiled. "Well, I must head back for Fort Steele."

As he spoke, he knelt beside Sky Eagle and grasped his hand firmly. "You get well, my friend."

Tears misted the young warrior's eyes. He squeezed McClain's hand. "It is only because of you that I can get well. If that other soldier had done as he wanted to, I would be dead. Thank you for saving Sky Eagle's life."

McClain smiled. "I'm glad I was able to do it. Farewell."

As McClain rose to his feet, Meadowlark stepped up to him with tears glistening on her cheeks. Laying a gentle hand on his arm, she said softly, "Meadowlark wishes she could fully tell you how she feels, but she cannot. You must understand it in the language of the heart. Thank you for giving us our son back."

McClain warmed her with a wide smile. "I understand the language of the heart, ma'am. I know what you are trying to say. I am glad I could bring your son back to you alive."

The sergeant felt a strong hand grip his shoulder. He turned to see Black Hawk looking at him tenderly. If ever McClain had seen gratitude in human eyes, he saw it then. "Sergeant McClain Reardon will always be welcome in this village. Black Hawk will not forget his act of mercy."

McClain smiled, turned, and moved in the direction of his horse.

The Cheyenne people made an opening for him in the press and watched him with kind eyes as he made his way toward the edge of the village. He mounted his horse and quickly disappeared in the gloom. The sound of the horse's dull footfalls gradually died away.

Soon McClain was on the broad prairie, heading southward. The day had been a hot one, and long after sundown the radiation of heat from the surrounding rocks persisted. A prairie bird whistled a wild, melancholy note from a tall cottonwood nearby and a distant coyote wailed mournfully. The stars shone white until the big round moon rose from the eastern horizon to burn out all their brilliance.

After some two hours, McClain topped a gentle rise and saw the fort spread out before him in the moonlight. Soon he drew near the guard tower at the gate, and could make out the two sentries in their lofty perch.

"That you, Sergeant Reardon?" one of them called out.

"Sure is!" McClain called back.

One of them hastened down the stairs and pulled the gate open. "We're glad you're back, Sergeant," he said as McClain guided his horse past him. "We were getting a bit worried."

"Thanks, Corporal," said McClain. "I'm fine."

McClain took his horse to the stable, where he removed the saddle, blanket, and bridle and put him in the corral with the other horses. He made his way toward Captain Jess Adams's house to give his report.

Stepping up on the Adams porch, he knocked on the door. Light footsteps were heard immediately. When the door opened, Leona Adams smiled and said, "Hello, Sergeant. I'm glad to see you're back. My husband is with Colonel Lamont at his office. He said to tell you to go over there."

McClain thanked her, quickly made his way to the commandant's office, and found the door open. Captain Jess Adams, Captain Lance Moore, and Lieutenant Carl Pierson were seated before the colonel's desk. Having heard his footsteps on the boardwalk, Colonel Ward Lamont looked his way. "Ah! You're back,

Sergeant. Come in. Tell us how it went."

Sitting down with the officers, McClain asked how the two wounded soldiers were doing. Lamont assured him they would be all right. Glad for the good news, McClain gave his report.

"Well, I'm glad Black Hawk and his squaw feel that way toward you, Sergeant," said the colonel. "And even though the Cheyenne will continue to fight us, I'm glad Sky Eagle will live."

McClain smiled and nodded without comment.

Lamont looked at Pierson. "I believe, Lieutenant, you had something you wanted to say to Sergeant Reardon."

Pierson cleared his throat and sat up straight, looking at McClain. "Sergeant, I owe you an apology. I was wrong for wanting to kill that wounded Indian."

Another smile creased McClain's handsome features. "I'm glad you see that, Lieutenant."

"Well, both of these captains talked pretty straight to me on the way back to the fort." He paused and adjusted his position on the chair. "I want to say, Sergeant, that what you did to stop me out there has made me admire you very much. Thanks for standing up to me and keeping me from doing something I would have regretted."

"You're welcome, sir. And you would have regretted murdering Sky Eagle. God's Word says, 'Whatsoever a man soweth, that shall he also reap.' Whatever seed we sow in life eventually comes back to us. If we sow bad seed, when the harvest comes—and it always does—we reap bad results. On the other hand, if we sow good seed, the harvest produces good results. It's God's natural law."

Pierson scratched his head. "Never thought of it that way, Sergeant. But I can see the truth of it."

11

Two Years Later

Just after ten o'clock on Saturday morning May 10, 1879, Sergeant McClain Reardon stepped out of the barracks into a flood of golden sunshine and headed across the compound toward Fort Steele's chapel. A warm, dry breeze touched him as the sound of twittering birds from the surrounding trees met his ears.

A moment later, McClain saw Colonel Doug Chandler coming off the quartermaster's porch. "Hey, Sergeant!" called the fort's new commandant. "You nervous?"

McClain chuckled. "Maybe just a little, sir."

"I have confidence in you. You'll come through it all right."

"Thank you, Colonel."

As McClain continued toward the log building with the small steeple on its roof, his thoughts ran to Colonel Ward Lamont. The place wasn't the same without him. McClain liked Colonel Chandler, but a bond had been molded between Colonel Lamont and him. He looked forward to the day when he would see him again.

McClain's attention was suddenly drawn to Captains Jess Adams and Lance Moore, who were coming his way, just passing by the chapel. As they drew up and stopped, McClain smiled. "Good morning, sirs."

"And good morning to you, Sergeant," said Moore.

Adams grinned slyly. "You got the jitters?"

McClain chuckled. "Do I look nervous, Captain?"

"Yes, you do. But then the wedding is at three o'clock. You've got less than five hours."

McClain pulled at an ear. "I assure you, sir, I'll be fine."

"Sure you will," said Adams. "A soldier who can look in the faces of wild, screeching hostiles with hatred burning in the eyes and guns blazing, and never flinch, will certainly make it through a wedding ceremony."

"You going to the chapel now?" said Moore.

"Mm-hmm. I want to see how the ladies are coming along with the decorations."

"Sure. Well, we'll see you at the wedding."

With that, the captains moved on, and McClain entered the chapel. There he found Edith Chandler—wife of the new commandant—and three other officers' wives putting flowers in vases and baskets and placing them across the front of the chapel's platform.

"Good morning, ladies," he said in a cheerful tone.

The women returned the greeting, warming him with smiles.

"It's looking great," said McClain. "I sure appreciate what you're doing to make the place look nice for the ceremony."

"We're happy to do it, Sergeant," said Edith. "When one of our finest men takes himself a bride, we want to do our part to make the wedding a special one."

McClain was about to comment when the door of the chaplain's office opened at the rear of the building and the sound of voices filled the air. He quickly looked that direction and saw Chaplain Curtis Fremont, his wife Elaine, and Carrie Duncan moving into the small auditorium.

Carrie ran her appreciative gaze over the flowers and said, "Oh, ladies, the flowers are beautiful! You've done a wonderful job."

Edith took hold of Carrie's shoulders. "Sweetie, the flowers will pale in their beauty when the eyes of everybody in the chapel fall on the beautiful bride!"

Carrie blushed. "You're very kind."

"You're the first mail order bride I've ever met. I think it is so wonderful that you and your husband-to-be found each other that way."

McClain stepped up close. "It really is wonderful, Mrs. Chandler. Especially in this instance, because when a man puts an ad in the Eastern newspapers and stipulates that he is seeking a born-again bride, it severely narrows the field. Carl—I mean, Lieutenant Pierson—put ads in a dozen newspapers back East, and Carrie was the only one who responded."

"The Lord was good," said Chaplain Fremont. "He had it all planned."

"That's right," said Carrie. "The Lord had already chosen Carl and me for each other, so it doesn't matter that I was the only one who responded."

Carrie then turned to McClain with misty eyes and gave him a sisterly embrace. "And you were the willing vessel God used to lead Carl to Jesus. If it wasn't for your concern for Carl's eternal destiny and your shining testimony to him, he wouldn't be a Christian and I wouldn't be here to become his bride today. Thank you, McClain."

The sergeant patted her hand. "I'm honored that the Lord allowed me to bring Carl to Him, Carrie."

Chaplain Fremont laid a hand on McClain's shoulder. "Let me tell you, Carrie, McClain has led several men to Christ in this fort over the years. And I'm glad Carl was one of them. He certainly has been a blessing to me since he got saved."

Carrie thumbed a tear from the corner of her eye. "I'm glad, Chaplain. Carl has told me how much both you and McClain have helped him to grow in grace since he became a child of God."

Fremont smiled, then looked at McClain. "Is the best man nervous?"

"I am, sir. I've never been best man in a wedding before. But I'll be fine."

Elaine Fremont chuckled. "Well, being best man in this wedding will help prepare you to be the groom in your own wedding, Sergeant."

McClain laughed. "I have to find the girl the Lord has picked out for me, first. Now, if I was an officer, I would've tried the mail order bride system myself. But since only officers can have their wives in the fort, I guess I'll have to wait till I'm out of the army before I can start looking for that right girl."

Chaplain Fremont's brow furrowed. "Are you planning on leaving the army soon, Sergeant?"

McClain started to reply, but his words were cut off by the chapel door opening. A corporal came in and said, "Sergeant Reardon, Lieutenant Pierson sent me over here to tell you that he needs to see you right away."

"Must be important," said McClain.

The corporal grinned. "Oh, it is, Sergeant. I think he needs you to hold him up. It's still four hours till the wedding, but he's really nervous already. You'll probably have to carry him over here to the chapel for the ceremony."

Carrie laughed. "You'd better get over there to him, McClain. I want him here, even if you do have to carry him!"

On Thursday morning June 5, 1879, Richard Garrett guided the team into the Richmond depot lot under a bright blue Virginia sky and pulled rein. Catching the attention of one of the baggage handlers on the terminal porch, he waved and pointed to the luggage in the back of the wagon. The man wearing the white cap nodded and began pushing his cart that direction.

Richard hopped down, went around to the other side of the wagon, and helped Laura from the seat. When she was on the ground, he reached up and took hold of Rya's hand.

"Thank you, Papa," she said as he helped her climb down.

Richard noted the pensive look in her eyes.

The baggage man drew up with his cart and looked at the trunk and two pieces of luggage in the bed of the wagon. "How many traveling, sir?"

"Just this young lady," said Richard, nodding toward Rya.

"May I see the ticket, please?"

Rya reached into her purse and produced the ticket. The baggage handler looked at it. "Kansas City."

"Yes."

He wrote the ticket number on three tags, handed the ticket back to her, and as he tied the tags to the handles of the trunk and luggage, he said, "These pieces will be unloaded by the baggage coach at the Kansas City terminal, miss."

Rya thanked him, and walked into the terminal with her parents while the baggage handler was loading her luggage on his cart.

Richard looked up at the large chalkboard above the ticket windows. "Track number three."

As they were heading for the platform that served track number three, they noted that the train was already there. Other baggage handlers were loading luggage into the baggage coach.

Suddenly a female voice called from the milling crowd, "Rya!"

Rya turned to see two familiar faces. "Oh! Allie! Lucinda!"

The young women glanced at Richard and Laura, then Allie said, "I know these are your parents. I remember seeing you with them on graduation night."

"Right. Mama, Papa, I want you to meet Allie Gower and Lucinda Locke. They were in my college graduating class."

The Garretts greeted the young ladies warmly. Rya asked, "Are you meeting someone?"

"Yes," said Allie. "We're here to meet my brother, Ed. He's coming from Wilmington, Delaware."

Noting that only Rya was carrying a small overnight bag, Lucinda asked, "Are you going somewhere?"

"Yes. This is my train here. It will take me to Kansas City, Missouri."

"Did you get a teaching job in Kansas City?" queried Allie.

"No. Actually, I have a high school teaching job waiting for me in Sacramento, California."

"Really?"

"Uh-huh. When I get to Kansas City, I'll be taking a short ride to Independence, Missouri, where I'm scheduled to join a wagon train that's going to California. I have friends there—Roy and Elsa Gibbs—who used to be members of our church in Bowling Green. They've invited me to come and live with them in their home."

"Well, honey, I'm glad for you," said Lucinda. "Allie and I haven't landed our teaching jobs yet. But Rya, why aren't you traveling by rail all the way to California? Certainly that would be faster and easier than taking a wagon train."

"Faster and easier, yes, but not nearly as enjoyable. I'm going on the wagon train because through Professor Wilkes at college, I was hired by the wagon master to teach the children during the three to four months it will take us to get to Sacramento."

"That's a long time," said Allie. "They tell me it gets awfully dusty on those wagon trains."

"Not to mention the threat of wild Indians," put in Lucinda. "Aren't you afraid you'll get scalped, Rya?"

Laura and Rya exchanged a flicking glance, then Rya said, "I'm not afraid, Lucinda. The men on the wagon trains are all well-armed. And from what I've read, few of the wagon trains are ever attacked by the Indians anymore."

"So will your wagon train be taking the famous Oregon Trail?" asked Allie.

"To begin with, yes. We'll head northwest out of Independence after crossing the Missouri River, and move across the northeast corner of Kansas into Nebraska. We'll continue across Nebraska, and go all the way across southern Wyoming into Idaho. Not long after we enter Idaho, we'll come to a fork, where the trail splits in two: the California Trail and the Oregon Trail."

"Oh, that's right," said Allie. "I remember reading about it. So at that point, your wagon train will take the California Trail."

"Mm-hmm. We'll drop south into Utah, past Salt Lake City, then directly into Nevada. When we've covered Nevada, the wagon train will make its way up and over the Sierra Nevada Mountains into California through Placerville, all the way to Sacramento."

"Sounds like a long, hard journey," said Lucinda. "But knowing you, Rya, you'll be so wrapped up in teaching those children, you won't even notice the hardships."

Rya giggled. "I hope you've got that right!"

The sound of a train chugging in on track number four met their ears.

"Well," Allie said, looking that direction, "we'd better go, Lucinda. That's Ed's train."

Both young ladies wished Rya happiness in California, told the Garretts they were glad to have made their acquaintance, then moved to meet the train on track four.

Laura set anxious eyes on her daughter. "Honey, you be sure to write us from Independence, so we'll know you made it there, won't you?"

"Of course, Mama."

"And we want you to post letters to us from the towns where the wagon train stops to pick up supplies," said Richard.

Rya smiled and patted her father's cheek. "I'll do that, Papa. I promise."

While Rya and her parents were talking on the platform, Jason Lynch guided his horse among the wagons, buggies, surreys, and carriages until he spotted the Garrett wagon. He dismounted beside the wagon and tied his horse to a hitching post.

Inside the terminal, Laura was having a difficult time containing the tears that were just under the surface.

Rya took hold of her hand. "Mama, please tell me you'll be all right."

The tears began to run down Laura's cheeks. "I don't mean to make this hard for you, sweetheart. It's just that…well, you're my youngest child, my baby. Your siblings all live right here in Virginia. It's a long, long way from Virginia to California. When you were in college, you were only about three hours' drive away and we got to have you home every weekend. But now, I—"

"Mama, we'll be close in our hearts. And you and Papa can come see me. We've already gone over this, but as I prayed about the offer of the job in Sacramento, I had such peace in my heart that it is the Lord's will."

Laura nodded, wiping tears from her cheeks. "Yes, I know."

"We both know you're following the Lord's leading, honey," said Richard. "But it's still hard to let you go."

"I understand, Papa."

Laura sniffed. "Part of my problem is that long, arduous journey you're facing. And…and Lucinda touched on another thing. The Indian danger. I just tremble inside when I think of the possibility of those savages attacking your wagon train."

"Mama, the Lord will take care of me. I know you and Papa have prayed that He will. Now we must trust Him to do it."

Laura closed her eyes and said, "Dear Lord, it's so hard to let my baby go so far away. But I know I must step aside and let her try her wings. She's such a...such a little bird."

Rya put her arms around her and hugged her tight. "Yes, Mama, to you I am still just a little bird. But do you remember what Jesus said? 'Are not five sparrows sold for two farthings, and not one of them is forgotten before God? But even the very hairs of your head are numbered. Fear not therefore: ye are of more value than many sparrows.'"

Laura held her daughter equally tight. "Thank You, Lord, for Your wonderful Word and the way it calms our fears."

Richard looked on, having his own problem with keeping his composure.

Armed with the great peace that only the Saviour can give, Laura eased back so she could look into her daughter's eyes. "Rya, what a wonderful experience this will be for you. Just don't forget to write us often, even after you get to Sacramento, so your papa and I can share this new adventure in your life."

Rya let her gaze go to her father, then looked once again at her mother. "Mama, my heart will always be here with you and Papa, and when I am settled in Sacramento, I will write at least once a week and keep you posted on what's happening in my life."

Though Rya kept it concealed, her own heart was wavering between the excitement of the future that lay ahead of her in California and the homesickness that was already beginning to grip her.

Suddenly, Rya and her mother were startled to hear Richard's voice cut like a knife as he said sharply, "What are you doing here?"

Still hanging onto each other, they turned to see Jason Lynch boldly facing Richard. "I came to see Rya before she leaves for Sacramento."

Rya felt a pain lance through her midsection. It caused her to flinch a bit, and Laura felt it. Her brow furrowed as she looked at Rya.

Richard's voice was tight but controlled as he said to Jason, "How did you find out she was going to Sacramento?"

"I happened to be in Bowling Green yesterday, and ran into

your neighbors, the Scullys. They told me that Rya was taking the morning train to Kansas City today, then was joining a wagon train to travel all the way to Sacramento. They said she has a job teaching at the Sacramento High School. I just wanted to see her before she left."

Richard regarded Jason. "All right. You've seen her. Now you can go."

Jason licked his lips, looking as if he was going to say something caustic, but instead, he set his eyes on Rya, gave her a slanted smile, then quietly walked away, into the crowd.

Richard stared after him with disgust. His attention was brought back to Rya when she bent over, her hand going to her midsection.

"Honey, is it that same pain you've been having?"

Rya pressed fingers against the spot and nodded. "Yes, Mama. But it's easing up. I'll be fine in a few minutes."

"Honey," said Laura, "maybe we'd better take you to the doctor like I wanted to last week. If he says it's nothing serious, you can take tomorrow's train. You could still make it to Independence in time to join the wagon train."

Straightening up, Rya shook her head. "I'll be all right, Mama, when my nerves settle down. I know other things have brought it on, but most of the time, it was when Jason came near me with that indescribable look in his eyes. With him out of my life, the pains will probably go away for good."

"All abo-o-o-oard!" The call of the conductor sounded from beside the train. "All abo-o-o-oard!"

Laura looked deep into Rya's eyes. "Are you sure you'll be all right?"

"Yes, Mama. I'll be fine."

Rya hugged and kissed her parents, promising once again to write to them along the way, then hurried to board the closest coach. Tears streamed down her cheeks as she waved to them from the window while the train chugged out of the depot.

12

ON SATURDAY, JUNE 7, Rya Garrett awakened at sunrise to the sound of the steel wheels beneath her and seconds later, she heard the conductor call out, "Kansas City! Twenty minutes! Kansas City! Twenty minutes!"

Rya then realized it was the conductor's entrance into the coach that had awakened her. She had fallen asleep shortly after the train had pulled out of St. Louis just after 2 A.M.

She stretched her cramped legs out as far as the seat in front of her would allow, moving her ankles in circles, trying to establish some circulation in them. Then she arched her back against the seat and twisted her body first to the right and then to the left while swiveling her neck. It had been a long trip from Richmond, and her tired body was now feeling every mile.

It's been fun, though, she mused to herself. *I've enjoyed the scenery and the ever-changing landscape.*

Soon the train began slowing down. Rya pressed close to the dirt-encrusted window in an attempt to catch a glimpse of Kansas City. There were farms dotting the green, grassy land as far as she could see. Moments later, she caught sight of the stockyards, with pens of shifting cattle stirring up dust. The stockyards seemingly went on for miles as the train continued to lessen speed. Soon it pulled into the railroad terminal and ground to a halt. Since this was the end of the line, all passengers were making ready to leave the train.

Rya stood up, adjusted her dark green travel suit, and smoothed the wrinkles out of it. Reaching overhead, she picked up her hat, and placed it just right on her auburn hair that was pulled back into a loose bun, and fastened it with a hat pin.

Reaching into the overhead rack once again, she gathered her overnight bag, noticing a man threading his way down the aisle amid the passengers who were collecting their belongings. "Go ahead, miss," he said, pausing to allow her to move first.

She smiled, thanked him, and made her way to the door. When she stepped down from the platform, she squinted as the bright sunshine greeted her. A porter was answering a question for two men who were traveling together as Rya looked at the baggage coach. Four or five men were busy removing baggage from the coach and placing it on the depot platform. Her eyes then went to the line of wagons that stood along the side of the dusty street.

As the two men were walking away, the white-haired porter said, "May I help you, miss?"

Rya smiled. "Yes, please. I need to hire one of those wagons out there to take me to Independence."

"All right," he said, raising his hand and signaling the driver of the first wagon in line. "Do you have luggage to be picked up, miss?"

"Yes, sir," she said, taking out her ticket and handing it to him. "A trunk and two pieces of baggage."

"You wait here," said the porter. "The driver and I will get your luggage."

As the porter pointed toward the baggage coach and the driver guided his team in that direction, Rya stood in the glaring sunlight, wishing for shade and a cool breeze.

She watched other passengers as they greeted relatives and friends. A lump rose in her throat as she thought of her family and friends way back in Richmond, and a strong wave of homesickness seemed to engulf her. *Oh, what have I done?* she asked herself.

A still, small voice spoke to her heart. "It's all right, my child. You are in My hand, and I am in control."

She closed her eyes and whispered, "Thank You, Lord."

Opening her eyes again, Rya looked toward the wagon and saw the two men loading her luggage into the bed of the wagon.

Moments later, the porter headed back into the depot, and the grizzled driver pulled the wagon up close to Rya. He handed her the ticket. "The porter said you are wanting to go to Independence, missy."

"Yes."

He lowered himself to the ground, helped her into the wagon seat, climbed up beside her, and wiped his brow with a red-and-white handkerchief. "Just where in Independence do you want to go?"

"Where the wagon trains gather, sir."

"All right," he said, and put the team into motion. "That'll be right close to the east bank of the Missouri."

As they made their way south through the city, the driver said, "So you're takin' a wagon train West, eh?"

"Yes, sir."

"Joinin' up with friends or relatives who have a covered wagon, are ya?"

"No, sir. I'm from Virginia. Going to California alone. I was made aware by the wagon master's agent that I'll be assigned to a wagon with someone who has room for me."

The driver gave her a sidelong glance and grinned. "You one of those mail order brides?"

Rya chuckled. "No, sir. I'm a schoolteacher. I'll be teaching in the high school in Sacramento."

"I see. Just figgered since you're young and pretty that you might be goin' out West to get hitched to one of them lonely fellas out there."

Rya smiled thinly, but did not comment.

The driver kept a running conversation going, but Rya paid little attention as she let her eyes take in the sights around her. Missouri was quite different from Virginia.

When they arrived at the west edge of Independence, Rya's attention was drawn to a long wagon train that was pulling away from the large open area near the river. The leading wagons were already in the stream, heading for the west bank.

"Looks like one's just pullin' out," the driver said. "Lots of wagon trains headin' west from now through September. It's that time of year."

Rya noted that there were two other wagon trains forming, each in a circle. One had seven wagons and the other had four. She wondered which one was hers.

"Do you know your wagon master's name, missy?" asked the driver as he pulled rein.

"His name is Chet Place."

Two men were passing by on foot. The driver called to them, "Hey, fellas! Do you know which one of them trains belongs to Chet Place?"

"Yes, sir," said one, pointing to the one with seven wagons. "It's that one."

The driver thanked him, then drove up to the spot and said, "Well, missy, let's see if we can find the wagon master."

He slid to the ground, then shuffled around the rear of the wagon and helped Rya down. A man and woman who appeared to be in their late forties were walking by.

"Pardon me, folks," the driver said. "Are you part of this wagon train?"

"We sure are," said the man. "How can we help you?"

"Well, Mr. Place is expectin' this young lady to join his train. She's from Virginia. I just brought her from the railroad station in Kansas City."

The couple looked at each other, smiling.

"Does your name happen to be Rya Garrett?" asked the man.

"Why, yes," said Rya, smiling.

"You've been assigned to our wagon for the journey," said the man. "I'm Burt Keegan, and this is my wife, Dorothy."

Rya offered her hand to Dorothy first, then to Burt. They told her they were from Lafayette, Indiana, and would be traveling all the way to Sacramento. From there, they would be going by rail to San Francisco.

While Rya, Dorothy, and Burt chatted and walked toward the Keegan wagon, the driver followed at the reins. Burt helped him unload Rya's trunk and baggage, placing it beside the covered wagon. Rya paid the old man and thanked him for the ride. As he drove away, Burt said, "Well, let's find Chet and let him know you're here."

The Keegans led Rya to the lead wagon, where Chet Place and his son, Ken, were patching a rip in the canvas cover. Chet was in his midfifties, and Ken, by Rya's estimation, had not quite reached thirty.

Chet lifted his hat, ran a sleeve over his sweaty brow, and said, "Miss Garrett, it's really gonna be great having you on the wagon train to teach the children. All the parents are happy that there'll be a teacher along to help keep their children from getting bored on the trip and to make the trip profitable for them."

"I'm honored to have the opportunity, Mr. Place," said Rya.

"How about if you come back here to my wagon right after lunch, and you and I can work out the details of when you'll have your class sessions during the journey?"

"I'll be glad to. How many students will I have?"

"Well, it looks like about fourteen, between the ages of five and sixteen. We're scheduled to pull out on Tuesday morning right after breakfast, so I hope everybody who's signed up will be here by then."

For the next two days, covered wagons pulled in and joined both trains that were forming. The other train was not leaving until Thursday. On Monday morning, Rya wrote a letter to her parents, which Ken Place posted for her when he went into town.

By Monday afternoon, all scheduled wagons had arrived for the Place wagon train. That evening after supper, Chet Place called for a meeting of the parents and children. Several fires were burning in the circle, giving off sufficient light for everyone to see. Chet had Rya stand before parents and children and introduced her as the teacher for the trip. He explained that she was from Virginia, and had just graduated from Virginia Teacher's College in Richmond and was on her way to Sacramento, where she would be teaching at Sacramento High School.

The wagon master went on to explain that they would have classes four evenings a week along the trail, after supper. Each session would last two hours, and the parents were welcome to attend the classes with their children if they wished.

Rya made it clear that she would teach each lesson so that the material would be on a graded basis in three sections: five- to eight-year-olds; nine- to twelve-year-olds; and teenagers.

When the meeting was over, parents and children passed by to introduce themselves to Rya. As she met each child, Rya concentrated on learning their names and committing to memory something distinctive about each one.

As the line was dwindling, Rya saw the smiling faces of a boy and his parents move up. "Hello," she said to the boy with a wide smile. "And what is your name?"

"Bobby Jensen," came the friendly reply. "I'm twelve years old."

"That's exactly what I was thinking!" said Rya. "And these are your parents?"

"We are," said the father. "My name is Dick Jensen, and this is my wife, Donna. We're from Virginia."

"Oh, really? Where?"

"Roanoke. We're going to Yuba City, California, which is north of Sacramento. Is your home in Richmond?"

"No. I was born and raised on a farm just outside of Bowling Green."

"Oh, Bowling Green!" said Donna. "My parents live in Doswell."

"I know right where it is. Just about fifteen miles southwest of Bowling Green. Well, it sure is nice to meet some fellow Virginians. And, Bobby, I'm happy to have you in my class."

"I'm looking forward to it, Miss Garrett," said Bobby.

As the Jensens walked away, Rya saw that there was one little girl left to meet, who was accompanied by her mother. Rya guessed her to be the second of two five-year-olds who would be in the class.

The child appeared to be somewhat bashful. Her head was lowered as she gripped her mother's hand, and she was scuffling her small bare feet, stirring up little puffs of dust before her. Her faded dress was shabby but clean.

"Hello, sweetheart," said Rya, bending down in an attempt to meet her eye level. "You're five years old, right?"

She looked up at Rya through her bright blue eyes and let a

smile curve her lips. "Uh-huh. I'll be six in August."

Rya took hold of the girl's free hand and said softly, "My name is Miss Rya. Can you tell me yours?"

The child dropped her eyes to the ground again, shuffling her dusty feet in the dirt.

"Tell Miss Rya your name, dear," the mother gently admonished her.

The little girl slowly lifted her head and set her eyes on the teacher. In a tiny voice that was almost a whisper, she said, "Emily Grace Custer." She quickly looked back at the ground.

"That is a beautiful name," said Rya, "and it matches such a beautiful little girl."

"Really?" said Emily Grace, looking up into the pretty lady's eyes.

"Yes, really. And there's something else."

"What?"

Rya reached out and took one of Emily Grace's pigtails in her hand and brought it up close to her own head. "Our hair is the same color, and to me, that's pretty special."

A beam glowed on the child's face. "I think you are special, Miss Rya."

"Thank you, sweetheart," said Rya, giving her a hug. "So I'll see you in school?"

"Yes, ma'am," replied the little girl, her voice growing stronger.

Rising to her full height, Rya smiled at the mother. "Mrs. Custer, you have a wonderful little girl."

"I know," said the mother, smiling and patting her daughter's head. "My name is Grace, Miss Rya. My husband is busy at our wagon, but I know he will want to meet you in person, too."

Rya's brow furrowed slightly. "Does your husband happen to be related to General George Armstrong Custer, who was killed three years ago in the battle of the Little Bighorn?"

"Yes. George was Mike's cousin. We're from the same town: New Rumley, Ohio."

"I see. Does it bother you that we'll be traveling through Indian country on this trip?"

"Well, Mike and I are a bit nervous about that, but we're trusting God to get us through safely to California."

"Me, too," said Rya.

"Well, Emily Grace," said the mother, "we'd better get back to the wagon. Your papa may need us to help him. Nice to have met you, Miss Garrett. I'm sure my little gal will enjoy your classes."

The little redhead nodded. "Bye, Miss Rya."

Rya leaned over and kissed the top of her head. "I will look forward to having you in my class, sweetie."

Both mother and daughter sent smiles to the teacher as they walked away toward their wagon.

The next morning, everyone in the wagon train was up at dawn. Breakfast was eaten by firelight, and by sunrise, Chet Place was in the saddle, leading the train of sixteen covered wagons and fifty-four people toward the Missouri River. Ken Place drove the lead wagon, just behind his father.

They crossed the river to follow the Oregon Trail and headed northwest across the corner of Kansas toward the Nebraska border.

As the miles passed slowly, Dorothy Keegan sat between her husband and Rya Garrett on the wagon seat. Rya asked questions about Indiana, while letting her eyes take in the broad sweep of the land around her. The farther they got from Missouri, the more level the country became. She saw only miles and miles of flat land, dotted here and there with cattle, and acres of waist-high wheat and corn. She was entranced with the sight of a land that seemed to go on forever, and the cloudless blue sky that stretched westward into infinity.

There was no class that evening, but on the next three evenings, Rya found herself in a happy state as she gathered the children around her for their lessons.

On the sixth day out, the wagon train crossed into Nebraska and stopped for the night beside a small brook. There had been no classes on the fifth night, but on this night, the eager children assembled to have their lessons once again. Several lanterns burned close by to give sufficient light. A few parents sat in, but most were mingling with the other people in the wagon train, getting better acquainted.

When Rya finished the lessons, she led the children in a happy song, then dismissed them. Many of the children went to Rya, expressing how they felt toward her. They thanked her for the lessons, some saying they wished she could be their teacher all the time.

Smiling warmly, Rya hugged each one, telling them she loved them.

Soon Rya was down to two students. Next was Emily Grace Custer, who reached up toward her teacher, opening her arms. Rya bent down and hugged her. The little girl kissed her cheek and said, "I love you, Miss Rya."

Warmth spread through Rya's heart. "I love you, too, sweetheart. I hope you sleep well tonight."

Emily Grace smiled. "I will, ma'am. You, too."

As the little redhead skipped away, Rya's attention went to the last one in line. A bright smile lit up her face. "Hello, Bobby."

"Hello, Miss Rya," said Bobby Jensen. "I...I just want to tell you how very much I appreciate your teaching. Especially your history lessons. You really make history come alive. It has always bored me before but not now."

"Well, I'm glad I've made a difference in your attitude about history. Maybe by the time we get to California, I'll have a boy who'll want to go to college and become a history teacher."

Bobby shrugged his thin shoulders. "Maybe. Good night, Miss Rya."

The boy ran away and soon disappeared among the wagons.

With her notes and books in hand, Rya headed across the circle of wagons toward the Keegan vehicle. As she neared the central fire, she moved past two young men who were seated on the ground a few feet from the fire, talking. She heard one say, "Well, I'm originally from Virginia, near Bowling Green. I was born and raised on a farm there."

Rya glanced at the young man who had spoken, but could only see part of his face. What little she could see was not familiar. She hurried to the Keegan wagon and placed her notes and books inside. The Keegans were in conversation with an older couple and only glanced at her.

Eager to meet the young farmer from the Bowling Green area, Rya rushed back toward the central fire. The two men were still talking as she drew up, but she stood near, waiting until their conversation was over so she could make a polite approach. The one from the Bowling Green area had coal black hair and his back was still toward her.

Some two or three minutes later, the two men rose to their feet. The dark-haired one said, "Well, Charlie, it's been nice talking to you. We'll have to spend some more time together."

"Let's do that," said Charlie. "Good night."

"Good night."

As Charlie walked away, Rya stepped up to the dark-haired young man, who caught her movement in the corner of his eye, and turned to look at her. "Hello," he said, smiling.

Now that she could see him clearly, there was something familiar about him. "Excuse me, sir," said Rya. "I was passing by a moment ago, and I heard you tell that other gentleman that you're from Bowling Green, Virginia."

"Yes. I was born and raised on a farm a couple of miles outside of Bowling Green. Are you from—"

"McClain!" gasped Rya, cutting off his words. "McClain! Is…is it you?"

McClain Reardon's eyes widened. "Yes, but do I know you?"

Rya clamped her hands over her mouth, her eyes misting.

McClain squinted and bent his head to one side, studying her. "I've seen you teaching the children, but—R-Rya? Little Rya Garrett? It can't be!"

Suddenly, without hesitation, they were embracing.

"Oh, McClain!" Rya said as he held her tight. "I thought I would never see you again on this earth. It's been such a long time!"

"How long has it been, Rya? Twelve…thirteen—no! It was 1865! Fourteen years!"

"Yes," she said as he released her, and they looked at each other. "Fourteen years, McClain. When you moved away, you were thirteen, and I was ten."

He took hold of her shoulders and turned her toward the firelight to get a better view. Her soft eyes were like the azure reaches of the sky.

Rya could only smile at him.

Licking his lips, he said, "How about your family? Is everybody doing all right?"

"Mm-hmm. Jack, Ella, and Saul are married. They and their mates and children live in different parts of Virginia. Mama and Papa still have the farm. They're doing fine."

"Good. You'll have to tell me more about all of them later."

"Sure. And how about your mother, and Lena and Ruby?"

"They still live in Blue Springs. Mom has never remarried, but both the girls are married now. I was just there to visit them."

"So you live elsewhere."

"Well, yes, but it's too long a story to tell you right now. I want to know what you're doing in this wagon train, and you'll be asking why I am. But since it's getting late and Chet wants us up at dawn, we'll have to get together soon and talk."

"Well, tomorrow evening there's no class. We can talk then."

"All right. We'll do it." He grinned and shook his head.

"What?"

"Rya, I've glanced at the wagon train's teacher several times, but I had no idea it was you."

She smiled. "Well, it's been fourteen years."

"Yes. You're riding in the Keegan wagon, aren't you?"

Rya giggled. "Well, I guess you did glance at me sometime, since you know that."

He grinned sheepishly. "I'll walk you over there."

"Have you met the Keegans?" she asked.

"No. I haven't had that privilege."

"Well, let's take care of that right now."

When they reached the Keegan wagon, Burt and Dorothy were at the tailgate. They glanced at McClain, then set their eyes on Rya.

"Burt and Dorothy Keegan," said Rya, "I want you to meet McClain Reardon. McClain and I grew up in the same farming community in Virginia and just recognized each other a few minutes ago."

As McClain shook hands with Burt and tipped his hat at Dorothy, Rya said, "McClain was my older brother's best friend all through childhood. He and I became very good friends, too. We haven't seen each other since 1865."

Burt chuckled. "I guess you two have a lot of catching up to do."

"We sure do," said McClain. "But not tonight. Glad to have met you folks. Rya, we'll get together tomorrow evening right after supper."

"All right," she said softly. "What a wonderful surprise, McClain. It's so nice to see you again."

"You, too, Rya. Good night. And good night to you, Mr. and Mrs. Keegan."

With that, he turned and walked away.

"Pretty warm tonight, Rya," said Burt. "I'm pinning the flaps open so if we get a breeze across these plains, it can find its way inside. We'll sleep better that way."

Rya's attention was on McClain as he crossed the open area toward the other side of the circle. Without taking her eyes off him, she said, "That'll be nice, Burt."

Dorothy smiled to herself as she observed Rya watching McClain.

Later that night as Rya lay in her cramped bed next to the tailgate inside the Keegan wagon, sleep eluded her. The soft, even breathing of both Burt and Dorothy deeper in the wagon bed told her they were fast asleep. She closed her eyes and listened to the crickets giving their nocturnal concert. There was no breeze so far, but it wasn't the heat that was keeping her awake.

Rya raised her head, fluffed the pillow, and turned onto her back. She gazed up at the great canopy of stars twinkling in the Nebraska sky. Her mind went back over the events of the evening.

"I can hardly believe he's here," she said to herself. "What a coincidence, that after so many years we would run into each other like this."

A night owl hooted somewhere in the distance.

Now, wait a minute, Rya, she thought. *With God nothing is coincidental. He has a plan for every Christian's life. It is no accident that you and McClain are together in this wagon train.*

Lord, she prayed, her eyes fixed on the heavens, *You know as a young girl I had such admiration for McClain. Especially after that John Wilkes Booth incident. And...and You remember, Lord, how I was crushed so deeply when he and his family moved away. Lord, You knew McClain would be in this wagon train. Is he to be a part of my new life?*

With this thought, Rya's heart skittered and she emitted a long, shuddering breath.

"Could it be, Lord? Could it possibly be?"

Suddenly she realized she had spoken aloud. Dorothy roused, whispering, "Are you all right, Rya?"

"Oh, Dorothy, I'm sorry I woke you. I...I guess I'm just a little restless tonight. The air is so hot and still."

Dorothy's reply in the darkness came with a smile in her voice. "Honey, are you sure it's the temperature? Or could it possibly be that handsome young McClain Reardon's presence in the wagon train?"

A small sigh escaped Rya's lips. "Well-l-l-l...it...ah...it might be."

"Mmm. Well, whatever it is, dear, I suggest you put it to rest and get some sleep. Morning will be on us shortly, and we'll have another hot, tiring day."

As she was trying to let sleep overtake her, Rya thought of what she had said to the Lord only moments ago about McClain becoming a part of her new life. *Girl,* she admonished herself in her thoughts, *how foolish can you be? You're going to Sacramento to start your new life. McClain no doubt lives hundreds of miles from there...maybe thousands.*

Don't let yourself cling to something that will only let you down hard and break your heart. Enjoy the time you will have with your old friend on this journey, and let the Lord guide your life. You know He has led you to accept that teaching job in Sacramento. Keep that firmly in mind.

McClain Reardon was traveling in a covered wagon owned by a middle-aged couple named Vance and Rhonda Larkin from Oak Park, Illinois. Each night since leaving Independence, McClain had slept on the ground in his bedroll beside the wagon in order to give the Larkins more room for sleeping inside.

Since McClain had first been assigned to Fort Steele in Wyoming, he had fallen in love with the West. And now that he was headed that direction again, he felt the sweet satisfaction that nights on the prairie could give.

Lying on his back in the darkness, he enjoyed the strange silence that stretched away under blinking white stars. However, he found it difficult to fall asleep.

A face haunted him. A young woman's face. Whether he closed his eyes or left them open, Rya's features hovered in his mind.

"Where are you headed, Rya?" he whispered. "Why have you left your home in Virginia? Is this some new chapter in your life? Oh, sweet Rya."

THE NEXT MORNING, RYA GARRETT sat on the wagon seat with Burt and Dorothy Keegan as the wagons broke the circle behind the mounted Chet Place and headed northwest across the prairie. The long green grass tossed about in the morning breeze like waves of the sea, highlighted with bright-colored wildflowers in the golden sunlight.

Some of the men in the wagon train walked alongside their wagons while their wives or teenage sons handled the teams. Others rode saddle horses, sometimes trotting up and down the line to chat with the occupants of other wagons, but most of the time they stayed close to their own families.

The day passed slowly for Rya, but finally, as the sun was setting red in the west, the wagon master gave signal for the wagons to make a circle on the bank of the Little Blue River. Riding along the line as the circle began to form, Place announced that they were only about two miles from a small town called Endicott. If anyone needed supplies, they were to let him know as soon as the wagons were parked. He and Ken would be taking the lead wagon into town for supplies before supper.

Rya had written a brief letter to her parents before breakfast that morning, telling them about McClain being in the wagon train and explaining that she would fill them in on more later. She had no idea she would get to mail it so soon.

When Burt hauled the team to a halt, she climbed into the back of the wagon and hastily addressed an envelope. She hurried to the lead wagon and handed the letter to Ken Place, asking him to post it for her in Endicott.

She was returning to the Keegan wagon when she saw McClain coming toward her. There was a fluttering in her heart as she smiled and hurried to him.

"Hello, lovely lady," McClain said, his eyes sparkling. "The people I'm riding with have heard me talking about you all day, and they'd like to meet you."

Rya's face tinted. "McClain, you embarrass me."

"Just because I'm proud to have known you since we were children, and I've bragged about it?"

"Well, I'm flattered that you feel that way, but—"

"Can you spare a few minutes to come and let me introduce you to them right now?"

"Well, I guess so." She turned to the Keegans, explained that she would be back to help Dorothy cook supper in a few minutes, and let McClain usher her across the circle.

As they moved along, he said, "You'll love these people, Rya. They are both wonderful, dedicated Christians."

"Great! I wish the Keegans were Christians, but when I bring up the Lord and quote things from the Bible, they find a way to change the subject. Nice people but cold toward the Lord and His Word."

"There are a lot of those kind of people in the world, Rya. Nice folks, but lost. I'll remember the Keegans in my prayers."

"Please do. I'm doing the same, and I'll keep trying to talk to them about the Lord."

When they reached the Larkin wagon, Rya found a warm welcome. She felt an instant kinship with the Larkins, and what few moments she had with them, found the fellowship sweet.

As McClain was walking Rya back toward the Keegan wagon, they met up with Bobby Jensen, who flashed a smile at his teacher. "Hello, Miss Rya. I see you and Mr. Reardon have become acquainted."

Rya looked up into McClain's face, then back at Bobby. "Well, actually, we have known each other since we were children. We were both born and raised on neighboring farms in Virginia. Mr. Reardon was thirteen when he and his family moved to Missouri in 1865. We haven't seen each other since then."

"Wow!" said the boy, eyes wide. "So you must've been surprised when you saw each other."

McClain chuckled. "Well, Bobby, it took us a few minutes to recognize one another, but when we did, it sure was a pleasant surprise."

"That's really neat. You must have a lot to talk about."

"We sure do," said McClain, glancing at Rya. "We sure do."

Bobby set admiring eyes on his teacher. "I'm really gonna miss having class tonight, Miss Rya. I really like the way you teach. Some of the other kids have told me that, too."

A smile spread over Rya's face. "I'm glad to hear that, Bobby."

"Well, I gotta get to the wagon," said the boy. "See you both later."

At supper, Rya sat beside the Keegan wagon at the small folding table with Burt and Dorothy, trying valiantly to eat the meal that she and Dorothy had prepared. A slight breeze had picked up, and was cooling the air. A few thunderheads could be seen on the northern horizon, gaining in size.

"That breeze sure feels good," commented Burt. "We just might get some rain."

"I hope so," said Dorothy.

"A nice rain would be great," Rya said, laying her fork down. Her stomach was so full of butterflies at the prospect of spending the evening with McClain that there was little room for food. She cleared her throat gently. "Would you...ah...excuse me, please? I need to go freshen up a bit."

"Of course, dear," said Dorothy. "You go ahead."

Looking perplexed as Rya hurried away, Burt frowned. "Dottie, is something wrong with our little gal?"

Dorothy grinned. "Oh, nothing that an evening with McClain Reardon can't fix."

Burt grinned. "Oh, so that's it. Their little date tonight." His grin broadened. "Well, as I think back on our courting days, I was the same way. All jittery and no appetite."

"Why, you ol' sweetheart," Dorothy said, reaching across the table and squeezing his hand. "It kind of seems like yesterday, doesn't it?"

Rising to his feet, Burt bent over and kissed her brow. "Guess I'd better tend to the horses."

After helping Dorothy wash and dry the dishes, Rya leaned against the wagon and waited for McClain. The cool breeze felt good. A glance to the north showed her a growing mass of dark clouds. The rest of the sky was clear.

When she looked back amid the wagons, her heart skipped a beat. McClain was weaving his way toward her through the milling people, a wide smile on his face.

She rushed to him, eyes aglow.

As they met, McClain said, "How about a little stroll along the river?"

"Oh, that would be nice."

He took hold of her arm and they walked outside the circle of wagons to the bank of the Little Blue. The sun had dropped beneath the western horizon, leaving its golden radiance on the prairie.

For a few minutes, they strolled quietly along the bank, each deep in their own thoughts. When they came to a fallen tree, McClain said, "How about we sit down?"

"All right." As McClain took her hand and helped her sit down, Rya willed her wildly beating heart to slow its pace.

The gurgling sound of the river and the reflection of the sunset on its rippling surface added to the beauty of the moment as McClain sat down beside Rya and they looked at each other.

"Well," he said softly, "tell me first about my ol' pal, Saul. What's he doing? Who did he marry, and how many children do they have?"

When Rya had answered his questions about Saul, he then wanted to know all about what had happened in her life in the past fourteen years.

Rya filled him in on the early years after he moved to Missouri, then told him about her college days and having earned her degree in education.

"So that's why Chet is having you teach the children on this journey," said McClain.

"Uh-huh. And I'm enjoying it very much." She paused. "You see, McClain, I'm on my way to Sacramento. I've been hired to teach at Sacramento High School."

McClain jerked. A strange expression flitted across his face.

Rya frowned. "What's wrong?"

Shaking his head while a grin captured his mouth, he said, "Rya, you're not going to believe this."

"What?"

He laughed gaily. "Before I tell you, let me give you some background on myself since we last saw each other. You see, I've been in the army for the past several years."

Rya's eyebrows arched. "The army?"

"Yes. Let me tell you about it."

Rya listened intently as McClain told her about his years in the army—both at Fort Larned and Fort Steele—then said, "I'm out of the army now. I was honorably discharged two months ago."

"Oh. So what are you doing now?"

He chuckled. "Most of my time at Fort Steele, the commandant was a wonderful Christian man, Colonel Ward Lamont. A couple of years ago, he retired from the army at forty-nine years of age to go to California, where he took over his older brother's construction business. The Lamont family has been in the construction business for over forty years. Colonel Lamont's father started it in the Chicago area when he was a young man. I still call him 'Colonel,' although he told me to call him Ward. Anyway, Ward was brought up in the construction business, as was his older brother, Warren, who is now retired. Warren had moved to California as a young man and established his own company.

"This is the one Ward has taken over. And here's what's happening: Colonel—I mean, Ward—and I grew very close during those years at Fort Steele, and when he made his plans to retire and take over Warren's business, he sat me down and made me an offer.

He said if I would muster out of the army in a couple of years, he would give me a good-paying job and teach me the construction business."

"So that's why you're in this wagon train. You're on your way to California to go to work for Mr. Lamont."

"Right. But let me tell you the rest. There are no other Lamont heirs. Ward is the last. So the deal is this. When I've learned the business, he will make me vice president of the company. Then someday when he retires, he will sell the business to me. California's on the grow, Rya. The Lord has made a way that I'll be in a good business for the rest of my life."

"Oh, McClain," she said, "I'm so glad for you. Where in California is this?"

He set eyes on her and smiled. "Here's the part you won't believe. It's in Sacramento."

Rya gasped. "Oh…oh, McClain. I've never had a more pleasant shock in all my life! It's…unbelievable, but I believe it! Oh, praise the Lord. I'll be able to see you often then, right?"

"You sure will, little Rya Garrett."

Putting her hands to her temples, Rya shook her head. "Isn't it something that we both should end up in Sacramento?"

"Rya…"

"Yes?"

"I…ah…need to know something."

"Sure."

There was a quiver in his voice. "Well…ah…well…"

Laying a hand on his arm, she looked him straight in the eye. "McClain, what is it?"

"Do…do you have some young man back in Virginia who will be coming to California to…to join you?"

"No. Is there some young woman somewhere who will be coming to join you in Sacramento?"

He met her gaze evenly. "No."

Elation swept through Rya like a warm ocean wave, and suddenly raindrops began to fall. Both had been so engrossed in each other that they had been oblivious to the heavy clouds covering the sky directly above. A strong wind whipped rain against them as

McClain helped Rya to her feet and they headed for the shelter of the wagon train.

As the days passed and the wagon train made its way further across Nebraska—keeping a northwesterly angle toward the southeast corner of Wyoming—Rya Garrett and McClain Reardon were spending much time together in the evenings. This was especially true on the evenings she had no classes. They talked about their childhood days, their times in school and church, and of the times when McClain stayed overnight at the Garrett house with Saul. Every night, they read the Bible and prayed together by firelight.

One evening when there was no class, the Larkins invited Rya to eat supper with them and McClain. The conversation led to Rya and McClain reminiscing during the meal about the incident with John Wilkes Booth and David Herold at the Garrett farm. Rya proudly told Vance and Rhonda how McClain had taken her out the back window of the barn, risking his own life to save hers.

Rhonda smiled at Rya. "McClain must have a very special place in your heart."

"He most certainly does," said Rya, flicking an affectionate glance at McClain.

"That's commendable, McClain," said Vance. "Especially for a thirteen-year-old boy. Help me with this. My memory is a little sketchy with the details of the capture and fate of the men who helped John Wilkes Booth assassinate Lincoln."

"Well, there were six accomplices, including David Herold," said McClain. "Herold, George Atzerodt, and Lewis Paine were hanged on July 7, 1865. Life sentences were handed down to Samuel Arnold and Michael O'Laughlin, and Edman Spangler was given a six-year sentence."

"I'm surprised they didn't hang every one of them," said Rhonda.

McClain shrugged. "I guess when all the evidence was in, the court made their decisions based on just how much each man was involved in the plot."

"Makes sense," said Rhonda. "Well, it looks like we've eaten everything on our plates. McClain, you take Rya for a walk or something. Vance will help me clean up."

Vance made a mock scowl. "Yes, dear."

McClain and Rya laughed.

"Guess we'd better do as Rhonda says," said McClain, chuckling, "or she'll have me doing the dishes."

Vance laughed. "You're right about that, boy! You'd best shake a leg."

McClain quickly made his way to the rear of the Larkin wagon, took his Bible from his bedroll, and returned. "Okay, Miss Garrett, I'm ready to go."

Rya thanked the Larkins for the meal, and walked away on McClain's arm as they crossed the circle.

"Those really are precious people, McClain," said Rya as they neared the central fire.

"They sure are," he agreed, spotting a semiprivate space near the fire. "Let's sit down over here."

Rya and McClain greeted people sitting near the fire. They talked a few minutes about their families, then McClain opened his Bible and read a passage from the Psalms. When he finished, they prayed together, asking God to guide them in their lives and to protect the wagon train, especially when they reached Cheyenne, Sioux, and Blackfoot territory. The names of Burt and Dorothy Keegan were also brought to the Throne of Grace.

When the amen was said, McClain rose to his feet, offering his hand to Rya. "Thank you for a very pleasant evening."

"My pleasure, Sergeant Reardon. Oops! I mean Mr. Reardon. You are a civilian now. And thank *you* for a very pleasant evening."

McClain walked her to the Keegan wagon, where Burt and Dorothy were already inside preparing for bed.

"See you tomorrow, Rya," said McClain. "Pleasant dreams."

"You, too," she replied, warming him with her fetching smile. "Good night."

"Good night."

"Oh! McClain!" called Rya, hurrying to him.

"Yes, ma'am?"

"Do you remember back when you got me out of that barn,

that I said you would always be my hero?"

"Yes, I do."

"Well, I just had to tell you that those were no idle words. You are still my hero."

McClain's face tinted. He playfully clipped her chin. "Little Rya Garrett, I would do it again if you needed to escape another John Wilkes Booth."

Her heart was thumping her rib cage. "I have no doubt of that."

Two days later, the wagon train made its circle for the night at sundown on the south bank of the Little Blue River, near the small town of Deweese.

While all the women in the train were cooking a combined meal at the large fire in the center of the circle, Ken Place approached his father, who was in conversation with Dick Jensen and a wagon owner in his late fifties named Archie McCrum.

"Dad, three men just rode up and asked me if they could talk to the wagon master. I said I would bring you to them."

"All right, son," said Chet. "Please excuse me, gentlemen."

When Chet passed behind the lead wagon, he set his eyes on the three riders, who were still in their saddles. They were dirty, with scraggly beards and shaggy hair dangling beneath their sweat-stained hats.

"This is my dad, Chet Place," said Ken.

"What can I do for you?" asked Chet, smiling.

One of the three was a muscular man with a neck like a tree trunk. "My name is Gabe Hute, Mr. Place," he said politely. "This fella on my right is Bob Monell, and the one on my left is Wally Arbuckle. We've been travelin' for days and are runnin' low on food and money. Could you possibly find it in your heart to share a meal with us?"

"Well, you hit it good this evening, fellas. Our ladies are doing a combined supper. Climb down and come on in."

The people were gathering at the food tables when Chet led the riders into the circle and introduced them. He explained that the trio was low on food and money, and had asked if they could share in this evening's meal.

Chet could tell by the faces of his people that they were a bit uncomfortable at the sight of their guests, but when he asked if anyone had any objections, none were given.

During the meal, Rya and McClain were seated together near the three men, and unknown to either of them, Gabe Hute kept looking at Rya. The guests took their fill, then stood around and chatted with some of the men while the women were cleaning up after the meal.

After a while, Wally Arbuckle said, "Gabe, we need to get goin' so we can cover a few more miles before dark."

"You're right, pal. Gentlemen, it's been nice meetin' you, and Mr. Place, thanks for the meal."

"You're quite welcome," said Chet. "Hope the rest of your trip is a pleasant one."

The wagon master and the small group of men who stood with him watched the trio until they passed between the lead wagon and the one behind it. Soon they saw them riding away.

Burt Keegan shook his head. "I wonder how long it's been since those three have taken a bath."

The others laughed, and Chet said, "Well, guys, I've got work to do."

When the three riders passed over a hill and were out of sight from the wagon train, Gabe Hute pulled rein. "Wait a minute, fellas."

The other two stopped, looking at Hute quizzically.

Flicking a glance back in the direction of the wagon train, the man said, "I ain't never seen a woman as gorgeous as that redhead they called Rya. You know, I've been seriously thinkin' about set-tlin' down and gettin' married. I'd sure be proud to call that beauty my missus. I'm gonna to go back there and grab her when it gets dark."

"Aw, Gabe," said Wally, "ain't no way you're gonna get her away from that wagon train."

"Right," said Bob. "When we get to where we're goin', we can each find us a wife, Gabe. Let's keep movin'."

Hute set his bearded jaw. "I said I'm goin' back there to grab her."

Bob shook his head. "Don't be a fool. That guy she was sittin' with doesn't look like any pushover. You grab her, and he'll be on your trail in a hurry."

Gabe guffawed. "I can handle him."

"You're askin' for real trouble, Gabe," warned Wally.

Gabe grinned, showing a mouthful of crooked yellow teeth. "She'll be worth it."

Darkness had fallen and a three-quarter moon was rising in the east.

After Rya and McClain had finished their Bible reading and prayer time, he walked her to the Keegan wagon. When McClain was gone, Rya and Dorothy were talking about the three riders who had been the train's guests for supper.

While they talked, Rya stepped to the side of the wagon, picked up the long-handled tin dipper that hung on a nail beside the water barrel and dipped it into the barrel. She sipped on it while she moved back to Dorothy.

Burt was doing some work at the front of the wagon by the moonlight. "Dottie," he called. "Would you come and help me here for a minute, please?"

"Sure, honey. Be right back, Rya."

Rya nodded and took another sip of water.

Suddenly she gasped as strong hands seized her, one clamping over her mouth. She dropped the dipper as she was dragged between the wagons. Struggling against her captor, she tried to let out a loud whine to alert somebody of what was happening, but the powerful fingers that pressed against her face prevented it. The man who had her in his grip picked her up and carried her into a clump of trees, where his horse waited. When he took a bandanna from his pocket and stuffed it into her mouth, she saw by the moonlight that it was one of the riders who had been in the camp earlier.

Terror clawed at her heart, and she felt a sudden sharp pain lance her midsection like a hot dagger. The pain made her want to cry out, but she could manage only a tiny whine.

Gabe Hute used another bandanna to tie around Rya's mouth, knotted it behind her head, then hoisted her up into the saddle and swung up behind her. Holding her so tight she could hardly breathe, he put the horse to a gallop.

14

At the Keegan wagon, Dorothy handed her husband the wrench she had been using. "What would you ever do without me?"

Burt chuckled and laid the wrench in his toolbox. "I'd never make it, sweetheart. Especially when it comes to doing repairs on the wagon. You have a knack for mechanical things like few women ever have. Thanks for helping me."

Dorothy smiled. "Anytime, Mr. Keegan. It's getting close to bedtime. Better finish up there pretty soon."

"It'll only take a few minutes since I had that expert help."

Dorothy wheeled and moved around the corner of the wagon. Expecting to see Rya where she had left her, she said, "Well, Rya, we'd better get ready for b—" Running her gaze around the area with her brow furrowed, she headed for the rear of the wagon. "Rya…"

Suddenly her attention was drawn to the dipper lying on the ground.

The furrows in her brow deepened as she picked it up, remembering that Rya was drinking from it when she left her. Quickly she moved to the tailgate. When there was no sign of her, she looked at the dipper in her hand again and moved out between the wagons onto the moonlit prairie.

She saw a horse galloping away, carrying two riders. Her heart leaped in her chest as she rushed back to the wagon. "Burt! Burt!"

Burt came around the corner, holding a screwdriver in his hand. "Honey, what's the matter?"

"It's Rya! I found this dipper on the ground where she was

standing a few minutes ago, and I saw a horse galloping away, carrying two people. I'm sure one of them was Rya. The other was a man. Burt, Rya's been abducted!"

Dorothy's excited voice could be heard throughout the camp. People began moving that way, but the first to reach the Keegans was McClain Reardon.

"Dorothy!" said McClain. "Did I hear you say Rya's been abducted?"

Dorothy made a quick explanation about the riders on the galloping horse.

With Burt and Dorothy on his heels, McClain dashed out onto the prairie, and in the distance to the west, he saw the horse racing away.

At that moment, Chet Place drew up.

"Chet," said McClain, "I know your horse is fast. Can I borrow him?"

"Sure! He's in the rope corral. Still has the bridle on him."

McClain pushed his way through the gathering crowd and ran to the rope corral. Untying the reins of Chet's bay gelding, he swung aboard, and riding bareback, he put the horse to top speed.

The pain in Rya's midsection was causing her to bend over in the saddle.

Gabe Hute guided the horse to a small brook and pulled rein where his two friends were sitting casually on the ground. "Hey, guys! Lookee here! My new bride!"

Rya made a whining sound, looked back at him, and shook her head vigorously.

As Menell and Arbuckle rose to their feet, Rya struggled to free herself from Gabe's grip.

"Now, just settle down, honey," Gabe said as he slid off the horse and took her out of the saddle.

When Rya's feet touched ground she tried to run, but Gabe grasped her wrist and held it tight. Her eyes were wild.

The big man laughed, removed the gag, and said, "Go ahead and scream, honey. No one will hear you now."

With her free hand, she reached up to claw his eyes, but he was quick enough to avoid her. He grabbed the free wrist and laughed. "Hey, sweetie pie, you're really a spitfire! You wear that red hair well. You're gonna make me an exciting wife!"

Suddenly Bob Menell's attention was drawn to movement on the prairie. "Gabe! Look! There's a rider comin' from the camp. And he's in a real hurry!"

Hope rose up in Rya as she swung her line of sight that way. The rider was bent low and she couldn't make out the figure. But she knew in her heart the identity of the man on the racing horse.

Wally Arbuckle headed for his horse. "Gabe, you should've listened to me and Bob. There's gonna be trouble now. I'm leavin'!"

Menell also headed for his horse. "I don't want no part of this!"

As the two men swung into their saddles, Hute bellowed, "Hey! Stay and help me fight this guy off!"

"It's your fight, Gabe!" said Arbuckle.

Both men touched spurs to their mounts and headed south at a gallop. Holding on to one of Rya's wrists, Hute shook a fist at them. "You dirty traitors! I'll get you for this! Y'hear me? I'll get you!" As he dragged Rya toward his horse, he swore. "C'mon, redhead, we gotta get outta here."

When Hute let go of Rya's wrist in order to pick her up and put her in the saddle, she surprised him by digging the fingernails of both hands into his eyes. He howled and lifted her off her feet, twisting his head to the side to avoid her clawing hands. She slipped from his grasp and fell to the ground as the sound of pounding hooves filled the air.

Hute was swearing at Rya when he saw horse and rider bearing down on him. He clawed for the gun on his hip, but before he could bring it up, McClain sailed through the air and hit him full force. The revolver flew out of Hute's hand, skittering across the prairie grass.

Both men hit the ground with McClain on top.

Rya looked on, eyes wide. She watched McClain quickly jump up and stand over him, fists clenched, his face bearing resemblance to a thundercloud.

Hute scrambled to his feet, growled like a wild beast, and

lunged for McClain. McClain drove a fist to the man's belly, causing him to double over. McClain stepped in with a quick left hook to the bearded chin that shook Hute to his heels. He followed with a right cross that staggered Hute backward on wobbly legs.

Eyes glassy, Hute tottered forward, swinging one meaty fist then the other. McClain avoided the fists, then sent a pistonstyle punch to the man's jaw, snapping his head back. Hute went down like a dead tree in a high wind.

The sound of thundering hooves was suddenly in the air.

Rya burst into tears as McClain rushed to her. "Rya, are you all right?"

She wrapped her arms around him and clung tightly. "Yes, I'm fine. Thank you for rescuing me!"

At that moment, they both looked up to see five riders closing in on them. They quickly recognized Chet Place in the lead as seconds later they skidded their horses to a halt.

Dick Jensen slid from his saddle, his attention on the big man who lay motionless on the ground. "It's one of those grubby drifters! The big one."

Chet looked around. "Where are the others?"

"They're gone," said Rya. "It was that one who abducted me."

Chet looked at McClain. "Remind me to stay on your good side." Then to Rya he said, "Are you all right?"

"Yes, thanks to God and McClain."

Gabe Hute groaned and slowly rolled his head back and forth.

Chet glanced at him, then looked back at McClain. "You take Rya back to the camp. We'll take Hute into Deweese and turn him over to the town marshal. I've met Marshal Blackburn before. When I tell him what Hute did, I guarantee you, he'll lock him up for a good long time."

While McClain was lifting Rya up and placing her in his saddle, Chet and the other men tied Gabe Hute's hands behind his back. He was mumbling profane words at them.

McClain swung up behind Rya and reached around her to grasp the reins. "Thanks, Chet, for the use of your horse."

Rya was still trembling as McClain put the horse to a steady walk. The familiar pain in her midsection was still there, but she did not let on. She leaned her head back and rested it against McClain's broad chest.

"Are you comfortable?" he asked softly.

"Yes, thank you."

"Good. You just relax."

By the time they were halfway to the camp, Rya's trembling had ceased, though the pain in her abdomen was still there. The moon showed them the circle of wagons in the distance.

Rya sat up straight, twisted on the saddle, and looked into McClain's eyes. "Well, Mr. Reardon, this is the second time you've rescued me from trouble. You are now my hero twice over!"

Later that night, after being welcomed back by the people, Rya lay in her bedroll next to the tailgate inside the Keegan wagon. The pain in her midsection was excruciating. Rolling onto her side, she drew her knees up in a fetal position. Asking God to ease the pain, she relaxed in His care, and soon the discomfort had eased to a steady ache instead of the horrible breathtaking pain.

As she was whispering words of thanks to the Lord for answered prayer, she heard the wagon master and the other men return. Knowing her abductor was in the hands of the law, she thanked her heavenly Father for sending McClain to rescue her and settled down to go to sleep.

But sleep eluded her.

She could only think of the man who rescued her…again.

Rya thought of the warm affection she used to have for McClain as a child and found the warmth of something akin to that affection in her heart at that very moment.

But it is no longer just affection, she thought. *I have fallen head-over-heels in love with my childhood hero and friend.*

In his bedroll across the circle, similar emotions were stirring within McClain Reardon. He thought back to his growing up years on the farm in Virginia, and how he had always had a tender spot in his heart for little Rya Garrett.

And now little Rya Garrett had grown up into a beautiful and vivacious young woman.

McClain thought about the evenings he and Rya had spent together since finding each other on the wagon train; of the moments they had spent reading the Bible and praying. In a whisper, he said, "Rya, not only are you beautiful, but you love the Lord and walk close to Him. I've been looking for that girl the Lord had chosen for me, and you are everything I've dreamed of. The tender spot I've always had for you is still in my heart, but now there's more. Rya, I am in love with you."

The next evening after a long day on the trail, the wagon train was camped once again on the south bank of the Little Blue River near a small town called Ayr.

While Rya was teaching her class, McClain sat by one of the fires talking to Dick Jensen and his twelve-year-old son, Bobby. The boy had already covered the arithmetic material she was teaching that evening in his school at home, so she had excused him from attending.

Bobby had been asking McClain to tell him stories about when he was in the army and fought Indians in Wyoming. As they sat by the fire and McClain told story after story, Dick smiled as he observed his wide-eyed son. Bobby was totally captivated, and often asked questions that the events brought to his mind.

When class was over and the children were scattering to their wagons, McClain finished a story, then looked toward the spot where Rya was talking to a couple of her students. "Gentlemen, I'll have to ask you to excuse me now. I need to talk to that lovely teacher." He rose to his feet.

Smiling broadly, Bobby jumped up and said, "Thank you for telling me those stories, Mr. Reardon. They were really exciting!"

McClain messed up the boy's hair. "I've got plenty more, Bobby. I'll tell them to you later."

"Oh, boy!"

"See you later, Dick," said McClain, then headed toward Rya.

The students who had been talking to her were gone now, and

she was picking up her notes and books as McClain drew up. "May I carry those to the wagon for you?"

She warmed him with a smile and handed them to him. "Of course. Thank you." McClain took hold of her hand and led her across the open area within the circle of wagons.

"How did class go?"

"Good, as usual. They're such precious children. I missed Bobby, though."

"I kept him busy. He's been wanting me to tell him some of my experiences fighting Indians when I was at Fort Steele."

Rya grinned, loving the feel of her hand in his. "I'm sure Bobby liked that better than the dry and boring arithmetic lesson he would have heard in my class."

They reached the Keegan wagon. Rya took the books and notes from McClain and put them away.

When she turned back to him, he thrilled her by saying, "It's still early. How about we take a walk along the river?"

"Sounds like a good idea to me."

"All right!" he said, taking her hand once more.

Moments later, Rya and McClain were walking on the river bank in the silver light of the moon. A cool refreshing breeze rustled the leaves of the trees along the bank.

When they were out of earshot from anyone in the camp, McClain pointed to a fallen tree. "Would you like to sit down?"

"Sure."

McClain helped her ease onto the tree, then sat down beside her and surprised her by taking hold of her hand once more. "Rya...I..."

She noticed his sudden nervousness. "Yes?"

"I...ah...have something to tell you."

Rya sat with a throbbing pulse and listened as McClain started back in their childhood days and told her he had always had a tender spot in his heart for her. He reminded her of special times when things she said and did endeared her to him even more.

"And I want you to know that you often crossed my mind over these fourteen years, Rya. Of course, the only picture I had of you in my mind was of the ten-year-old sister of my best friend. What a wonderful moment when I discovered you in this wagon train!"

Struggling with her racing heart, she said, "It was a wonderful moment for me, too."

He tightened the grip on her hand. "Rya, I—well, what I want to tell you is…is that the tender spot is still there. But now there is more. It has only taken these few days with you to know that I have fallen in love with you."

Tears filmed her eyes. She squeezed his hand. "McClain, back in those early childhood days, I had a powerful admiration for you. I used to watch you at church when you had no idea I was looking at you. And…and I used to get so excited when you came to stay all night with Saul. It would give me special times to tease you and be teased back. I loved it when you pulled my pigtails. The attention you paid to me made me like you even more. And then—"

She choked up, biting her lips. "And then came that night when you saved me from John Wilkes Booth at the barn. At that point, my admiration for you changed to—well, to deep affection. In my little-girl way, I fell in love with you."

McClain was holding her gaze, a lump rising in his throat.

"I missed you terribly when you moved away, McClain," she said, "and I thought of you so often through the years. I was so thrilled to find you again here in the wagon train and to feel the freshness of the affection I had for you. From that first moment we recognized each other, my affection began to grow." She reached up and caressed his cheek. "And then you so bravely saved me last night from that awful Gabe Hute. I really knew it before last night, but your unselfish act just put the icing on the cake."

The next words that came from her lips ran like a slow measure of music through McClain's heart.

"Oh, McClain, I have fallen desperately in love with you."

The happy couple was in each other's arms, and their lips came together in a tender kiss.

While he held her close, McClain said, "Oh, sweetheart, the Lord is so good! His mighty hand has been on us all this time, and He has planned our lives together in His perfect way. Just think: we were both going to Sacramento to begin new chapters in our lives, not knowing that God was going to bring us together!"

"Yes!" she said. "Thank You, Lord! Thank You!"

The next evening after supper, Rya and McClain were sitting by the central fire, talking to Archie and Della McCrum and the young lady who was traveling with them in their wagon. Betty Hilmes was nineteen, blond, petite, and quite pretty.

"Rya and I were talking about you folks a little while ago," said McClain. "Since neither of us have had the opportunity to get to know you, we decided we'd invite you to sit down with us here by the fire after supper."

"I'm glad you did," said Archie. "We've been saying the same thing about both of you."

Rya looked at the pretty blonde. "Betty and I have exchanged good mornings and good evenings a few times, but that's about all. Someone told me, Betty, that you are traveling with the McCrums like I'm traveling with the Keegans."

"That's right," said Betty. "I'm from New Haven, Connecticut. I traveled by rail to Kansas City, and was assigned to the McCrums' wagon by Chet Place when I arrived in Independence."

Archie grinned at the young couple. "Betty, Della, and I saw you two reading the Bible and praying together by the fire a few nights ago. We figured you just might be born-again children of God."

"You're right about that," said McClain, a smile spreading over his face. "Rya and I have known each other since we were children back in Virginia. We hadn't seen each other since 1865 till we met by surprise here in the wagon train. We were both raised in the same church by our born-again parents and were saved when we were very young."

"Wonderful!" said Della. "It was the same way with Archie and me. Being in Christian homes and in a church that preached the gospel of our precious Lord Jesus Christ, we came to know Him when we were children."

"I was six years old when I got saved," said Betty. "My dying grandmother led me to Jesus. My parents were killed in a train wreck when I was only four, and Grandma Hilmes took me into her home to raise me. Grandma only lived four days after she led me to the Lord, but before she died, she saw to it that I was taken into a Christian home. It was a family in Grandma's church. They're wonderful people. They gave me a good home." She took a deep breath. "The Lord has been so good to me. What a joy when I learned from the McCrums that they are Christians. It's been marvelous to travel with them and to enjoy the sweet fellowship."

"Praise the Lord," said McClain. "Now, Della, Archie, someone told me you're from Dayton, Ohio. Is that right?"

"Sure is," said Archie.

"And you're going to California?"

"Right. We'll be leaving the wagon train at Placerville. Our only son and his wife live there. Dale owns a stable, and I'm going to work for him."

"I see," said McClain. "Placerville is at the foot of the Sierras. What about you, Betty? Will you need another wagon to ride in? I assume you're going elsewhere in California."

Betty smiled at him. "Actually, Mr. Reardon, I'll be leaving the wagon train at Fort Bridger, Wyoming. That's going to be my new home."

McClain's eyebrows arched. "Fort Bridger? Really?"

"Why, yes. Are you acquainted with it?"

"I sure am. Up until a couple of months ago, I was in the United States Army stationed at Fort Steele, Wyoming."

"Well, isn't that something? So you've been to Fort Bridger?"

"Sure have. It's a hundred and seventy miles from Fort Steele to Fort Bridger, but my commandant, Colonel Ward Lamont, had business with the commandant at Fort Bridger and included me in the cavalry escort who accompanied him there."

Rya said, "You're going to be living at Fort Bridger, Betty. I've read some about it. Are you speaking of the actual army fort or the town?"

"The fort."

Rya's brow furrowed. "But don't you have to be an officer's wife to live in the fort?"

"Sure do."

"I...I don't understand."

"Well, you see," said Betty, a bright smile on her face, "I'm going there to become the mail order bride of one of the officers."

Rya's hand went to her mouth. "A mail order bride? Oh, how romantic! I want to hear about this!"

15

McClain Reardon smiled at Betty Hilmes. "A close friend of mine at Fort Steele married a mail order bride two years ago, Betty. He was a lieutenant then but a captain now. He and his mail order bride are very happy, and when I left Fort Steele a couple of months ago, they had a baby on the way. They're both Christians, and when he put an ad in a dozen Eastern newspapers, saying he only wanted a born-again bride, he got exactly one response."

Betty's eyebrows arched. "Only one?"

"Mm-hmm. But as they corresponded, it quickly became apparent that the Lord had chosen them for each other. So it has worked out perfectly."

"Well, I'm glad."

"Tell us about how it happened with you and this officer at Fort Bridger, Betty," said Rya, her eyes sparkling with excitement.

"It's quite simple. There just wasn't a single young Christian man in my church or in any other church in town who interested me. Oh, I dated several, but I just knew in my heart that none of them were right for me as a husband. I knew the Lord would bring Mr. Right into my life when He was ready.

"Then one day, I just happened to be looking in the classified ad section of the *New Haven Chronicle,* and I spotted this string of ads for mail order brides. I was acquainted with the mail order bride system and was fully aware of the shortage of women in the West." She laughed. "I never had even given a thought to myself becoming a mail order bride until I read Chris's ad."

"Chris?" said McClain. "Are you talking about Lieutenant Chris Cooper?"

"I sure am! You must know him."

"Most certainly! I know he's a born-again young man and is dedicated to the Lord. During my two visits there, I got to know the family very well. Chris's stepfather, Colonel Dane Kirkland—who is Fort Bridger's commandant—is a solid Christian, as is Chris's mother, Hannah, and the rest of the family."

"Well, isn't this something?" Betty said with a lilt in her voice. "You know my prospective groom and his whole family!"

"And you'll love all of them. I had the privilege of spending some time with Colonel Kirkland and his family, and I got to know them quite well."

"Oh, this is so exciting!" exclaimed Betty. "You know my future husband! And it's good to hear you say he is a dedicated Christian. This is the impression I have about him, having exchanged several letters."

"Well, you're absolutely right. And he's a born soldier. All he's ever wanted to do was be in the army."

"Yes, he told me that in one of his letters. He said that his father had been an officer in the army back East. His father was killed while taking his family to Wyoming from Missouri in a wagon train. Chris went to West Point when he turned seventeen. When he graduated four years later, his stepfather did a little string-pulling, and Chris was assigned to Fort Bridger so he could serve under Colonel Kirkland and be near his mother and siblings."

"So Chris is how old, Betty?" queried Rya.

"He's twenty-one."

"Do you have a picture of him?"

"Yes. In the wagon."

"And he's quite handsome," said McClain.

"Oh, yes!" Betty said. "But even if he wasn't, it's what is on the inside that attracted me to him…long before he sent me a picture. When we began corresponding, he told me nine other Christian young women had responded to his ad, but the Lord had impressed him strongly that I was the one. I knew he was the one for me, just as certainly, and told him so in my next letter. When this was settled, we exchanged photographs."

"Oh, Betty, I'm so happy for you!" said Rya. "I've read a lot about mail order brides, and I think it's wonderful that the Lord has used the system to bring you and Chris Cooper together."

"Me, too," Betty said with a sigh. "Of course I wanted to get to Fort Bridger as soon as possible once Chris and I agreed that the Lord was leading us together, but Chris told me there is no rail service in that part of Wyoming, so I'd have to come by wagon train. It works out real good, though, since the Oregon Trail goes right past Fort Bridger."

"The Lord knew that," said Della. "He put you in this wagon train so we could have you in our wagon and get to know you."

"And vice versa, Della," said Betty. "You and Archie have been such a blessing to me." Her eyes went to Rya and McClain. "And now, I've had the privilege of getting acquainted with you two."

"It's a privilege for us, too, Betty," said McClain. "So where will you be staying when you first get to Fort Bridger?"

"Chris is going to put me up at the Uintah Hotel. I'll stay there while we're getting to know each other. I have no doubt it's going to work out. Chris and I are already as much in love as it's possible to be by exchanging letters."

"I'm sure that's true. And as I said before, you're going to love the whole family."

"I have no doubt of that. Chris's mother has written to me twice since it was settled that I was coming to Fort Bridger. She seems like such a sweet lady."

"Hannah is definitely that," said McClain. "Everybody in the town and the fort loves her."

"How many siblings does Chris have, Betty?" asked Rya.

"Four. Two sisters and two brothers. Chris is the oldest. His sister, Mary Beth—who is twenty—is married to a young Christian attorney who recently established an office in the town. Mary Beth teaches fourth, fifth, and sixth grades at the Fort Bridger school. I'm sure the two of you will have a lot to talk about if you get to meet her when the wagon train stops there. Chet told me they always stock up good at Fort Bridger, so you'll probably be there a half-day or so."

"I hope I get to meet her," said Rya.

"The next oldest is Brett Jonathan. Chris says they call him B.J. He's fifteen. Then there's Patty Ruth, who's thirteen. Chris says she's the droll of the family."

McClain laughed. "She is definitely that! And she's a cutie, too."

Betty smiled. "And lastly, there's Eddie, who's six years old. I'm sure looking forward to meeting all of them. Chris's maternal grandparents live there, also, and he speaks so highly of them. I just know the Lord's hand is in it all. As you can see, I'll have a pretty good-sized family."

"I'm sure that will be a blessing," said Della. "Archie, we'd better head for the wagon. It's almost bedtime."

"Guess I'd better head for the Keegan wagon," said Rya. "Dawn has been coming in the middle of the night lately."

Everyone laughed.

McClain stood and offered his hand to her. "I think maybe you're the wagon train's droll!"

Rya playfully dug an elbow into his ribs, then gave him a winsome smile as she stepped to Betty and hugged her. "I'm so glad for you, Betty. It's so romantic. Just think! A mail order bride!"

McClain then took Rya by the hand and led her to the Keegan wagon. Burt and Dorothy were already in bed. McClain looked around to see if anybody was watching, then kissed her good night, helped her into the rear of the wagon, and walked away.

As the weeks passed and the wagon train moved farther west, they traveled close to the south bank of the Platte River and camped on it at night. When they reached the spot where the river split into the North Platte and the South Platte, they followed the South Platte until it veered toward Colorado, then proceeded westward along the bank of the smaller Lodgepole River.

Although Rya stayed busy teaching four evenings a week, she and McClain made time to be together. They found themselves falling deeper in love with the passing of each day. McClain was privately praying that the Lord would help him to know when the time was right to ask Rya to marry him, and just how to do it.

On several occasions, McClain overheard Rya and Betty talking, and Rya often repeated her feeling that to be a mail order bride must be terribly romantic. Once when McClain heard it, Rya added: "And maybe just a little bit scary."

This caused him to smile to himself.

The wagon train was within four or five days of the Wyoming border when Chet Place led them to form a circle on the bank of the Lodgepole, just outside the town of Sidney. All the women pitched in to make one meal so everybody could eat together.

During the meal, McClain had butterflies in his stomach. The Lord had impressed him that this was the night to ask Rya to marry him. He knew the way he was going to ask her would both surprise and please her.

When the meal was over and the women were getting ready to wash dishes, Rya called for her students to join her for the evening's class.

Having kept an eye on Bobby Jensen during supper, McClain hurried to him as he left his parents and headed for the Jensen wagon to get his books and notebook.

Drawing up to the wagon just behind the boy, McClain said, "Bobby, could I talk to you for a minute?"

"Sure, Mr. Reardon."

"I need you to do me a big favor."

"I have to go to class now, but I'll do it right after."

"Well, you can do this favor when you go to class."

"Oh. All right. What is it?"

"Go ahead and get your stuff, then I'll need you to come to the Larkin wagon with me."

Bobby climbed inside and retrieved his books. As he walked beside McClain across the open area, he asked, "What is it you want me to do?"

"I'll explain in just a minute."

When they reached the Larkin wagon, McClain reached in over the tailgate and took out a leather case. Opening the case, he pulled out a sealed envelope and said, "I want you to give this to your teacher immediately after class is over."

Looking a bit puzzled, Bobby nodded. "Yes, sir."

"Go ahead and read what it says on the envelope."

Angling it toward the light that came from the nearest fire, Bobby read the words written by the hand of McClain Reardon:

Miss Rya Garrett

c/o Chet Place's Wagon Train

Somewhere in Nebraska, USA

Brow furrowed, the boy said, "This looks like a letter you would send through the mail."

"Exactly. You're a smart boy!"

Bobby laughed.

"Here's what I want you to do: when you hand Miss Rya this letter after class is over, tell her you are the official postman of the wagon train, and you have a letter for her."

"Is this a love letter, Mr. Reardon?"

"You could call it that, son. Now what are you going to tell her when you hand it to her?"

"That I'm the official postman of the wagon train and I have a letter for her."

McClain patted him on the back. "Excellent! I really appreciate this."

A grin lit up Bobby's young face. "I'm happy to do it, sir." With that, he hurried off to class.

McClain watched him go and whispered, "Well, Lord, the wheels are in motion. How can I ever thank You for bringing Rya back into my life? Please help me to be the husband she deserves."

For nearly two hours, McClain moved about the camp, making conversation with different people. When it was almost time for class to be over, he hurried to that side of the wagon circle. Moving into the shadows where no one could see him, he watched the last few minutes of the session. He chuckled under his breath when Rya dismissed her students and Bobby hurried up to her.

"Miss Rya…" said the boy, with a wide smile on his face, while holding the envelope behind his back.

"Yes, Bobby?"

"Ma'am, I am the official postman of the wagon train, and I have a letter for you." He handed it to her.

Looking puzzled, Rya took the envelope. "Why...ah...thank you."

Bobby told her she was welcome and quickly darted away.

Rya opened the envelope and took out the letter. Moving close to one of the nearby lanterns, she angled the letter toward its glow and began reading.

July 22, 1879
My darling Rya,

It is with an eager mind and an adoring heart that I pen these words. You have spoken often to Betty Hilmes, letting it be known how romantic you feel it is for a young lady to become a mail order bride. Because I love you more than you will ever know, I have arranged the same for you. Please note that you are holding a piece of mail in your hand, delivered by the official postman of this wagon train.

I am hereby asking you to become my mail order bride. Will you marry me? I will breathlessly await your answer.

Your loving McClain

When Rya finished reading the letter, she sensed movement at her side and looked up through her tears at McClain.

"Oh, you wonderful darling!" she said, and started to throw herself into his arms. But from the corner of her eye, she saw people passing by. She sniffled, wiping tears. "Let's take a little walk."

"Yes, ma'am! I'll take your books and notes to the Keegan wagon. You wait here. I'll be right back."

Tears flowed down Rya's cheeks as she doused the lanterns. "Oh, dear Lord, You have given me the most wonderful man in the whole world! He's so sweet! How many men would have thought of this?"

There were still people passing by when McClain returned. Without a word, he took her hand, led her between two wagons, and they made their way to a private spot on the bank of the river under an expanse of dark sky glittered with twinkling stars and a pale half-moon.

Rya threw her arms around the man she loved. "I love you so

much! You're the most wonderful man in all the world!"

McClain held her tight. "As long as I've got you believing that, nothing else matters."

Pulling her head back so she could look him in the eye by the dim light, she gave him a sly grin. "All right, Mr. Reardon, who made Bobby the official postman of the wagon train?"

"I did." McClain put a palm under her chin and gazed into her eyes. "Well?"

"Yes! Yes! Yes! I will be your mail order bride, you wonderful romantic!"

After sharing a sweet kiss, they held each other tight.

McClain put his lips against the soft hair on top of her head. "Let's pray and ask the Lord to bless our lives and our marriage."

When they finished talking to the Lord together, they kissed again, then McClain took her by the hand and said, "Since dawn has been coming in the middle of the night, my future mail order bride needs to get in her bedroll."

"Now, who's the droll?"

As they were heading back to the camp, holding hands, McClain said, "It is my opinion that we should get married as soon as we get settled in Sacramento."

"Oh, it is, huh?"

"Yes. It is."

"Well, Mr. Reardon, I happen to be of the same opinion."

"Good! Then it's settled."

"I'll write my parents tomorrow, and let them know that we're engaged. We'll be passing by Kimball tomorrow or at least the next day. I'll mail it there."

They passed between two wagons, and as they neared the Keegan vehicle, they saw Burt and Dorothy sitting on chairs beside the wagon, each sipping a cup of coffee. A fire crackled close by, giving off a glow of yellow light.

"Something's in the air, Burt," said Dorothy. "Just look at these two!"

"Mm-hmm," said Burt. "The love light is shining tonight."

Dorothy rose to her feet. "Are you lovebirds going to share what has you looking so delighted?"

Rya and McClain looked at each other, nodding their agreement.

"Well," said McClain, placing an arm around Rya and drawing her close to him, "you two will be the first to hear it. Rya has consented to be my wife!"

"Oh, I'm so happy for you!" Dorothy squealed. She laid her tin cup on the chair and put her arms around both of them. "I was wondering when you were going to get around to asking her, McClain!"

"Me, too," said Burt. "It sure took you long enough, boy!"

Dorothy let go of them, eased back, and in a voice clogged with emotion, said, "The best wish Burt and I can have for you is that you will have as happy a marriage as we've had."

That night as Rya lay in the Keegan wagon next to the tailgate, she didn't even feel the usual lumps and bumps. It was as if she were floating on a cloud. Giving God praise for His abundant blessings and for bringing McClain back into her life, she asked for wisdom and guidance so she could be the best wife possible to the man she loved so dearly.

Lying there with the sound of the crickets all around her, she relived the glorious evening, shedding tears once more as she thought of how McClain had made her his mail order bride. She told herself she never knew that falling in love could be so marvelous. Her lips moved in barely a whisper. "Rya Reardon. That sounds so good! Mrs. McClain Reardon. Oh, there's music in it!"

Lying on the ground in his bedroll beside the Larkin wagon, McClain was also reliving the evening. He thanked the Lord for planning his life, and so lovingly making Rya the biggest part of it.

When he thought of how she had said yes three times and of the sweet kiss that followed, his pulse quickened and he felt the staccato beat of his heart through his whole body.

His mind went back to the morning of the day when Carl Pierson and Carrie Duncan got married at Fort Steele. He recalled Chaplain Curtis Fremont asking him if the best man was nervous and he had said he was. He also remembered the chaplain's wife saying that being best man would help him to be the groom in his own wedding.

As he turned over in the bedroll next to the Larkin wagon, McClain recalled his reply to Elaine Fremont. "I have to find that right girl the Lord has picked out for me. Now if I was an officer, I would have tried the mail order bride system myself. I guess I'll have to wait till I'm out of the army before I can start looking for that right girl."

He smiled in the darkness. "Lord, You work in such marvelous ways. I didn't even have to look for her. You put her in this wagon train and handed her to me on a silver platter. Thank You, Lord! Thank You!"

The next morning before the wagons pulled out, Rya got Betty Hilmes alone and told her about McClain's letter, asking her to be his mail order bride. Betty hugged her, saying how happy she was.

Late that afternoon, the wagons made their circle, and Ken Place hopped on his father's horse to go into Kimball to post some mail while Chet was helping one of the men make repairs on his wagon.

McClain was talking to Rya at the tailgate of the Keegan wagon when he happened to look out on the prairie and see a small cavalry unit riding toward the circle.

Following his line of sight, Rya said, "There are soldiers coming."

"Mm-hmm. There's an army camp just north of Kimball. No doubt that's where they're from."

"What do you suppose they want?"

"I don't know, but I'd better go get Chet. They'll want to talk to him."

Rya watched McClain cross the open area to the wagon where Chet was helping with repairs. When Chet heard McClain's words, he nodded, and the two of them stepped outside the circle to meet the soldiers as they drew up. People all over the circle were watching.

Rya stood with Dorothy and Burt as they observed the scene.

"I don't like the looks of this," Burt said.

"What do you mean, honey?" asked Dorothy.

"Take a gander at that lieutenant's face. Like he just came from a funeral. Chet and McClain may be getting some bad news. I wish their backs weren't toward us. I'd like to see their faces."

Even as Burt was speaking, Chet and McClain turned and headed back to the wagons. Both looked somber as they talked in low tones. When they came inside the circle, everyone was looking at them.

"We need to have a meeting, folks!" called Chet. "Right out here in the middle of the circle!"

As the people were gathering, McClain spotted Rya coming with the Keegans and hurried to her.

"McClain, what is it?" she asked, worry showing in her eyes.

"I'll let Chet tell you, honey. It isn't good."

When everyone was present in a large half circle, Chet stood facing them. "As you saw, McClain and I just talked to a cavalry unit. They're from an army camp over by Kimball. All of you know we're nearing the Wyoming border, which means we'll soon be in Cheyenne Indian territory. Lieutenant Barlow just told us that the Cheyenne are in an uprising right now because the government is trying to put them on reservations, and they're very hostile. Every gun in this wagon train must be ready at all times. Starting tonight, we'll double the men on watch.

"After supper, we'll meet around the fire, and I'll fill you in on just how to be prepared for Indian attack. All of you men have been wearing sidearms since we left Missouri. Let's have those rifles loaded and handy at all times. See you after supper."

Rya took hold of McClain's arm as they walked toward the Larkin wagon. A small shiver of fear lodged in her heart. McClain put an arm around her shoulder and gave her a squeeze.

When they drew up to the Larkin wagon, McClain pulled his revolver, checked the loads, and dropped it back in the holster. Reaching inside the wagon, he pulled out his Winchester .44 and worked the lever, checking to make sure it was fully loaded.

Rya cringed as she looked at it. "I didn't even know you were carrying a rifle."

"It's too bad the Cheyenne are stirred up. I never did feel we should put them on reservations. I can't blame them for being angry. They're rapidly losing the freedom they once had. All we can do is be prepared."

"I hope you never have to use the rifle or the revolver."

McClain spoke in a whisper. "I hope not, either, sweetheart."

16

THREE DAYS LATER, CHET PLACE'S WAGON TRAIN crossed the Wyoming border at high noon. The brilliant sun was at its peak overhead. The sky, pale on the eastern horizon, deepened in hue directly above, becoming a sapphire blue as it stretched to the western horizon.

McClain Reardon was walking alongside the Keegan wagon. Rya was on the wagon seat, sitting beside Dorothy, who was next to her husband.

Burt eyed the sturdy wooden sign that reminded them they were on the Oregon Trail and were now entering Wyoming Territory. He looked past the women at McClain. "You're experienced at fighting Indians here in Wyoming. What tribes have you fought?"

"Well," said McClain, "I've done battle with Blackfoot, Sioux, Shoshoni, and Cheyenne."

"Do you think we could face all four?"

"It's possible. They're all upset that the government is working at putting them on reservations."

"What about the Crow? It seems I've read that they're also in these parts."

"Some of them are, but the Crow aren't the fighting kind like the others. They've made peace with the white man. They'll go on reservations without a fuss."

"So which of the four hostile tribes do you consider the best warriors, McClain?" queried Burt.

"It's a toss-up between the Sioux and the Cheyenne."

"Why didn't that Lieutenant Barlow mention the other tribes when he warned Chet about the Cheyenne threat?"

"Because the Oregon Trail only goes through Cheyenne land. I said it's possible that we could face all four, but only if the other three happen to be riding through these parts. Our greatest threat is the Cheyenne."

"So they're pretty tough?"

"That's putting it mildly. They are fierce fighters. They are courageous and they are savage. I hope we don't have to fight them."

Fear showed on Dorothy's face. "McClain, do they kill women and children when they attack?"

"Yes, they do. They don't discriminate when they attack white people. They mean to kill every one of us. Like I said, I hope we don't have to fight them."

Dorothy's lips trembled and her eyes filled with tears. "Oh, this is horrible! I'm so frightened I can hardly breathe!"

Rya moistened her lips and took hold of Dorothy's hand. "Honey, none of us can say we aren't frightened with this Indian threat hanging over us. The butterflies are rioting in my stomach right now. But I have peace in my heart that if the Indians should attack and kill me, I will go to heaven. I know that for sure. If you will open your heart to Jesus, He will save you, forgive all your sins, and give you peace about facing eternity."

Dorothy sniffed and wiped tears from her cheeks with a hankie. "Rya, I want to hear more about being saved. I know I've changed the subject every time you've brought it up and haven't given you a chance to explain it to me. Burt has done the same thing. I'd like for you to—"

"Aw now, Dorothy," cut in Burt, "there's no reason to get so upset. There are plenty of guns on this train, and a good supply of ammunition. We can handle anything those savages throw at us."

Dorothy stared at him for a moment, then turned her line of sight straight ahead and rode in silence, dabbing at her tears.

Rya looked down at McClain as he kept pace with the wagon. When her gaze locked with his, he saw her brow furrow. *We'll talk about it later,* he mouthed silently.

—∞—   —∞—   —∞—

When the wagons made their circle that evening, the men began building a large central fire so all the women could cook another communal meal.

Rya was helping Dorothy slice potatoes at the Keegan wagon when McClain came by and asked if he could talk to her for a moment. She excused herself to Dorothy, and they stepped away until they were at a spot where no one could hear them.

McClain said, "Honey, I think if you could talk to Dorothy when Burt isn't around, you could lead her to the Lord."

"She sure seems ready to listen. It's an answer to our prayers. As stubborn as Burt is about it, I believe we're going to have to reach Dorothy first. Once she's saved, it may make it easier to win him over."

"Right."

"Well, we will have to pray for wisdom from the Lord and ask Him to lead us so we can handle it correctly, and to give me the opening I need when we're alone."

"Yes. And while we're praying that way, we'll ask God to give us wisdom even now when we're with Burt, that we can plant and water the seed. Since there's no class tonight, let's sit with them at supper so if the Lord gives us any kind of an opening, we can take it."

"I was about to suggest that myself. Seems like all great minds run on the same track."

McClain playfully clipped her chin. "That's what I love about you. You're so smart!"

She smiled. "I'd better get back to Dorothy. See you at supper."

While Rya, McClain, and the Keegans were eating together, they talked about the Indian threat for a few minutes, then Dorothy said, "Rya, I told you earlier today that I want to hear more about salvation. Would you and McClain talk to me after supper?"

Burt was chewing his food and frowned. Dorothy saw the frown, but ignored it as Rya said, "We'd love to."

"Good. We'll go inside the wagon so we won't be bothered."

McClain looked at Burt. "We'd love to have you sit in on it, too."

The frown on Burt's brow melted into a sour look that spread over his entire face.

Burt Keegan still had a sour look as the four of them sat inside the wagon with two lanterns burning. Rya was sitting next to Dorothy with her Bible in hand, and McClain was sitting next to Burt as he opened his Bible and said, "Let me show you what God says about our state before Him as sinners who are headed for eternity and judgment. Rya, if you will follow in your Bible so Dorothy can see it, I'll let Burt look on mine. Let's go to 1 John chapter 3. I want to give you God's definition of sin."

Rya angled the page so Dorothy could easily see it.

Putting a finger on the spot he wanted, McClain said, "Look at verse 4. 'Whosoever committeth sin transgresseth also the law: for sin is the transgression of the law.' Now, the law God is referring to here is this Bible. His written Word. He calls it His law over and over again. David wrote about it repeatedly in the Psalms. In one place he wrote and said to God, 'The law of thy mouth is better unto me than thousands of gold and silver.' In another place he said, 'Horror hath taken hold upon me because of the wicked that forsake thy law.'

"So we see that when we transgress His Word, we sin. Now, let's look in Romans chapter 5 and see what God says about it there."

When both Bibles were open to the designated passage, McClain said, "Burt, how about you reading verse 12 for us?"

Burt's voice was weak as he read it aloud, 'Wherefore, as by one man sin entered into the world, and death by sin; and so death passed upon all men, for that all have sinned.'"

"All right, Burt," said McClain. "Are any of us sinless?"

"No."

"So we have all transgressed God's law, haven't we?"

Burt cleared his throat. "Uh...yes."

McClain looked at Dorothy. "We're all sinners, right?"

Dorothy nodded, her lips pressed tight. "Yes."

"Now, you will notice," McClain proceeded, "that it says by one man sin entered into the world, and death came as a result of sin. All men have to die, don't they? And that one man referred to is named in verse fourteen. Adam. So Adam's sin brought physical death on himself and all of his descendants, right?"

The Keegans nodded.

"And, of course," said McClain, "we deserve death, ourselves, because we are sinners by choice, just like Adam was. Now, we're talking about physical death that came upon all mankind because of sin. But there is also spiritual death, and this was passed on to us by Adam. Just as sure as physical death. We were all born physically alive, but spiritually dead. Therefore we must be born of the Spirit to be alive spiritually.

"Paul wrote to born-again people in Ephesians 2:1 and said, 'And you hath he quickened who were dead in trespasses and sins.' What you need, Dorothy, Burt, is to be brought to life spiritually so you don't have to spend eternity in the lake of fire, which God calls the second death. Born only once, you die twice. Born twice, you can only die once—physically.

"Okay, let's see how a person gets born again. John 1:12 and 13. Of Jesus Christ, it says, 'But as many as received him, to them gave he power to become the sons of God, even to them that believe on his name: Which were born, not of blood, nor of the will of the flesh, nor of the will of man, but of God.' It's God who gives the new birth. And please notice that we sinners have to become the sons of God. We are God's creation, but we are not His children until we're born again, and only God's children go to heaven when they die."

"That's right," said Rya. "And when we receive Jesus, according to Ephesians 3:17, we receive Him into our hearts."

"And we do that by calling on Jesus," said McClain. "We repent of our sin, and believing the gospel, receive Him into our hearts as our personal Saviour."

Tears were streaming down Dorothy's cheeks. "I want to do that right now!"

"Wonderful!" said McClain, then he looked at Burt. "How about you, my friend?"

Burt shook his head. "It makes sense to me, all right, but I'm not ready to do it."

"All right," McClain said. "Dorothy, let's bow our heads. If you would like help in what to say to the Lord, Rya will do that."

Dorothy wiped tears. Looking at Rya, she said, "Help me, please."

Burt looked on while Rya led Dorothy to the Lord. While the two women were embracing, shedding tears of joy, McClain turned to Burt and laid a hand on his arm. "Burt, won't you open your heart to Jesus, too?

Burt drew a deep breath and set steady eyes on McClain. "I've got plenty of time to tend to this. There's no need to be concerned about getting saved now."

McClain quickly flipped to Psalm 90. Putting his finger on verse 12, he said, "Read that to me. This is Moses talking to God."

Burt licked his dry lips. "'So teach us to number our days, that we may apply our hearts unto wisdom.'"

"Now, think on those words, Burt, while I go to another verse." McClain turned to Psalm 39 and put his finger on verse 4. "Read that to me."

Burt's voice was shaky as he read it aloud: "'LORD, make me to know mine end, and the measure of my days, what it is; that I may know how frail I am.'"

McClain then tried to convince Burt that every person on earth lived their life one frail heartbeat at a time, never knowing when the last beat would come. He pointed out that for saved people, it only meant that when their hearts beat for the last time, they were immediately absent from the body and present in heaven with the Lord. But for lost people, it meant their last heartbeat would deliver them into the flames of hell.

McClain's voice broke as he said, "Burt, you need to apply your heart unto wisdom by repenting of your sin and receiving the Lord Jesus into your heart as your Saviour before it's too late."

Still clinging to Rya, Dorothy looked at her husband. "He's right, dear. You need to settle it right now."

Burt pressed a weak smile on his lips. "Dottie, I'm not ready to do that. Besides, there's plenty of time to take care of it later."

Tears filmed Rya's eyes. "But Burt, you don't know that. This is why God says now is the day of salvation."

"Well, won't tomorrow, or next week, or next year be now when they get there?" argued Burt.

McClain chuckled. "Sure, if you live that long. But what if you don't?"

Burt looked at him blankly.

"Let me tell you about an ancient custom they used to have in some of the central European countries. Chaplain Fremont at Fort Steele told us about it in a sermon. The custom was, that they would put an hourglass into the coffin of the dead to signify that their time on earth had run out. Chaplain Fremont's comment was, 'The hourglass was a useless notification to the dead person. Much better to put an hourglass into the hand of every living person and show them the grains of sand gliding steadily to the bottom, signifying that soon life will be gone.' What do you say to that?"

Burt squared his shoulders. "I don't say anything to it right now, McClain. Like I said, I'm not ready to get saved."

As the days passed, Rya and McClain fell deeper in love while making plans for their future. They discussed Roy and Elsa Gibbs, in whose home Rya was to live when she reached Sacramento.

The Gibbses had come to Bowling Green after McClain and his family were gone, but Rya had told him that they were dedicated Christians and wonderful people. She knew they would be happy for her and would let her stay with them until the wedding. Rya had also told McClain that in her correspondence with Roy and Elsa, they told her they belonged to a solid Bible-believing church in Sacramento, so she and McClain would have a good church.

Late one afternoon, Rya was sitting in the back of a wagon belonging to a young couple named Brodie and Jane Hyland, who were from a farming community near St. Louis. With Rya were Jane Hyland and Betty Hilmes. While the wagon rocked and bumped along the trail, Jane was suggesting some ideas to Betty

and Rya about their weddings, and the two brides-to-be were listening intently.

All three were laughing about something funny Jane had said
when they looked up to see McClain appear at the rear of the
wagon on Chet Place's horse.

"Darling, did you take over Chet's job?" said Rya.

"No. We're about to pass by Fort Steele. Chet is letting me use
the horse to ride over there. I want to see some of my friends. I'll
catch up to the wagon train when it stops to make camp for the
night."

"Oh, of course," said Rya, leaning over the tailgate to look
northward. She could make out the stockade fence that surrounded the fort and the gate tower with Old Glory on a pole,
flapping in the breeze.

"I'll see you at suppertime." He glanced at Jane and Betty, then
looked back into Rya's blue eyes. "I love you."

As Rya was watching McClain gallop the horse toward Fort
Steele, Betty said, "I can hardly wait to hear Chris say those three
little words to me."

Fort Steele had passed from view about an hour previously when
the wagons completed their circle. The sun's fiery rim was still visible
on the horizon as some of the men were building fires and others
were making a rope corral. The women were busy preparing supper.

Rya and Dorothy were working together when Dorothy
glanced at the setting sun and looked at Rya. "Shouldn't McClain
be getting here?"

"Yes, he should. He said he'd see me at suppertime. I'll go see if
he's coming."

Moving between the Keegan wagon and the one behind it, Rya
looked eastward, and a smile broke across her face when she saw a
rider galloping toward the wagon train. He was close enough that
she decided to wait for him and welcome him home with a kiss.

After a minute or so, she saw that the horse was gray. Chet's
horse was a sorrel.

She started to turn back between the wagons when she saw the rider lift his hat and wave. She paused, focusing on him, and moments later, she could make out his face. Her heart seemed to stop and her stomach went sour.

It was Jason Lynch.

"Lord help me," she breathed.

Jason brought the gray to a halt, slid from the saddle, and hurried to her. "Rya! I've finally found you! It's so good to see you!"

When he moved up with open arms, she took a step back. "Go on back home, Jason."

"Aren't you glad to see me?"

"No, I'm not glad to see you. You have made this trip for nothing."

Jason put on a hurt look. "But, Rya, I still love you and want to marry you."

Rya saw another rider galloping toward the wagon train from the east. "Jason, I'm engaged to marry a man who is in this wagon train. We're going to get married when we reach Sacramento. The best thing for you to do is turn around right now and leave."

"You belong to me!" Jason said. "You have no right to marry this other guy!"

"Jason, I have never been in love with you. And I never told you that you had any claim on me."

Jason grabbed her by the shoulders and shook her. "I know you love me! I've come to marry you and make a new life in Sacramento!"

"I'm not marrying you!" Rya snapped as she tried to wrest herself from his grasp.

Chet Place and some of the men were hurrying across the circle, having heard the angry voices.

McClain was thundering in on the sorrel, his eyes set on the stranger who was manhandling the woman he loved.

"Let go of me, Jason!" Rya said. "Let go of me!"

Just as Chet and the others came between the wagons, McClain was out of the saddle. He threw a neck lock on Jason, squeezing him in a viselike hold. The sudden pain made Jason let go.

Rya backed away, her midsection on fire.

McClain let go of Jason, who slumped to the ground, holding his throat.

McClain stood over him and looked at Rya. "Are you all right, sweetheart?"

Rya rushed to him. "Yes, I'm fine."

He took hold of her hand and looked back down at the gagging man. "Who is this guy? Do you know him?"

Before Rya could answer, Jason kicked McClain's leg, toppling him.

McClain hit the ground but sprang to his feet, eyes fixed on Jason. Rya felt Chet Place's hand on her arm. He pulled her back a few steps.

Jason cursed McClain as he scrambled to his feet then lunged at him.

McClain dodged the blow and pounded Jason with a right, a left, and another right. The last punch lifted Jason off his feet and dropped him on his back. He was out cold.

Rya rushed to McClain again. He took her in his arms and looked into her eyes. "Did he hurt you?"

"No. I'm not hurt."

By this time men, women, and children had come from the wagon circle and were looking on. Rya said in everybody's hearing, "His name is Jason Lynch. He's from Virginia." Rya went on to tell McClain of Jason's harassment of her.

A moan came from the man on the ground.

"I have told Jason plainly many times that I do not love him and will not marry him," Rya said, "but he won't take no for an answer. When he rode up here, I had come out to see if I could get a glimpse of you riding in. He said he had come to marry me and make a new life in Sacramento. When I told him I was engaged to marry a man in the wagon train, he went crazy."

McClain turned to see Jason Lynch sitting up, shaking his head. Both lips were split and bleeding.

"Excuse me, Rya," McClain said, and moved to Jason while everyone in the crowd looked on.

Grasping his shirt collar, he jerked him to his feet and said, "Get on your horse and ride. Go back to where you came from.

Rya is my fiancée. Don't you ever come around her again."

Jason's eyes were still a bit glazed, but he focused them on McClain as best he could. He wiped blood from his lips and growled, "You can't tell me what to do."

There was a flush to McClain's face. "I'm telling you to stay away from Rya. She and I are getting married shortly after we arrive in Sacramento, and you're not invited to the wedding."

Chet Place stepped up and set cold eyes on Lynch. "I'm the wagon master, and I'm telling you to get away from this train and stay away. If you ever show up again, you'll be tied to a tree and left for the wild animals to feed on. Do you understand?"

Jason turned to Rya with a hurt look as he wiped more blood from his mouth. Then he stabbed McClain with a hateful look as he walked unsteadily toward his horse. Without looking back, he mounted up and rode away, heading east.

"All right, folks," spoke up the wagon master, "show's over. Let's eat supper!"

McClain touched Rya's arm to walk her into the circle. Suddenly she buckled, putting a hand to her midsection.

Grasping her to keep her from falling, McClain said, "Honey, what is it?"

Betty Hilmes rushed up as Rya said through clenched teeth, "It's just a problem I have now and then when I get upset. I'll be all right."

Dorothy Keegan was there instantly. "McClain, let's take her to the wagon."

McClain picked Rya up, cradling her in his arms. "We'll make you comfortable, honey. Then if you feel like eating, I'll bring supper to you."

"It will help if I can lie down," said Rya. "The pain will subside in a few minutes. I'll be fine."

17

TWO DAYS PASSED. AT MIDMORNING, as the wagons were moving along at their usual pace, Rya Garrett was on the seat of the Keegan wagon next to Dorothy.

Rya had her Bible in hand, and with Dorothy looking on, was reading Matthew chapter 27 aloud. When Rya read of how the Roman soldiers made a crown of thorns and put it on Jesus' head, and called Him King of the Jews while spitting on Him and hitting Him on the head with a reed, Dorothy began weeping. "Oh, Rya! How terribly they treated Him!"

"Yes," said Rya, her own voice choked with tears. "The Lord Jesus had only shown them love and compassion, but they hated Him and rejected Him. It's the same today, Dorothy. When people hear the gospel and learn that Jesus suffered, bled, and died to provide salvation for them, but they still reject Him, it's like mocking Him and spitting on Him, even as the Roman soldiers did."

Burt kept his eyes straight ahead as if he had not heard her words.

At that moment, McClain Reardon came riding up on Rya's side of the wagon aboard Dick Jensen's black gelding. "Chet wants me to ride point with him for a while," he said, smiling. "I just wanted to see how you're feeling."

Rya put a hand to her abdomen. "It's better than it was at breakfast. I'll be fine."

"I'm sure praying that you will," said McClain. He pointed northwestward. "See that town just coming into view?"

"That's Rawlins, isn't it?" said Burt.

"Sure is. We'll come within about two miles of it when we pass it."

"I guess we're about on schedule as Chet planned it," said Burt.

"Pretty close, I think," said McClain.

"Look!" said Rya, pointing straight ahead. "It's Chet. And he's riding hard."

"Uh-oh," said McClain. "There may be trouble." With that, he put the gelding to a gallop and soon intercepted the wagon master just as he was pulling rein at the lead wagon.

"Cheyenne!" Chet said. "I was about half a mile ahead of the train when I saw a small band of them on top of a hill about five hundred yards to the north. I watched them closely, but they wheeled and rode away behind the hill. They may be going after more warriors so they can attack us. I need to let the people know so they'll be prepared. How about you taking the back half of the train?"

"Sure."

"Tell them to keep a sharp eye. No telling which direction they'll attack from. Every man needs to have his rifle handy."

McClain turned the horse around and trotted back along the line of wagons. People were calling out to him, asking what was going on. He called back that Chet would be along shortly to tell them.

When he reached the Keegan wagon, which was in the front half of the train, he paused long enough to tell Rya and the Keegans what Chet had told him.

"Keep your eyes peeled, ladies," Burt said after McClain rode on.

While both women were scanning the land in every direction, Dorothy said, "Rya, I'm still frightened at the thought of an Indian attack, but I have peace now, knowing that if I should be killed, I would go to heaven."

Rya patted her hand. "That's peace that only a child of God can have. Paul said in Philippians 4:7, 'And the peace of God, which passeth all understanding, shall keep your hearts and minds through Christ Jesus.' There's nothing wrong with being afraid of an attack. I'm frightened of it, too. It's only natural. But thank God for the peace He gives to His own about facing eternity."

Moments later, with everybody alerted, Chet and McClain rode past the Keegan wagon to ride point together. When they were about half a mile ahead of the train, both men glanced northward at Rawlins, basking in the late morning sun.

"Things look quiet over there," said McClain.

Chet nodded. "And I hope they stay quiet, too. You soldier boys may enjoy fighting Indians, but us wagon train boys don't cotton to it."

"It isn't something we enjoy, Chet, but—"

McClain's words were cut off at the sight of a covered wagon pulling away from a patch of trees off to the right and angling toward them.

"What's this?"

"I dunno," said Chet, "but we're about to find out."

As the wagon came to a halt, both riders drew up to the driver's side. Two men who looked to be in their thirties sat on the seat.

"Hello, gentlemen," said the driver. "We figure you're riding point for that wagon train back there."

"That we are," said Chet. "My name's Chet Place. I'm the wagon master. This here is McClain Reardon."

The driver smiled, nodded, and said, "I'm Ted Yoder, and this is my brother, Colin. We're from the St. Louis, Missouri, area. We were in a wagon train passing through here about ten days ago on our way to Oregon when Colin took sick. I had to take him into Rawlins so a doctor could take care of him."

"I'm sorry to hear that," Chet said.

"Colin hasn't felt like traveling until a couple of days ago. We've been waiting for another wagon train to come along in hopes of joining it. We spotted yours from Rawlins a little while ago and hurried out here to meet up with you. With the Cheyenne on the warpath, it's too dangerous to travel alone."

"That's for sure," said Chet. "A couple fellas alone wouldn't have a chance. I assume there's no one else in the wagon."

"No, sir. It's just us."

Chet nodded. "I've got a family in the wagon train who are from somewhere around St. Louis. Now, this train is going to

California, but you can join us till we reach the point in Idaho where the California Trail veers off from the Oregon Trail. No doubt you can join an Oregon-bound wagon train there."

Smiling broadly, Ted said, "We really appreciate this, Mr. Place. How much will it cost us to travel with you that far?"

Chet rubbed his chin, calculating the distance. "Be forty dollars."

"Fine," said Colin, standing up in the box and pulling his wallet out of his hip pocket. He handed Chet the money. "We really do thank you for taking us in."

Chet stuffed the bills in his shirt pocket. "Glad to help. You boys are wearing sidearms, I see. Do you have rifles?"

"Sure do," said Colin. "We know how to use them, too."

"Good. I saw a small band of Cheyenne warriors off to the north a while ago. They rode away, but they might be coming back with more of their pals. You'd best keep your eyes peeled and your guns ready. I'll put you right behind the lead wagon, which my son, Ken, drives. If I give signal to form a circle, just follow Ken."

The wagon train was drawing close. Chet trotted toward the lead wagon and Ken pulled rein as his father drew up. Chet explained about the new wagon joining the train, and that he had instructed the driver to pull in behind Ken.

Moments later, the Yoder brothers' wagon was in place. Ken led out, and as the wagons were rolling, Chet trotted to the rear of the train, turned around, and rode along the line, telling the people that he had taken on a new wagon.

When Chet drew up alongside the Hyland wagon he said, "Brodie, Jane, that new wagon we just took into the train is a couple of brothers from the St. Louis area."

"Oh, really?" said Brodie. "What's their names?"

"Ted and Colin Yoder."

Jane gasped, her eyes bulging, and Brodie's face darkened.

"What's the matter?" asked Chet.

"I don't want the Yoder brothers in this train, Chet," Brodie said.

"Why's that?"

Brodie's eyes flashed fire. "Because the Hylands and the Yoders have been feuding for three generations."

Chet adjusted himself in the saddle. "Look, I can't turn them away. I've already accepted their money. Besides, if they go on alone, they'll be vulnerable to the Cheyenne. They wouldn't stand a chance."

"How come they're alone?"

"They were in a wagon train but had to pull out because Colin was sick. Ted had to take him into Rawlins to a doctor. They've been waiting in Rawlins for another wagon train to come along."

"Then they can wait till the next one comes along," Brodie said.

Chet studied him for a moment. "I'll be right back." Even as he spoke, he nudged the horse into a trot and headed toward the front of the line.

Pulling alongside the Yoder wagon, Chet said, "Do you fellas recall I mentioned that I have a family in the train who are from somewhere around St. Louis?"

"Yes. I meant to ask you their name in case we might know them," said Ted, "but it slipped my mind with all that was going on."

"Well, their name is Hyland. Brodie and Jane Hyland."

Ted visibly paled.

Colin's eyes turned cold.

"The Hylands just told me about the longtime feud between your families. They want me to put you out of the train. Will you go back there with me so we can talk?"

The Yoder brothers looked at each other.

"What do you think?" Ted asked Colin.

The younger brother shrugged. "Guess we can try."

Ted set his eyes on Chet. "Okay, Mr. Place, we'll go with you."

Chet nodded. "Be right back. I'll tell Ken we're stopping the train for a few minutes."

The wagon master hurried his horse up to the lead wagon, told his son that he was stopping the train while he had a discussion with the new men and the Hylands. He gave the signal for the drivers to stop, then told Ken to hurry down the line and tell everyone it was only for a short time.

Brodie pulled rein when he saw Chet's signal. "Honey, he's gonna bring those no-good Yoders back here."

Jane moaned and shook her head. "I thought we'd escaped the Yoders when we left Missouri."

"You stay in the seat," said Brodie, climbing down. He planted his feet beside the wagon and felt his blood heat up as Chet walked toward them with the Yoder brothers flanking him.

As they drew up, Chet said, "I think we need to have a little talk."

"Nothing to talk about!" Brodie said. "I don't want anything to do with these low-down skunks! Jane and I won't tolerate them in the same wagon train with us!"

Chet stiffened. "I told you I already accepted payment from them."

"Then give it back! They can wait till the next wagon train comes along."

Colin drew a deep breath. His words came out slowly and controlled. "Brodie, we've already lost better than a week because I got sick. Our brother, Cecil, is in Medford, Oregon, waiting for us to come and take over his lumber business. Cecil is dying of stomach cancer. He needs us desperately, as do Louisa and their four children."

There was a moment of silence while Brodie tried to think of something to say.

"Look, Brodie," said Chet, "certainly you and Jane can put the feud aside in a case like this."

Brodie looked up at Jane, who sat on the seat like a statue, her hands clasped tightly. "What do you say, honey?"

Jane shrugged. "All right, Chet, but they'd better keep their distance from us."

Ted's said, "Jane, Brodie, I promise. We won't cause any trouble. Thank you both for not keeping us out of the wagon train."

Fixing them with a hard look, Brodie nodded, pulling his lips into a thin line.

"All right," said Chet. "Let's get this train moving."

The wagon train pulled out, with Chet riding point.

—⁓— —⁓— —⁓—

When the train stopped for the night and everyone was around the central fire after supper, Chet Place introduced the Yoder brothers. He explained about their having to pull out of their previous wagon train and about their brother Cecil in Oregon, who was dying of stomach cancer, and their need to get there as soon as possible.

Rya and McClain were sitting on the ground by the fire, their arms touching. At the mention of stomach cancer, Rya's blood ran cold. She was having the familiar pain in her abdomen at that very moment. It had subsided for most of the day, but had come back during supper.

McClain felt Rya's body tense up and turned to look at her with questioning eyes. She smiled at him, forcing her body to relax.

When McClain put his attention back on Chet, Rya prayed silently, *Oh please, dear Lord, don't let these pains in my stomach be cancer.*

McClain looked at her again. She gave him another smile, promising herself that she would see a doctor soon after they arrived in Sacramento.

A week passed without any more Indians being sighted.

When they made camp just outside the town of Green River, Chet Place called everyone together around the fire after supper. "I know you are all relieved that no Indian attack has come. I am, too. But we must all keep a sharp eye. Sometimes the hostiles will follow a wagon train for days, keeping out of sight, then they'll attack when they think the train is most vulnerable."

There were fearful glances between family members at Chet's words.

He went on. "Now, in the morning, most of us will be going into town to beef up our supplies. I want you to go in small groups of no more than three or four families. That way, those who are still here with the wagons can watch for any sign of approaching hostiles. The Indians never attack a town, but they might come after the wagon train, even though it's close to Green River. So let's all be alert."

The next morning, all kept a close watch as the small groups alternated going into town.

The Hylands waited until they knew the Yoder brothers had gone and returned. Rya and McClain went in with the Keegans, the McCrums, and Betty Hilmes. When they reached Main Street, the group stopped and looked up and down the dusty thoroughfare.

"We need to go to the general store," said Archie.

"I guess that's where all of us are headed," said Dorothy.

"I need to go to that boot shop up there," McClain said, pointing with his chin. "The heel on my left boot is coming loose. Rya, do you want to go with me, or would you rather stay with the group?"

"I need to mail this letter to my parents. How about I just meet you at the general store, darling?"

"Okay," said McClain, heading up the street. "It shouldn't take long."

As Rya drew near the post office, she noted a physician's shingle hanging in front of a small white clapboard building.

I wonder if I should slip in there and talk to the doctor about my stomach pains. I could probably get it done while McClain is getting his boot fixed. I just can't let him know how much pain I'm having.

Rya was about to move toward the doctor's office when she saw the door open, and two men came out. One was obviously a farmer or a rancher. The other was dressed in a dark suit and tie and carried a black medical bag. The doctor hurriedly climbed into a buggy that stood at the boardwalk, and the other man mounted his horse at the nearby hitch rail. Both put their horses to a gallop and headed out of town.

Guess that takes care of that idea, Rya thought. *I'll just wait till we get to Sacramento.*

Thinking of her new home brought a sweet peace to her heart, and she hurried on to the post office.

That night after supper, Brodie and Jane Hyland were standing at the tailgate of their wagon, going through the goods they had purchased in town that day. They heard footsteps approaching, and turned to see the Yoder brothers drawing up by the light of a nearby fire.

Brodie took hold of Jane's hand as both of them gave the Yoders icy stares.

"Brodie, Jane," said Ted, "can we talk to you?"

"About what?" snapped Brodie.

"Well, it's about the age-old feud. It started long before the four of us were born. Colin and I have come to ask if we can't—well, you know…just bury the hatchet."

Brodie scowled, his features hard. "I'd like to bury the hatchet…in both of your heads! Get out of here!"

Ted and Colin looked at each other, then walked away.

At the close of the next day, Chet Place gathered the people around the fire. "Well, folks, we're now within three days of Fort Bridger. I know that some of you weren't able to get things you needed in Green River because the general store was a bit low on some items. If you need more supplies, there's a well-stocked general store in Fort Bridger. I usually stop my trains for a couple days there just to let everybody get a little rest. With the army right there, we don't have to be concerned about Indians attacking."

When it was time to pull out the next morning, the wagon train was abuzz with excitement about the upcoming stopover at Fort Bridger.

At the Jensen wagon, Dick had harnessed the team, and was hooking them onto the doubletree when he saw Chet Place coming his way. He smiled as Chet drew up. "I know what you want, Chet. You want to borrow Blackie so McClain can ride point with you again."

Chet grinned sheepishly. "You've got me figured out, don't you?"

"I guess so. Since McClain is experienced with Indians, and

we're in the heart of Cheyenne country, you like having him up front with you."

"You hit the nail on the head, Dick. He...well, he seems to have a sixth sense about Indians. I just feel better having him at my side, and I sort of get the idea the people feel the same way. Several have commented about it."

"Chet, he's welcome to ride my horse anytime. He's tied to the rear of the wagon. Take him."

McClain was standing at the Larkin wagon in conversation with Vance and Rhonda when he caught sight of the wagon master coming his way, leading Dick Jensen's black gelding.

Vance chuckled. "Looks like you've got a steady job riding point with the boss, McClain."

"You're pretty smart, Vance. How'd you figure that out?"

Just as Chet drew up, the black set eyes on McClain, whinnied, and bobbed his head.

Chet snickered. "McClain, it's not hard to tell that this horse likes you. Funny...I was just walking past the Jensen wagon, and this big black fella snorted and said, 'Hey, Chet, I'd sure like to carry McClain today so he can ride point with you.'"

McClain stepped up and stroked the gelding's long face. "Blackie, how come you talk to Chet but you don't talk to me?"

The horse blew and shook his head, rattling the metal rings on the bridle.

Chet laughed. "I guess you got the message, didn't you? Blackie will only talk to me. C'mon. Let's get this train moving."

Moments later, the wagon train was in motion with Chet Place and McClain Reardon riding point. The sound of hooves clopping on the soft earth and the squeak of wagon wheels filled the air as the train rolled steadily westward. Every eye was peeled as the people kept a vigilant search around them for any sign of Indians.

Up front, Chet and McClain kept themselves about a half mile in front of the lead wagon. Chet was asking questions about McClain's life at Fort Steele when suddenly McClain stiffened in the saddle.

"What is it?" Chet asked.

McClain stood up in the stirrups and let his eyes flit across the rolling prairie. "I…I think trouble is in the air. I just had a feeling we're being watched by hostile eyes."

Chet's head moved from side to side as he searched the area. "I don't see anyth—"

Suddenly they both saw a party of Cheyenne topping a hill off to the left about five hundred yards away. They drew rein, stared toward the two riders, then looked at the wagon train.

"They're going to attack!" Chet said. "Let's get the wagons in a circle!"

McClain touched his arm. "They're not going to attack yet. Best we keep moving."

"How do you know?"

"By the way they're sitting their horses. They play their psychological game first."

"What do you mean?"

"Well, you don't see Indians unless they want you to see them. Sometimes it's simply to make white men nervous, and they're not planning an attack at all. Other times, they like to get your nerves on edge before they attack. Since we don't know their plans, let's ease our way back to the wagons so we can make sure everybody understands what I've just explained to you."

"Whatever you say, my friend," said Chet. "This is exactly why I wanted you riding point with me."

Casually trotting their horses back to the wagon, Chet and McClain split up and rode alongside the train, making the explanation. Everyone in the wagons had already spotted the Indians on the distant hill.

With everyone admonished to stay alert, Chet and McClain once again took up their positions at the head of the train, but this time, they stayed within thirty yards of the lead wagon.

They watched as the Cheyenne warriors rode off the hill and disappeared. Within a half hour, they appeared again. This time, they were about a mile to the south, riding parallel to the wagon train single file, obviously making sure the white travelers could see them. Nerves were strung tight in the wagons as the occupants kept a close watch on the Indians.

The Cheyenne party continued to parallel the wagon train as

the morning wore on. As it was coming up on noon, the long line of warriors began to angle closer to the train.

"What do you think of that?" Chet asked McClain.

"Hard to tell. It may just be more of their little game, designed simply to frighten us."

"Or they're getting closer so they can attack."

"Can't rule that out. Let's see just how close they come. If they come any closer than a half mile, we'll put the wagons in a circle."

Shortly after McClain had spoken, the Cheyenne were moving parallel with them once again, at a point just about a half mile in distance.

The afternoon dragged interminably while a sense of strain closed down on the people of the wagon train. The sun beat down, making the prairie bright. The creak of saddle leather, the clink of harness metal, the squeak of wagon wheels, and the muffled beat of hooves on the soft floor of the prairie was jarring in the uneasy silence.

Once again, the line of warriors slowly began to angle closer to the wagon train.

"See that, McClain?" Chet asked.

"Yes. And see the war paint on their faces? Let's put the wagons in a circle."

Chet and McClain wheeled their horses and trotted back to the train, with Chet signaling for the wagons to form a circle.

Even as Ken Place began circling the lead wagon, everyone heard the far-off whoops and shouts of the Cheyenne reaching them on the wings of the warm afternoon breeze.

The hostiles were galloping at top speed toward the wagons, waving their feathered rifles and barking like wild dogs.

MAIL ORDER BRIDE SERIES
NO. 9
1877
USA
AL & JOANNA LACY

KEN PLACE WAS ABLE TO LEAD THE WAGONS into a full circle before the charging Cheyenne were within firing range.

The men quickly saw to it that the women and children were lying flat on the floors of the wagons, then chose the spots where they would do battle against the war party. Some were bellied down beneath the wagons, while others positioned themselves between them. The children were crying and their mothers were doing their best to quiet them.

When McClain had made sure Rya was flat on the floor of the Keegan wagon next to Dorothy, he took a position at the rear, between it and the next wagon. Burt was bellied down underneath the wagon, rifle ready.

The Cheyenne were drawing near and the heavy beat of the galloping horses vibrated the earth beneath the wagons. It was like a hundred drums beating out a savage rhythm. When the Indians were within firing range, they bent low over their horses' backs and put rifles to their shoulders. At the same time, the men of the wagon train made ready for the coming attack.

Chet Place had asked McClain Reardon to give the command to fire when it was best to begin. McClain was sure the warriors would spread out and go on both sides of the circle. Just as he shouted for the men to commence firing and unleashed his own rifle, they divided.

The air came alive to the menacing crack of rifles and the whisper of hot lead. Bullets chewed into wagons, splintering wood and ripping canvas tops. Amid the roar of guns and the thunder of hooves, the shrill whoops of Cheyenne warriors echoed across the prairie.

A blanket of terror settled over the women and children in the wagons. Gun smoke filled the air. Through the clouds of blue-white smoke and the haze of brown dust, the men blazed away as they saw the painted faces and the bronzed bodies of the warriors on their pintos.

In the Keegan wagon, Rya and Dorothy lay flat, faces down, while they held hands and prayed. Cheyenne bullets ripped through the canvas above them.

Ted Yoder was firing from between their wagon and the lead wagon. Colin was underneath, blasting away at the whooping warriors. Not far away in the circle, Brodie Hyland was hunkered between his wagon and the next one.

Ted fired from his position and saw his bullet drop a warrior from the back of his pinto. He caught sight of another one through the dust and smoke, raised his rifle, and squeezed the trigger. The hammer made a dead, clicking sound, and Ted stepped behind his wagon while he reloaded.

Just as he reached into his pocket for more cartridges, he saw a Cheyenne warrior sneak inside the circle, behind Brodie Hyland, who was down on one knee. Ted dashed that direction, shouting, "Brodie! Look out!"

Brodie heard Ted's cry and whirled around to see the Indian practically on him, raising a long-bladed knife. Ted swung his empty rifle, striking the Indian solidly in the head. He went down and Ted hit him again, finishing him off.

Brodie's face was sheet white. Rising to his feet, he looked at Ted with tender eyes. "Thank you. You saved my life."

Ted smiled and ran back to the Yoder wagon.

While McClain Reardon was reloading his rifle, he called toward the bed of the wagon, which was covered with tattered canvas. "Rya! Dorothy! You all right?"

"Yes, we are!" came Rya's voice. "We're praying for a miracle!"

McClain thought, *We're going to need one if this lasts much longer.* Aloud, he shouted back, "Keep praying!"

With the magazine full again, McClain jacked a cartridge into the chamber, moved around the corner of the wagon, and put the rifle to his shoulder. A fresh wave of mounted warriors was swarming down on his side of the circle.

McClain had noted the Cheyenne chief among the warriors two or three times, but this time, as he looked along the barrel, he brought the warrior who wore the chief's headdress into his sights.

What he saw stunned him. He was focusing on a familiar face.

At the same instant, the chief saw McClain's face.

McClain had him in his sights, but could not bring himself to squeeze the trigger.

Sky Eagle wheeled his horse about and signaled for his warriors to pull away. He shouted something in the Cheyenne language to a subchief on the other side of the wagon circle and quickly led all of his warriors across the prairie at a full gallop. Even the riderless pintos followed. Within seconds, Sky Eagle and his warriors topped a gentle rise and vanished from sight.

Some of the men who had been fighting close to McClain had observed the incident. As Rya and Dorothy were shakily climbing down from the wagon bed, the men gathered to McClain. One of them was Dick Jensen, who said, "McClain, why did that chief look so surprised when he saw you? Why did he immediately call off the attack?"

Rya moved up close to the man she loved, her features pale. McClain set tender eyes on her and pulled her close to him, then looked at Dick. "That chief's name is Sky Eagle. I once saved his life. Apparently he couldn't find it in himself to make war against this wagon train because I'm part of it."

Chet and Ken Place had drawn up with others and heard McClain's words. Chet was about to comment when suddenly a bloodcurdling scream pierced the air. Every eye went to Dorothy, who was on her knees beneath the wagon, her fingers clutching Burt's shirt. "He's dead!" she wailed. "Burt's dead!"

The sun was lowering in the west as the people of the wagon train stood in a circle around Burt Keegan's grave outside the wagons.

Five dead Indians lay sprawled where they had fallen on the prairie during the attack. A sixth—the one killed by Ted Yoder—lay just outside the wagon circle where his body had been dragged. Three men of the wagon train had been wounded, but Burt was the only one who had been killed. The wounded ones were being cared for in their wagons by their wives.

Chet Place had asked McClain Reardon to read Scripture over the grave and say a few words. McClain's heart was heavy as he stood at the head of the grave and read from 1 Corinthians 15. He did what he could to make sure everyone within the sound of his voice knew how to be saved. He told the crowd what a kind man Burt was, and that he died bravely trying to do his part to protect everyone in the wagon train.

McClain closed in prayer, asking God to be especially close to Dorothy in her grief and sorrow and to spare the lives of the three men who had been wounded in the battle. When he closed the prayer, he headed for Rya, who was standing beside Dorothy, holding her hand. Heads hanging low, the others started filing back inside the circle.

As Ted and Colin Yoder moved inside the circle and headed for their wagon, Colin said, "If we'd tried traveling alone, that bunch of Indians would have killed us in a hurry, big brother."

"For sure," agreed Ted.

Colin was about to say something else when a familiar voice came from behind them. "Ted, could Jane and I see you for a moment?"

The Yoder brothers turned around to see Brodie and Jane Hyland drawing up.

"Sure," said Ted.

Tears misted Brodie's eyes. "I want to thank you again for saving my life. There's no question that Indian would have killed me."

Jane sniffed and thumbed a tear from her cheek. "Yes, thank you. It was a very brave and unselfish thing for you to do, Ted. Especially in view of the way we have treated you. We're sorry."

"Very sorry," added Brodie.

Ted smiled. "Then the feud is over?"

Brodie offered his hand. When Ted gripped it, Brodie said,

"For this part of the Hyland and Yoder families, it is indeed over."

"Good!" said Colin. "I think we should tell Chet. This has been a real worry for him."

"All right," said Brodie. "He's over there by his wagon. Let's go tell him."

When all others had gone back inside the circle, Dorothy Keegan stood over Burt's grave, weeping. Rya was on one side of her and McClain on the other.

Dorothy dabbed at her tears with a handkerchief. "Oh, Rya, McClain, if only Burt had listened to us. He said he had plenty of time to get saved." She sniffed, choked up for a moment, then added, "He didn't know it, but there was so little time."

Rya squeezed her hand.

Dorothy turned to McClain and looked at him through her tears. "I keep thinking of what you said about the hourglass. If only Burt would have heeded your plea to open his heart to Jesus."

McClain bit his lower lip and nodded, staring down at the fresh mound of dirt.

Rya and McClain stayed with Dorothy until she was ready to leave the grave, then each held onto her as they walked her back inside the circle. Several people spoke words of condolence to her as the trio made their way toward the Keegan wagon. Each time, she tried to smile as she thanked them.

Across the circle, they saw an elated Chet Place in conversation with the Yoder brothers and the Hylands. He was smiling and shaking their hands.

"I wonder what that's about," Rya said.

"Maybe the Yoders and the Hylands settled their differences," McClain said. "Vance Larkin told me he saw Ted save Brodie from being stabbed by that Indian who got into the circle."

Rya's eyes widened. "Oh, so that's what happened. While we were making our way out to the grave, I heard a couple of the women talking about Ted having killed that Indian. I didn't realize he had saved Brodie's life."

As they drew up to the Keegan wagon, McClain said, "Dorothy, would you like for me to drive your wagon for the rest of the trip?"

Dorothy lifted dull, reddened eyes to his. "That would be wonderful. Thank you."

"Dorothy, you get in the wagon and lie down," said Rya. "I'll fix supper."

"I'm really not hungry," Dorothy replied softly. "Why don't you fix supper for the two of you?"

"All right."

McClain helped Dorothy into the bed of the wagon, then helped Rya in so she could get her settled before starting supper.

Suddenly the loud voice of Ken Place cut the air from where he stood by the lead wagon. "McClain! That Cheyenne chief is coming back all by himself!"

"I'd better see about this," said McClain to the women, and hurried outside the circle.

Chet Place was on his way, followed by several of the men. They moved outside the circle and stepped up behind McClain and Ken Place. Sky Eagle was trotting his pinto toward them, holding a white flag that flapped in the breeze. He had no weapon. Some of the women crowded between a couple of the wagons, looking on with curiosity. Rya was among them.

Sky Eagle drew up, pulling rein. He wore only a loincloth and the bright-colored headdress, whose feathers had been taken from birds of a dozen plumages. The red-gold of the setting sun emphasized the copper of his skin. His black eyes stared out over high cheekbones.

Fixing McClain with those dark eyes, Sky Eagle said, "Sergeant McClain Reardon, Sky Eagle asks for permission to dismount."

McClain looked at Chet, who nodded his assent.

"You may dismount," said McClain.

Sky Eagle slid from the pinto's back, holding the white flag in his left hand, and took a step toward McClain. "Sky Eagle has no weapon, Sergeant McClain Reardon. I come in peace." As he spoke, he offered his right hand, and he and McClain shook hands Indian-style.

"Sky Eagle wishes to make apology for attacking wagon train with Sergeant McClain Reardon aboard. If he had known the man who saved his life was in wagon train, Sky Eagle would not have led his warriors to attack. Black Hawk die since the day you kept your fellow soldier from killing Sky Eagle. Sky Eagle now chief of village.

"Cheyenne and other tribes continue to suffer at hands of white men. They take our land, kill our buffalo and deer, attack our villages. Now, they determined to put Indian on reservations. Confine us. This why we attack wagon trains, farms, ranches."

McClain nodded. "I understand, Sky Eagle."

The young chief looked into McClain's eyes. "Sky Eagle owe his life to Sergeant McClain Reardon. Wish to protect his wagon train from attacks of other Cheyenne and other tribes. If Sergeant McClain Reardon wish, Sky Eagle and warriors will escort wagon train until it cross into Idaho."

Chet Place spoke up quickly. "Sky Eagle, I am the wagon master. My name is Chet Place. I will gladly accept your offer."

The chief looked at McClain.

"As the wagon master, Mr. Place has the authority to accept your offer, Sky Eagle," McClain said.

Sky Eagle nodded. "When you plan to move on?"

"Tomorrow morning. We must pull out at sunrise."

The chief nodded again. "Sky Eagle will be here at rise of sun with many warriors."

"All of us really appreciate that, Chief," said Chet, offering his hand.

They shook hands Indian-style, then Sky Eagle turned to McClain and shook hands with him again, saying, "Sergeant McClain Reardon is Sky Eagle's white brother."

McClain smiled. "I'm honored."

The chief almost smiled. "Sky Eagle has some warriors watching from hill," he said, pointing to the hill they had ridden over earlier. "They wait for signal so can come pick up dead warriors."

"Go ahead, Chief," spoke up the wagon master.

The young chief turned and waved toward the hill. Four warriors rode in, each leading a riderless pinto. The six dead Cheyenne were draped over the pintos' backs, and Sky Eagle and his warriors slowly rode away.

Soon people were milling around inside the circle. Some had shattered nerves, but there was relief that Sky Eagle had made the offer and that Chet Place had accepted it. Chet and Ken Place visited the wagons where the wounded men were being cared for.

When Rya climbed into the Keegan wagon, she explained about the Cheyenne escort to Dorothy, who was lying down. Dorothy showed her relief at the news, then they talked about how they had prayed for a miracle while the battle was going on and agreed that God gave the very miracle the wagon train needed by bringing the fighting to a halt.

Dorothy's lips began to tremble and tears filled her eyes. "Oh, Rya, I know it was God's time for Burt to die, but...if only...if only—"

Rya took both of Dorothy's hands in her own. "I know, honey. If only Burt had been saved."

Dorothy broke down and sobbed.

Rya stroked Dorothy's head, thinking how hard it was to give comfort to a Christian who had lost an unsaved loved one.

After supper, Chet Place gathered the people together around the central fire and gave them a report on the three wounded men, saying they seemed to be stabilized.

"I want all of you to know," he said, running his gaze over their faces, "that I've told the wives of these men that there's a good doctor in Fort Bridger, and we'll be there in two days."

As Chet walked away from the fire and began talking to people who had questions, McClain noticed that Rya had her hand on her midsection.

Rya smiled at McClain. "Well, darling, I guess I'd better see to Dorothy. Maybe when you walk me to the wagon, we can sneak a good-night kiss."

McClain's eyes lit up. "I'll go for that."

She took hold of his hand, ready for their short walk to the Keegan wagon.

He gripped it firmly, but when she started that direction, he pulled her to him.

Rya's eyebrows arched. "Yes?"

"Are you having that pain again?"

"Why do you ask?"

"Because I saw your hand pressed against your stomach just a moment ago."

"Oh. I guess I was doing it absentmindedly."

"So it was hurting you?"

"Well, yes. It still is a little."

McClain said firmly, "Miss Garrett, when we get to Fort Bridger, you are going to let the doctor there check you."

Rya noted the tone of authority in McClain's voice. Smiling through her pain, she said, "Yes, sir!"

McClain chuckled. "You might as well get used to it, sweet lady. When we are husband and wife, I'm going to take good care of you."

"I wouldn't have it any other way."

Dawn was breaking on the eastern horizon when Rya awoke in her bedroll at the foot of the Keegan wagon. Rubbing sleep from her eyes, she raised her head and looked to see if Dorothy was still asleep. There was enough light coming through the tattered canvas cover to see that Dorothy's bed was unoccupied.

Hurriedly, Rya dressed and climbed out of the wagon, feeling quite sure where she would find her friend. As she moved between the wagons, she said, "Please, Lord, give me wisdom as I try to help her."

Suddenly, she found herself facing Vance Larkin, who had been on watch for the past three hours.

"Oh. Good morning, Mr. Larkin."

"Good morning to you, Miss Rya. You're probably looking for Mrs. Keegan."

"Yes. I just woke up and found her bed empty."

Vance pointed toward Burt's grave, where Dorothy knelt, her head bent low. "I've been watching her. She's been there for about two hours. Figured she wanted to be alone. You know."

"Yes. And I appreciate that. But I'd better go to her now."

Rya made her way toward the grave.

Dorothy heard her footsteps in the grass and turned to see who was coming. When she saw it was Rya, she dabbed at the tears in her eyes and put her head down again.

Rya knelt beside Dorothy and put an arm around her. "Honey, I'm so sorry."

Dorothy turned, buried her face against Rya's chest, and sobbed.

When the sobbing subsided, and Dorothy was wiping tears and thanking Rya for being such a good friend to her, they heard excited voices in the camp. Both women turned to see Chief Sky Eagle and a large number of warriors riding across the prairie toward the wagon train.

Rya rose to her feet. "We need to get back to the wagon."

Dorothy nodded, and Rya took her hand to help her up. When Dorothy was on her feet, she paused over the grave for a few seconds, then they walked slowly toward the circle.

As they drew near the wagons, Rya said, "You remember that McClain is driving your wagon?"

"Yes. Bless him."

"While we're riding in the wagon seat today, I want to read you some Scriptures that will help you in this difficult time."

Dorothy smiled at her. "I'd like that."

"I meant to tell you that I asked McClain if Fort Bridger has a store that sells Bibles. He said he heard that Cooper's General Store carries Bibles. I'm going to buy you a Bible when we get to Fort Bridger."

"I desperately want my own Bible, honey, but I can buy it."

"No. I want to present it to you as a gift."

With tears shining in her eyes, Dorothy said, "You are so sweet, Rya. Thank you."

Sky Eagle and his forty warriors drew up to the wagon train and were met by McClain Reardon, Chet Place, and a few other men.

Chet explained to the chief that some of the people had yet to finish their breakfast, and when they did, the wagon train would be ready to roll. While he was speaking, he let his gaze take in the forty warriors. "You brought a small army, Sky Eagle."

From his perch on the pinto's back, Sky Eagle nodded. "Yes. It is Sky Eagle's plan to place ten warriors behind wagon train, ten on each side, and ten in front with Chet Place and Sky Eagle riding ahead of them."

Chet glanced at McClain, grinned, then said to the chief, "I like that plan. Thank you, again, for providing this escort."

"You can thank Sergeant McClain Reardon, Chet Place. It is because he saved my life that I provide this escort." He paused. "It is all right if Sky Eagle dismounts?"

"Of course," said Chet.

As the chief slid from his pinto's back, he looked at McClain. "I ask favor."

McClain smiled. "Name it."

"Sky Eagle wishes to present his white brother to his warriors."

"Well, all right."

Taking McClain by the arm, Sky Eagle walked him to a spot where all the warriors would get a good view of him. He explained to them that this was the man who saved him from being killed by a white soldier when he lay wounded after a battle with soldiers from Fort Steele. He then told them that Sergeant Reardon had carried him on his horse all the way to the village so Tall Tree could tend to him.

The warriors looked on McClain as Sky Eagle told his story. Some remembered the occasion. Others had heard about it.

Soon the wagon train was moving out with the Cheyenne warriors positioned as planned by Sky Eagle. The chief and the wagon master rode out front.

McClain drove the Keegan wagon. Rya sat next to him with Dorothy at her side.

As they passed Burt's grave, Dorothy's eyes were fixed on it, her lips moving silently. Rya gently placed her hand over both of Dorothy's, which were clasped tightly in her lap.

As the grave passed from view, the grieving widow leaned over the edge of the seat, still looking back in that direction. She breathed a deep sigh—which was almost a groan—and a shudder ran through her. Rya tightened her grip on Dorothy's hands.

Soon Rya felt the tenseness leave Dorothy's body.

Dorothy turned, straightened herself on the seat, and looked into Rya's eyes. Though tears streaked the widow's cheeks, there was a God-given peace in her aching heart. Dorothy then fixed her eyes on the western horizon where her uncertain future awaited her.

Rya let go of Dorothy's hands and picked up her Bible. "Let's read now."

A thin smile graced Dorothy's lips. "Yes."

As the wagon groaned and squeaked on the prairie's rough surface, Rya showed Dorothy one Scripture after another to give her comfort, strength, and to increase her faith in the Lord's love and care for her.

Later, when Rya had closed her Bible and put it away, she turned to McClain. "Dorothy and I talked about it last night. We'd love to hear the story of how you saved Sky Eagle's life."

TWO DAYS LATER, LIEUTENANT CHRIS COOPER was leading his patrol unit of a dozen men along the west bank of Black's Fork of the Green River, heading due north toward Fort Bridger. The sun was driving its heat down from a brassy sky.

The uneven rooftops of the town were coming into view in the distance as one of the troopers raised a sleeve and wiped the sweat out of his eyes. "Lieutenant, since Chet Place's wagon train is supposed to be showing up any day now, I imagine you're on needles and pins."

Another laughed. "Wouldn't you be, Rex, if you had a mail order bride comin' your way on that wagon train?"

The others laughed.

The dark-haired lieutenant had just uncorked his canteen. He took a long pull, wiped his mouth with the back of his hand, and smiled. "Well, gentlemen, I admit I'm on needles and pins. I'm excited that Betty is coming, but I'm somewhat nervous, too."

Another trooper said, "I think we understand that, Lieutenant."

Sergeant Keith Morley, who rode next to Cooper, said, "Lieutenant, do you have a picture of Betty? I mean, you keep talking about what a good-looker she is. You must have a picture of her."

Chris turned around on his McLellan saddle, unbuckled a saddlebag, and took out a small photograph. Flashing it at Morley, he said, "Here, feast your eyes on this."

The sergeant reached out his hand. "Let me get a close look."

"Okay, but be careful. It's the only one I've got."

Morley studied the photograph intently, then looked at his lieutenant. "She really is a looker, isn't she?"

"Well, pass it around," came a voice from the column behind. "Let the rest of us see what she looks like."

The picture was passed around, and each man had a favorable comment about Betty.

Chris was slipping the photograph back into the saddlebag when one of the troopers said, "Lieutenant, look out there!"

There was a wagon train to the north, angling in the direction of Fort Bridger and surrounded by painted warriors.

"Lieutenant, what do you make of that?"

Chris signaled for them to halt as he pulled his binoculars from a saddlebag. "Strange, to say the least." He quickly raised the binoculars to his eyes.

"What is it, sir?" asked Sergeant Morley.

"I've never seen anything like this! Those are Cheyenne, and they're actually escorting that wagon train. I can make out Chet Place there in the lead, riding beside the one wearing the chief's headdress. I don't recognize him. Must be a chief from farther east."

He ran the binoculars back along the train. "This really is amazing. Some of the people on the wagons are talking to the Indians riding close to them. They all seem to be at peace with each other!" He lowered the binoculars. "Come on. Betty is in one of those wagons!"

As the wagon train neared the area where Chet Place would lead them to make camp, his attention was drawn southward to the cavalry unit galloping toward them.

"We've got company, Sky Eagle," said Chet, pointing toward the dust cloud raised by the galloping hooves.

"Umm," said the chief, nodding. "Soldiers from Fort Bridger, I am sure."

"You wait here," said Chet. "I'll go meet them and explain my Cheyenne escort."

Sky Eagle joined those in the train who watched the wagon master galloping toward the oncoming cavalry patrol.

They were about two hundred yards from the wagon train when Chris raised a hand to stop his men as Chet drew near. "Howdy, Lieutenant Cooper!" Chet said.

"Howdy to you. Would you mind telling me what's going on up there? Who are those Cheyenne?"

"That's Chief Sky Eagle, from the Fort Steele area."

"Sky Eagle? Isn't he Chief Black Hawk's son?"

"Right, though Black Hawk has died. Sky Eagle and his warriors are escorting my train all the way to the Idaho border to protect us from any other tribes who might attack us, or even some Cheyenne who could have it in mind."

"How did you manage this?"

Chet grinned. "It wasn't me who managed it, Lieutenant. It was a friend of yours—Sergeant McClain Reardon, though he's a civilian now."

A smile spread over Chris's face. "He's riding in your train?"

"Yep. On his way to California to get married to a little gal who's also in the train."

"Well, isn't that something? And you say it was Serg—I mean, McClain who arranged this Cheyenne escort for you?"

Chet took a few minutes to tell the lieutenant and his men how it came about that Chief Sky Eagle and his warriors were escorting the train.

Chris shook his head in wonderment. "So McClain saved Sky Eagle's life some two years ago, and it resulted in stopping the attack on your train a few days ago and bought you protection through Cheyenne, Blackfoot, and Shoshoni territory. That's amazing!"

"To say the least!" said Chet.

"Well, it'll be good to see McClain again."

Chet chuckled, and his brow furrowed. "But isn't there someone else in that wagon train you want to see even more?"

Chris's face beamed. "Which wagon is she in?"

Twisting around in the saddle, Chet looked back at the wagon train, noting that people were out of their wagons, watching him and the army unit. "Start with my wagon and count till you get to wagon number six. Betty's riding in that wagon with Archie and Della McCrum."

Chris looked at Keith Morley. "Sergeant, bring the men on in. I've got to see Betty right now!"

With that, the young lieutenant put his horse to a gallop and headed for the sixth wagon in the train.

Archie, Della, and Betty were standing together beside the McCrum wagon watching the scene out on the prairie.

"One of them's riding this way," said Archie. "Looks like an officer from here."

Betty's heart seemed to leap into her throat. "You don't suppose it's—"

"I've got a feeling it is," said Della.

As the galloping man in the dark blue uniform drew within about sixty yards, Betty's hands went to her mouth. "Oh, it is! It's Chris! He looks just like his picture."

Archie chuckled. "Seems he's in a hurry to meet you."

The Cheyenne warriors who were in Chris's path moved their pintos to make room for him. When he drew to a halt, Betty took a couple of steps toward him.

Dismounting quickly, Chris set his gaze on the comely blond. "Betty!"

She took another step, cutting the distance between them to some ten feet. "Hello, Chris."

Chris hesitantly opened his arms, and Betty met his embrace. Suddenly he saw McClain Reardon hurrying toward them, sided by a young woman with the sunshine dancing on her auburn hair.

McClain and Chris shook hands, saying how good it was to see each other. McClain introduced Rya, telling him they had not seen each other for fourteen years, then by the Lord's hand, they met on the wagon train and were going to get married when they reached Sacramento.

Chris congratulated them.

Rya offered her hand to Chris, saying she was glad to meet him.

He took it gently and said, "Miss Garrett, you are getting a good man!"

"Yes," said Rya, looking at the man she loved. "I know."

Chet Place and the cavalry unit were drawing up.

Chris said, "Chet will want to get the train closer to Fort Bridger, Betty. May I help you into the wagon seat?"

Betty gave him her hand. Chris helped her up to the seat then reluctantly let go of her. "I'll see you where the wagon train makes camp near Fort Bridger. I have to report to Colonel Kirkland and attend a brief officers' meeting, then I'll be there. I want to take you to the fort to meet my family."

"I'll wait anxiously," she said, smiling.

McClain and Rya returned to the Keegan wagon, and with Chet Place and Sky Eagle out front, the wagon train moved to Chet's chosen spot just outside the town. There, he announced that they would not hit the trail again until day after tomorrow. He wanted everyone to get some rest.

The Cheyenne warriors found a spot close by and prepared to make their own camp.

The three wounded men were carried into town, and some of the other people left their wagons to buy supplies.

Archie McCrum was one of the men who helped carry the wounded men into town, and Della stayed with Betty, who was expecting Chris. Betty took a few minutes to wash the trail dust from her hands and face and to touch up her hair. Then she slipped out of her brown wrinkled and dusty homespun cotton dress and put on a clean blue dimity dress, dotted with white flowers. She ran a hand over the skirt of the dress and said, "I wish it didn't have these wrinkles."

Della laughed. "Don't you worry so much, girl. Remember, Chris's family traveled this same trail a few years ago. They know all about the hardships and conditions that go with it."

Della's wise words calmed Betty some, but nothing could calm her wildly beating heart.

Hannah Cooper Kirkland was busy mopping the floor in the kitchen of the commandant's two-story house, humming a hymn. She blew a wisp of dark brown hair off her forehead as she dipped the mop into the bucket of sudsy water and moved to another spot. She paused when she heard the screen door at the front of the house open and close.

"Mama!" came the voice of her oldest son. "Where are you?"

"I'm in the kitchen, honey!"

"Could you come out here, please? It's very important!"

Quickly drying her hands on her apron, Hannah hurried into the hall and made her way toward the front of the house. "I'm coming, Chris," she said as she neared the foyer. "What are you so excited ab—"

Her words came to a sudden halt when she saw that her son was not alone. "Oh! Betty!" she gasped, and went to her, arms open wide. Hannah kissed her cheek. "It's so wonderful that you're here!"

Betty squeezed her tight. "Thank you!"

Tears misted Hannah's eyes as she held Betty at arm's length then glanced at her son. "Chris, she's even more beautiful than her picture!"

"I agree, Mama."

Betty blushed. "You're both so kind."

Chris ran his gaze toward the back of the house. "Are the kids here?"

"No, but they should be real soon. Patty Ruth is over at the Fordhams with Belinda. I expect her any minute. B.J. took Eddie over to the corral to help him curry your daddy's horse. They should be about finished by now."

Suddenly they heard young voices. Hannah stepped to the door and saw B.J. and Eddie coming toward the house with Patty Ruth. "It's all three!" she said excitedly.

Betty received a warm welcome from Chris's brothers and his youngest sister. Betty immediately felt a kinship with them.

"Mama," said Chris, "there's somebody else in the wagon train that you know."

"Oh? Who?"

"McClain Reardon."

"McClain? What's he doing in the wagon train?"

"Well, he's out of the army now. He's on his way to Sacramento to take a job with Colonel Lamont in the construction business. Only, he's not a colonel anymore."

"Yes. I heard they have a new commandant at Fort Steele."

"And something else—McClain has his fiancée with him. They're going to get married after they arrive in Sacramento. Her name's Rya Garrett. McClain said he's anxious to see all of you and for you to meet Rya. She seems to be a fine Christian young lady. They've known each other since they were children back in Virginia."

"I'm happy for him," said Hannah, "and we'll look forward to seeing him and meeting Rya. Sometimes the wagon trains stay over a day or two when they reach this point on the trail. Do you know how long this one will be here?"

"The wagon master told us they'd leave day after tomorrow," Betty said.

"Good! Tell you what, Chris—"

Heavy footsteps were heard on the porch.

"It's Daddy!" said Patty Ruth, and rushed to meet her stepfather.

Colonel Dane Kirkland was introduced to Betty, and he welcomed her to Fort Bridger. He told her he was looking forward to the wedding, when he could welcome her into the family.

"Mama, you were about to say something when we heard Dad coming," said Chris.

"Oh, yes! Since the wagon train will be here all day tomorrow, I'd like to prepare a special dinner tomorrow evening to welcome Betty and invite McClain and Rya."

Betty's face beamed. "Oh, Mrs. Kirkland, I'm honored."

Hannah hugged her again. "As soon as you and Chris are married, you can call me Mama like the rest of this brood does."

Betty smiled. "Yes, ma'am. I sure will." She put a finger to the corner of her mouth. "Ah…Mrs. Kirkland…"

"Yes, dear?"

"Our wagon train was attacked by Cheyenne a few days ago,

and…well, we had one man killed in the attack. His widow just became a Christian. McClain and Rya led her to the Lord. Her name is Dorothy, and I was wondering…"

"Yes?"

"Would it be possible for Dorothy to join us for the dinner tomorrow evening? Her husband died without Christ, and she's really hurting. Rya and McClain have been staying very close to her, and—"

"Betty, you don't have to say any more. Dorothy is invited, too."

In town, Rya, McClain, and Dorothy were moving slowly down the boardwalk on Main Street, heading for the general store.

"There it is," said McClain.

Rya and Dorothy saw the sign that hung above the door: *Cooper's General Store, Jacob Kates, Prop.*

McClain opened the screen door, allowing the women to move inside ahead of him. Several other wagon train people were in the store, picking up items from the well-stocked shelves. At the counter, a small, thin, silver-haired man in his early sixties was waiting on Vance and Rhonda Larkin.

The Larkins greeted the trio, picked up the paper bags the proprietor had stuffed full of goods, and headed for the door. The little man smiled at McClain, Rya, and Dorothy. "May I help you find something, folks?"

"Yes, sir," said McClain. "We understand you sell Bibles."

"Sure do," said Jacob Kates. "Let me show them to you."

Jacob rounded the end of the counter and led them toward a table near the front window, where a number of Bibles were on display.

"Here they are," said Jacob. "Are you folks with the wagon train?"

McClain said they were and introduced himself, then the ladies. Jacob shook hands with McClain, introducing himself as the proprietor. McClain explained that as a soldier at Fort Steele, he had come to Fort Bridger on two occasions with his commandant and had met Colonel Dane Kirkland and his family.

"Oh, so you know our Colonel Kirkland, and dear Hannah and her children, too."

"Yes. Wonderful people."

Jacob grinned. "You folks have that look about you. I sense it in my heart."

"What's that?" asked McClain, smiling.

"You are born-again people."

"We sure are!" said McClain. "Rya and I have known the Lord since we were children. And, praise the Lord, Dorothy was saved several days ago back on the trail. We came in here to get her a Bible."

There was a twinkle in Jacob's eye. "Please, may I give this dear new-born child of God a Bible?"

The trio stared at him.

"Please?"

"Well, all right, Mr. Kates," said McClain. "We'll allow you to do that."

"Good! Please, ma'am, pick out the one you want."

"I don't know how to thank you, sir," said Dorothy.

"There is no thanks necessary. It's my pleasure as your brother in Christ. You see, I'm a Jew from New York City."

"I thought the name *Kates* was Jewish," said McClain. "We'd love to hear how you came to know the Lord."

Jacob told them in brief that he came to Fort Bridger a few years ago and was hired by Hannah Cooper to work in the store. In time, through the witness of the Cooper family—especially the oldest girl, Mary Beth—he saw that the Lord Jesus Christ was the Messiah and received Him as his Saviour.

McClain, Rya, and Dorothy rejoiced to hear it. Jacob then told them that six years ago, widow Hannah Cooper married Captain Dane Kirkland.

"Shortly thereafter," said Jacob, "she sold the store to me. Captain Kirkland was promoted to major a few months after that, and within about four years, he was made a colonel and commissioned by the army as commandant of Fort Bridger upon the retirement of the previous commandant, Colonel Ross Bateman."

"I knew some of these things," said McClain, "but I'm glad to get the whole picture. More than anything, Mr. Kates, I'm glad to know that you're a Christian."

Noting that customers were lining up at the counter, Jacob told Dorothy to pick out her Bible.

"I will, sir," she said, "and thank you for your generosity. I will treasure it always."

As the trio stepped out onto the boardwalk, they saw Chet Place and the men who had carried the wounded to the doctor's office coming toward them. When they drew up, Chet was smiling.

"So how are they doing?" asked McClain.

"Just fine," replied the wagon master. "Dr. O'Brien says he'll have them patched up sufficiently so they can travel day after tomorrow. He'll keep them at the clinic until late tomorrow afternoon, just to make sure there are no complications."

"Well, this is good news!" said McClain. "I'm so glad to hear it."

"We all are," said Chet. He set tender eyes on Dorothy. "I only wish it could've been the same for your husband, ma'am."

Dorothy nodded, pressing her new Bible to her heart. "Thank you, Mr. Place."

After supper with Dorothy that night at the Keegan wagon, Rya and McClain stepped outside the circle to spend a little time together. They observed the small fire that glowed in the twilight where Sky Eagle and his warriors were camped.

Walking slowly and holding hands, Rya and McClain discussed Chris Cooper's family, and how well they thought Betty would fit in.

"I don't think it will be very long before wedding bells ring," Rya said.

"I'm sure of that," said McClain. "In fact, it won't be long after we're in Sacramento that our wedding bells will ring."

Rya smiled up at him. "I love you so much."

Returning the smile, he said, "I love you so much, too, sweetheart."

Their eyes were locked in a gaze of adoration when suddenly Rya winced.

"Is it your stomach again?" asked McClain.

She nodded.

"Well, in the morning, I'm taking you to Dr. O'Brien."

Rya managed a smile. "Yes, sir."

The next morning, McClain waited in the outer office while Dr. Patrick O'Brien examined Rya with his nurse at his side.

While lying on the examining table, Rya explained to Dr. O'Brien about the recurring pain in her stomach that she had been experiencing for the past few years. She told him that it occurred mostly when she was nervous or upset, but that it was increasing in frequency.

"I'll give you some powders to ease the pain, Miss Garrett," said Dr. O'Brien, "but when you get to Sacramento, you should immediately establish yourself with a doctor and let him run some tests."

"I will do that, Doctor," she assured him.

When Rya and Dr. O'Brien entered the office, they found Sundi O'Brien chatting with McClain.

Dr. O'Brien introduced his wife to Rya.

When the ladies had greeted each other, McClain said, "Honey, Mrs. O'Brien has been the schoolmarm here in Fort Bridger for several years."

Rya's eyes lit up. "Oh, really?"

"Yes," said Sundi. "Your fiancé was just telling me that you have a teaching job waiting for you at Sacramento High School."

"And I'm so excited about it!" said Rya. "Do you teach all grades, Mrs. O'Brien?"

"I used to, but the town and fort have both grown in population the past few years. I now teach tenth through twelfth grades."

The two discussed the joys of teaching for several minutes, then Sundi excused herself, saying she had some summer school students to meet at the school, and hurried away.

Dr. O'Brien told McClain what he had done for Rya. McClain assured him she would see a doctor soon after their arrival, paid him for his services, and escorted Rya back to the wagon train.

That evening, Hannah Cooper Kirkland had a virtual feast prepared for her guests.

Chris and Betty welcomed Rya, Dorothy, and McClain at the door, and guided them into the parlor, where introductions were made. Dorothy and Hannah found an immediate friendship. Hannah's parents, Ben and Esther Singleton, were there, as was Hannah's oldest daughter, Mary Beth Martin, and her lawyer husband, Dan.

Spotting Patty Ruth's long auburn hair, Rya compared the matching color of her own, and the two agreed that they had their own exclusive redhead society.

When they sat down to dinner, Colonel Kirkland asked McClain to offer thanks to the Lord for the food. A sweet Christian fellowship bound them together in their hearts.

Dorothy was seated next to Hannah, who asked her, "Now that your husband is gone, what are your plans?"

Dorothy bit her lower lip. "Well, I don't really have any plans. Since Burt is gone, I really have no reason to go on to San Francisco. But I figured I would stay with the wagon train till it gets to Sacramento, and see if something develops there."

"Do you have relatives back East?"

"None."

"I see. Well, since I learned of your husband's death yesterday from Chris, I've been thinking. Have you ever done any clerking work? You know, in a store?"

"Why, yes, I have. Before Burt and I were married, I worked in a grocery store."

Hannah smiled. "Well, even if you hadn't, I would've made this offer, but since you have, all the better. I talked to Jacob last night. He said he met you yesterday in the store."

"Yes," said Dorothy, her eyes shining. "That dear man gave me a Bible."

"Dorothy, Jacob needs help at the store. He had two ladies working for him up until a week ago, but their husbands were both transferred to a fort in northern Wyoming. Would you be interested in staying here and working for Jacob? He would like to have you."

While Dorothy was trying to find her voice, Hannah said, "We have a spare bedroom upstairs, since Mary Beth is now married. Dane and I agreed this afternoon that you could stay with us until you get on your feet financially, then we can guide you to a very nice boardinghouse here in town. What do you think?"

Face flushed, Dorothy said, "I'm a new Christian, Hannah, but it seems to me the Lord has opened a door for me. I can build a new life right here."

"We have a wonderful church in town and a wonderful pastor. You'll love it here, I guarantee you."

"Sure sounds like God has worked this out for you, Dorothy," said Rya.

A smile worked its way across Dorothy's face. "All right, Hannah. You can tell Mr. Kates he has a new employee!"

There was applause all around the table, then suddenly Dorothy threw palms to her cheeks. "Oh! What'll I do with the wagon and the team?"

"Tell you what," said McClain, "I'll buy them from you. Rya can ride with me in the daytime, and I'm sure the McCrums will let her stay with them at night since Betty is no longer with them."

"I have no doubt of that," spoke up Betty.

"Do you know what Burt paid for the wagon and team, Dorothy?" McClain asked.

"Yes. It was a hundred and ten dollars."

"Sold for a hundred and thirty dollars!" said McClain.

"No, I said a hundred and ten."

There was a glint in McClain's eyes. "Oh, but they no doubt have gone up in value since we left Independence."

Dorothy laughed for the first time since Burt had been killed. "All right, smarty! Sold for a hundred and thirty dollars."

"We'll get your belongings out of the wagon in the morning," said McClain, "and bring them here to the house."

When the wagon train was about to pull out the next morning, the Cheyenne escort was mounted and ready to go.

Dorothy and Betty were there at the Reardon wagon, along

with Hannah. Tearful good-byes were said quickly. Betty and Rya embraced, mingling their tears, and promised to write.

As Chet Place and Sky Eagle led the train out onto the prairie, Dorothy wiped tears and waved. Hannah slipped an arm around her waist.

Dorothy smiled at her and looked back at the rolling wagons. "Oh, Hannah, I sure hope Rya and McClain have a long and happy life."

IT WAS TUESDAY, SEPTEMBER 16, when Chet Place led his wagon train amid truck farms and fruit orchards under a clear California sky to an open grassy field on the eastern outskirts of Sacramento.

After good-byes were exchanged with the wagon master and friends, some wagons headed north while others headed south. Other wagons aimed straight into the heart of Sacramento, including that of McClain Reardon.

Sitting on the wagon seat beside the man she loved, Rya Garrett held on to his arm. "I wonder how Dorothy's doing in Fort Bridger by now. Wasn't it wonderful that she and Hannah became fast friends so quickly?"

McClain nodded. "I was very happy when Dorothy decided to stay in Fort Bridger."

A contented smile graced Rya's lips and her thoughts turned to the future she was going to enjoy with this man who had so captured her heart. She let her gaze take in Sacramento as it lay before her. "Oh, darling, we're finally here!"

"Yes, we are, m'lady. And yours truly will give you a personal guided tour."

"How are you going to do that? You've never been here before."

"Oh, but I have studied written information on this place, given to me by Ward Lamont, including a detailed map."

"Oh, you have, eh? Well, let's hear some pertinent information on our new home."

"Well, the town gets its name from the Sacramento River, which has a confluence with the American River on the town's north side. The American River is its largest tributary. Sacramento was settled in 1839. It grew slowly until gold was discovered at nearby Sutter's Mill in January 1848. This brought prosperity and notable growth to Sacramento, and it was incorporated in 1850. In that same year, it became the seat of Sacramento County."

"This is interesting," Rya said, squeezing his arm. "Tell me more."

"All right. By 1854, the town's population was more than six thousand, and it became California's state capital. Today, as it welcomes the most beautiful woman in the world into its fold, the population is over sixty thousand and growing."

Rya laughed and kissed his cheek. "The most beautiful woman in the world, huh? Aren't you the flatterer!"

"That's not flattery, my sweet. That's fact."

She kissed his cheek again as the covered wagon rolled into town on Main Street. The Sacramento River flowed out of the north with a crystal glitter in the brilliant sunshine as it joined with the American River and bisected the town.

Rya was amazed to see so much construction going on in the residential areas and in the business district. "Looks like you're going into the right business, darling."

"Ward told me the town was booming, and as the state capital, will continue to do so."

"Oh, the Lord is so good to us."

"That He is. And He has been extra good to me. He brought you back into my life, and soon you will become my mail order bride!"

"I'll never get over how you came up with the way to make me your mail order bride, Mr. McClain Reardon. Indeed, you are a genius."

He chuckled. "As long as I've got you thinking so, future Mrs. McClain Reardon, that's all that matters."

Rya laughed and tightened the grip on his arm. "Well, let's see, now. As you take me on this personal guided tour, can you find 1441 West El Camino Avenue?"

"Hmm? What's that?"

"That, my dear sir, is Roy and Elsa Gibbs's address. You know, where I am going to be staying until we get married."

McClain's handsome features tinted. "Well, ah…my map isn't that detailed. I'll…ah…have to stop and ask someone."

Rya giggled. "I understand having to ask someone for directions puts a crimp in the male ego. Would you like me to do it?"

McClain reached over, tweaked her nose, and said, "I can handle it."

They laughed together as McClain veered the wagon toward the side of the street, where a group of men stood on the corner.

Roy Gibbs was in his backyard, pruning trees, when he heard Elsa call from the kitchen door. "Honey, a covered wagon just pulled up out front! It's Rya!"

As McClain was helping Rya down from the wagon seat, they both saw the silver-haired couple emerge from the front door of the white frame two-story house.

Seconds later, Rya was embracing both of them. When they let go of each other, Rya said, "Roy, Elsa, I want you to meet the man I am going to marry."

Shock showed on both faces.

"Marry?" gasped Elsa.

"Wh-when did you get engaged?" asked Roy.

"Oh, quite a while ago. While we were crossing Nebraska."

"Then you met on the wagon train," said Elsa.

"Not exactly. When you were living in Bowling Green, I talked a lot about a boy who used to live there. McClain Reardon. Do you remember?"

"Oh, sure," said Roy. "You brought his name up many times. If I remember right, he was the one who was with you in the barn when John Wilkes Booth and his pal were holding the two of you hostage. McClain managed to get you both out."

"That's right."

"He had been Saul's best friend, if I recall correctly," said Elsa.

"You recall correctly," Rya said with a big smile. "Well, Roy and Elsa Gibbs, meet McClain Reardon!"

The Gibbses welcomed McClain, and Rya quickly told them

the story of their meeting on the wagon train after being apart for fourteen years and how they fell in love and became engaged.

The Gibbses congratulated the young couple, then McClain explained that Rya would need to stay with them until they got married. They were praying about the wedding date and would be talking to the Gibbses' pastor about it.

"She's welcome to stay as long as is needed," said Roy.

Elsa's eyes were shining. "And you're both going to love Pastor Mark Whitfield, his family, and the whole church. Pastor Whitfield has been looking forward to having Rya in the church. This will be a double blessing for him."

"McClain," said Roy, "there's a nice boardinghouse just a block east of here on this same street. You can get a room there until you two get married."

"Good," said McClain. "I want to be as close to Rya as possible." He looked at Rya. "Well, sweetheart, let's get your things unloaded."

While Roy was helping McClain carry Rya's trunk and luggage into the house, McClain asked if he knew where he might be able to sell the covered wagon and team and purchase a horse and buggy. Roy said he did, and whenever he wanted to go, he would take him. McClain said he would like to do it right away.

When Roy and McClain returned with the horse and buggy, Elsa told her husband about Rya's stomach pains, saying she had asked about a doctor. Elsa had recommended their family physician, Dr. Peter Yarrow.

"Couldn't recommend a better one," said Roy. "He's sure been a good doctor for us. He's very thorough and knows his business."

"Good," said McClain. "I'll take Rya to him tomorrow."

McClain then took Rya in the buggy and drove her to Sacramento High School so she could meet the principal and let him know she had arrived. Principal Gerald Baxter warmly welcomed Rya. Rya introduced McClain to Baxter, explaining that they would soon marry. The principal congratulated them, then took Rya into his private office to talk about her job.

As they talked about the classes she would teach and Baxter gave her further information about Sacramento High, Rya explained about her recurring abdominal pain. She told him that McClain was taking her to see Dr. Yarrow tomorrow and mentioned that she was sure she could go to work as planned.

Baxter had good comments about Dr. Yarrow, and said he hoped she would be all right. He had been very much looking forward to having her on his teaching staff.

It was a fifteen-minute drive to the Lamont Construction Company, where Ward Lamont welcomed his new employee. He met Rya and was pleased to learn that they were going to marry soon.

In Rya's presence, Lamont talked to McClain about their plan for him to one day own the company. Rya was thrilled to hear it and thanked the Lord in her heart for working out this opportunity in McClain's life.

The next stop was the boardinghouse, where McClain was able to rent a nice room.

That evening, the Gibbses took Rya and McClain to the church parsonage to meet Pastor Mark Whitfield, his wife, Marla, and his children. Rya instantly took a special liking to Marla. When the three Whitfield children learned that Miss Garrett was a teacher, they got excited. But the excitement lessened when they learned that she would be teaching at the high school. They were in grades two, four, and six.

When the Gibbses, Rya, and McClain were heading back to 1441 West El Camino Avenue along the lantern-lit streets, McClain said, "Nice people, those Whitfields. I was impressed with how well-behaved their children are."

"I really like all of them," said Rya. "What a sweet lady Mrs. Whitfield is."

"Both of you are going to love Pastor's preaching, too," said Roy.

"Well, if the pastor and his family are examples of what the rest of the church is like," said McClain, "we're going to love them, too."

"Then get ready to love the whole church," Elsa said. "We're so happy to be a part of it."

At nine o'clock the next morning, Rya and McClain entered the office of Dr. Peter Yarrow and approached the receptionist's desk. The receptionist was a bright-eyed woman in her late fifties. The nameplate on her desk bore the name Sarah Wickham.

Smiling up at them, Sarah said, "May I help you?"

"Yes, ma'am," said McClain. "My name is McClain Reardon. This young lady is Rya Garrett. We arrived yesterday on a wagon train."

Gesturing to the two chairs in front of her desk, Sarah picked up pencil and paper. "Please sit down. And welcome to Sacramento."

They thanked her, then Sarah asked if both of them needed to see the doctor. McClain explained that it was Rya who needed to see him.

After giving Sarah her temporary address, Rya told her about her abdominal pains, and that Dr. Patrick O'Brien in Fort Bridger, Wyoming, had told her to see a doctor in Sacramento to do some tests.

Sarah made notes, then asked the couple to sit down in the waiting area. It wasn't long till Rya was in an examining room with Dr. Peter Yarrow and his nurse, whom he introduced as Billie Blake.

Dr. Yarrow asked many questions, and learned about Jason Lynch and how his unwanted presence had often brought on the abdominal pains. Rya explained that even since she last saw Jason many weeks ago, she was still having recurrences of the pain. She told Yarrow the pain was excruciating during and after the Cheyenne attack on the wagon train.

The doctor made notes, rubbed his chin, and said, "Miss Garrett, before I put you through the tests, I would like to see how you do now that Jason is no longer around, and the long wagon journey is over."

Rya nodded. "Whatever you say, Doctor."

"I'm going to give you medicine to take whenever something upsets you. This is for your nerves, which can affect you physically. If the medicine doesn't take care of it, I want to know immediately.

I'll also give you some powders to take if the pain does come back. But I want to see you right away if it happens. If not, I still want to see you in a month. Please make an appointment with Sarah on your way out."

When Rya and McClain were heading back to the Gibbs home in McClain's buggy, she explained what Dr. Yarrow had said.

"I sure hope this will be the end of the problem," he said.

"Me, too. I've got to be about my teaching job and be busy making preparations to become Mrs. McClain Reardon."

A few days later, letters went out to Rya's parents in Virginia, and McClain's mother in Missouri, letting them know that they had arrived safely in Sacramento, and both loved their jobs. Nothing was said about Rya's stomach problems.

The next Sunday, the happy couple attended church services with the Gibbses and found the people warm and friendly. They also loved the music, and most of all, they loved Pastor Mark Whitfield's preaching.

At the close of the service, they walked the aisle and presented themselves for membership.

On Tuesday night, Rya and McClain met with the pastor and told him their wedding plans. The wedding date was set for Saturday, October 18, at seven o'clock in the evening.

The next day letters went out to Rya's parents and McClain's mother, telling them of the wedding date. Rya had written to Betty Hilmes in Fort Bridger, informing her of the date she would become Mrs. McClain Reardon.

In early October, Rya and McClain rented a small house near the Gibbs home, and Elsa helped Rya decorate it.

On Tuesday, October 7, when McClain came to the Gibbs house for supper, Rya met him at the door with an envelope in her hand, her eyes dancing.

Looking at the envelope, then into Rya's dancing eyes, McClain said, "I can see it's a letter. Who's it from?"

"Betty Hilmes!"

"Oh? And what's got you so excited?"

"She told me that she and Chris have also set their wedding date for October 18!"

"Well, now, isn't that some kind of coincidence? I'm glad for them."

The next day, a letter came from McClain's mother, congratulating them on the upcoming wedding, saying she wished she could be there. Two days later, a letter came from Richard and Laura Garrett, also sending congratulations, and saying they wished they could attend the wedding.

On Saturday, October 18, 1879, dawn was just beginning to paint its gray light on the eastern horizon when Rya sat up in bed and looked out her largest bedroom window. The sparrows in the trees were beginning to chirp as they welcomed the dawn.

Rya had spent a restless night, anticipating this most important day. Stretching her arms, she yawned and threw back the covers. She picked up her flannel robe from the chair beside the bed, put it on, and padded her way to the washstand. Splashing cold water on her face, she dried it with a fluffy towel, then went to the rocking chair that sat by the large window and sat down. The house was quiet, since Roy and Elsa were still asleep. Rya folded her legs beneath her and watched the dawn grow brighter.

This was her wedding day. She let her mind wander back to her home in Virginia, and as she thought of her parents and siblings, a melancholy feeling stole over her. Without even realizing she was weeping; she felt tears splash on the folded hands in her lap.

"We can't have this on such a happy occasion," she admonished herself in a whisper.

She used the sleeve of her robe to dry her cheeks and hands and put her mind on the preparations she needed to make for meeting McClain at the altar that evening.

Rya prayed to her heavenly Father, asking once again for His blessings on her marriage to McClain. She asked Him to continually fill her with a deeper and more powerful love for the man God had given her.

"Help me to remember Your Word, dear Father," she said

softly. 'Wives, submit yourselves unto your own husbands, as unto the Lord.' Help me to be like the wife You described in Proverbs 31, and lead me each day, precious Lord, as I yield my all unto You."

Rya prayed for her family back in Virginia and for McClain's family in Missouri. Just as she said her amen, she became aware of sounds indicating that the Gibbses were up and moving about the house.

She uncurled her legs, rose to her feet, and stood at the window watching the sunlight kissing the distant hills good morning. Wrapping her arms around herself, she twirled about with a wide smile on her lips. "This indeed is a glorious day. Thank You, Lord, for Your mercy and goodness."

That evening, Rya and McClain were married in a small, simple ceremony, and after the modest reception, they climbed into McClain's buggy and drove to their rented house. McClain parked the buggy in front of the porch, hurried around to Rya's side, and helped her out. Holding hands, they climbed the steps of the porch and stopped at the door.

McClain opened the door, swinging it wide, then smiled down at the lovely redhead in the beautiful white dress. "Well, here's the threshold. Ready?"

She laughed and raised her arms to shoulder height. "I'm ready!"

McClain swept her into his arms and kissed her soundly. "Chris Cooper isn't the only man who married his mail order bride today!"

On the following Thursday afternoon, Mrs. McClain Reardon was at the blackboard in her classroom, writing dates of important historical events for her students to put into their notes and memorize, when the bell sounded out in the hall, indicating that school was over for the day.

Laying the chalk down, Rya ran her gaze over the faces before her. "Everybody get these dates down?"

Heads were nodding as the students were closing their notebooks.

"All right. Now study hard, young people. The history test is tomorrow. You're dismissed."

As the bulk of the students were filing out the classroom door, two girls stepped up to the desk.

Rya smiled back. "Melissa, Lorene, is there something I can do for you?"

Melissa's smile broadened. "Yes, Miss Gar— I mean, Mrs. Reardon. You can just keep on being so interesting in your teaching. We just love the way you teach."

"Yes," said Lorene. "You make every subject come alive. Especially history. Thank you. We're so glad you're our teacher!"

Rya hugged them both at the same time as tears filled her eyes. "Thank you, girls. That means more to me than I can ever tell you."

The girls smiled, then left.

With joy bubbling in her heart, Rya picked up the two textbooks she needed to take home for study along with her small notebook, and left the classroom, closing the door behind her.

As she moved down the hall, she came to two women teachers, who were standing in the open door of a classroom. They both smiled and told Rya how glad they were that she was part of the faculty.

She smiled in return, thanked them, and moved outside. She began planning what she was going to cook for supper as she descended the stairs and headed for the boardwalk that paralleled the street.

Suddenly Rya stopped, her eyes wide and heart pounding, the hair rising on the back of her neck.

Jason Lynch was walking toward her across the campus lawn, his eyes like sharp points of steel.

Rya felt a shudder go through her as he drew up. "Hello, sweetheart."

"Don't call me sweetheart!" Rya snapped.

Jason stepped closer. "I've missed you terribly. I just couldn't stand it anymore. I had to come and find you and tell you that I still love you. I want you to forget this McClain Reardon and marry me. I'll find a good job here, and—"

"Stop it, Jason!" She lifted her left hand to his face, showing her wedding ring to him. "See that? I already married him. I am now Mrs. McClain Reardon. Go back home, Jason!"

Eyes blazing, Jason screamed, "You had no right to marry Reardon! You were always meant for me!" He grabbed her by the upper arms and shook her. "Do you hear what I'm saying? You were meant for me!"

Students who had not yet left the grounds were looking on, mouths agape.

Two adult couples passing by in a buggy saw Jason shaking Rya. Frank Sandoval quickly pulled the buggy to a stop and jumped out. Jay Dutton was on his heels as he ran across the lawn.

Sandoval rushed up. "Let go of her, mister! Right now!"

Jason swore at them. "Mind your own business!"

"Let go of her or we'll beat you to a pulp and carry what's left of you to the police station."

Jason released Rya and took a step back, eyeing both men.

Rya was weeping and rubbing her upper arms as the two women from the buggy rushed up and put their arms around her, speaking softly to her.

"Look, you guys!" Jason said. "I've been in love with this girl for a long time. She married another man and tore my heart out!"

"Well, since she's another man's wife, you'd better keep your hands off her," Frank Sandoval said.

Jason gazed at Rya with a burning look, then turned and stomped away.

Jay Dutton called after him, "You stay away from her, buster!"

Jason didn't look back.

Trembling in the arms of the two women, Rya ran her gaze to the men. "Thank you for coming to my rescue."

"Our pleasure, Miss," said Dutton, picking up Rya's books and notebook. "Are you a teacher here at the school?"

"Yes," Rya said.

"May we take you home?" asked one of the women, introducing

herself as Shawna Dutton. "Our buggy is right over here."

"I…I only live two blocks away, ma'am," said Rya, her voice shaking. "I can walk."

"I really think it's best if we take you home, honey," said Shawna.

Rya nodded, placing a hand over her stomach. "All right. Thank you very much."

MAIL-ORDER BRIDE SERIES · AL & JOANNA LACY
NO. 9
1877
USA

21

WARD LAMONT APPEARED AT THE OPEN DOOR of McClain Reardon's office. "Hey, young man, shouldn't you be on your way home? Everybody else left here twenty minutes ago."

McClain grinned, picked up the papers on the desktop, opened a drawer, and slid them inside. Rising from the chair, he rubbed his eyes and said, "Yeah, boss, you're right. I was just trying to get those papers for the new Myers-Westerman project done. I've got to spend tomorrow afternoon with the big cheeses and their board of directors."

"You look tired, son. You can finish those papers easily in the morning, can't you?"

"Sure. I just wanted to get started on the papers for the new firehouse building in the morning. But it can wait till Saturday."

Lamont stepped up to him and patted him on the back. "McClain, you're doing a marvelous job. Especially for a man who's never been in the construction business. You really catch on quick."

McClain grinned. "I try."

"Now, you get on home and tell that sweet girl I said hello, won't you?"

"Sure will," said McClain, heading for the back door. "See you in the morning."

McClain walked to his buggy, patted the horse on the neck, and untied the reins from the hitching post. As he guided the horse down the alley and onto the side street, he began whistling a tune he had learned in Sunday school the previous Sunday. Moments later, he turned onto Main Street and headed toward El Camino Avenue. He smiled when his eyes fell on the vacant lot where the Lamont Construction Company would be erecting the new firehouse. Sacramento was growing so fast it needed a company of firemen on the west side of town. The other was on the east side, where the town first began.

When McClain turned onto El Camino Avenue, his heart skipped a beat. In a few more minutes, he would hold the woman of his dreams in his arms once again. She always got home about an hour and a half before he did. They had been married only five days, but he was sure he already loved sweet Rya a thousand times more than he did when he carried her across the threshold last Saturday night.

The setting sun's fiery rim had the western horizon aglow with golden light when McClain guided the buggy into the driveway of the small two-story house and headed past it toward the barn at the rear. Moments later, he made his way onto the back porch and stepped into the kitchen, where he would find Rya cooking supper.

The kitchen was unoccupied, and there was no fire in the cookstove. There were no place settings on the table.

McClain frowned and headed into the hall. "Rya! Honey, where are you?"

He paused at the open door of the small sewing room where she did her studying, but it too was unoccupied. Heading toward the parlor, he called out again, but there was no answer. Maybe she was detained at school for some reason.

But a strange uneasiness ran through his mind. Trying to shake it off, he called Rya's name again, this time louder than before.

Nothing.

Why should she be delayed this long at school? Something was wrong.

He moved back out into the hall and paused at the foot of the stairs.

Suddenly his ears picked up a sound coming from upstairs. There were muffled sobs, accompanied by moans that almost sounded like they were coming from an injured animal.

Fear shot through his heart as he bounded up the stairs. As he hurried down the hall, he noted that the door to the master bedroom was closed.

The sobbing and moaning sounds were louder as he paused before the door then turned the knob and stepped into the room. His wife was curled up on the bed.

Hurrying to her, McClain eased onto the edge of the bed and laid a hand on her trembling shoulder. "Sweetheart, what's wrong? Has something happened?"

When she opened her tear-filled eyes, McClain saw terror in them. It was so stark, it sent a chill through him, weaving webs of ice in the hollow of his bones.

"Honey, what is it?" he asked, carressing her hair.

A shudder coursed through her. "It...it's Jason."

McClain's eyes widened. "Jason Lynch?"

Rya nodded slowly. "Yes. He...he was waiting for me when I came out of the school building. He was like a madman, McClain. He said he had come here to marry me. When I showed him my wedding ring, he went into a rage."

She sat up and rolled up the sleeves of her shirtwaist. McClain's eyes fell on the dark purple marks. "This is what he did to me."

McClain clenched his teeth until his jaw muscles throbbed. What had been ice in his bones was now molten lava. Anger pulled down the corners of his mouth.

Rya told him how Frank Sandoval and Jay Dutton had rescued her from Jason, and they and their wives had brought her home.

McClain folded Rya into his arms. "I must find those people and thank them for what they did. And then I'm going to find Jason."

Easing back in his arms so she could look into his eyes, Rya said, "Darling, I know you're angry. So am I. But please don't do anything that will hurt your reputation here in town. This is our home, now. You mustn't jeopardize—"

Rya winced and buckled in the middle, running a hand to her stomach.

McClain's brow furrowed. "Your stomach?"

Head bent down, Rya nodded, her hand gripping her midsection.

"I'll go mix your powders the doctor gave you for pain. Maybe you should take some of the nerve medicine, too."

Rya had not needed either since Dr. Yarrow had given them to her, but now she agreed it would be best to take them both.

Moments later, when the medicines had been administered, McClain said, "You just lie here and rest, sweetheart. Let the medicines do their job. I'm going to find Jason if he's still in town and have a talk with him."

"Don't do anything you'll be sorry for."

"I won't. I promise. You're right. I mustn't jeopardize my standing in the community. But if Mr. Jason Lynch is in town, he's going to be told in no uncertain terms that he had better leave you alone and that it would be in his best interest to get out of Sacramento."

Worry crowded into Rya's reddened eyes. "McClain, be careful. Jason could be dangerous. He wasn't wearing a gun when I saw him, but he probably is now. And with his twisted mind—"

"I'll be careful, honey. You rest. I'll be back in a little while. Did the Sandovals and the Duttons happen to tell you where they live?"

"Yes. Shawna Dutton wrote both addresses down for me. They're on a piece of paper at the very front of my school notebook. It's downstairs on the top of the chest in the entryway."

McClain pulled a soft quilt up over her shoulders. Bending down, he kissed her trembling lips. "Now, don't worry. When I first saw those marks on your arms, I was angry enough to—well, to inflict untold punishment on him. That won't happen now, but I am going to make sure he understands that he'd better never touch you again."

He kissed her once more, then walked toward the door.

Rya's eyes followed her husband as he left the room, a fervent prayer for his safety deep in her heart.

Since Sacramento only had two hotels, McClain decided he would try the newest and largest first. As he stepped out of his buggy, he thought of how warm and friendly both the Sandovals and the Duttons had been to him when he knocked on their doors and expressed his appreciation to them.

Entering the lobby of the American Hotel, he approached the

desk, where the clerk was just finishing with a middle-aged couple.

When McClain stepped up, the clerk smiled. "Yes, sir. Do you need a room?"

"No. I'm looking for a man who is visiting here from Virginia. I'm not sure which hotel he's staying in. His name is Jason Lynch. Is he registered here?"

"Yes he is, sir. But he's not in his room at the moment. He left about half an hour ago after asking me about some of the nearby saloons. I named three: the Golden Lantern, the Gun Barrel, and the Bulldog. I don't know which one he might be in."

"Thank you," said McClain, and returned to the street.

He ran his gaze up and down the street, and saw that the closest saloon was the Golden Lantern. The next closest was the Gun Barrel. When he didn't find Lynch in either of those, he walked a block to the Bulldog Saloon and pushed through the batwings.

Even before he could look around the place, he heard a familiar voice. At the bar, Jason Lynch was in a heated argument with another customer.

The bartender moved up between them. "If you two wanna fight, do it outside!"

Jason Lynch did not even notice McClain Reardon as he and his adversary stomped outside, followed by a half dozen would-be spectators.

McClain also stepped outside to observe.

As soon as the two angry men stepped into the dust of the street, they started punching. The fight lasted less than two minutes. An unconscious Jason Lynch lay on his back in the street, and the man who had put him out dusted off his hands, laughed, and went back inside the saloon with the others following.

Jason had lost his hat in the fight. It lay a few feet from him. McClain picked it up, walked to a nearby water trough, and filled it up. He carried the hat to where Jason lay and poured the water in his face.

Jason stirred slightly and made a groaning sound, slowly rolling his head back and forth. His eyes remained closed. The groaning stopped after several seconds, and he lay still.

People were collecting on the boardwalk, gawking.

McClain dipped another hatful and doused him with it a second time.

Jason opened his eyes and saw the tall, broad-shouldered man standing over him. The street lamps were bright enough to expose McClain's features, but it took Jason a few seconds to clear his vision enough to recognize him. He shook his head, blinked, and focused on him again.

"Yeah, it's me," McClain said. "You manhandled my wife today, and you and I are going to have a little talk."

McClain leaned over, grabbed Jason by the shirt collar, stood him on his feet, and jammed the wet hat on his head. Looking him straight in the eye, he said, "Your head clear?"

Jason licked his lips and nodded. "Yeah."

"All right. I have a message for you and I want to make sure it gets through."

Jason licked his lips again. "What's that?"

McClain gripped Jason's upper arms until the pain showed in the man's face. "Get out of town, Lynch. And don't come back."

More people were gathering on the boardwalk.

Wincing from the pain, Jason tried to free himself, but it was as if his arms were clamped in a pair of steel vises. "You don't own this town! I can stay here if I want."

"Not when you treat my wife like you did this afternoon."

Jason shook his head. "Aw, I never—"

"Don't deny it, mister! There were witnesses."

Again, Jason attempted to pull away from McClain's grip, but found himself unable to move.

McClain shook him hard. "Don't you ever lay hands on my wife again. Rya's name isn't Garrett anymore. It's Reardon. Do you hear that, Jason? She's my wife. You stay away from her, or you'll be sorry!"

With that, McClain let go of the man. Jason turned to walk away, stumbled, and fell. Mumbling something no one could understand, he scrambled to his feet and staggered down the boardwalk in the direction of the American Hotel.

One of the men in the group stepped up. "You're that new man Ward Lamont hired, aren't you?"

"Yes, sir."

"What's your name?"

"McClain Reardon."

"I'm Neal Caldwell," said the man, offering his hand.

McClain met his grip. "Glad to meet you, Mr. Caldwell."

Looking up the street where Lynch could still be seen staggering along, Caldwell said, "Did we hear it right? That guy manhandled your wife today?"

"Yes. Left bruises on her arms."

"Guess I can't blame you for talking straight to him. What're you going to do if he doesn't heed your warning?"

McClain shrugged and glanced at the small crowd. "I don't know, but he'd better not ever get near her again, or he and I will both find out."

"You know him, Mr. Reardon?" asked a young man in the crowd.

"Vaguely. He's wanted for quite some time to be suitor to the young lady I married. Well, you folks might as well move along, now. The excitement is over."

As the crowd was dispersing, Neal Caldwell moved close to McClain and said, "I sure wouldn't want be in that guys shoes if he ever comes around your wife again."

When McClain came home from work the next day, Rya had fried chicken, mashed potatoes and gravy, green beans, and hot bread on the table. McClain was glad to hear that her stomach had given her only a little pain that day.

While they were eating, Rya said, "Darling, I sure hope Jason is gone."

"Looks like it. I stopped by the hotel on the way home from work, and the clerk told me he had checked out about nine-thirty this morning."

"Good. I hope he goes back to Virginia and finds himself a girl to marry."

McClain let a thin smile touch his lips. "Well, whether he finds that girl or not, he'd better not come back here and bother you anymore."

The days passed quickly, and on Friday evening when McClain entered the kitchen from the back porch, Rya smiled at him from where she stood at the cookstove. "Hello, darling. Did you have a nice—McClain, what's wrong?"

He put his arms around her, held her close for a moment, then looked into her eyes. "Jason's still in town."

"Oh no."

"Remember I told you about a man who introduced himself to me as Neal Caldwell the other night?"

"Yes."

"Well, he came into the office today. He owns Sacramento Hardware. He knows Ward well, because Ward built the hardware store for him. The two of them were talking in the outer office when I happened to come out of my office. Neal told me he ran into Jason this morning at the lumbermill just outside of town. Bill Barton, the owner of the mill, was in the process of firing Jason when Neal walked into the office. After Jason stomped out in anger, Barton told Neal that Jason had started trouble with another employee, and he had to fire him. The other employee said Jason's been a troublemaker ever since he hit town. He's started fights two or three times a week in the saloons."

Rya shook her head. "Why does he stay around? I'd think he'd want to get out of Sacramento."

"You'd think so. There's nothing here for him. With his reputation as a troublemaker, nobody's going to give him a job."

"Well, at least he hasn't come around me. You must have gotten through to him."

McClain set his jaw. "If he knows what's good for him, that's the way it'll stay, too."

On Monday, Rya left her classroom at the close of the school day, and moved down the hall, books and notebook in hand. As she headed toward the boardwalk, her line of sight went to a man who stood across the street, looking at her.

Jason! What's he doing here? Immediately pain gripped her midsection.

She turned onto the boardwalk and moved down the street. She could feel his eyes on her as she reached the intersection and crossed the street as usual, but she did not look back.

Rya wondered if he was following her, but was afraid to turn around and find out. As she hurried toward home, she noted residents on their porches and in their yards and took comfort. Soon she was drawing up to the small two-story house, and breathed a sigh of relief when she mounted the porch steps, glanced down the block, and saw no sign of Jason Lynch.

When McClain came home from work, he stepped into the kitchen and smelled the sweet scent of supper cooking, but Rya was not there. He hung his hat on the peg by the door and called, "Sweetheart, I'm home!"

There were footsteps in the hall and Rya entered the kitchen, trying to work up a smile. McClain read her eyes. "What's wrong, honey?"

She moved to him, wrapped her arms around him, and laid her head on his broad chest.

McClain held her close. "Honey, what is it?"

"Jason."

McClain put a hand under her chin and tilted her face. "What about Jason?"

"When I left the school building to come home, he was standing across the street, watching me. I didn't acknowledge his presence. I just hurried home."

"Did he follow you?"

"No."

"Well, I'm at least glad for that." He studied her eyes. "You're in pain, aren't you?"

She nodded and stepped back. "I'll get supper on the table."

"I'll take you to Dr. Yarrow's house right after we eat."

"There's no need," she said, giving him a weak smile. "Jason's presence caused it, so nothing is different. I'll take a dose of both medicines, and it'll be better in a little while."

While they were eating supper, McClain said, "What do you suppose Jason's game is now?"

"I have no idea. I wish he'd go back to Virginia and leave me alone."

"Well, if this keeps up, he's going to force my hand. I'm not going to tolerate it."

"I appreciate that, honey. But if you get physical with him, he might go to the law and get you for assault and battery. I don't want anything like that to happen. One day you will own the Lamont Construction Company, and you'll need the respect of the people of Sacramento to succeed."

"I know, but one way or another, I'm putting a stop to the harassment Jason's putting on you."

Rya reached across the table and took hold of his hand. "Maybe today's little incident is all there'll be."

"I'd like to believe that, but I've got a feeling he's not through."

On Tuesday, when Rya came out of the school building, she looked across the street where Jason had been the day before and was relieved that he was not there.

It was the same on Wednesday, and as she walked home, she told herself that Jason's little game was over.

When she arrived home, she decided to do some cleaning in the parlor before she started supper.

While using a feather duster on the furniture in the parlor, Rya moved to the large window to dust the sill. Suddenly her attention was drawn to a figure standing in the middle of the street in front of the house. Jason was looking at her.

She gave him a heavy scowl and pulled the drapes. Her hands shook while she finished her dusting. When she had put the feather duster away, she eased up to the window, parted the drapes a tiny bit, and peered out. Jason was gone. She opened the drapes and went to the kitchen to start supper.

Though Rya was experiencing some stomach pain when McClain came home, she did not let on. Neither did she tell him about Jason's appearance in the middle of the street.

After supper, while McClain was taking a bath, Rya went to the kitchen and took the medicine.

The next day, she saw Jason standing across the street from the school again. This time, he smiled at her when she glanced at him. But he did not follow her. Her stomach pain was excruciating. As soon as she arrived home, she took more medicine. But when McClain came home, she kept it to herself.

Jason did not put in an appearance on Friday or Saturday. Sunday came, and being in church and hearing their pastor preach was a comfort to Rya.

On Monday, however, when Rya arrived home from work, Jason was standing across the street from the house. Again, he smiled at her.

She dashed inside the house, and after a few minutes, she went to the parlor window and looked out. Jason was still across the street.

Quickly she pulled the drapes, ran upstairs to the bedroom, and threw herself across the bed, weeping.

"Dear God," she sobbed, "please make this horrible nightmare come to an end. Make Jason leave me alone."

When she had her emotions under control, she crept up to a front window in one of the spare bedrooms and peeked out. Jason was gone.

When McClain came through the back door from the barn, Rya was in the kitchen, cooking supper. Rya kissed him. "Hello, darling! Did you have a good day?"

Holding her at arm's length, McClain said, "A very profitable one, honey. I lined up two good construction projects today."

"Wonderful!"

McClain's brow furrowed. "Sweetheart, when I pulled into the driveway, I noticed the drapes on the front window in the parlor are closed. Why's that?"

Rya's lower lip quivered. "Honey, I...I—"

"What?"

Tears filmed her eyes. "Well, I just didn't want to tell you because it upsets you so, and I don't want you to do something rash."

McClain caressed her cheek. "I appreciate your concern for me, but I must know what's going on. It's Jason again, right?"

"Yes."

Rya wiped tears while she told McClain of Jason's repeated appearances, both at the school and in front of the house. She drew a shuddering breath. "I forgot to open the drapes after he was gone."

McClain took her in his arms and held her. "I'm angry enough at Jason to do something rash, Rya. But I won't. I'll go to the sheriff's office tomorrow and ask Sheriff Drew to do something about this harassment."

Relief showed in Rya's eyes. "Oh, thank you, McClain. I'm glad you are going to handle it this way."

When McClain entered the kitchen the next evening, Rya hugged and kissed him. "Jason was across the street from the school again today," she said with irritation in her voice. "Did you get to see Sheriff Drew?"

"I did," replied McClain, his voice heavy. "He said there isn't anything legally he can do about these appearances. He can't arrest a man for standing on public property. Jason will have to make some hostile move before he can arrest him."

"So we just have to sit back and let him keep this up till he decides to make a move to hurt me?"

McClain nodded. "That's the law. I guess I showed some anger when the sheriff told me this. He warned me not to try to stop Jason's harassment on my own by some kind of violence."

Rya sighed. "Well, I don't want you doing anything like that either. So we just have to put up with Jason's nonsense."

"Not exactly. I'm going to have another talk with Jason. I don't know where he lives or where he might be working, but I'm going to find him. This harassment is going to stop."

"But, Sheriff Drew warned you—"

"I won't get violent, honey. But this is going to stop."

Rya clung to him. "You be careful. Jason might just be the one to resort to violence."

MAIL ORDER BRIDE SERIES · NO. 9 · 1877 · USA · AL & JOANNA LACY

22

ON WEDNESDAY MORNING, MCCLAIN REARDON sat in Ward Lamont's office and told him about Jason Lynch harassing Rya in Virginia, on the trail from Missouri, and in Sacramento.

Lamont leaned his elbows on the desk. "I've heard this guy's name time and again. He's a troublemaker, and people in this town don't like him. Maybe he needs to be tarred and feathered and run out of Sacramento."

"Believe me, Ward, I'd love to be the one to do it, but if I did, Sheriff Drew would have me behind bars. I talked to Drew about this and he said Lynch would have to make some kind of hostile move before he could arrest him. As long as he's merely standing on public property, he's within his rights. He also cautioned me about using violence to stop Lynch from harassing Rya."

Lamont chuckled. "Well, I never thought of tar and feathering as violence, but the sheriff might. And for sure, as Christians, you and I both know the Lord wouldn't want you to be violent toward him unless it was to protect Rya from harm, or in your own self-defense. We both fought Indian wars, McClain, but we knew in battling the hostiles, it was kill or be killed. But from what you've said Lynch has made no threatening moves of bodily harm toward you or Rya."

"He did bruise her arms some when he grabbed her and shook her that first day in front of the school, but I doubt a jury would consider it serious enough to jail him."

"For sure, they wouldn't excuse you for beating him to a bloody pulp. And according to that sermon from Romans 12:19 Pastor

Whitfield preached a week ago, the Lord wouldn't either. 'Vengeance is mine, I will repay, saith the Lord.'"

McClain nodded.

"So what are you going to do?"

McClain sighed. "Well, boss, that's why I'm here. I talked to Lynch about this once. He wouldn't listen. I guess the only thing I can do is talk to him again. He's got to leave Rya alone. This harassment is affecting her physically as well as emotionally. I need some time off work today so I can find him and have that talk."

Lamont eased back in his chair. "Take all the time you need. You're caught up on your work. And Lynch must be stopped."

McClain drove his buggy out to the lumbermill and asked Bill Barton if he knew where Lynch took up residence after leaving the American Hotel. Barton told him that Lynch had moved into Martha's Boardinghouse on the north side of town. McClain then drove to the boardinghouse, where Martha Wells told him that Lynch caused so much trouble with other boarders that she had to put him out. She had heard that he was now staying at the Sacramento Hotel.

Fifteen minutes later, McClain entered the lobby of the Sacramento Hotel and approached the desk

"May I help you, sir?" the desk clerk asked.

"I hope so. My name is McClain Reardon. I was told that you have a Jason Lynch as a guest here. Is that so?"

Looking at the guest register, the clerk ran his finger down the page, then looked up. "Yes, sir. Mr. Lynch is in room 212."

McClain thanked him and turned to head for the staircase. Suddenly he saw Lynch coming down the stairs. Many people were milling about the lobby, and Lynch did not see McClain as he headed for the front door. When Lynch was almost parallel with the desk, McClain stepped in front of him.

Lynch halted and they looked at each other for a moment. Then Lynch said loudly, "Get out of my way, Reardon!"

This caught the attention of everybody in the lobby.

McClain could once again see the fear and pain in Rya's face that Jason Lynch had put there repeatedly. His eyes measured the man coldly, and the words cracked with tension as he said equally as loud, "You'd better quit bothering Rya, Lynch. I mean it! If this keeps up, you're going to be sorry!"

Lynch hissed through his teeth, "Don't threaten me, Reardon! I'm not breaking any laws." With that, he stepped around McClain and hurried out the door.

When McClain arrived home that evening, Rya asked if he had found Jason.

McClain told her he had, in the lobby of the Sacramento Hotel. He warned Lynch to stop bothering her.

"Well, it didn't do any good. He was across the street from the school this afternoon, watching me."

McClain felt his blood heat up. "Guess I'll have to come up with some other approach. But right now, I'm concerned about *you*. You're hurting a lot, aren't you?"

Rya's hand went to her midsection. "Yes."

"I'm taking you to see Dr. Yarrow tomorrow after school. We've got to find out just how serious this problem is."

Jason Lynch was not in sight when McClain picked Rya up in the buggy at school on Thursday afternoon. When they entered the doctor's office, Sarah Wickham smiled. "Hello, Mr. and Mrs. Reardon. May I help you?"

"Dr. Yarrow told us that if Rya continued to have problems with her stomach, we should get her in here right away. She is having severe pain almost constantly."

"I'm so sorry to hear that, Mrs. Reardon," Sarah said, giving Rya a compassionate look. "Sit down. I'll tell Dr. Yarrow you're here."

Less than five minutes later, the Reardons were sitting in front of the desk in the doctor's private office. When Rya told him of Jason's appearances and the excruciating pain she was experiencing, he said, "No question about it, Mrs. Reardon. It's time to do the tests. We can do it tomorrow if you can make arrangements with Mr. Baxter."

"We'll go to his house on our way home from here," said McClain. "I'm sure he has someone who can substitute for her."

The doctor nodded. "Fine. Then I will need her at the hospital at eight o'clock in the morning. The tests will take about three hours. Since we have to work internally, there will be some discomfort."

"I figured that would be the case, Doctor," Rya replied. "I'm certainly willing to go through some discomfort in order for you to know what we're dealing with and to get this problem cured."

Yarrow nodded. "Of course. You should feel well enough to go home when the tests are over. I'll know the results of the tests by Saturday morning. Since I take my lunch break each day at one o'clock, let's have you come in at noon on Saturday. I'll tell you what we're looking at, and what we have to do in order to get you over this problem."

Rya had her tests done as scheduled on Friday morning. McClain had her home by eleven-thirty, and rushed off to work.

Rya lay down for a while, then arose and went about doing some light housework. While sweeping off the front porch, she thought of Ted and Colin Yoder, whose brother Cecil was dying in Oregon of stomach cancer. She wondered if they had arrived there in time to see their brother before he died.

As she carried the broom back into the house, a sharp pain lanced her midsection. She closed the door behind her, pressed a hand to her stomach, and said in a tremulous whisper, "Please, dear Lord, don't let this be stomach cancer. McClain and I are just starting our life together. He needs me. I want to give him children. I want us to have a long, happy life together."

Returning the broom to its place in the pantry, Rya turned to other small jobs about the house. The hours seemed to drag by as she vacillated between optimism and despair. Trying with all of her Christian might to give this burden to the Lord, she still found herself carrying it and grappling with emotions.

—⚡—   —⚡—   —⚡—

Neither Rya nor McClain slept well Friday night. They were both awake when the early light filled the room.

McClain took hold of her hand. "Sweetheart, we're both on edge. I know we prayed a long time before we put out the lantern last night. But let's pray some more."

"Yes," said Rya, squeezing his hand.

They rose from the bed and dropped to their knees beside it, still holding hands.

Rya felt her husband's body trembling and there was a sob in his voice. "Father, You know my concern for my precious sweetheart, and how desperately I want this problem to be a simple one that can be treated and cured in a short time. But…but in my heart, I know I must leave it in Your hands. Whatever will give You the most glory is what I want. I'm committing her to You, and asking that Your will be done."

"Yes, amen," said Rya, clinging now to her optimism. "May Thy will be done. We are Your children. Whatever You choose for me in this situation will be right."

They wept together and prayed some more, asking God for His strength and peace. Then rising from their knees, they prepared for the day and whatever God had for them in the future.

McClain pulled the buggy to a halt in front of the general store, tied the reins to a hitching post, and helped Rya out of the buggy. He glanced at the clock on the Bank of Sacramento a few doors down and noted that it was 11:47.

They entered the general store, made a small purchase, and returned to the boardwalk. McClain placed the paper bag on the floor of the buggy. "All right, sweetheart. Let's go see what Dr. Yarrow has to tell us."

Rya took hold of his arm. They stepped off the boardwalk and paused in the street, waiting for traffic to clear so they could get across.

While they waited, McClain patted the hand that held onto his arm and looked into her eyes. "I adore you. Do you know that?"

A smile spread over her features. "Yes, I know. And I adore you."

McClain looked at the clock on the bank's sign. "Oh, it's three minutes till twelve. We've got to get across here, now. Don't want to be late." McClain quickly guided her through the traffic as they made their way to Dr. Peter Yarrow's office.

When they stepped inside, they looked at Sarah Wickham, expecting her customary smile and cheerful greeting. Sarah forced a thin smile, but she was not her usual chipper self. "Hello, Mr. and Mrs. Reardon. Dr. Yarrow is waiting for you in his office."

They followed Sarah toward the doctor's private office. She tapped on the door, then opened it. "Mr. and Mrs. Reardon are here, Doctor."

Yarrow stood up behind his desk. "Please come in, folks." He managed a grim smile as he told them to sit down, then settled into his chair as Sarah stepped out and closed the door.

Biting his lower lip, Yarrow picked up the folder on his desk that had Rya's name on the tab. He opened it, looked at the papers inside, then set his eyes on the nervous couple. He cleared his throat. "The…ah…test results are not good."

McClain took hold of Rya's hand.

The doctor's eyes filled with tears. His throat was constricted as he spoke solemnly. "Mrs. Reardon, you have cancer in your stomach, and I'm afraid there's not much we can do. Surgery would do no good. In fact, it would only make the cancer spread."

There was an ever-tightening knot in the pit of Rya's stomach. Her tongue was thick and dry and clung to the roof of her mouth.

All of McClain's senses were wound tight. "Well, Dr. Yarrow, what does this mean?"

"It means—" He choked and cleared his throat. "It means her life is going to be cut short. She…she has a year to live…at the very most."

"Are you sure you've diagnosed this correctly?"

"Two other doctors have studied the results of the tests, Mr. Reardon. They are older and more experienced than I. They both agree with my conclusion. If you would like to talk to them, I—"

"You've done the right thing in getting their opinion, and I appreciate your being so thorough. Your word is good enough for me. It's just that—"

"I understand, Mr. Reardon. Naturally, you were hoping for a simple problem with a simple solution. But let me say this: I will give your wife the best of care, so she can stay at home as long as possible. And I will do everything I can to ease her pain, which is going to get worse. Her...ah...last few months will have to be spent in the hospital where she can get the care she will need by then."

McClain clenched his teeth and nodded.

"Mr. Reardon, you will need to have someone come in during the time she is staying at home. A woman who can look after her needs and take care of her while you're at work. She will need this care soon."

McClain patted Rya's hand. "I'll take care of it, Doctor."

Rya drew her breath in a short, pained gulp. "Elsa has told me two or three times that if this stomach problem ever got so bad that I needed help at home, she would be glad to come."

Yarrow set compassionate eyes on his patient. "Mrs. Reardon, I'm so sorry I had to give you this bad news. It's at times like this that I wish I was in another profession."

Rya pressed a tenuous smile on her lips, took a deep breath, and let it out slowly. "Dr. Yarrow, it's no fault of yours. I very much appreciate your being so straightforward with us."

"Thank you." Then rising from his chair, Yarrow said, "You're going to need more of both kinds of medicine. I'll get it ready for you."

Moments later, the Reardons stepped out of the doctor's private office, and as they headed toward the outside door, Sarah stood up at her desk. "Mr. and Mrs. Reardon, I...I'm so sorry. Dr. Yarrow told me the test results this morning."

They gave her grim smiles, nodded, and hurried out the door.

Without a word between them, they walked across the street to the buggy, and McClain helped her onto the seat. He untied the horse from the hitching post, then sat down beside Rya, took the reins in hand, and put the horse into motion. When the buggy was rolling down the street, McClain put his arm around Rya's shoulder. She saw tears streaming down his cheeks.

Struggling with her own emotions, Rya said, "Darling, we both told the Lord whatever would give Him the most glory was what we wanted. We agreed that our desire was for His will to be done."

McClain wiped away the tears that were dripping from his chin and nodded. He tightened the grip he had on her shoulder. She took hold of his hand and squeezed it hard.

Soon they were home, and McClain guided the buggy into the driveway and stopped at the front porch. "I'll go get Pastor and Marla. They will be a real help to us, I know."

"Of course. I would love to have them."

When McClain helped her out of the buggy, Rya took hold of his hand and looked up into his red-rimmed eyes. "I'm so sorry for what this is doing to you."

He laid a palm against her cheek. "You don't have to be sorry, honey. But I can't imagine what it's doing to *you.*"

"I…I don't know exactly how to put this, but it's like the Lord is holding me in His arms. I'm not afraid of dying. I know I will be with Jesus. But…I don't want to leave you. A year at the most, Dr. Yarrow said. So little time."

McClain bit his lower lip. He folded her into his arms, held her close, and said with a broken voice, "I will spend every possible moment with you. You'll have to quit your job right away."

Rya swallowed hard. "Yes."

"We'll talk to Roy and Elsa this evening, and see if she will take care of you during the daytime when I'm not home."

"I'm sure she will. I won't need her to do it yet. I'll just have to see how fast the cancer grows, and how it makes me feel."

When Pastor and Mrs. Whitfield arrived at the Reardon home with McClain, they were very kind and compassionate. The pastor read several passages of Scripture in an effort to comfort Rya and McClain, and prayed, asking God for comfort, grace, and strength.

Late that night, when Rya was asleep beside him, McClain dropped silent tears. Moonlight slanted through the windows, making a soft, silver glow in the room.

McClain laid a tender hand on Rya's silken hair. "Yes, my sweetheart. So little time."

Suddenly, he was overcome with grief, and had to slip out of the bed and go to one of the spare bedrooms, where he knelt at a chair. Between sobs, he asked God to help them in this most difficult time and even to heal Rya of the cancer.

Back in the master bedroom, Rya stirred in the bed, running a hand to touch her husband. Suddenly she was wide awake, realizing McClain was not in the bed. Rising, she put on her robe and headed down the hall. When her ears picked up his sobs, she hurried and found him on his knees.

Unaware of her presence, McClain continued sobbing and praying. He stopped short when he felt a tender hand on his shoulder. Rising to his feet, he took her into his arms. They sat down on the small bed in the room, clung to each other, and wept.

As the weeks passed, Rya slowly lost weight. On the first day of the third week, Elsa came to the house to stay with Rya while McClain was at work.

When McClain came through the back door into the kitchen after work, he found supper on the stove and the two women sitting at the table. "Smells good, ladies," he said, bending over to kiss Rya's cheek. "How are you feeling, honey?"

"Oh, not too bad. Except—"

"Except what?"

"Except that Jason Lynch was standing across the street looking over here," spoke up Elsa, disgust lining her voice.

McClain scrubbed a palm across his mouth, anger welling up in his eyes. "When was this?"

"I spotted him at about two o'clock," said Rya. "Elsa kept looking out the parlor window, and finally, at four-fifteen, he was gone."

"News spreads fast in Sacramento. I've lost count of how many people have stopped me to say they had heard about your cancer. Jason has to have heard about it, too."

"I cannot imagine why he stays in Sacramento," said Elsa.

"I can't either," said McClain. "He's gotten into countless

fights, from what I hear, and has many enemies. People look on him as a nuisance, and most of them shun him. If he's employed, I don't know where it is." He took a deep breath and set his eyes on Rya. "I'm going to have another talk with him."

That night, McClain searched among the saloons, and Jason was not in any of them. Just as McClain was coming out of the Bulldog, he saw Jason about to enter. People were milling about on the boardwalk, and looked on as McClain surprised Jason by grabbing his shirt with both hands. "I've had enough, Lynch!" he said. "You stay away from Rya!"

A sneer curled Jason's lips. "I have every right to stand anywhere on any street I want, and there's nothing you can do about it!"

"I'm telling you for the last time to stay away from my wife. If you don't, you're going to be very, very sorry!"

Jason laughed in McClain's face. "I'll be across the street from your house tomorrow!"

McClain pulled Jason's face up so close their noses were almost touching. "You heard my warning, Lynch. If you don't quit bothering my wife, you'll soon wish you had."

McClain let go of Jason's shirt, gave him a shove, and moved down the boardwalk.

Jason called after him, "If Rya had married me, she wouldn't be dying! It's your fault she's so sick!"

McClain looked back over his shoulder without breaking his stride, and saw Jason enter the Bulldog Saloon.

While he walked the dark streets toward home, McClain grew angrier and angrier at Jason's last words. He was almost home when he decided to go back to the saloon and drag Lynch to the sheriff's office. He quickly turned that way.

When he reached the saloon, he moved inside and ran his gaze over the place. There was no sign of Lynch. A man, who had been in the crowd that had watched the scene earlier, stepped up. "You looking for Lynch, Mr. Reardon?"

"Yes."

"He left a few minutes ago after arguing with Jack Bowles.

Lynch and Bowles have come close to fighting before."

McClain returned to the street, and as he passed by the dark, open space between the saloon and an adjacent apartment building, he heard a moan. Leaving the boardwalk, he moved toward the sound in the near darkness. The only light was from two apartment windows near the rear of the building. Suddenly, he was able to make out the form of a man lying on the ground. Just as he knelt beside the fallen man, a lantern was lit in a second-floor window directly above him, spraying the area with its yellow glow.

McClain saw that the fallen man was Jason Lynch. His eyes were closed, and he was moaning and gasping for breath. The long blade of a knife was buried in his chest. McClain leaned over and pulled the knife out just as Jason stopped breathing.

Suddenly people were gathered on the boardwalk looking at McClain, standing over the dead man with the bloody knife in his hand.

"Look!" a man said. "It's McClain Reardon! He stabbed that Lynch guy!"

"Charlie already went for the sheriff!"

"Now, look," McClain said, moving toward them. "I didn't kill him. I was passing by and heard him moaning. When I pulled the knife out of his chest, he stopped breathing."

"Likely story," another voice said. "We heard you threaten him, saying he was gonna be very, very sorry. We watched you leave, but you came back, didn't you? Must've gone to get your knife."

"That's what it looks like to me," said another. "Murder ain't the way to handle it, mister."

Galloping hooves were heard on the street, growing louder.

"That's not the way it is!" McClain said. "I told you, I found him lying here with the knife already buried in his chest!"

A horse drew to a halt on the street and Sheriff Jake Drew appeared, shoving his way between the people on the boardwalk. He took one look at McClain, standing with the knife in his hand, and whipped out his gun. "Drop it, Reardon!"

McClain looked down at the knife, then back at the lawman. "Sheriff, it isn't what it looks like. I didn't kill that man."

Drew glanced past him at Jason Lynch lying on the ground in

the spray of light coming from the window above. "I said drop it! You're coming with me. I've got a cell just your size."

McClain let the knife slip from his fingers and fall to the ground.

"Sheriff, you've got this all wrong. You've got to listen to me."

"I warned you not to solve your problem with this man by doing something violent. But you didn't listen, did you?"

McClain squared his shoulders. "I'm telling you the truth, Sheriff. I didn't stab him. I found him like that."

"Yeah, sure." Drew waved the muzzle of his revolver. "Let's go."

23

IT WAS ALMOST ELEVEN O'CLOCK, and Rya Reardon was pacing the floor in the parlor and wringing her hands. There was a dull pain in her midsection. Her lips moved, but barely a whisper came out. "Oh, McClain, where are you? Did you and Jason get into a fight? I know something's wrong. You wouldn't do this to me if you could help it."

She went to the window, pulled back the drapes, and looked out into the darkness. There was only one house across the street that had lights in the windows. Dropping the drapes back in place, she went back to pacing the floor. The pain was growing worse.

"Dear Lord," she whispered, "You know where he is and what has happened. Please take care of him, and—"

Footsteps on the front porch interrupted her prayer, and she froze in place. McClain would come in the back door. She would have heard the buggy go past the house on its way to the barn.

She jumped when a loud knock echoed through the house. Trembling, she made her way to the door, where a single lantern glowed in the small foyer. "Who is it?"

A muffled voice said, "It's Sheriff Jake Drew and Deputy Lance Myers, ma'am."

Rya slid the bolt and opened the door.

"May we come in, Mrs. Reardon?" asked Drew. "We have your husband in jail, and I need to talk to you."

Rya took a step back and swung the door wider. Closing the door behind them, she said, "I don't understand, Sheriff. Why do you have McClain in jail?"

"He's under arrest, ma'am, for murdering Jason Lynch."

Rya's heart thudded in her chest. "This can't be. My husband is no murderer."

"I'm sorry, ma'am, but for several weeks, people in this town have heard your husband threaten Lynch. Well, he carried out his threat. He stabbed Lynch to death and was seen by at least a dozen people, standing over the body with the knife in his hand. When I got there, McClain still had the knife in his hand. He gave a cock-and-bull story that he found Lynch alive and pulled the knife out of his chest, and then Lynch died. When your husband came to me weeks ago about Lynch bothering you, I warned him not to get violent. But he ignored my warning. He killed Lynch, all right."

"No!" cried Rya, shaking her head. "You're wrong, Sheriff! My husband is telling you the truth. He wouldn't have murdered Jason. It isn't in him to do such a thing."

"Like Sheriff Drew said, ma'am," Deputy Lance Myers said, "he was caught red-handed."

"But—"

"He'll face a jury trial," said Drew. "I just wanted to come and let you know what happened. You can visit him at the jail in the morning if you wish."

When Rya closed the door behind the two lawmen, she leaned her back against the door, and burst into tears. She slumped to the floor, her arms wrapped about her violently shaking body.

"This can't be happening!" she sobbed, rocking back and forth, thumping her head against the door. "Lord, help us! Please help us!"

At nine o'clock the next morning, McClain Reardon heard the steel door of the cell block rattle and looked through the bars of his cell to see a deputy enter with Rya at his side. His heart lurched in his chest. He jumped off the cot and hurried to the barred door.

"Fifteen minutes, ma'am," said the deputy, then moved back into the hall and closed the door.

Rya rushed to him, and McClain reached through the bars to enfold her in his arms. The other prisoners looked on as the couple clung to each other, weeping. After a few minutes, they eased back, grasping each other's hands.

Rya was wearing her prettiest dress and had used face powder to try to cover up the evidence of her sleepless night.

Drawing a shuddering breath, McClain said, "I didn't do it, Rya. I didn't kill Jason."

"Oh, my love, I know that," she said softly. "I never thought that for a moment. When the sheriff came to the house last night, I told him it isn't in you to do such a thing."

"Thank you for believing in me."

"I know you were angry at Jason, but murder? Never! Tell me what did happen."

After giving Rya the details, McClain asked, "How did you get here?"

"Roy and Elsa brought me. I went to their house this morning when I knew they would be eating breakfast. They're waiting for me out in the office. They want me to tell you that they know you're innocent."

"Bless them."

"They've offered to take me into their home until this awful nightmare is cleared up."

"Bless them again. Please thank them for me."

"I will." She squeezed his hands. "Darling, the Lord knows you're innocent. He will see that justice is done."

McClain tried to smile as he nodded. "Yes, He will."

"My time is almost up. I'll have Roy and Elsa take me to the company office so I can tell Mr. Lamont you're in here. He's probably wondering why you're not at work."

"I was about to ask if you would do that. And if you would, please go by and tell Pastor Whitfield, too."

Rya and McClain kissed through the bars.

As the steel door was rattling, she reached up and stroked his cheek. "The Lord will see that justice is done."

Less than forty minutes after Rya had left the jail, Ward Lamont appeared before McClain's cell. His first words were to assure McClain that he knew he was innocent; then he asked to hear the story. Before leaving, he told McClain he had no doubt that he would be cleared of the crime.

Lamont had been gone only a few minutes when Pastor Mark Whitfield arrived, affirming his belief that McClain was innocent. After hearing the story as it actually happened, the pastor read Scripture to encourage him and was praying with him as the deputy came and told him his time was up.

Rya visited her husband every day for a week, as did the Gibbses, Ward Lamont, and Pastor Whitfield.

On the eighth day, as sick as Rya was, she was in the courtroom with Roy and Elsa on one side of her, and the pastor and Marla on the other. Ward Lamont and his wife sat just behind them.

The prosecution produced many witnesses—including the owner of the Sacramento Hotel and his clerk—who testified under oath that they had heard McClain's threats against the murdered man. Every person who had found McClain standing over the body of Jason Lynch with the knife in his hand testified on the stand.

It was brought out in the trial that the sheriff had questioned Jack Bowles, who had been in an argument with Jason Lynch in the Bulldog Saloon that night. Jake Drew, on the stand, told the court that Bowles had denied knowing anything about Lynch being stabbed, and that there was no evidence to the contrary.

McClain's attorney gave an impassioned plea to the jury to take into account that his client was a respectable businessman and a model citizen, and that he insisted he had not put the knife in Jason Lynch's chest. He had found him that way, and doing the natural thing, had pulled the knife out.

When the jury left to deliberate, McClain turned around to look at Rya. Holding the hands of Roy and Elsa Gibbs, she tried to disguise the pain she was experiencing, in her soul and her stomach, but McClain could read both in her drawn features. He tried to smile, and she tried to smile back.

The jury was gone only twenty minutes. The judge called for the defendant to rise, and McClain did, with his attorney at his side. When the foreman announced that they had found McClain

Reardon guilty of second-degree murder, Rya let out a heart-wrenching wail. The Gibbses, the Whitmans, and the Lamonts did all they could to comfort her.

The judge then sentenced McClain to life in prison at California's San Quentin Prison.

Rya was quietly weeping and clinging to Elsa and Marla as a pair of deputies grasped McClain's arms to escort him out of the courtroom. Struggling to her feet, Rya stretched out her hands toward the man she loved more than life itself, while a flood of tears streamed down her cheeks. He looked at her through agony-filled eyes as the deputies hurried him away. Rya's knees gave way, and she collapsed on the seat, sobbing.

Back at home, Rya asked Pastor Whitfield why God would allow this to happen to her innocent husband. Whitfield told her he did not know, but showed her in the Bible that God cannot do wrong, and that He doesn't make mistakes. He then took her to Romans 8:28 to show her that God, in His wisdom, had some purpose in allowing it.

"Pastor, would you pray for McClain and me right now? Pray that the Lord will sustain him in that awful prison, and that I will have the strength to go on without him during the little time that I have left on this earth."

When Pastor Whitfield finished praying, Rya found a sweet serenity in her heart. She thanked him for praying. "Pastor, I don't pretend to understand any of this—my sickness or this mock of a trial and what has happened to McClain. But I do know this: God knows the end from the beginning, His grace is sufficient, and He never does wrong."

"You're right about that," the pastor said.

Rya put trembling fingers to the corner of her mouth. "I don't know how long I have to live, but every day, though I cannot be with him, I will love the precious one that God has given to me for such a brief time."

McClain Reardon sat on the cot in his cell, his face buried in his hands. "Lord, why has this horrible thing happened to me? You know I didn't murder Jason Lynch, but You know who did. Please see to it that the guilty man is caught. Rya needs me, Lord, and I need to be with her."

At that moment, Pastor Mark Whitfield appeared at the cell door.

They talked for a few minutes, then the preacher shared the same Scriptures with McClain as he had with Rya, trying to comfort him.

A little while later, Ward Lamont came to see McClain and assured him once again that he knew he was innocent. He told McClain that sooner or later, the truth would surface, and when it did, he would have his job back, and the plans for him to one day own the company would proceed. McClain thanked him sincerely.

Rya visited her husband at the jail the next two days, as did the Gibbses, Pastor Whitfield, and Ward Lamont. During those visits with Rya, McClain commented that she was still losing weight, and asked if her pain was getting worse. She said she was down to eighty-nine pounds, and that her pain was definitely getting worse. She had seen Dr. Yarrow, and he had told her she would be spending at least half-days in bed very soon.

The next morning, the Whitfields and the Gibbses brought Rya to the jail just before McClain was to be put in a police wagon and taken to the railroad depot.

They entered the office, and Pastor Whitfield asked the deputy on the desk if he could see Sheriff Drew. When the sheriff came out of his office, Whitfield asked if Mrs. Reardon could have a few minutes alone with her husband, explaining that she had stomach cancer, and her doctors had predicted that she had less than a year to live.

Drew granted the couple ten minutes alone in a deputy's office. When Rya and McClain stepped into the office and one of the deputies closed the door behind them, they were instantly in each other's arms, tears flowing. After several minutes of silence between them, Rya reached up, took McClain's face in her hands and looked at him with a world full of love in her eyes. "Darling, unless our heavenly Father does some kind of miracle, we won't see each other on this earth again. We have had so little time to be together, but...but we have all eternity to look forward to."

McClain leaned down and pressed his lips on hers, their tears mingling. He held her close once more. "I will always hold you in my heart. Oh, Rya, I love you so much!"

The office door opened. "Time's up," said the deputy.

They kissed again, and as they stepped back from each other, Rya whispered, "Go with God, my darling."

As they stepped through the door, where the deputy stood with a pair of handcuffs, McClain echoed her words. "Go with God, my love."

Rya joined the Whitfields and the Gibbses, and Marla and Elsa took her in their arms.

Rya watched through a veil of tears as Sheriff Drew introduced McClain to Deputy Bart Milford, who would be escorting him to San Quentin. The deputy then placed a cuff on McClain's right wrist and the other on Milford's left wrist.

Milford hastened his prisoner out the door to the police wagon. Rya and her group followed and stood on the boardwalk, looking on.

When deputy and prisoner were seated inside the wagon, the driver snapped the reins and put the horses to an immediate trot. McClain was looking at Rya through the small barred window in the rear of the wagon as it rolled down the street. Tears were streaming down his cheeks.

Soon the wagon passed from view. Rya let out a sob, and her knees gave way.

At the Sacramento depot, Deputy Milford took his prisoner aboard the train under the curious eyes of the passengers.

Moments later, the train was rolling southwest toward San

Francisco. They were seated on the left side of the coach, which put the prisoner next to the window.

They both looked out the window for some time, watching the beautiful countryside roll by, then Milford said, "Sheriff Drew told me about your wife's sickness, Reardon. Too bad. You really messed up by killing that Jason Lynch. You could have been with her for her last few months."

McClain looked at him from the corner of his eye. "I didn't kill Jason Lynch, Deputy. We had been at odds, yes, but he had already been stabbed when I found him. All I did was pull the knife out of his chest. People saw me with the knife and assumed that I had stabbed him. The jury believed them."

"Sure. Because right out in public, you'd threatened several times to kill him."

"I didn't threaten to kill him. I merely said if he didn't stop harassing my wife, he would be sorry. I wouldn't murder anybody, Deputy. I've been a born-again child of God since I was a boy. I live by God's standards as laid down in His Word. Jesus Christ lives in my heart. I'm not a murderer."

Milford gave him a cold look.

"While we're on the subject, Deputy," McClain said softly, "how about you? Have you put your faith in God's Son to forgive and wash away your sins and save your soul?"

"Enough of that, Reardon. A cold-blooded murderer sits here and tells me he's a Christian. Yeah, sure. Don't make me laugh."

As time passed, McClain Reardon languished in San Quentin Prison, weeping in his cell night after night, praying and asking God for help.

"Lord," he said over and over, "Rya has so little time. Please clear me of the charge so I can go to her. Lord, I need a miracle!"

During the wearisome days, McClain worked in the prison kitchen, where he witnessed to his fellow inmates and began leading them one by one to the Lord.

—⁓—   —⁓—   —⁓—

At the Gibbs home, Rya wept continually over McClain's unjust imprisonment, begging God to perform a miracle and expose the real killer, so she and her husband could be together for the short time she had left.

She was visited daily by the Whitfields, who prayed with her and did all they could to comfort her. Rya was getting very thin and was growing weaker.

One day at the prison, when McClain had been there seven weeks, Warden Harry Piedmont had him brought to his office. As he sat in a chair before the warden's desk with two guards flanking him, Piedmont said, "Reardon, you know, of course, that I have a copy of your trial record in my file."

"Yes, sir."

"I don't know exactly how to put this, but you have had a powerful influence on so many of the prisoners you work with in the kitchen. Since you've been here, we have seen a definite change in those men. What is it?"

"I've given them the gospel of the Lord Jesus Christ, sir. They have become Christians, and when Jesus moves into a man's heart, he is a brand-new person. Those men won't be hard to handle anymore."

The warden shook his head in wonderment. "Mr. Reardon, I have a hard time believing you murdered that man. By your trial record, I see that you claimed innocence—that you found the man already stabbed and dying."

"Yes, sir. I am innocent. I did not kill Jason Lynch."

"I believe you. But, of course, that doesn't change anything. The judge put the life sentence on you because the jury pronounced you guilty. But let me say this: keep up the good work you're doing among the men in this prison."

"I plan to, sir."

The next day, Pastor Whitfield arrived at the prison and was allowed half an hour in a private room with McClain. Since men with life sentences could receive no mail for their first six months, he told McClain of Rya's worsening condition, believing he had a right to know.

The pastor prayed with McClain, and when the half hour was up, they embraced, and McClain went to the prison kitchen to work.

When McClain walked into the kitchen and was putting on his apron, four of the men he had led to Christ approached him. Max Trujillo, Gene Woods, Luke Odom, and Gus Hines formed a circle around him.

"McClain," said Max, "we've worked out a plan to help you escape so you can go to Rya."

McClain frowned and blinked. "You're kidding."

"We're serious," said Gus. "Every man who works with you knows you're not a murderer. Especially those of us you've led to Jesus. Your little wife is dying. We want you to have some time with her before she goes to heaven."

"Just listen to this," said Luke. "When the grocery wagon comes tomorrow, Max and I will fake a fight and cause a diversion so you can get under the wagon, hold on, and ride outside the prison. We'll have the guards so busy breakin' up the fight, they won't even notice you."

McClain scrubbed a shaky hand over his mouth. "Fellas, I can't let you jeopardize yourselves for my sake. If the prison officials figure out you faked the fight to help me escape, your sentences will be extended."

"McClain," said Max, "we can get you out without anyone knowing there was anything but a fight between two convicts. The warden and his guards will think you simply saw an opportunity and took it."

"As Christians, we wouldn't do this if you were guilty of murder," said Luke. "But we know better. Go…and take the time God allows you to be with Rya."

"But, fellas, the warden had me in his office just yesterday, thanking me for the influence I've had on you. I explained that it was because I had led you to the Lord. If you two guys get into a fight—"

"We'll apologize to Warden Piedmont," said Max. "And I have a feeling he'll be glad you got out of here so you could be with Rya. I heard him tell a guard the other day that he thought you were innocent."

McClain took a deep breath. "Okay. I've been praying that the Lord would get me out of here. I just didn't think He would do it this way."

The next day, the fight broke out in the kitchen. While the guards were occupied, McClain made it to the grocery wagon just outside the kitchen door and got underneath it without being detected.

Elsa Gibbs had just put Rya to bed for the night and joined her husband in the parlor when they heard a tap on the window that overlooked the front porch.

Roy and Elsa looked at each other, frowning. "What can this be?" asked Roy as he moved to the window.

Elsa was on his heels as he pulled back the drape. Both were shocked to see McClain's face at the window. He was in his prison garb.

Roy darted to the door and when he opened it, McClain hurried in. Both of them embraced him, and Roy said, "How did you escape?"

McClain quickly explained, then said, "Folks, I've got to take Rya somewhere so we can have what's left of her life."

"She's been feeling somewhat better the past few days," Elsa said. "She hasn't lost any more weight, either. We check her weight every day."

"We don't mean to get your hopes up by telling you this," said Roy. "Dr. Yarrow told us yesterday when we had Rya at his office that cancer often works this way. It will seem to ease up at times, then gets worse again until the person finally dies."

McClain nodded. "I've heard that before."

"I just put Rya to bed," said Elsa. "She's probably awake. You should go in and see her."

McClain rubbed the back of his neck. "Roy, Elsa, I don't want to get you into trouble for aiding and abetting a criminal. Just do this for me. Go in and tell Rya I'm here. I'll give her a chance to dress and pack a few things she needs, then I'll kidnap her and take her out the window. Unlock it for me, will you? That's all I ask. Then just forget you saw me, okay? I want to spend the time with her that she has remaining. After that, I don't care what they do to me."

Roy touched McClain's arm. "What else can we do to help?"

McClain cleared his throat. "Well…ah…if you'd have any spare money—"

"We've got some. Would three hundred be enough?"

"Plenty. Somehow, I'll pay you back."

"Nope. It's a gift, not a loan."

McClain started to say something else, but Roy interrupted. "Where are you planning to go?"

"Los Angeles. They have excellent doctors and medical facilities. Some of my prison mates are from there, and they told me about it. I can get lost in the crowd there."

"We've got to get you out of those prison duds," said Roy. "Since you and I are about the same size, I'll give you some of my clothes."

"While you're doing that, honey," said Elsa, "I'll go tell Rya who's here and what's happening and get her ready."

Roy nodded. "McClain, just how are you going to get to Los Angeles?"

"By train. There's a train out of here at midnight."

"But what if somebody who knows you sees you at the depot? They'll have the sheriff on you in a hurry."

"Well, I—"

"Go on in there and see Rya, boy. Elsa and I will drive you down to Stockton. Nobody will know you there. We'll put you on the morning train to Los Angeles at Stockton."

McClain grinned. "All right. You win."

Elsa was still standing there. "Go on, McClain. After you surprise her and tell her what's happening, I'll help her pack. Then Roy can outfit you with some of his clothes."

—⁓— —⁓— —⁓—

In her bedroom, Rya was almost asleep when there was a tap on the door. Turning her head that direction, she said, "Yes, Elsa?"

The door swung open, and Rya saw her husband silhouetted against the light in the hallway. She gasped. "McClain?"

He rushed to the bed, bent over, and folded her in his arms. Rya broke into tears. "Darling, how…how did you escape?"

"I'll explain it on the way to Stockton, sweetheart. Roy and Elsa are going to help us. I'm taking you to Los Angeles where there are good doctors and hospitals. It's a large city, and I can live and work there with less chance of being caught. We'll catch the morning train in Stockton for Los Angeles."

"I…I can't believe this is happening! I asked the Lord to get you out of prison, but I didn't think it would happen by your escaping from there."

McClain planted a soft kiss on her lips. "Elsa's going to help you get ready. We have to leave right away."

Thirty minutes later, Roy Gibbs drove his buggy southward through Sacramento under the cover of darkness. Elsa sat next to him.

In the back seat, McClain held Rya and began his explanation of how he escaped. On his body were Roy's clothes, and in his pocket was a wad of money. In his heart was the hope that he could elude the law at least until the Lord took Rya home.

WHEN RYA AND MCCLAIN REARDON ARRIVED in Los Angeles, they rented a small house near downtown, and the next day, McClain found a job with a construction company. They gave him two days to get Rya settled and under the care of a doctor before he started work. The pay was good, and on the evening of the same day, he hired a middle-aged widow named Helen Newell, who had advertised for domestic work in the classified section of the *Los Angeles Times*. They were pleased to learn that Helen was a Christian, and she recommended her church to them.

They explained to Helen that Rya was dying with cancer, and they would need her there Monday through Saturday each week during the day. Helen's heart went out to them, and the compassion she showed to Rya was a comfort to both of them.

As Helen was about to leave for home, which was less than three blocks away, McClain said, "Helen, I need to get Rya under the care of the best doctor in this city. Who do you recommend?"

"You take her to the Worley Clinic over on Rosemead Boulevard. Dr. Ralph Worley heads it up. He's the one who took care of my dear husband, Fred, right up until his death from consumption. Dr. Worley has a staff of four doctors and six nurses. Mrs. Reardon will get the best care right up until...until she goes to heaven to be with Jesus."

The next morning, McClain walked to a stable and purchased a horse and buggy.

It was almost ten o'clock when they pulled into the parking lot of the Worley Clinic. McClain helped Rya out of the buggy, and holding on to her arm, walked her into the building and up to the receptionist's desk. He explained that they had just moved to Los Angeles, that the doctors where they lived in northern California had diagnosed his wife with stomach cancer, and they had given her less than a year to live.

A few minutes later, they found themselves in the office of the head doctor. Dr. Ralph Worley looked at what the receptionist had written down about Rya and told them he wanted to hear the whole story. When Rya finished telling it, Worley asked for the name of the physician who had diagnosed her cancer. Both of them were relieved when Dr. Worley said he wanted to do his own tests so he would know exactly what he was dealing with.

"We can do the tests right now, if you folks have the time," Worley said.

"We sure do, Doctor," said McClain. "I start my new job tomorrow, so we're free for the rest of today."

"Good. We're very thorough, Mr. Reardon, so it'll take about four hours to do the tests."

"That's fine, Doctor. I'll be right out there in the waiting room."

Worley excused himself, left the office, and was back in two minutes with one of his nurses. He introduced the nurse to the Reardons, then said, "Our laboratory is a bit overloaded right now. Ordinarily we would have the results of the tests day after tomorrow. Let's see…this is Wednesday. Will your work schedule allow you to bring her back at…let's say…eleven o'clock Monday morning, Mr. Reardon?"

"I'll arrange it with my employer," said McClain. "We'll be here at eleven o'clock on Monday."

They stepped out of Worley's office. The nurse took Rya down a long hall, and Dr. Worley told his receptionist to set an appointment for the Reardons to see him at eleven o'clock Monday morning. McClain took a seat in the waiting area.

In the following few days, Rya and McClain were happy to have their evenings together. But there was always the niggling awareness that time was slipping through their fingers like sand in an hourglass.

Rya rested most of the time on Thursday, Friday, and Saturday, but still did little things to help Helen around the house. She also spent part of the afternoons praying and reading her Bible. She committed Psalm 121 to memory, and daily drew strength from God's Word.

On Saturday afternoon when McClain came home from work, he found Rya and Helen sitting at the kitchen table, sipping hot tea.

McClain greeted Helen and bent down and kissed his wife's pale cheek. "Have you been a good girl today, sweet stuff?"

"I have. I've rested even more than usual today so I'll feel like going to church tomorrow morning."

"Are you sure you can handle it?"

"Oh, I'll be fine. I want to be in God's house and hear His Word taught and preached."

"Taught and preached, huh? So you think you can handle both Sunday school and the preaching service?"

"Yes."

He bent down and kissed her cheek again. "All right, sweetheart. I'm glad you feel well enough to do both."

On Monday morning at eleven, the receptionist led the Reardons into Dr. Worley's office and seated them in front of the desk, telling them the doctor would be there shortly. She hurried back to her desk, leaving the office door open.

McClain took hold of Rya's hand and squeezed it. "You look a bit peaked, honey. As soon as we're through here, I'll get you home so you can lie down and rest."

She gave him a loving look and nodded.

They heard rapid footsteps in the hall, and Dr. Worley entered his office.

"Good morning, Mr. and Mrs. Reardon," he said, rounding the desk and sitting down. He opened a drawer and took out a folder with Rya's name on the tab. He smiled and ran his eyes from one face to the other. "I have some very good news. Mrs. Reardon, you do not have cancer. You never did."

A lump rose in McClain's throat.

Rya's eyes filled with tears, and she was speechless.

"What...what does she have, Doctor?" asked McClain.

"Her problem is a stomach ulcer, which has dealt her all this misery. I've seen it happen just like this many times. Tests sometimes seem to show that the patient has cancer, when all the time, it's an ulcer. Please do not blame Dr. Yarrow. We probably have more advanced testing techniques than he does, but until medical science improves a whole lot more, this same error will occur time and time again."

"But you're absolutely sure of your diagnosis, Doctor?" McClain said.

"Yes, sir. Absolutely. Our laboratory technicians were elated when they announced it to me. My staff of physicians all looked at the test results, and we are in agreement with the technicians. This dear young lady has an ulcer, but she does not have cancer."

McClain jumped out of his chair, and Rya stood up. They held onto each other and wept, praising the Lord together, while the doctor looked on, excess moisture in his own eyes.

Worley told them about a new medicine that had just come from some doctors in Switzerland, which he was sure would heal the ulcer in time, if Rya took it as he would prescribe.

Rya assured him she would.

The doctor added that with plenty of rest and the proper diet, she would gain some weight, and though the ulcer would act up once in a while until it was completely healed, she would be fine.

As they drove toward home, McClain put an arm around Rya and pulled her close. "Sweetheart, I have begged God for a miracle, and here it is, sitting right next to me! He, indeed, is the Great Physician!"

Rya was weeping for joy and couldn't speak.

She looked up through her tears into her husband's face and suddenly his countenance changed. "Sooner or later the law will catch up to me. I'll go back to prison for the rest of my life. We...we still have so little time."

Rya wiped tears and sniffed. "As soon as I get better, we've got to pack up and go elsewhere. The Lord knows you didn't kill Jason. Certainly He will help us elude the law, even as He helped you escape from San Quentin."

They were drawing near the house.

"It'll have to be God's hand to do it, Rya. There's no way on earth I can take care of you and hide from the law for very long. I—"

Rya frowned as McClain narrowed his eyes, looking straight toward their house. "What's wrong?"

Her own eyes fell on the man and woman standing in the front yard as McClain said, "That's a lawman with Mrs. Jeffries, who lives next door. See his badge? That's his horse there in the driveway."

The neighbor woman pointed at the oncoming buggy and the lawman looked straight at McClain.

"What are you going to do?" Rya asked in a fearful voice.

"There's nothing I can do," McClain said, pulling back on the reins. "We can't outrun him in this buggy. I'm going back to prison. I'll have to send you home to your parents."

Rya's heart sank.

The lawman started toward the buggy, and the neighbor woman hurried into her house.

Rya bit her lower lip. *Please, oh, please, Lord. Not after what we just learned from Dr. Worley! Don't let them take McClain back to prison. This has been such a glorious day with the wonderful news that I'm not dying with cancer.*

McClain felt nauseous as he drew the buggy to a halt in front of the house. They both saw by the lawman's badge that he was a deputy United States marshal.

"Mr. and Mrs. Reardon, I'm Deputy U.S. Marshal Clint Forbes," the lawman said. "Mr. Reardon, I've been on your trail for a week, and I'm sure glad I found you. It's my happy privilege to tell you that you are a free man! Jason Lynch's killer was a man named Jack Bowles."

Rya looked at McClain then at the deputy U.S. marshal in stunned surprise.

"They caught him?" said McClain, his voice strained.

"Yes, sir. Bowles was in a work accident several days ago, and the doctors told him he was dying. Not wanting to die with the murder on his conscience, Bowles asked for the sheriff and confessed that it was him who put the knife in Lynch's chest after they had been arguing in the saloon."

"The miracle I prayed for has happened!" Rya cried. "Oh, praise the Lord!"

McClain jumped out of the buggy. "Deputy Forbes, let's go in the house so we can talk further."

Rya had the men sit at the kitchen table and put a coffeepot on the stove. She sat next to her husband, and while they held hands, Forbes explained that after McClain's escape from San Quentin and word came from Sheriff Drew that McClain had been cleared, his office commissioned him to find the innocent man and let him know he had been cleared.

Forbes reached into his coat pocket and handed McClain an envelope. "There's a letter in here from the governor of California, Mr. Reardon. It's an apology for the wrongful verdict of the jury, and it also declares you innocent of the murder charge and a free man."

Rya shed tears as she hugged her husband's neck. "Oh, glory to God! He is truly the God of miracles!"

Forbes smiled. "Mr. Reardon, everybody in Sacramento knows that you are innocent and a free man. I talked to Ward Lamont. He is eager for you to return to Sacramento so the two of you can follow up on his plan."

Rya went to the stove and poured coffee around. After Deputy Forbes had downed two cups of coffee, he thanked the Reardons for their hospitality and rode away.

Standing on the front porch as Forbes disappeared at the corner of the block, McClain turned to Rya and said, "Now I know why the Lord let me be convicted and go to San Quentin. I told you about the four convicts who helped me escape."

"Yes. Because you had led them to the Lord."

"And that's just it, honey. There were actually more men I was able to lead to the Lord, too. If I hadn't been there, the nine men I had the joy of leading to Jesus might have gone on through life and died lost."

Rya laughed happily. "All things really do work together for good to them that love God!"

They stepped back into the parlor, and neither said a word, but both fell to their knees at the couch, holding hands.

"Thank You, dear Lord, for the valley," said McClain. "In the valley, You allowed me to win those lost men to You. I can see that Your plan was perfect. Help us to remember always, as Your Word says, 'As for God, his way is perfect!'"

"Amen," Rya said in a whisper. "May we always praise, honor, and glorify You, dear Lord."

They prayed for the new Christians in San Quentin Prison, asking the Lord to help them to grow in grace and to lead other men to Jesus.

They stood up and wrapped their arms around each other, tears flowing.

"Praise the Lord!" Rya said. "Now we can have our life together!"

Multnomah Publishers

The publisher and author would love to hear your comments about this book. *Please contact us at:*
www.allacy.com

Mail Order Bride Series

Desperate men who settled the West resorted to unconventional measures in their quest for companionship, advertising for and marrying women they'd never even met! Read about a unique and adventurous period in the history of romance.

An Exciting New Series
by Bestselling Fiction Authors

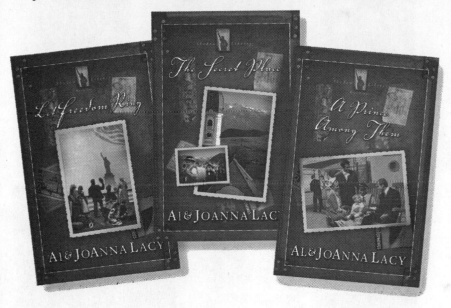

Hannah of Fort Bridger Series

Hannah Cooper's husband dies on the dusty Oregon Trail, leaving her in charge of five children and a general store in Fort Bridger. Dependence on God fortifies her against grueling challenges and bitter tragedies.

#1	*Under the Distant Sky*	ISBN 1-57673-033-6
#2	*Consider the Lilies*	ISBN 1-57673-049-2
#3	*No Place for Fear*	ISBN 1-57673-083-2
#4	*Pillow of Stone*	ISBN 1-57673-234-7
#5	*The Perfect Gift*	ISBN 1-57673-407-2
#6	*Touch of Compassion*	ISBN 1-57673-422-6
#7	*Beyond the Valley*	ISBN 1-57673-618-0
#8	*Damascus Journey*	ISBN 1-57673-630-X